BLACK WING

A NOVEL BY

DAVID CAMPICHE

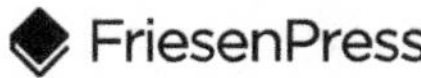

One Printers Way
Altona, MB R0G 0B0
Canada

www.friesenpress.com

First Edition — 2023

ISBN
978-1-03-914146-9 (Hardcover)
978-1-03-914145-2 (Paperback)
978-1-03-914147-6 (eBook)

1. FICTION, INDIGENOUS

Distributed to the trade by The Ingram Book Company

To all First Nations peoples, particularly to an elder who wishes to remain anonymous, a man of wisdom and patience and a voice both eloquent and caring. I will forever remain grateful for his kind words.

I am beholden to many friends who supported me through the writing of this novel, particularly to Laurie, my steadfast and beloved partner, and to Jim.

Native people speak elegantly for themselves. Simply put, I wish to bear witness to their story. My respect runs deep. During the twelve years that I have worked on this novel, there has been much progress made to further Native culture and language. At the same time, acknowledgements have been made for the atrocities committed against them by the non-indigenous culture. With this novel I hope to add my support to these First Nations peoples.

CHAPTER ONE

I qu. aa yax x'wán—Go forward with courage

—Tlingit saying

British Columbia, 1896

Pressed into a fissure in a sheer mountain wall, two men huddled inside a womb of stone and ice. The wind tormented them. After hours of climbing, they were hardened to the landscape, a vista stunning to the eye and sleeved in ice.

The sky was steel blue, and that winter day the weather remained as uncompromising as the barrel of a rifle. The men's spirits were daunted. Their lives hung by a rope tether. They were the hunted. One of the men remembered an admonition, "Never, never drop your guard."

Occasionally the men turned from their climb and gazed down the cliff into a deep river valley. From above, a spangled ribbon of fast-running water appeared still and silver hued. Shadows moved down the sheer granite wall. As the light faded, gray erased blue. The sky paled to pewter, then gunmetal. Darkness approached as quickly as the men adjusted their eyes.

"Get in here, André. Get out of that dang wind. Mother of God, it's cold."

André shuddered, his hands shaking.

The men were tormented by a chilling frost. The severe weather sought out every hidden pore in their hardened bodies. As night settled into the valley below, their mood turned desperate.

Dan and André Skinner were brothers. Dan was the older of the two, a lean, muscular man with sandy hair and a scar that curled across his left cheek to the corner of his eye. The scar was the handiwork of a grizzly bear. That encounter left Dan with a wariness and respect for the harsh, mountainous wilderness he inhabited.

Just now his hands were bruised and torn from climbing. They were large hands, strong and calloused. His stomach was tight, his long legs lean and muscular from years of living and working in a mountain environment. Even in the fading light, his gray eyes were empowered with a trajectory that held other humans in their grip. In that winter of 1896, Dan Skinner was thirty-four years old.

With his strong arms and thick wrists, he pulled his younger brother onto a thin granite shelf that was buttressed from the wind by a perpendicular slab of fissured stone. The austere nest cut some of the wind but refused to hold back the cold.

Over six feet apiece, with weathered faces, the two were ruggedly handsome. Their faces were haggard from a week in the wilderness, and a coarse brown stubble darkened their chins.

When a gust of wind turned the corner and called out its icy chant, the younger brother, André, exploded with a stream of expletives. His eyes were dark and brooding. A mane of long blond hair lay matted on his square forehead.

He pulled himself as close to the wall as possible, folded his knees into his chest, and wrapped his arms around them, but nothing could stop the trembling. Nothing curbed his anger or his profane language.

"André, that talk doesn't help a thing. Before this night gets finished with us, it'll be a darn sight colder than this."

"Great. That's just great, Dan. This one time just save me one of your lectures. OK!"

For just a second—for the first time in days—his older brother snapped. "Dammit to hell, André, I didn't exactly get us into this mess, remember? You brought this misery down on yourself. You killed that man—not me.

Think about it. Maybe you would rather deal with those four lawmen all by yourself."

Dan turned his back on his brother. Like the gusts of wind that assailed them, his anger crested and then subsided. He was sorry for his outburst. He was always sorry when he lost his temper. No good came from his uncontrolled emotions. He was not a man to lose his temper easily, but the situation was dire.

Dan was so exhausted that his insides felt shaved as if by a steel adz. Still, fury etched his face muscles, but unlike his brother, his temper never lasted long.

As the wind twisted around the granite slab, Dan turned to private thoughts. His eyes swept across the vista below. Somewhere lower on this nearly impassable cliff, four armed men hunted them. He knew the men and one in particular. A few times he had worked that side of the law. He had crisscrossed the wilderness with them, a silver badge decorating his chest. And now the posse was chasing them.

Dan could guess how the lawmen thought. Their strategy was simple enough; the law was unambiguous. They would bring the brothers in, dead or alive. When that job was done, the officers would all head home—get out of the harsh weather, away from the danger. For the lawmen, most of the suffering would be over.

André remained sullen. That didn't surprise Dan. Even in the best of times, André was a handful. Dan knew him better than anybody, and he knew they were headed for a battle of wills.

At that very moment, Dan had bigger problems to deal with than André's temperament. He was calculating their slim chances of reaching the summit and chose not to think much beyond that. *Take it one step at a time. Stay loose. Stay aware. Move cautiously.* A litany of survival skills played out in his mind. To this man of the mountains, survival had become second nature, and discipline remained vital.

Dan weighed his options. One thought remained clear: André was not an accomplished climber. Still, he had overcome the odds. He had climbed most of the way up the steep cliff. They would climb on. Dan prayed his brother would stay aware and watch his footing. After all, there were no alternatives.

Surviving the ascent remained paramount. Unfortunately, the men had lost their firearms and most of their supplies when their canoe capsized in a violent chute of water two days earlier, leaving them stranded under the granite wall with a posse closing in behind them. In a wilderness as tough as this, those supplies might well mean the difference between life and death.

But they still had their wits. And if André wasn't functioning as well as Dan might have hoped, he didn't appear ready to give up. No sir! They were still out of range of the lawmen's rifles, and they had to keep it that way. Somehow, they had to find the strength to move even faster.

Dan pulled some cheese and misshapen bread from his rucksack and handed pieces to his brother. The cheese broke sharply in their mouths like an ice-cold vegetable. His mouth felt numb, as did his whole body. The bread was moldy, but Dan would never complain. However paltry or tasteless it was, both men knew the value of even the most meager of foods. Many things might kill a pioneer in this cold. Exposure was one of the stronger possibilities. A man in the wild had to stay warm. Had to eat and keep up his strength.

"Get out that blanket, Dan."

Relieved from his crouching position, André's feet dangled over the precipice. With his back squeezed against the wall, he continued to shake. He watched his brother's head turn in his direction. Their eyes met and held. André knew from experience and from his older brother's firm expression that another decision was imminent. If it were possible for anyone to lead him to safety, it would be Dan.

"Listen, I spotted a narrow chimney about an hour's climb from here. It will be a damn sight easier climbing from there. A man can get a grip on the stone—anchor his body. It'll be better. I promise."

It was difficult to think beyond the narrow stone shelf. The weather, the steep cliff—André was frightened and exhausted. All he thought to say was, "God Almighty, it's cold. Holy Mother."

Uncertainty continued to pester the scar-faced brother—Dan couldn't help himself. What would happen when—if—they reached the top of the cliff? What then?

Even if they both made the summit, where the hell might two outlaws run from there? Where would they hide or run? Wilderness and more wilderness—those seemed to be the only options. Dan knew he was capable of surviving the winter, but he didn't like the long-term commitment. Didn't like the ante. But this was no poker game. Besides, the hand they had been dealt was weak. He reasoned that the only two jokers in the pack were his kid brother and himself.

Finally, he could only guessed about André, how it might be if either brother—through the grace of God and Dan's mountain skills—survived. Dan took a deep breath and felt his lungs protest. In this cold, the scar on his cheek festered. Dan realized there was no sense in worrying about too much too soon. *One step at a time*, he reminded himself, and then stared back across the valley. Stone-cold darkness erased the palette of somber colors. *Never, never drop your guard.* He remembered that the words belonged to Tom LaCross, the Tsimshian Native. And now that very man was tracking him. Dan stared down the cliff. He failed to see him, but Dan knew: the scout waited below. And the lawmen. Few fine woodsmen escaped the likes of Tom LaCross. The next day would try Dan and his brother. *And what then?* he wondered. As he deliberated, fresh snow began to fall.

"And getting there, brother?" André interrupted his brother's thoughts. André was still thinking about the chimney, still struggling with his fear.

"Huh? Oh . . . well, that will take a little doing, but no worse than today."

"Yeah, that's a thought. Sure 'nuff. Not possible to be any worse than today, brother. Saints be damned if things get any tougher. Jesus, you know heights scare the piss out of me. Give me flat ground or an angry river and I'll test the currents. Pit me against a man—any man—I can stand my own."

With that, a mischievous smile slid into place. André had beautiful teeth and a handsome smile. A dimple punctuated his chin.

Dan remained silent, his thoughts hankering back to his kid brother's habit of fist arbitration. Already, he sensed frustration flooding back into André's voice, into his brooding eyes.

"André!" Dan gathered as much patience as possible but was slow to finish the sentence. He was a careful man, always positioning himself with fastidious attention to detail. "I've gotten out of big trouble before. You're doing just fine, André. Believe me."

Against his careful nature, Dan nearly broke into a chagrined half smile but then he caught himself. *Devil's in this here weather.* Normally, he would have chosen to do nothing that might aggravate André's temper. Up there, events tumbled out of his control.

A long silence passed before André spoke again. "Yeah. Sure thing, Dan. Listen, I'm sorry. Listen . . . uh . . . Dan, I wouldn't have a sinner's chance in hell if it weren't for you."

Like Dan, André's mind drifted away, moving like chimney smoke back down the long valley. Back home.

As he meditated, darkness thickened.

The final acknowledgment floated between the pair. Words trembled in the thick, chilling air. The snow that had fallen throughout the short daylight gave a reprieve, but the sky was heavy with the promise of a return performance. That promise hung over the brothers like a cleaver.

André's last words faded suddenly, breaking like a covey of grouse under gunfire. Wind disposed of them neatly.

Both brothers were aware of the final moments of twilight, and they expected harsh weather that night. The temperature plummeted like a broken-winged raptor. Two days earlier, Dan had seen a falcon swoop upon a larger raptor, breaking the back of a great eagle. Oddly, the image haunted him, as did the reality of another night of bitter cold. No matter how he tried, little else postured into a single positive thought. Nothing except soothing memories of his wife, Rebecca.

He turned those thoughts aside. The brothers huddled close together now, darkness spreading like ink across a paper blotter.

At least under the cover of darkness, Tom LaCross won't be lowering his rifle sights on my back, Dan thought. Then he pondered the question of lady luck. He hadn't expected the lawmen to follow them up the cliff. Few men would have attempted such a climb. But then, few men were as capable as Tom LaCross. Had he goaded the others up the shear cliff?

Night fell upon the men. Dan thought again about the falcon and the eagle. The air grew colder. Gusts of wind tangled erratically.

Frigid air penetrated their wool blankets, the single garment of warmth each brother wrapped about their dirty, pale skin, over their wool shirts and leather capotes. It was all the clothing they had left. Luck had deserted them when their canoe floundered.

Neither man had bathed in the last ten days. The leather on their backs was shredding. Stains and dirt had replaced the natural luster. Rain had further decayed the smoke-cured skins. Dan wore a fur hat. André's had blown away earlier in the day. Blown down the cliff. He had strapped a bandana over his scalp, but that offered little comfort. Both men cursed their circumstances.

Down the valley, a wolf let out a howl that spoke to a solitary existence. As nightfall closed upon the predator, the weather turned colder. The large male wouldn't make too much of that. He felt the penetrating freeze but knew no voice of complaint. A hunter with keen senses and night eyes, he was a creature of action. Winter was upon him, and he was hungry. Under the cloak of darkness, the predator would hunt.

While his mate and her two youngsters hunkered inside a cache fashioned beneath a tree in soft clay, dirt and detritus, the male opened his mouth, and wild sounds curled out. That call was strong and high-pitched, and ricocheted off the cliffs. This was the wolf's world, his mountain, his valley.

Twice more the howl rose, echoing from the sheer stone walls and out into the crisp freezing air. Miles away, six men heard the wolf. Among those men, only one attempted to demystify the animal's message, but he wasn't talking to the others, to the three lawmen or to the two brothers above, high on the precarious cliff.

Again, the wolf let loose his howl. Again and again. Around him, the wilderness listened.

Dan spent the night contemplating his chances for the coming day. But his thoughts were flighty. After a minute or two, his early reflections would skip away, his thoughts wandering down the valley to his small farm, to his wife of ten years. He would picture her then, standing on the cabin porch at dusk, calling him for supper. Around the farm, he was always hungry. After a twelve-hour day, he was tired to the bone and ravenous. Each day was the same. Each day was challenging. This was his life, his choice. He never thought to complain.

Perhaps he had been clearing the great trees from their field when she called. Maybe he had been building a corral, roofing a barn with rough-hewn cedar shakes, or just shuffling straw to the animals. Farm life consumed his waking hours, the bulk of his energy. The stumps took months to burn. Sometimes he chose dynamite, but Rebecca hated the sound. Dan was sensitive to her wishes. By dinnertime, he smelled of cedar and spruce, of sweat, pitch, and rich, fertile earth.

She would touch his slick, sweaty skin. Wipe the dust or grime from his face with a damp kitchen cloth. Touch the scar that darkened his face into a harder mask. Rebecca knew his gentleness; she coveted that side of her man. She always acted as if the scar was still fresh and sensitive, as if the injury had just happened. Her touch never failed to soothe him.

Even now he felt her warm fingers on his arm. Sensed the affection in her touch. Felt his arousal.

Another gust cut him. Quick as a snakebite, the elation of her memory slipped away. Dan felt alone on the cliff, separate even from his brother.

In the darkest hour of the night, Dan's heavy brows pressed together, the lines on his face furrowing deeper and deeper. Even in his dreams, he was drawn to her. He loved her dazzling eyes, her silken auburn hair. The graceful way she walked and spoke—her determination, the set of her wide mouth, her full, soft lips. He loved the feel of her silky skin in bed next to him, the intimate laughter that frequently preceded their lovemaking.

The brothers pressed together, shoulder to shoulder. André fidgeted through the interminable night. Here there was no sleep, only contorted, restless dreams. The wind beat out a stern message. Rain and sleet followed. The weather bullied them.

"Dammit to hell!" In and out of his sleep, André kept repeating the words. They became a convoluted statement, wind sounds agitating terse human mews.

The snow returned. Their lives were forever intertwined with winter and a fatal mistake that harangued their souls, their every move.

Spring 1994—British Columbia

She picked up the baby. Oh, how the tiny infant struggled. The brown-eyed girl was endowed with an extra parcel of energy. The baby's eyes suggested as much. They danced and sparkled. The infant was hankering to get an early start on life. The little darling was impatient to leave her mark on the world.

Across the room, the woman's raven-haired lover rose, a cup of hot-brewed coffee warmed his hands. As he approached the table to sit down, his chair made a high-pitched dragging sound, an exclamation mark above the Native flute music that played softly over the two small speakers at each end of the tiny cabin. The brew steamed a trail of cloudlike vapor into the chilly air.

Outside, it was snowing. A murder of crows had settled into the trees. An eagle glided overhead, calling forth a message that spoke to something deep and compelling.

"Well, my little wolverine," the man said to the baby while winking. "What have we gone and done?" Wrinkling his brow, he posed the question to his new wife.

A wide smile crossed his handsome face. The man was a dream catcher and her best friend.

CHAPTER TWO

"Never, never drop your guard."

—White Bear

Six men rested high above the deep valley. If the granite wall imparted a music of its own, the two Mounties and their sergeant weren't listening. The fourth man among them rested at a distance. He was a man of strong countenance, a warrior from the Tsimshian nation. His thick-boned body with its hardened, leathery face said as much. He was tall for his clan. Under the cliff, separated from the others, he was listening to the howl of a lone wolf. In the dusk, his eyes reflected the dense black-green of jade stone.

"Ain't no corn-picking weather today, boys," one of the lawmen muttered. Silence as deep as nightfall ensued. "Conversant bunch of critters, ain't ye?"

"Shut up, Al!" The second deputy spoke irreverently to the first. "Give us all a break for a change."

"For Christ's sake, let me pretend I'm asleep, and this is Heaven. That's enough now, damn it! Let's get some shuteye. Tomorrow will be another long day."

The last authoritative words were spoken by a seasoned officer of the Northwest Mounted Police, a hard man of English extraction—William Casey by name. The officer wasn't naïve. Against his better wishes, he realized there was little chance of sleeping that night. Even as he finished speaking, darkness descended upon them, an invisible dancer cloaked in midnight gray. Pushing the harsh weather was a severe, northerly wind. The weather accosted each of the officers separately, just as it did the two brothers above.

There were three Mounties on the cliff, three hardened constables. The fourth among them was the tracker, a Native scout named Tom LaCross. His Tsimshian name was White Bear, though in this crowd, that name remained unspoken. All four men lived in or up the coast from the small village of Kilnook, nearly as far northwest as British Columbia extended. But like most of the folks who lived around that isolated sliver of habitable land, they knew little about this taciturn man, this scout of half-Tsimshian blood called Tom LaCross. All agreed the man was mighty quiet.

Almost half a century before, Tom's father had galloped out of Quebec, a posse tight on his tail. He quickly adopted the trapper's craft, French-Canadian style, learning his wilderness skills as he moved across the Canadian continent, east to west. The passing years cloaked his sinewy body like fur on an animal.

Two decades later, on the northwest coast, he took a bride from the Tsimshian. The girl was Tom's mother. She was an unwavering Native girl with jet-black hair and fine features, soft skinned with a step like a wary deer. It was the woman's sensuous mouth and brooding eyes that struck the attention of a stranger and said, *Notice me.* Or suggested something more. But she held her distance, particularly toward the queen's men whom she so disdained.

Nobody teased her as a young woman, not for a second. Her beauty painted a picture that only a blind man might miss. And her eyes were blue, the blue of an abalone shell, a color rare among her people. The color harkened back to the last century, a chance encounter that no one remembered.

She held her head high and proud. She wore a fine cedar skirt, a vest of dentalium shell that spoke to Tsimshian royalty.

But her eyes rarely followed his, this gnarly trapper from Quebec. That was the custom, though the trapper failed to understand the protocol. His brashness and gruff mannerisms were in sharp contrast to this proud daughter of a chief. But she couldn't help but be drawn to his voice, as thick as the trapper's coffee.

Her marriage had been arranged between her father and the trapper. She was bartered for a good rifle, plenty of powder and lead, a steel chisel, and a small barrel of bad whiskey.

"Cost a slew of foofaraw." The trapper repeated his verdict for years to anyone with ears to listen.

He found her beautiful, *l'objet* worth the barter. The Natives called her by the Tsimshian name for the abalone shell that deferred to the mottled blue her eyes reflected in the blaze of a campfire. The Tsimshian name translated into English as "Blue Shell." The trapper went only by his last name, "LaCross." Nobody ever heard his first. "Just call me LaCross," he would mutter. "Don't need no other name."

And that was it, as far as he intended. The trapper usually got in the last word. A taciturn man. Likewise, his son, who grew up in two worlds. In the changing times of the late nineteenth century, Tom acclimated and survived as best a young Native might. He preferred his Tsimshian name, White Bear. Once outside of the Native village, the young man was always addressed as Tom.

Squatting on the granite precipice, the Tsimshian scout was as silent as the icy wall itself. But if bird or beast listened closely, they would have noted that he was chanting a prayer to his Creator under his breath. If the wind had subsided—if his words had risen above the audible howl of the storm—nobody would have cared, least of all his companions. The lawmen were indifferent to the Tsimshian. And did it really matter? The mountain storm whisked away White Bear's hallowed words, and all the others too, as each was unceremoniously deployed into oblivion.

White Bear was chanting a winter song passed along through generations of coastal peoples—his ancestors. It had been passed along for as long as the ancient cedars had lived. It was a Tsimshian song, sung to him in his infancy by his mother. The song unfolded inside his head, bracing him against the cold.

His father taught him the lessons of stealth and survival. "Keep the devil's thoughts to yourself," the gnarly trapper would repeat frequently, like book lessons the boy would later be compelled to learn at the residential school. Tom never cared about school learning, but when it came to the wilderness, his eagerness to learn the lessons it imparted never wavered. His school remained the sacred lands of his people. At that he was an adept student, a star pupil. Even as he grew into adulthood, he swore allegiance to the wild lands.

His old man was of a different sentiment. "Me don't believe in no Indian magic. Those red-faced coyotes are crazy."

His father taught him the mountain man's lessons. The boy respected his father's cunning in the wilderness, though he hated the trapper himself. White Bear traveled his own road.

"Boy, you are a dumb beast. Cold as your mother's teats."

The trapper frequently took drunken swings at Tom, but the boy easily dodged them. After those encounters, the old man would down more of his bad whiskey, then swagger away from the campfire, swinging from side to side, unsteady and profane. Tom's father was devoid of doubt. Until the end, a tight-grained trapper's disposition guided him like his one true friend.

In a hunting accident, the trapper suddenly lost his breath. His son, Tommy, was twelve years old. Tom refused to cry over his dead father.

The Tsimshian people raised the boy after that. They called him White Bear, after the Spirit Bear, the white Kermode, and for the boy's wily wilderness skills. Even as a young man, hunting, trapping and stalking with his peers, he had no equal. In the forests of the Pacific Northwest, his steps left no trail, no sign or sound. He prowled the shadow world of forest and glade with the cunning of a she-wolf.

Sitting cross-legged on a granite shelf—alone with his thoughts—Tom was feeling sure of himself, sure of his ability to find his prey, to bring the brothers in or stop them, notably with a .30-30 slug. The lawmen's rifles would do the killing. By choice, Tom carried no firearm. His job was to get the officers close enough to take a decent shot. The lawmen figured that wouldn't be much of a problem. No man knew this wilderness better than Tom LaCross. No man was a better scout.

This was his people's land. Had been for centuries, for millennia. It was Tsimshian and Haisla land. North was Tlingit territory—south, Bella

Coola and Kwakiutl. Straight west on the Queen Charlotte Islands, the Haida Gwaii, the fierce Haida—the sea raiders—dominated. At least, all this had been Native land. Had been until the Whites came in their great sailing ships and with armies of pale-faced men and took it all away.

Tom knew one thing for sure: the nearest anyone came to matching his mountain skills was the man who scampered up the cliff just a few hundred yards over his head. The Tsimshian knew the older of the two brothers well. Some men called him "Skinner," others by his first name, Daniel or Dan. Tom rolled the name over in his mind, *Skinner . . . Dan,* and he liked the sound of it.

Oddly enough, that was the same name the Natives had chosen for Tom's father, the wily trapper, calling him "the Skinner." The title harkened back to the French-Canadian's obsession with the trapping and sale of thick winter fur or plew from the otter, beaver, marten, or bear. His old man had trapped and skinned the four-legged animals by the thousands.

Tom knew Dan Skinner well. Not so many years before, he had been the young man's mentor.

The scout had closed the gap. He had tracked the two brothers across nearly two hundred miles of wilderness, pressing hard and fast. He knew that if he was half lucky the following day—the tenth of their journey—the posse might get the two sure shots they needed. Then, just ahead of the half-cut moon, the lawmen could retreat to Kilnook. Although Tom seldom complained, the bludgeoning weather took a toll on him as well.

He relished the thought of a hot fire and the smoky flesh of fresh kill: a backstrap of venison or the rump or tongue of a young elk. Shivering, he recollected the relative comforts of his small cabin and the large potbelly stove he prized above other domestic comforts. But no matter how he justified his mission, the thought of killing the two brothers continued to sadden and confuse him.

Tracking was his profession. Tom always did his job carefully. He was guided by a strong sense of pride and hard-earned mountain skills. But long ago, he had taken kindly to the two brothers and didn't fancy the notion of killing either one of them. His honor was in conflict with his craft, a skill that he held proudly and close to his chest. And why had he left his Winchester propped against the wall inside his small cabin? His decision: he would lead; the lawmen could do the killing.

Of the six men on the cliff that night, only Tom slept. Once again, his relatives sought him out and found White Bear in the world of nocturnal dreams. Ancestral spirit-helpers sheltered him in his unconscious moments, flooding his mind with visions and prayers. Like drifting smoke, they emerged through long caverns of night sky, speaking in Native tongues and dialects both rich and ancient.

He slept restlessly. In the dreamworld, White Bear saw objects falling. Though he failed to make out the shapes, he thought they were human. The sky was the mottled blue of a sun-bleached clamshell. Sometimes those colors were painted on elegant Tsimshian masks. Sometimes the Natives embedded abalone shell into the soft-grained cedar wood, into elegant masks, endowing the eyes of their fantastical carvings with an otherworldly presence.

Minutes later, he dreams of a carved mask with a wolf's face. In his dream, the predator bites his extended hand. That same hand he offers in greeting and friendship. He thinks of the English adage, "Don't bite the hand that feeds you." Well, the wolf is wild, isn't it? But its world no longer remains stable. In either world—waking or sleeping—there are fewer and fewer havens for the wild animals of the north country. The White man's rifles, sharp-toothed traps, and steel logging tools have usurped the animals' sanctuaries.

A great eagle floats in and out of his dream. The eagle knows the part of the story lost in White Bear's waking world. The eagle's head is the same pure white as the ermine's silky fur. Its body is fine feathered and as dark as charcoal except where its tail waves its wide white flag. Even deep in the Tsimshian dreamland, White Bear knows the eagle will come.

Tom was startled awake. Chagrined, he cursed himself. He was usually first up. The three constables were gathering up their "possibles," leather sacks containing survival equipment: flint and steel, brass-cased bullets, elk jerky, and smoked fish. Coffee and a canteen filled with clear stream water. Tied on each belt, a leather sheath sheltered a Green River knife, a razor-sharp weapon that remained a favorite among trappers. Snaking around their shoulders and necks, two of the lawmen carried a lengthy hoop of rope. Each officer carried a .30-30 rifle, hanging by a leather strap. The sergeant coveted a flask of bad whiskey that pressed against his hairy chest. He had also requisitioned a bronze spyglass.

Long before first light, Dan and André were on the move. Hours before sunrise, Dan was prodding his younger brother up the granite wall and through the dark. The lack of daylight further terrified André, but the brothers were out of options. They had to stay ahead of the lawmen. Ahead of their bullets.

"Listen to me, André. Use your hands and feet like claws. Never move one until the other is firmly planted. Never move too rapidly. Anchor first, then move. Follow my steps exactly."

At that, André issued a few of his patented guttural sounds, twisted words and grunts all as dark and as cavernous as the pit of a wolverine's stomach. Dan hardly noticed. He had been subjected to his younger brother's verbal entanglements for years.

André had little patience left. He was exhausted and testy. The brothers had barely slept the night before. A man couldn't exactly call a catnap "sleep." André was nearly frozen with fear and by the icy blasts of wind that stung him. Dan led, and André followed.

If any man needed to know, André had been influenced by his older brother since he was a kid pup. Big brother to little brother—well, with their father dead, no one else was left. Certainly not their mother whose prissy personality never adjusted to frontier life.

What André failed to admit to himself was that he was hiding his inadequacies behind a powder keg of anger. And he had never felt so scared. André was petrified of heights. He was climbing into his worst nightmare.

Foot followed foot—hand followed hand. Each man moved alone in his private world. A strong hemp rope bound the two brothers together. The rope became the sole physical link between the two men, a talisman of security. Dan climbed surely. André suffered with each foot and handhold. Dan was goat footed. On the cliff, André was clumsy, hounded by a revulsion for the mountain and its sheer icy face.

His breath spurted out raggedly. On the sharp granite precipice, his fingertips bled. Ice and grime cauterized his wounds. He knew he must move forward—that he must climb through his fear. He pressed higher and higher, refusing to stare back down the cliff. André felt little sense of accomplishment for how far they had come. He knew there was no retreat. Climbing down such a cliff without proper equipment was tantamount to suicide. Besides, the officers waited below.

He aimed his eyes high above. He knew. He had to survive. Dan spurred him on. Down the rope snaked a message. *Follow me, little brother. You will be alright. Are you listening to me? Make no sudden moves. Show care. By the grace of God, we will get through this together. You know you can trust me, André. I would never lead you astray.*

André edged upwards, putting his faith into Dan's hands. He was pressed to admit it, but he admired his big brother above all other men. His veneration remained silent. It wasn't natural for either brother to verbalize their common affection.

Dan climbed like a goat, and André followed awkwardly. Their mission was plainly simple. The only alternative was the fall itself. Every man on the mountain knew what that meant.

Light crawled slowly above the horizon. Morning warmed. Still, the wind froze, and the ascent remained deadly.

"Hey, little brother, pass me a cup of hot coffee."

André chortled. That tiny shard of mirth was the most pleasant emotion he had experienced over the last several days.

While dawn crested the snowy mountains, pale sunlight streamed across the snowy landscape and into the Kilnook Valley where Native people had gathered for centuries, netting eulachon, the candlefish, and rendering the rich oil. Corralling the great salmon, the swimmers, and dozens of plants and animals that nourished these ancient hunter-gatherers. There, they harvested the rich resources, berries and roots, fish and game, that had fed the people of the great valley for eons beyond memory.

At last the fissure that Dan sought opened its breach. André fought back his terror. Hope skittered down the hemp rope. He grasped it. For the first time in days, he began to perceive his deliverance. His climbing grew steadier. From time to time, the summit crept into sight. A rare sunburst warmed his neck and hands.

The two brothers stopped and rested briefly.

"How far, Dan? How far now?" André thrust out his words while he gathered in hearty gulps of frigid air. His breath came in rasps, a mingling of exhaustion and fear. They had climbed hard and fast for the last two days, but no matter how quickly they climbed, Dan felt the threat of a .30-30 slug penetrating his back.

"Two or three hours at the most. The fissure probably won't run all the way to the top. But the climb will be kinder." Those words encouraged André.

"Dan?"

"Yeah?"

"Listen, I'm sorry. I . . ." Then he stopped. He failed to muster any more words.

Dan knew the end of the sentence. He spoke now in a soft, cushioned voice. "It's okay, brother. If you mean you're sorry for your anger, you don't have to say any more. I know. You're my brother. Brothers stick together. We always have."

"Listen, I want to offer a thing or two. Just in case something happens." There was urgency behind André's words.

"Alright, André. I'm hearing you." Dan was feeling the need to press on, but he knew his brother wanted to speak. Against his better judgment, he held up.

"Dan, you remember on Teal Slough that time I nearly bought the farm? How I got dragged down by the current? You swam in and pulled me out. I was nearly a goner. That water was swift and cold. Near stole my breath away. You remember that time, Dan, don't you? Son of a badger, I nearly drowned."

"Sure, little brother. Sure. I remember." Dan quieted. He knew André had more to say.

"Remember when I was a kid, how you always defended me in fights? Took my lickings with me, for me. And just last year—remember? That time we both got the living tar knocked out of us 'cuz I drank a bit much and pushed that lard-ass Kevin Spanner and his clan of loggers into a brawl. Seven to two. Badly outnumbered and we nearly won the fight. A draw, maybe?"

Dan remembered well enough. He had the scars to prove it. "What are you driving at, André?"

"Listen, I've gotten both of us into big trouble this time. Hell, wasn't no cause of yours. Listen to me, Dan. You always been too good to me. That's God's truth. I just wish I could take back this one mistake. I never meant to kill that man. He just deserved a whippin'. All I did was cause mighty trouble for you and Rebecca. She ain't never going to speak to me again. She's sure to hate me."

Dan jumped at the sound of her name. For a change he hadn't been thinking about her. His present troubles were plenty enough. He didn't need to burden himself with the added weight of her absence. Rebecca would have to wait—wait until he got his little brother over the top of the cliff. Until they broke away from the posse. Besides, she loved André. Any fool could see that. But Dan couldn't waste time on such thoughts. Time to press on. A man had to remain disciplined.

"That's just fine, little brother. Rebecca never hated you. Never. Not for a second. I wish we all could take back our mistakes. But you can't—I can't—and that's just how the dice roll. The world just isn't like that, no how. Listen to me. We'll get through this together. We'll get off this damn mountain alive."

Dan took a deep breath and looked up the mountain. He felt more than a glimmer of hope. He turned again to André. "Just someday . . . someday . . . I just wish you could hold that temper of yours in check. Save us both a slew."

"Yeah. For sure. Dan? I'm mighty sorry. You get that?"

"Yes, I do, André. Thanks for saying so."

André looked off then, far down the valley. A silky silver sheen cloaked the distant horizon. He uttered something under his breath. A gust of wind scattered his words. He reached his cold fingers above his head and grabbed a handhold.

"What?" Dan shouted. "What did you say?"

André looked up, gathered in some more private thoughts. "I want you to know. After Mom died . . . well, you were always there."

After that, André said no more.

Above the precipice, a lone eagle circled. Two, three, four times, it floated across a half-dozen spots of living flesh, six men ascending painfully up the cliff face, praying for wings like his. Then the raptor fell away. Its great winged body moved effortlessly until, in a huge gliding arch, the raptor returned to the spot where the men perched in twos and fours. Black ring, gold ring, black dot—a piercing eye penetrated the persona of these western pioneers, these strange trespassers into the valley of his ancestors.

The eagle circled with the patience of the tides. Particularly, the huge bird sought out two of the men. One was the hunted and the older of the two brothers. The second man was caught between two worlds, one White and the other Red. He had inherited a world of conflicting natures and confusion.

Whatever thoughts the eagle possessed, they remained as private as the wind that bolstered him. Back and forth the eagle flew, cutting effortlessly through the gunmetal sky. Hard snow began to fall.

No weather for man or beast, it thought, its cognition strangely human. Even the raptor felt the penetrating claw of winter.

Who is the beast, the eagle wondered, *man or animal*? As it wrangled with deep thoughts, wide, flat flakes of snow began to paint a white face across the winter sky.

Tom sensed the fall before the sound reached his ears. Something unconscious jostled his sixth sense. He felt the return of his dream from the night before—suddenly remembering the black-and-white vision with clarity and shock.

Objects were slicing through the thin winter air. Tom could make out the shapes now. The two lawmen were tied securely, one to the other. The weapons were their precious repeating rifles. The blue-stained barrels, still bright and eager, sailed past his eyes like severed limbs from an ancient evergreen, each weapon tumbling toward the ground, far below.

The rifles flew freely and then thumped sharply into the cliff's edge, producing a high, chattering sound. Seconds later, the rifles would spring forward again, out into the air, out and down, gravity drawing them. The sound slapped at Tom's ears as if to prod his oversight. The ricochet of the weapons wounded his pride much like a mistake that shadows a man forever or accompanies him to an early grave.

Behind the pummeling rifles, came the bodies of two constables, tied together by a rope that marked them partners in the same twist of fate. As one body slammed into the granite wall, the other lurched forward like a marionette on a string.

An extended silence hung in the sovereign air. Tom felt the same chill that frequently descended upon him as he watched the Boston men leveling an ancient evergreen forest—as he watched the great trees stagger, moan, and then fall. Below, the earth waited, as accommodating as a gravedigger.

For the first time in days, the wind lulled, and for a short time, he heard the men's cries.

In the distance, the valley faded, receding into evergreen hues and soft, swollen grays. Tom shifted his weight and stuck one hand beneath his wool shirt. His fingers were numb, his skin cold. Again, his eyes followed the route where the lawmen had fallen.

Tom thought of the wives and families of the two lawmen. Suddenly, he thought about home, his home and theirs. Tom had loved ones too, and their ghosts hovered in the same air around him, admonishing his decision to harness the lawmen together. As Tom diverted his eyes up to Casey, he felt the hard tease of fate. He felt the odds closing in around him like a noose. His confidence had turned a corner and taken a hard fall.

A tight knot penetrated his chest. His gut hurt. His breath steamed out in short, convoluted bursts. He cursed his decision to track without a firearm. Only one Winchester rifle remained. That would have to be enough. Dan Skinner and his brother had none. Dan was handicapped by his brother's inexperience. Odds still favored the hunters. "Dan Skinner," he said, his words cursed by the promise of more snowfall. "Danny Skinner." *So many good memories and one bad.* "Dammit to hell!" The three words spurted out from the taciturn man's mouth but found no ears listening.

In a rare moment of indecision, he stopped momentarily and called up to the man on the wall, a dozen feet above him, the last lawman. "Cut it free, Joe."

The braided rope was severed, and the two men immediately became victims of their private fates.

Tom was a loner. Climbing independently of the sheriff, he felt a renewed sense of freedom. He turned once more, staring down the cliff where the officers had disappeared. Then he carried on: leghold, handhold, and up the cliff, as deftly as a mountain goat.

The Skinner brothers never heard the death cries. That was far below. If they had been conscious of the accident, they might have applauded their sudden spate of luck. They knew nothing.

Clinging by their fingertips, the odds were a little better than they had been over the last several days. Above them, closer now, freedom waited. Above them, the summit called for a temporary deliverance.

The brothers climbed steadily. The world at the top of the cliff—a sheared, flat-topped mountain plateau—loomed closer and closer.

With each foothold, cold and fatigue sapped André's strength and willpower. But with every agonizing step—one step closer to the summit—he felt the return of hope, and with that, a revitalized sense of determination. Life became a battle between the two, a rivalry of opposing forces. All the while the brothers ascended. Chance—the slimmest of chances—called their names.

There were chinks in the granite chimney. Dan would wrap his fingers and toes around any handhold. Pull his body upwards, hand over hand. His confidence was contagious. At times he found a rope hold on the granite face. From there he would anchor the braided hemp line. Once secured, the hold allowed André to shinny awkwardly up the cliff face. Dan would slap his brother's shoulder, encourage him with every stroke. Then Dan would turn and climb, weaving hope and skill into a survivor's mantra.

Twice André slipped. Both times the rope held. Both times fear surged through his body. Each time he stumbled, André felt the return of penetrating desperation.

"Damn it to hell!" His words rang out, reverberating into distraught echoes. André was a soldier. The wall was his enemy.

From time to time, Dan admonished his brother for his rough-edged words. But the parade of curses remained as consistent as the icy wind.

Fingers first—grasp, foothold next. Lift the body higher and higher. Another foothold. Another finger hold. Another curse. André repeated the litany over and over. The talk of taverns and beer halls nudged him toward the summit.

Overhead, an eagle circled high above the frozen mountain, two piercing eyes, following the brothers' movements as sure as shadow follows light.

A pinnacle—the two brothers sought a pinnacle—and that coveted space remained an elusive rendezvous. Finally, in a renaissance of muscle, mind, and luck, the summit drew near. Hard hours had flooded by. Dusk mixed with the snow-laden sky. Clouds roiled. A miasma of mist and snow melded into a veil that covered the mountain with a silky skin, as casually—as mysteriously—as a magician covered a shill with smoke, making bodies disappear before the imagination of a human audience.

As surely as if it had walked down the cliff to greet the two brothers, the summit postured and then arrived. Dan pulled his fatigued body onto flat-footed rock. He felt his strained muscles relax. Felt a prayer of thanksgiving slip from his tongue. He began to pull André up the few remaining feet. The mountain summit reverberated with the promise of their newfound freedom.

There and then a rifle blast filled the air. The rifle's echo rebounded off the granite wall and was hurled down the valley, a volley of thunder leapfrogging like a forest fire from tree to tree.

André hung limply from a tether of taut rope. By then the valley was haunted with the silenced voices of the dead.

Dan watched his brother's face lose its color. Before his eyes, the flushed, ruddy complexion that had painted André's face after so many hours of exertion on the precipice evaporated into gray pallor. There was no time for reconciliation. No time to say goodbye or offer a prayer to the abject and impersonal Gods of that mountain lair. A single word escaped André's lips. For the rest of his life, Dan would hear the word and wonder. The last word framed Dan's wife's name, spoke to a private litany of love and desire. André's last word was "Rebecca." Then the word danced off the icy wall and folded like all the others into twilight. Dan had never felt so great a loss.

Wool armor never stopped a .30-30 slug. One brother cut the other loose. The steel blade made a mewing sound like scavenger birds tearing flesh. Then André's body fell like the officers before him. Dan had no choice. He couldn't pull two hundred pounds of dead weight up the wall. And he refused to wait. The next slug might call his name. Dan didn't hold up. He reacted instinctively.

No time for tears. My brother is dead.

And that decision saved his life.

His brother free at last, Dan fled. No time for tears; those might come later, fermenting into deeper anger or hatred. Maybe time would calm him, untangle his emotions. Perhaps from the experience, Dan would find deeper strength, and his life would be changed—that was, if he survived.

Dan felt squeezed like a horseshoe clamped in a vise. If only he had skipped the brief conversation on the wall. If only he had foregone André's confession. What if he had convinced André to turn himself in? If only!

Dan was free now. *Free*? He imagined that he was with Rebecca. Working his farm. Trapping beaver in the early springtime. Splitting cedar rounds into shakes.

What had this skirmish accomplished? Only the loss of his kid brother and, most likely, his wife. Now, Dan was alone. So alone. And his tribulations were hardly over.

Dan fled. At that moment he ran from pain as much as from the posse, or what was left of it. And what was left was the best part. What was left was the famous scout, his Tsimshian mentor.

Snow swooned into an army of white flakes, falling thicker and harder until his vision was consumed by the opaque landscape.

Snow and ice hid the body but not pain. Around him, large snowflakes fluttered like a swift covey of songbirds driven by high mountain winds.

Then Dan stopped—suddenly, inexplicably—turned and began to trudge back to the edge of the cliff. A thought had settled in. A deadly thought. Again the man followed his instincts.

The intricate patterns of dusk, *pa nee khuit* to the Natives back in Kilnook, gathered up his lone shadow. Dan was lost in a deadly storm between mind and body.

May 1992

Forest is a forest is a forest

—Katherine Skinner-Patterson

She was never an easy-going person, never laid back. As a child and as a teenager—later as an adult—personal goals drove her. Katherine Skinner-Patterson always knew where she was going. She was precocious. She was determined. She was smart.

Even her face spoke to that same determination: intense celadon eyes, a square, strong jaw, a visage appearing sculpted or chiseled. Yet there was nothing dominating about her presence: petite, neither comely nor homely. She had a soft, quiet voice. But her persona spoke to something greater. She was a woman who trusted her intellect. A wolverine spirit cloaked in a woman's small body.

On a bright summer day in 1992, the wheels of her rented Mazda sped along the asphalt highway between Prince Rupert and Terrace, BC. About her the landscape spoke of deforestation, of another forest, felled, drawn, and quartered. That initially was one of two reasons she had come north.

Grandfather—Grandmother—trees she thought, knowing that the spirit of the old ones bound her like a talisman. She regarded that as odd but stuck to the certainty of her convictions.

And the old man with a voice like a deep well. That was the second reason for coming. Over the telephone his voice had touched her deeply. Transformed her, at least momentarily. Still, she reasoned, she was being irrational, impetuous. Katherine was a woman who followed her instincts.

Deep in British Columbia, her eyes danced over the landscape. Her eyes appeared excited, as if painted with an extra serving of sparkle. Katherine's deep, searching gaze generally caught an observer's attention.

She pushed the gas pedal toward the floor. The car responded with a series of ineffectual hiccups. "Ping, ping, ping," her voice echoed as she mocked the rented auto's lack of courage. God, she hated that. Slowly, the car picked up momentum. Katherine liked speed. She felt invigorated by a life menu of adventure. That included a salting of danger.

Katherine thought again about the old man, the portent of his message. She figured the elder was a craftsman, a master of the spoken word.

She thought suddenly about her daddy. Katherine wiped away the tiny moisture that precedes tears. Funny, for it had been years since she had cried over him, years since he had passed away. She knew this land and her father were braided together. She wondered if the elder fit into the same pattern, fit the intricate web of her life and the infectious call of virgin landscape. Well, she thought, soon there would be answers.

She pulled onto the side of the road, then scribbled more notes onto the blank, yellow page of a writing tablet. On the previous page were two dozen new lines, the beginnings of a poem.

Someday, she postulated, her words might become her story.

She wrote for about five minutes before pulling back onto the highway. The car wallowed in its ineffectual slow-motion acceleration. Again—impatiently—she pressed the gas pedal to the floor, soliciting more speed. She thought about transportation. Not so long ago, people depended on their feet or a cedar canoe. There had been no horses, no wagons, no roads. She liked that idea.

In her head, other ideas began to form. While scanning the highway before her, Katherine continued to scratch out words onto the blank yellow page in large clumsy letters, her hands moving without the aid of her eyes. The road charged into long, looping curves. Just beyond and downhill, she saw a small village. She pressed the pedal harder. Katherine put down the pencil. She envisioned the elder waiting. Here was the Native village of Kilnook.

CHAPTER THREE

Snow surrounded him. Hunkered around his body the way an angel might flirt with visitation. If this man had been watching the pattern of snowfall from the security of a warm log cabin, he would have experienced elements of sensuous beauty. But there was little beauty left in his beleaguered soul. Anger anchored its talons into his mind much as a storm haunts the deepest hours of a dark, silent night. Angels, he thought. These are angels of death.

A man is what he perceives.

—Katherine Skinner-Patterson
Notes for a novel

As Sergeant William Casey lowered the smoking barrel of his .30-30 rifle, he allowed himself a moment of satisfaction. The lawman had shot one of those brothers; that was for damn sure. He had witnessed the body as it plunged unceremoniously down the cliff. Likely, he had killed the same son of a bitch who had started the whole fracas just ten days before.

Casey's mind was racing.

Already, a disturbing sense of retribution prodded him. He had lost two friends, good men, both. Two brothers—now one brother—were responsible. Sure, they hadn't directly pushed his officers down the cliff, but they were the sole reason the Mounties had happened there. The brothers had murdered half his detachment as sure as the fall down the cliff had broken their bones. Casey was wondering what he was going to say to the lawmen's wives, to the community. All the while, justification was stirring in his mind.

Too bad I didn't get off another shot, he thought. But the older brother was nearly over the top of the cliff, and Casey had been caught in an awkward position.

Hell, no marksman could have done any better, could he? Done better under such circumstances? None, except maybe that silent Indian, and he ain't packin'.

Time was running out as Casey squeezed off the long shot. He would be the first to admit that he had been lucky, but the younger brother had fallen. *Luck be damned. After all, a man needs some bragging rights.*

He had watched the brothers with his looking glass—watched for hours—waiting for the Skinner boys to falter or stumble back into rifle range. The older brother had held the pair together. Like a voyeur, Casey felt as if he had gotten to know each of them better. Then the thought struck him: h*ell, it ain't over yet*. The older brother still had to be reckoned with. *Well, one down at least*. That evened the odds. "Good riddance," he whispered under his breath. Then he began to wonder out loud. Wonder where all the events might lead. "Hard weather ahead. Damn it to hell."

Suddenly, the wilderness opened bigger and wider and decidedly more dangerous.

Like the web of waterways that crisscrossed these mountains, Casey's thoughts meandered. Was he feeling satisfaction about killing André Skinner, or was the ante too steep? He couldn't ignore the fact that two of his men were dead. "Damn it to hell," he muttered. "Damn it anyways!"

Casey was a creature of habit. His ego was bolstered by the stripes that pierced his soiled woolen shirt, by his size and his indomitable spirit. He had not changed his garments in two weeks. Tattered long underwear clung to his muscular frame, anointing his body all the way up to his dirty neck. His odor was rank.

Casey was not an agile man, neither dexterous nor athletic. He was big-boned and muscular, and he used his size the way a boxer strikes with his fists. He had bullied himself up the cliff. He was relentless. He had a task to accomplish. He controlled his body but not his mind, and even now, clinging to the granite face, his thoughts galloping back and forth like the furtive gusts of wind that twisted up the valley. "God damn it," he muttered, his eyes leveled on the scout, his memory ambling toward their last conversation. "Closed-mouth, son of a bitch."

He reached up, palmed another stone handhold, and climbed higher and higher toward the summit.

The Tsimshian's actions had struck Casey as peculiar. Immediately following Casey's first fatal shot, Tom had insisted that Casey hold off on the second. The request seemed more like a demand. The dictate had annoyed Casey, but he had capitulated. He stewed over it now. *Probably wouldn't have gotten it off anyways. Would have been a long shot, a lucky shot. Far luckier than the first.*

Seconds fled by. Casey's ego fountained. He was angry, but he spoke his words so quietly that the wind scurried them away. As his anger cooled, he began to ponder the inevitable question: *Just who is running this show, me, or that no-account Indian?* Well, the breed demanded respect, sure 'nough. *The best tracker in the north country. He is the best, by God. And where would I be without him*? When all was said and done, a good man had to make concessions.

What the hell, he thought, his thoughts skittering like a crane fly on a still beaver pond. *I'll get another shot.* Just one more try—that was all he needed. He had killed one of those bad boys. He and the scout were closing in. Casey's mouth began to inaugurate the shape of a tight-lipped smile, a grin goaded with satisfaction. He caught himself. Instead, he shrugged and turned toward Tom as if hoping to extract an acknowledgment for his fine shooting.

Tom was watching Casey intently. He had caught the smirk. Tom was reminded of the way a retriever seeks his master's affection. Was this what the red coat—Casey—expected? Personally, Tom preferred the company of dogs and coyotes. He found Casey to be nothing but a braggart.

But Casey was proud of his marksmanship. He had done what a lawman was paid to do. He had shot straight and true. But Tom had tracked down the criminals—no man would question that.

Tom's face remained emotionless. Casey felt thwarted. Chagrined, he wondered what the taciturn man was thinking and silently cussed the scout's stubborn ways.

Tom's emotions were confused. Maybe out here the big country did that to a man. For sure, things weren't going as expected. *Move on*, he thought. *Finish the job.*

Then Tom heard the lawman murmur, "What do you expect from a breed?" Tom had keen ears. He felt his anger stir. Abruptly, he turned his eyes away from Casey. Under his breath, murmured an insult in Tsimshian. Casey noticed. Tom saw that the lawman felt chastised. That wasn't his problem. Over the years, Tom had learned to keep his feelings corralled. He was forced to turn inward then, and that was just one more burr under his saddle.

Minutes swept by. As if he had a change in tactics, Tom's head swiveled. His gaze held. His mouth opened. To Casey, the scout's gaze was direct and disconcerting. Tom's lips parted slightly, as thin as a pencil fracture across a sheet of ice. He never wasted a motion.

Well, that is his way, ain't it?

Maybe the Tsimshian's look was derisive. Maybe Casey was overreacting. A scant hiss of words slipped out effortlessly. Strangely, they disturbed the mountain's mood. *Cussed bastard,* Casey thought. But the deputy was expecting other words than the ones he got.

Two succinct words crossed the narrow space between the lawmen. "Let's git." Without waiting for Casey's reaction, Tom began to ascend the cliff.

"I'll be damned," Casey hissed under his breath. "What the hell?"

Yards away, Tom caught the dangling edge of Casey's declaration. He knew what sentiment lay behind the lawman's words, but Tom didn't much care. At least he told himself that. A private man, he didn't have a lot of friends. And Casey had just shot one of the few. *Well, that's my job, alright?* Justification stirred. Tom thought again of the afternoon when the younger Skinner had abandoned him. He thought of the boulder that had just sailed past his head, missing him by mere inches. Tom's mood remained dark. *This is no friend*!

Mountain shadows lengthened. The two climbers struggled up the icy wall. Occasionally, Tom stole a look into the sky above. Out of the corner of his eye—the flitting gaze was only an imperceptible interruption in his steady ascent—he caught the circuitous movement of a raptor. An eagle. *Same dang one.* Tom was certain. He had seen the magnificent bird several times earlier that day and twice the day before. This had to be the same bird. Tom had never seen an eagle of such size or wingspan. He housed a suspicious feeling about the raptor but refused to pin too much on his observation. Tom was a disciplined man. The mountain had already taken three. This was no time to let his thoughts wander.

Quickly, he turned his full attention back to the cliff. It was easy enough to define his charge: he had to get to the top alive. Tom knew that sooner or later he would find Dan Skinner. Find him. Bring him in. Bring him in, dead or alive. *They'll probably hang him anyways. Best to fight it out. Let the best man win.* His thoughts tumbled out. Find him if the wilderness didn't take one of them first, that is, if winter and the sheer cliff didn't kill them both.

Suddenly, he remembered his dream. Remembered the eagle. *Stay steady, man. Pay attention.* But thoughts rallied. Once again he was lost in two worlds.

Tom and the Sergeant followed the same route inaugurated by the brothers. As with the Skinners before them, the chimney proved a relief from both the dangers and the exhaustion of the arduous climb. Casey led. He was thirty-two years old that very day, standing four inches over six feet and two hundred sixty pounds—a big man in a big wilderness. Tom was fifty-three and sprouting a bit of a belly. Too much eulachon grease, he reasoned. He was capable of climbing steadily for many hours, but he continued to fall behind the lawman.

Casey was thinking about a hot meal. Tom about a sweetheart from years before. He was seeing the young woman's moody eyes reflected in a mottled, windswept landscape. For nearly forty years, he had been haunted by the loss of his first love. The thought remained as chilling as the frigid northern wind.

Ravenous, Casey imagined smelling the hot marrow of venison ribs simmering over campfire coals, a fine sheen of fat on his thick fingers and mustache. From the wall, Casey grunted, cursing the ache that etched his empty belly. Muscle fatigue tore at his strong legs and arms. The big man was weary.

Yards away on the frozen cliff, Tom's memory was possessed by the memory of the young woman's skin, a touch as soft as ermine fur. That was as far as it had gone. *Dead over thirty years now.*

Tom didn't remember if the girl had been a young woman or the young woman a girl. Well, she was Tsimshian for sure. And she was gone, buried as surely as his family and neighbors in a communal grave, a shallow pit. What had there been, a hundred? A hundred fifty? He turned his attention back to the wall, but there was no dislodging the thought or the memory of many tears. Had he cried since? He thought not.

For the second time in as many minutes, Tom swiveled his head. Above him, the sky darkened. Like a sweep of thick, dark pigment layered on canvas from a painter's brush, dark blue quickly bled into gray. *Grayland,* he thought. *The land, this landscape—Grayland.*

He turned his attention back to the climb. Above him, Casey's pace pressed him. The lawman's expression was rigid and mocking. So what? Casey was a bully. Tom had known many. He didn't much like this man, but as far as that went, he didn't like many. Casey was still his boss. He was responsible for Tom's paycheck and, to a certain degree, his reputation. *Climb on, man. Move on.*

Tom pulled himself up another notch, a yard higher. His fingers were numb. His legs ached. A warrior didn't waste his time on body pain. White Bear, the Tsimshian warrior known to the White world as "Tom," let his thoughts sweep back to his family, to the girl.

Smallpox—he envisioned the deep, broad pit filled with bodies, Native bodies, all from *his* village. Many were loved ones, several from his family and clan. No honor in the ritual. Death had come frenzied. The village had numbered nearly five hundred. Only a week later, eighty-three survivors buried the dead along with the major legacy of the tribe. As an efficient social unit—a fighting force—their efficacy was broken. As a man—as

White Bear or as the scout that the Bostons deferred to as a "breed"—the loss of his family marked him forever.

His thoughts shifted, his steady climbing missing a beat. Maybe the death of the younger Skinner brother had shaken loose old memories. Maybe he blamed this sudden flurry of woolgathering on the death of the two lawmen. *Don't I carry some blame?*

He wondered how those losses might shape his future. If he was feeling harangued by his past, the landscape of coming hours and days would be defined by the events of the last several hours. He grabbed for a handhold and pulled himself higher. The wind was as biting as ever he remembered. Of that one reality, he was certain.

Just as suddenly, Tom was remembering a second woman, remembering another place and time. He was seeing the face of a White woman. Her name was Ruth Anne. *Ruth Anne McCauley.* He had nearly forgotten her family name. He stopped his ascent mid-stride, his right hand extended but motionless, his eyes unfocused. Maybe her memory startled him. It had been decades. Tom had been a young man of nineteen.

He took another deep breath and faced the stone wall again. He was intimate with its hardness now. Intimate with the cold reality. He followed the veins and fissures of the dense granite like the delicate trail of a mink or a coyote. Even as dusk pushed down the mountain, Tom climbed with cat-like instinct.

Hand followed foot. He pushed himself even harder now. Through exertion, Tom hoped to circumvent unwanted memories. He didn't need distractions. The cold truth of his circumstance hounded him. He figured he had better keep up with Casey. If he punished his body hard enough, he might forget the woman, or both women, and those memories that scathed him. *Well, maybe*?

As he climbed on, there was little reprieve. Life and death were separated by the narrowest of circumstances. Was his fate to survive? The other option unsettled him.

He climbed higher and higher. The wind continued to punish him. He grasped at any stone outcropping he found. Pulled himself upward.

Above him the eagle swept across the darkening sky, its shadow swallowed by the miasma of gray.

1960

Martin Skinner, was named for the ferocious mammal, a critter of strength and determination. Or so went the story. The name clung on Katherine's daddy, long gone now, along with so many memories, and so many unanswered questions. Where had her father come from? What were his origins? Her mother had supplied a few answers, but the book of their lives remained nearly incomplete.

Her father's father had disappeared into the Canadian wilderness. Her grandmother was another incomplete story. All she knew for certain was that her grandparents were linked to the North. Even her father had been quiet on the subject, though he had shared a few names and stories. Snippets! Was he hiding a family secret? This much she knew: Rebecca Skinner had been a pioneer woman. She had both moxie and wilderness skills not particularly associated with a stereotypical 1950s woman.

Katherine wanted to know more, but her mother, her father's wife, remained vague on the subject. Somewhere was the full story that Katherine craved. That mystery haunted her. Katherine was determined. Sooner or later she would weave the disparate pieces together. She would discover the full story.

CHAPTER FOUR

Help me remain calm and strong in the face of all that comes toward me. Help me find compassion without empathy overwhelming me. I seek strength, not to be greater than my brother but to fight my greatest enemy: myself. Make me always ready to come to you with clean hands and straight eyes. So when life fades, like the fading sunset, my spirit may come to you without shame.

Translation by Lakota Sioux Chief Yellow Lark in 1887

When William Casey's bullet found André Skinner, the lawman was less than three hundred yards from the mountain summit. That paltry distance took Casey and Tom well over four hours to climb. Dusk was turning into night. Tom was deeply fatigued. Casey was too proud to admit it, but he too felt played out.

As twilight dropped an opaque curtain across the landscape, Casey raised his weary body inch by inch to the very spot where his bullet had slain André Skinner. Night shadows flooded the landscape with a deep purple cast. The cliff was stained with the reality of a man's blood. The lawman's long shot had found the younger Skinner brother and silenced him. By now, Casey was too tired to feel remorse or elation.

In the first hour of night, a spray of blood etched the rock wall like graffiti. For just a moment, a half-moon crept out from behind the dark clouds. In its pale-yellow cast lingered the haunting spirits of three dead men, soon becoming four.

Casey never saw the stone that crushed his body. From above came a swift wind, the song a ten-pound boulder makes as it whistles down a steep mountain. No time to react or call out—no time to say goodbye. He fell. Darkness and deadly surprise tracked his descent. Darkness, four spirits, and an eagle. Long before his body ever reached its final resting place, Casey's soul had crossed into the land of the dead.

Thirty feet below him, the last member of the posse, the Tsimshian whose mother's spirit was singing a death chant, sprang like a mountain goat, startled but lightning quick. A second rock nearly collided with his body. Tom felt a bolt of nausea. His fingers grasped another handhold, and he swung precariously before pulling his body up against the cold rock face. No sooner had he done so than another missile bounded past, decamped from its ancient resting place.

The moon crept back under the curtain of dark clouds. The rock saw no better in the dark than the marksman, and the stone swerved past Tom, missing by mere inches.

The Tsimshian scout known by his people as White Bear cached into a sliver of a depression chiseled into granite by eons, by undeterred wind and persistent rainfall. He swung under a pregnant ridge of stone, frightened and wary, his heart pounding like the clatter of a mountain goat's hooves. *So close*! For the second time in two days, Tom cursed his decision to track the brothers—cursed his lack of care. Huddling in a stone cache that reminded him of a coffin, the night passed as slowly as the movement of a glacier.

There were no more boulders, but for hours his muscles anticipated collision. Throughout the long northern night, a mountain of doubt marked an indelible message on his mind. A circus of questions and answers plagued him: *why wasn't I more cautious? Was I too cocky? Dan Skinner is up there, or maybe he's gone. Long head start, for sure. I'm a fool! Go back. But go back to where? Go forward. Where might that be? The sergeant, bâton merdeux* (one of a handful of French slang words he had garnered from his father), *dead now. But how will I explain that? I've got to find Dan Skinner. Now ain't that something. Find my student. Bring him in. Sacré bleu—I'll be lucky to just survive this damn cliff.*

His normal steady mind was drowning in afterthoughts. He had hours to contemplate his mistakes and options. The night bore down, interminable in its rancor. The temperature dropped well below freezing. The cold crept over him like ghosts from his past.

What will the town think if I return without Dan Skinner? He was my friend, once. Once?

What had happened to that friendship? What had turned the master tracker and his wily student away from each other? Tom knew the answer, but pride collided with reason. He shifted the thought away, but memories continued to rankle.

His brother's poor body is lying at the bottom of this stinking cliff. Will I gather him up? Bring in his body? What then? What if I return without the Mounties, without William Casey? How do I tell the families that their men are all dead? TELL THEM THEY ARE ALL DEAD! All of them. Damn it to hell!

Don't go back, he thought. *Move south. Take a fast boat to Seattle. Wherever the hell that is.*

Tom didn't quite know how to put a shape on a city of such size. Couldn't conjure up the tall buildings and the web of winding streets. He was highly capable of penetrating an untamed wilderness, but the thought of such a city caused him anxiety.

Run far and fast. No. You just can't; you can't back down, not now. Can't go back empty-handed. His mind sought hard answers, sprang ahead, then fell back. *Do what you've got to do. What's that, for God's sake? No rifle. Damn it! That was a dumb mistake.* He reached for the knife on his side—that would have to do. A stew of confusion confronted him.

Tom declined to hear what the relatives were saying, but he sensed their presence. They hovered around him, spirit angels or apparitions—ancient souls for sure. And family? The ghosts of his family? Suddenly, he doubted even that. Doubted everything at once.

He heard the echo of his dead father talking. Felt their minds colliding. Felt the staggering impact of the trapper's vain and racist judgments.

He conjured up a Sisiutl, the double-headed serpent of the deep ocean, a creature with shapeshifting abilities. Did he not possess two separate lives? After that White Bear felt shamed and wished to pull back his words and shroud his negative thoughts. His strength wavered. Then his faith found new meaning.

He endured and the night passed.

I have chosen this, he thought in one final revelation. *I have chosen who I am. I am White Bear. From now on I am White Bear.* But in a night shrouded in blackness and doubt, he soon questioned even that. After all, he was Tom LaCross. He was the White man's scout.

For a while, Tom pondered an ancient story of loyalty between brothers. A story passed down from his uncle. A story of courage and sacrifice. Simultaneously, he envisioned the two Skinner brothers, one leading the other to safety, one sacrificing a good life to defend his brother's mistakes. *Well,* he thought, *all that is over. One has already gone under. Now I search for the second while he hunts me.*

His thoughts gyrated like a Tsimshian dance.

Speaking out loud in his native tongue, he lamented, "Should have shot the bastard when we had the chance."

Confusion reigned.

After that, Tom was sure that the weather stung him out of retribution for his lack of honor. He felt flushed with shame. Already, he had forgotten a lesson deeply seated in his culture. He had abandoned a friend.

If stone had breathed that night, Tom would have heard its slightest murmur. His ears were keen.

In the deepest hour of night, he fled into a new hiding place. No stones came. He fled again. There was no shuffle of feet, no bark of broken snow. Indeed, not even the deadly whistle of stone dented the acoustics of the night.

Is he up there?

Tom decoyed again. Feigned movement. Twice. A third time. Not a breath of wind stirred against him, the Tsimshian warrior, White Bear. If Dan Skinner was above, he didn't take the bait. Tom moved perpendicularly up the rock face. His stealth would have startled even the wily cliff dwellers. He had turned predator.

He crouched in warrior's alertness only inches from the summit and gathered his thoughts. Tom was prepared for violence. Four fingers and a thumb grasped a final handhold and found balance. Then, like an acrobat, he drew his body up and over the sharp rock face, his arms and legs thrashing viciously with his knife at an invisible enemy.

No man waited. Dan Skinner was already hours away. He was nearly off the mountain. He had just evened the odds. Now only two men were facing each other in mortal combat. Two old friends hell bent on destroying each other. None of it made sense. Both men were drawn into an inexplicable gyre.

Snow baptized Tom. He was alone. The weather was too harsh for even the four-legged critters. Most were in hibernation now. Soft, fat snow crystals bound man, mountain, and sky together as one.

Tom knew it was time to be strong. Winter was the season to stand tall. Even so, he remained confused. He had made a fatal mistake. Okay! That was over. Or was it?

Though deep snow and darkness handicapped him, Tom moved with a quickness and agility that might have startled a younger man. Even so, he was falling behind Dan. That reality didn't worry him. Not in the least. Tom had many other skills. In the end, speed didn't matter all that much. Mountain survival skills were his strong suit. So was tracking.

Tom had long ago discovered that the wilderness had its own schedule. Dan's footsteps left a delicate path across the snowy earth. An accumulation of fresh snow wouldn't hide everything. Besides, Tom didn't need the full light of day to illuminate Dan's trail. Tom's toes ferreted out the faint marks, a language as clear as Braille to the keen tracker. Light would soon grace both the hunter and the hunted. A short day, but time was on his side.

Plenty of time to catch up. Plenty of time. *What then*? he wondered as the snowflakes swirled around him like ghosts from his past.

When their paths finally crossed, which man would be stronger? Tom figured one of the two would likely go under.

Struggling through the snow drifts, he thought he heard the echo of his thoughts. *Which one*? *Which man will prove the winner?*

Not even the forest spirits knew that answer. Tom did what he knew best. He moved forward with determination and undisputable skill.

The sheriff was dead. Dan had witnessed his fall. The two officers were gone as well. From above, Dan had imagined a single image struggling up the sheer cliff. His old mentor. Again, anger smote him. Two men remained. A showdown was in order.

Dan moved on, racing deeper and deeper into the wilderness, pondering a new reality: *who will survive? Which man is stronger*?

Dan was galloping down the mountain's south flank. Moving rapidly through deep hummocks and plateaus of snow, he felt at home. There, a man had freedom to move. His brother was gone. The debacle on the cliff had passed. He moved swiftly now. His only encumbrance was the mental loss of André, and of course, the weather. For the moment he planned to put distance between himself and Tom LaCross.

Dan suspected what his old mentor knew: sooner or later, the gap between the two woodsmen would close around them like a steel trap. That word hung in the dense frigid air. "Trap!" No matter how fast he moved, Tom would find him. Dan knew that as a certainty. A man could only run so far from the likes of Tom LaCross. In such a wilderness, the scout was a craftsman, an artist. Tom possessed both a bag of tricks and deep mountain lore.

Thoughts trickled in*: Attention, Dan. Pay attention!*

Dan knew the Tsimshian's strength. Knew it better than any living man. Hadn't Tom been his teacher? Hadn't he taught Dan not only how to survive in the wilderness but also, how to excel?

Dan believed that Tom had a rifle. That intensified his caution. *Got to find cover. Get into the deep woods. Run. Hide. Maybe, just maybe the hunted might become the hunter.*

Dan still had his knife. He would carve other weapons. He might even fashion a snare. The revelation struck him suddenly, like breathing air after being trapped underwater—*I will lure the hunter into a trap.*

There was no true dawn. Morning light was held captive by thick fields of snowflakes, by dense, snow-laden clouds. Light and dark wove intricate patterns through first light. In a rare and brief respite, Dan stopped and stared. The landscape about him was as pale as ancient ivory. And deadly—if a man got caught in its talons.

Dan thought about Christmas, the first with his lovely wife. In their new cabin, they had huddled before the stone fireplace. Flames galloped up the stone chimney—lots of dry firewood stacked under a lean-to on the lee side of the small cabin. Lots more where that came from. Below, they heard kindling snap as flames galloped toward the heavy sky. They snuggled closer yet. Outside, snow covered the pasture, the cedar roof, and finally, muffled many of the wilderness sounds. It also muted their love-making. At that moment, few couples had ever been happier.

As he moved deeper into the wilderness, farther from home, the beauty and the harshness that was the northern wilderness enveloped Dan in a slow-motion dance. Excruciating cold settled into his skin and then his pores like the curse of a determined adversary. Snow and a driving wind stung his face.

A deep, penetrating ache settled into the marrow of his bones, or so he imagined. His feet were numb, his fingers too. The stubble on his face was frozen in place. He realized the seriousness of his predicament. *A man might easily die out here.* He needed no reminder. Four already had.

There were no trails to follow unless he chose the earth-worn paths of the four-legged animals, and most of those markings were long buried. The wilderness was silent. Little stirred in this weather. Dan considered his next move. He carried no compass, but he was sure of the direction.

He skirted over mountain plateaus and moved silently through the thin, windswept groves, occasionally spotting the fine scratching of animals. He knew the individual prints: badger, deer, elk, mink, and yes, the Grizz. Fortunately, most would be in hibernation. As for the bear, their grand siesta was a blessing.

Dan inadvertently rubbed the scar on his cheek.

The conifers' heavy, snow-packed limbs might reach to the ground, might be trapped under mounds of snow. When the wind whipped the exposed branches, the needles left their mark, a fan pattern both delicate and fragile. From that Dan knew the wind direction. Snow was thinner on the lee side of the evergreens. The bark was lighter and dryer.

Dan only guessed at his destination, but at least he knew the direction in which he was traveling. *Traveling.* He liked the tenor of the word. But all the while, he was moving farther and farther from his one true love. The thought stung him with all the force of the northern winds.

The translucency that was a snow-camouflaged sunrise brightened the landscape, then lightened it more. For the next six or seven hours, he might more easily find his way. But which way? The obvious choice only led him deeper and deeper into the wild.

Bushwhacking across the harsh terrain, his mind was ripe with thoughts of his wife. Musing, he began to fill his mind's eye with her features, starting with her fingers and toes, her breasts and ivory-colored skin, until inevitably, he stopped at her face, her sun-dappled eyes, those faint freckles that highlighted her high cheekbones. He was seeing her standing in a copse of trees. It was summertime. She was wearing a summer dress. She owned but three.

Somehow, the bruising weather softened when he remembered her. Somehow, his melancholy disposition momentarily gladdened.

Forms stepped out of the grayness, only to be taken back. Migrating snow enveloped the shapes. As Dan moved closer, the same images were thrust forward one more time, until finally, they were committed to his eyesight. Wilderness was running wild. Wild, like a wolf he saw in the distance. Quickly, the stealthy animal disappeared. Was this the same one he had heard the night before? *No, that was miles away.*

The mountain terrain was painted with many hues of gray. Smoke and charcoal. The wolf's fur—gunmetal with a snow-white blaze—bled away from his thoughts. But Dan refused to forget those penetrating yellow eyes.

Images became apparitions, his journey a mirage.

In the long hours that Tom hung from the granite cliff, Dan descended the mountainside's softer, sloping ridges. Soon, he arrived at that place where the first barren plants and low-growing bushes clustered, circling like pioneer wagons seeking protection against a coming tempest. Dan remembered the way the elk gathered during the coldest threats of winter, forming larger bands of animals, bunching together. *Self-protection*, he reasoned. He wished he had some friendly faces around him now. He shrugged and then turned the aberrant thoughts away. No sense feeling sorry for himself. Dan had a mission now. He would stop Tom cold in his tracks. Stop him if any man was capable.

1962–Seek and You Shall Find

In the school library, Katherine stumbled across a legend of two brothers. The story opened a portal into the Native world, a legend passed from father to son, most likely, late at night around a campfire.

In the story, two brothers were preparing for a hunting trip. Their father cautioned the young men to only sleep on an uncomfortable rocky perch. "Sleep there," he said, "and you will not be bothered by trickster spirits."

Youth being impetuous, they chose to bed down in a mountain meadow covered with thick green grass. The setting was alluring. Spring flowers burst into view, raising like the dead after a long harsh winter. As night descended, songbirds flitted happily across the high mountain meadow. The world was at peace.

As dusk flooded the mountains, a dervish of melodious birdsong lulled the brothers into a deep slumber, but their dreams turned fitful. Awakened abruptly, they discovered they were stranded on a precipitous pillar of stone that had grown magically under their bodies during the night. It rose like a great cedar tree, tall and slender and precipitous.

Twining two ropes together, the older brother lowered the second to safety, but now the older was stranded. He had no way to anchor the rope. It wasn't long enough to lower him to the ground. There was no way to follow his brother.

Another day passed. The older brother slept sporadically, and during the second night, awoke to an animal sound. He peered from under his cedar cloak at an apparition. Before him was an ermine. The small animal was as white as mountain snow.

The ermine admired the young warrior's bravery, his sacrifice. "Put your hands and feet where I go," it said. "Lay them on my paws and follow me to safety."

The stranded brother trusted the animal helper and followed its lead. Soon, the brothers were reunited.

CHAPTER FIVE

The hunter was the hunted—the hunted, the hunter. In the wilderness there is always a predator and a prey. The weak overcome by the strong. Here, both men were strong. Both men sought the other. Ultimately, there could be but one true victor. Both were guided by the same force. That force moved through the forest and across the granite mountains and rode the wilderness currents like a phantom tyee. And here, that force might take your life.

—Katherine Skinner-Patterson
Notes for a novel

Dan was enchanted by the wild beauty of the northern wilderness, enchanted by the swift rivers that ran through the thick virgin evergreens, still beyond the reach of the cross-cut saw and the double-bladed axe. Few men ever loved the wild more, or so he imagined. This land belonged to the animals. As hard as the weather tore at him, he continued his love affair with the sensuous beauty of this uninhabited and mystical land.

He moved steadily now, the stunted stands of cedar, fir, and mountain pine obliging him passage. Again, he thought of Rebecca, alone at the farm. Loneliness crushed against his chest. He struggled forward guided by unflinching determination and hard muscle. Alone and susceptible, his mind shifted back to his kid brother.

A man wasn't capable of hiding from memories or pain—hadn't Dan learned that lesson years before? Here the harshness of the wild lands only enforced the loss of his brother. Dan knew: a warrior had to stare danger in the face. Had to chase it down. If not, he was doomed. Dan knew he had to shoulder the reality of the harsh environment as well as the pain of deep loss. He felt the weight of solitude, a heavy burden. Neither present nor past would let him be.

Now—and hardly for the last time—Dan tripped, a root or snow-covered limb taking him down. Rising from the snowdrift, he struggled to his feet and swept the cloak of snow from his body with his frozen hands. The fall hardly interrupted his reverie. He plunged ahead, memories piggybacking on his frozen soul.

Caught between deep snow and deeper memories, he was a child again, he and André, just ten and twelve. In his mind's eye, he envisioned his smaller brother standing resolutely on the weathered cedar boardwalk that paralleled the muddy streets, those man-made arteries that dissected the village of Kilnook, running north and south, east and west.

André wore britches two sizes too large, Dan's hand-me-downs. Even though it was autumn, and the coming tide of winter courted a bitter wind that whipped down the middle of the street, André's shirt was open halfway down his hairless chest, his thumbs hooked into his tattered belt loops. There was determination in his stance and something more. The younger brother wasn't about to give an inch.

André was watching a fight between two boys. One was his friend, the other a bully, an older boy. The larger boy was relentlessly pounding André's buddy into submission. Slowly, André dropped his hands from the belt loops. Drew them into clenched fists. He crept forward. And then he jumped, jabbing suddenly, unexpectedly. The larger boy went down, his nose bloodied. André hit the boy twice more, kicked him once for good measure, then scurried away, gleeful at his success. Already, André Skinner had developed the moves of a street fighter.

He was a tough, angry kid, and he was proud. The early glories of battle had already begun to shape him.

As Dan slogged across the snowfields, he felt a new sense of optimism. For the first time in days, he reckoned with his future. He was forming a plan of attack.

The first bushes appeared like conscripted leftovers from the thicker and taller forests below. This high in the mountains, the conifers grew intermittently. The weather had humbled and shaped them into wind-fashioned sculptures.

Another hour passed. As Dan descended, bushes became mountain pine, became stunted hemlock, cedar and fir. Growth was still restricted, midget in shape and height compared to the giant ones, the grandfather cedar and fir. The thicker, taller groves were still far below him, but as he skirted down the mountain's steep flank, larger evergreens drew up higher and met him. The land began to flatten out. Quickly, foothills plateaued and became lean forest.

Another hour passed. He moved deeper into the thicket. His stride was full and sure. He swung his arms in a resolute fury. Sweat gathered inside his leather shirt. The dampness worried him. In cold weather like this, a pioneer couldn't afford to get wet. Everything froze, even sweat. *Exposure.* Dan knew the word, knew the consequences. For the first time all day, he slowed his pace.

The grove thickened. Standing tall and proud before him was a deep, lush forest. Tree limbs were heavy with snow. Dan stopped and turned. In the limb of a tall cedar, an owl chortled, "Who. Who," Was it laughing at the man? Or was the bird expressing natural caution?

And Dan wondered, *who, after all*? *Just who* am I?

If Tom was close behind, Dan didn't suspect him. He knew that dusk was near. He turned north. He was sure of his direction. Another hour—then two—flew by. Dan trudged forward. No time to lose. Time was his enemy, and Dan already had one too many.

The thicket called his name, then—yes, he heard it—a bird call, perhaps a hawk or a jay. Ahead, somewhere deep in the glade, the bird made a high-pitched screech. Wind currents and distance twisted the bird's song. Was it a woodpecker? Another owl? The weather only convoluted the sounds.

For the second time in as many hours, he stopped. Dan felt extreme fatigue tugging at his heels, flooding up his legs and arms. The icy wind pummeled his face and chest, his muscles overwhelmed with fatigue. His feet were numb, numb right up to his knees. Dan realized that it had been days since he had really slept. Those few moments he had stolen on the cliff face hardly qualified as sleep. Winter frost and the proximity of the scout denied him of the rest he so craved.

He listened intently. For a moment there was only dead silence, followed quickly by another hard gust of wind. Again the evergreen forest called to him. He was in a grove of conifers now. *Thank God*! There he felt shielded from the scout's prying eyes. Tonight he would craft a plan. Polish it to perfection. Not even Tom LaCross could track him through this forest at night, not during the long darkness that enveloped much of the sound. And even if Tom succeeded, it would be slow going. *Tom needs sleep too.*

I will make a fire.

The vision of that luxury propelled Dan forward, deeper and deeper into the green.

"Sleep. *I must have sleep.*" He mumbled the words out loud, although it felt more like a request than an affirmation. His body craved warmth. All the while another instinct was at play—a base instinct. While the forest smothered him in its icy grip, revenge was seducing his spirit.

Only another hour of light, he thought, measuring out his circumstance. *Make haste.*

He moved steadily and quickly, deeper into the grove. Always deeper. The forest was his friend, his only ally. And as he moved, his mind and his instincts danced nimbly, like a bobcat on a tree limb.

Dan moved with purpose and precision. He sought a direction and stayed committed to the course. Pushing aside his exhaustion, his gait remained strong and even. Though the snowstorm obscured his view, he still knew he was moving north and east. He picked his direction from clues left in the forest: from heavier bark and moss growth on the north side of the trees; from the heights of a snowdrift, bigger and taller on one side of those same trees; from the movement of the pale, intermittent sun, north to south, low on the horizon. The sun rays were faint and infrequent, but from time to time, he determined the whereabouts of the snow-paled orb.

From the locations where the animals chose shelter—by migration patterns—he picked his direction. Above all else he trusted his instincts and the mountain lore that Tom had shared with him years before.

What have I missed? I should have listened harder.

He trudged on.

He knew he was leaving tracks. At times he struggled knee-deep through snowdrifts. Tom would never miss that. Falling snow would obscure most of the evidence, but nothing would stop the Tsimshian. Tom would follow his trail easily and—Dan reveled in anticipation—he would be waiting. He would invent a plan. He would kill the turncoat.

As the hours marched on and the afternoon sky changed hues, silver to the smoky gray of dusk, Dan's design gained credibility. Its invention became clear. All the while the grove called to him. As daylight fell, he ventured deeper and deeper into the lush dark place where secrets waited, each as patient as the grim reaper.

When his thoughts wandered off revenge, Rebecca would come to him. Dan felt her gentle eyes, the way they would caress a visual trail down his tall, lean body, scrutinizing the lay of his muscles, the whiteness of his taut belly. Her eyes massaged his handsome, wind-burnished face, his pioneer soul. Often she touched the scar on his cheek. Just then, he imagined her fingers tracing that jagged, bear-inflicted wound.

Dan's eyes were soft gray, flushed with darker shadow. Rebecca loved to go there. Loved to rove into his soul. Her heart guided her. *God*, he thought, *she can have all of me.*

And she could have him if . . . if only he got back to her. At that very moment, alone in the harsh and unforgiving wilderness, nothing mattered more.

He was finding a rare strength in a paradoxical pact between love and revenge. He moved on, refreshed with a plan for vengeance and the memory of her love.

Minutes later, Dan found a trickle of a stream. He stood, sturdy but forlorn, and studied the opportunity. With Tom in mind, he continued to craft a strategy.

"Stay natural," he repeated out loud, as if there was an audience, and upon the forest stage he was the solitary actor.

"Stay natural for LaCross. Lure him in."

At that moment he was wondering what Tom might be thinking as he followed Dan's trail, a trail that led both men farther and farther from the safety and comfort of their homes.

"Be careful," he said, liking the company of his voice.

Tom would be suspicious if Dan left too obvious a clue. He had to pretend he was eluding the scout. He had to be subtle. The stream was small now, probably artesian at the source, thrust from a hole deep in the earth. He knew the stream would enlarge. Here was an opportunity. Small water led to big water. It was only natural that a man would follow its path. Any pioneer would expect that.

He moved down the middle of the trickle, steady and sure. The water gained momentum, the stream enlarging, its song expanding from murmur to trill. Dan had long ago succumbed to the adage: *follow the water path. It will lead you home.*

Ultimately, unless ice locked up the water in its frozen grip, small freshets fed larger streams, then rivers, and finally saltwater bays. Beyond that was the ocean.

Most men with a wit of mountain sense would be reasonably sure to lose a pursuer if they committed to the water path—if they remained in the stream and left no trail. That is, if feet and legs could endure the excruciating cold. Dan thought of Rebecca and once again drew inner strength from her memory.

Cold plied him. Frozen rain pelted. Ice-cold water wrapped around his legs, knee-high. The stream offered an audible swishing sound as he kicked forward, pushing hard against the water's natural weight. A covey of pine siskins scattered before the strange foreign sound, at this peculiar human shape from beyond.

Dan expected Tom would follow him downriver nearly as easily as he had followed him through the snow. He was sure that Tom was tracking him, even now. He hoped the Tsimshian was coming on. Dan's anger had intensified. He now blamed Tom for the separation from his wife, for any number of his personal calamities. He certainly blamed Tom for his brother's death. Maybe Tom had been the one who shot André. Why not? Tom was a fine marksman. One of the best.

Well, here was a contradiction: Dan had been taught to shoot a rifle by the wily tracker. He contemplated the man's aim. *None better.* He was an uncanny marksman.

Dan thrust his jaw forward. Took another step. He had no way of knowing that the Tsimshian was unarmed.

Even as he struggled against the rising stream, he reckoned he would be ready when the time came.

"Don't get cocky," he cautioned himself. "Be careful now."

His words sounded out of place. Chances were, in remote back country like this, no man had walked, and if one had, the traveler had not spoken the queen's English.

Dan knew that Tom didn't think like most men, even the best of woodsmen. Tom might gamble on his instincts and cut a circuitous path across the wilderness and flank him. He might set his own snare.

Dan chewed on that thought for several minutes. Tom wasn't that fast, was he? *He's older now.* Once again the thought of the scout close on his trail pressed Dan forward, strengthening his resolve.

Dan knew that Tom was more than capable of following his tracks. Follow them nearly anywhere. *Maybe I'll march into hell. Let's see him follow me there.* If there happened to be a hot fire waiting, Dan figured he might be willing to suffer the consequences.

Tom had trained Dan well. No matter—both men surely appreciated the other's craft, and they both knew that sooner or later there must be a showdown with but one winner.

Dan lifted his fatigued legs and plunged forward. He felt the drift of deeper water, the hard, biting current. He realized he was thinking too much. *Take it one step at a time,* he warned himself. "Relax."

The word echoed across the icy water, buoyant with expectation. Dan hadn't spoken much in the last several hours. He had turned inward. The word sounded luxurious on his tongue.

He realized that nearly a full day had passed since he had cut his brother loose. *Relax*—that single word, as fundamental as it was, bolstered his optimism. He repeated it, as if to ward off bad memories. As he moved on, he thought of an old poem from his school days. He remembered a fragment and heard the school marm repeating it. "Once committed," the poem went, "there is no turning back. Weathered paths shadow old stone fences."

Well, there were no fences here, but he had a path to follow. Not exactly shining times, but a beggar had to take what was offered. He remembered his father reciting, "If wishes were horses, then beggars could ride."

In his weaker moments, Dan felt that he had made a terrible mistake by leading his brother into the wilderness. He kept stumbled upon the thought. Guilt goaded him. He thought of her again, seeing Rebecca over his shoulder as he and his brother scampered from the farm. Seeing her desperate eyes, the brooding anger at his decision. At a hundred yards, how could he be sure?

Water muscled hard and cold at his thighs, but the pain he was feeling was over the loss of his beloved wife, over André's death. His thoughts were tangled. He knew the danger in that. Out here a man had to stay focused.

Dan called his newfound stream the "Inconsistent." In the snow and ice, the stream had a habit of appearing and disappearing into underground chasms. Hidden beneath the ice and a blanket of snow, the stream plunged through long frozen tunnels, then, like a man surfacing from underwater and in need of air, the sluice rose dramatically to the surface.

Tom can't miss this, he thought, as he stepped onto a snowy patch that hung tenaciously over the water, leaving obvious footprints.

But soon the stream picked up enough force that the crusts of snow dropped away. There, the ice was thinner, *inconsistent*.

Soon he was thigh-deep in the freshet. The streambed spread almost thirty hands wide and moved faster and faster as gravity tugged at the water.

Another mile, another hour—the stream doubled its width again and soon, tripled the stake. The force of the water elbowed him hard now, as did the cold. As the stream roiled waist high, ice-cold blasts penetrated his loins with sharp, painful jabs. It reminded Dan of being hit with a gloved hand: pain but no scars. The ache moved up to his head. A splitting headache tagged behind, loyal to the end.

He would stumble on a stone or a waterlogged limb. Shaking from the excruciating cold, he scrambled onto a gravel bar. Dan felt mated to the icy freshet, its frigid fingers. He knew it would be impossible to endure the cold torture much longer.

He was certain that Tom would spot his steps if he left the water, even if he disguised his exit. Dan questioned his plan.

Smart! Tom's senses were razor sharp. *Careful, Dan.*

Wild thoughts hurled about like a mouse avoiding a fox.

Hell, Tom might even find evidence of his passage on the stream's rocky bottom. It might be a stone carelessly kicked aside (moss or algae marks face-down now) or a small alder or crabapple branch twisted just so. A limb out of its natural setting. Tom's ability was keen. A tracker of his stature collected information from the clatter of a mallard's wings as they sped across the water and vaulted into the air. Their urgency. Whether they were feeding or fleeing some pending danger, natural or unnatural. The animals always sent a signal: the way a deer stood, hid, or ran. Whether the creatures were skittish or content. Feeding, mating, traveling—all the clues were contained in a seasoned woodsman's bag of tricks. Dan also knew that a commitment to careful tracking would slow Tom down. Time was on Dan's side, at least for the moment.

The lay of the land lent a similar communication. If a stick were kicked into the water, it sent a different message than one that had fallen through natural circumstances. Had grasses been trampled by man or beast? Tom would know the difference. Would a clumsy man leave footprints as he passed? Leftovers? The land had an alphabet, a language, and Tom was fluent.

Dan was clear about all this because he was capable of spotting many of these signs himself. At that moment, he was certain that Tom was the better woodsman. *How much better,* he wondered? A whippoorwill wind mimicked his uncertainty, kicking a blast of snow and ice into his face while further ravaging his body and mind. He countered those thoughts with the knowledge that Tom was facing the same obstacles, fielding the same pain.

The short winter afternoon passed like water flowing, carried along by something mighty and insistent. A pewter sky brought more snow, a lovely white powder that dominated the landscape. Then, intermittently, open sky would trickle back. The weather was unpredictable in its predictability.

Suddenly, a glib sun ball hung in the pale sky, only to disappear, uncertain of its simple mission. In the next hour or two, it might scramble through again. Such patterns were impossible to predict.

Night began to close in, circling like a vulture.

As he moved forward—hypnotized and crippled by the icy freshet—the sandy-haired hunter's steady eyes searched the periphery of the stream bank for a place to cache. Dan craved shelter from the cold, a dry soft bed of earth, flat hemlock limbs for his mattress, and finally, a fire, a small one to be sure.

Dan figured that he had to hide the flame. But the smoke? He would have to find dry material: twigs, pitch, and small limbs from a fallen cedar. He knew how to pull that off. He knew all the tricks.

Dan craved warmth. After hours in icy water, his life depended on it.

Dusk unfurled its gray cape. The weather turned colder than before.

Just before dark, he left the stream, winding his way back into an ancient grove of cedar and Sitka spruce. Less than a quarter mile into the woods, he found what he wanted.

A massive cedar tree had been etched by lightning. Fire had followed. The tree's insides had been stripped of its wooden marrow. The circumference of the cedar was better than twenty feet—a giant—and the tree's age more than likely extended beyond a millennium. A natural chimney wound up through the center of the ancient one, a path where smoke would follow.

Like any earth animal, Dan burrowed inside. The floor of the great cedar was soft with forest duff. A huge trunk defined the tree, except for a man-sized opening that allowed entrance into the giant's bowels. Regardless of the huge gaff, a thick skin of bark moved life up the tree. Even with the center burned away, the wooden arteries kept the grandfather alive and nourished.

Skinner needed some nourishment himself. With his prized chunk of flint, a metal rasp, and dry shredded bark that he stripped from the cedar's innards, he built a tiny fire and then huddled close. Never had warmth felt so good. He added small chunks of firewood, broken limbs, and dry kindling that he had gathered at dusk from the forest that surrounded him. Once again he felt his fingertips.

Dan ate what little remained in his knapsack. He carried a small kettle. He boiled water from snow just outside the tree and brewed some tea. Meager as they were, he thanked the saints that he still had provisions. Soon he would have to gather food. That meant small game or a snared animal. But first he had to deal with Tom. Luxuries had to wait.

He banked the fire, then gathered another armful of firewood and small cedar limbs. Nearby, he found a chunk of spruce, thick with pitch. *Save it for the next fire,* he thought.

Night fell suddenly. An owl hooted from the safety of the thicket. He threw his dirty, tattered blanket over his weary body and placed more firewood beside his natural earth bed. Then Dan slipped into sleep like a man in a trance. Dreams smothered him.

Dreams cover him with silky seductive shadows. The backdrop of his dreamworld is the translucent blue of a summer sky. In dream or trance, warm ocean breezes touch his face. Into this dream a woman appears. He realizes immediately that the apparition must be his beloved wife, Rebecca.

He watches her riding his big mare into an old village he knows distantly as Old Kilnook. The abundance of cedar longhouses represents nearly any Native village from an earlier century. Little reminds him of his village, Kilnook, a small outpost composed mostly of White Anglo-Saxon citizens and a smattering of Native peoples. This settlement is inhabited by First Nations people long before Euro-Americans arrived in their massive sailing ships, in wagons, on horseback, and on foot.

Along the shore an extended row of cedar longhouses are anchored bravely against brisk ocean winds. Canoes rest like cattle sleeping in a field. Here stand the glorious totems—some recently carved. Many are painted with bright primary colors. Others are ancient, gray, and decaying. Colors have faded, victims of hard coastal weather and the natural unraveling of time. The colors are mixed from ripe berries and charcoal, from red clay and plants. Mortar and pestles are carved and shaped from soft volcanic stones that occasionally turn up along coastal waterways.

In this village there are drying racks for fish. And cedar-plank lodges with pouty gray smoke escaping through small holes arranged between disheveled planks that compose the roof tops. The longhouses face the ocean to the west, just as in real life.

The abstract paintings on the buildings are of animals from the natural world: whale, eagle, raven, salmon and more: crow, frog, grizzly bear and wolf. In the dreamworld, they appear ferocious with bright flashing teeth and long thin tongues extending from feral mouths. The images startle Dan.

Dozens of totems have been embedded along the beach, and other stately poles grace the entrances of the cedar-plank lodges. Many are mortuary totems. Cedar boxes at the top of the poles are permanent resting places for the bones of the dead. They are intended to remind the living of the old ways and family history. These totems are nothing if not testimonials to the elders, beloved family members, and the deceased leaders of the tribe. But here the forms are exaggerated.

The remaining totems are memorial, and the carved faces serve to remind the faithful of the four Haisla clans. Weather is the grand marshal of decay. Whether dulled from age or recently painted in bold primary colors, the carved masks glare down ferociously. In the primordial vestige of his dreamland, the images trouble Dan.

From the edge of the village, Dan calls to the woman on the horse. He can go no further. Fear binds him like a physical barrier. It is as if he is bound with a cedar rope woven from tree bark by Native women. The horse mysteriously turns into a princely wolf. Dan gasps. Rebecca rides bareback now. She is naked above the waist. She wears a woven skirt of cedar bark and tree roots. The soles of her feet are bare.

Dan remains invisible to his beloved. She cannot hear his voice or perceive his person.

In the dreamworld, his voice mixes with the wind. The louder Dan yells, the more ferociously the wind doubles back. Soon the wind is transformed into a howl, or a cry belonging to a wolf or coyote or some supernatural beast that he cannot identify. The sound is terrifying.

She rides the wolf through a manhole in the mouth of one of the painted animal faces, through the lodge entrance and into the dim interior. Dan's actions are stifled by panic. His voice has gone mute. The faint resonance of faraway drums floats on the wind. Suddenly, the wind drops, scuttling into whispers that remind him of the muffled sounds of the cautious forest creatures. The pounding of the surf resonates like his beating heart. Finally, there remains only the deepest and blackest of nights. Dan has never seen so many stars or experienced such a revelation. His heart is frozen. He has never felt so alone in the vast and mysterious universe.

From a mattress of soft tree duff, Dan bolted awake. The dream lingered, but the magical images quickly faded as exhaustion pulled him back onto the soft bedding. But before he succumbed to further fatigue, he stuck his head out of the tree and peered into the night. Several hours would pass before dawn graced the snowy landscape. Outside, the sky was filled with brilliant stars and a bright, half-cut moon. For the first night in many, the sky had cleared. "Get up," he mumbled to himself. "Let's get a jump on Tom. Let's get moving."

The remote memory of a dream tugged at his mind, but he couldn't shape the story. Facing the trapper was hard reality. Staring up at the stars, he cogitated. Doubts plagued him like the feral winter wind that promised only a further dousing of snow.

Not so many miles from the man he hunted, Tom stopped his pursuit. Having reached the forest, he relinquished his pace. As night descended, he realized the futility of further movement. Like the man before him, he picked his resting place under a giant bull of a tree and settled down for a much-desired rest. Though fatigued, he built a fire. The grove wrapped him in a ghostly trance. As it had for Dan, sleep slipped quickly over his eyes, and he fell deeply. He too, would sleep later than he intended.

His dreamworld is cloudy and gray. There is no moon, but the sky's texture is striated like the subtle fur of a silver-gray wolf. He finds himself on a beach. A village of split-cedar longhouses has been constructed just above the high tide line. Between the plank houses and the ocean, his ancestors have formed a human gauntlet of two parallel lines. They are dressed in rich ceremonial clothing. Their faces are hidden behind awesome cedar masks. The man of two worlds is being summoned. He is to test the gauntlet. Initially, the thought frightens him. He realizes this is to be a test for the Tsimshian warrior, not the White man from the settlements called Tom LaCross.

In the dreamworld, his body is painted in earth tones: clay-red, burnt-orange, campfire-black. He wears a loincloth, the warp and the weft woven of shredded cedar and goat's hair. Although the gauntlet appears threatening, the scout passes through unmolested. White Bear walks calmly. Not a single weapon is raised against him. The Natives can't see him, see the infamous son of Blue Shell. As he exits the westerly end of the double line, the ocean beckons. With a start he realizes that his spirit is being held captive in a White man's body. In the waking world, he belongs to the Bostons, but here, in the Tsimshian dreamland, his soul belongs to his people, to his mother, Blue Shell, and her ancestors. Spirit helpers all.

The beach is lined with totems. The carved poles have sharp claws and hooked beaks. Yellow-rimmed eyeballs with keen ebony centers stare down at him, challengingly. Find yourself, *they seem to say.* Come back to your people.

The most piercing of those carved wooden eyes belongs to an eagle. White Bear remembers one specific eagle from a waking dream. A huge bird. He wonders if the spirit bird materialized from this village and whether they will meet again. Is the eagle a spirit helper? He suspects so.

White Bird gazes westward. Before him, an elegant cedar canoe with a bowsprit highlighted with an ocean beast with gaping mouth and ferocious teeth sails easterly toward the sandy beach where he stands. They are coming for him, for White Bear. The tribe gathered on the beach appears to be his family, friends, and elders. Every man and woman standing along the shore turns their eyes seaward and then turns suddenly back to their Native son. They are seeing him now. They know that the canoes will carry their beloved warrior to the other world, the one that awaits far across the sea. Every eye rests on White Bear.

Far away, a grieving woman dreams. From her warm bed—her sturdy cedar cabin—she stumbles upon a Native village.

The village lies between four sturdy rock pinnacles in a distant valley that she has never seen before. Although she can't say exactly why, the village calls to her. Strangely, there is strong familiarity. She is drawn into the dreamworld.

As Rebecca watches from her out-of-world perspective, a Native girl emerges from a long wooden house, a lodge built of split cedar planks. Smoke curls through a hole in the planking. The entire house is supported by four enormous cedar posts, front and back, ancient trees felled from the nearby forest with heartwood wedges and stone axes. She can see into the longhouse as if it were an abandoned skeleton of some large-ribbed animal. She thinks of a whale, its cavernous rib cage.

Outside, the young Native girl with enormous sable-brown eyes is half running, half skipping across the dry sandy soil in such a playful manner—Rebecca finds her movements so appealing, so childlike—that even in Rebecca's dreamworld, affection binds her to the apparition. The Native girl has jet-black hair and penetrating eyes. Her legs are smooth, long, and muscular. As she runs, rays of sunshine cut threads of light through her shimmering, lustrous hair. Rebecca thinks about the daughter she has dreamed about. The one that she and Dan are incapable of having. That gap has cut a hole into their marriage, but they have filled the breach as best they can. Their love remains strong as the perpendicular fibers that run up a giant fir tree. Roots that feed and nourish life.

As she watches, the girl's raven hair turns into short, bristly fur. The young girl's body metamorphoses into a small black bear. In her sleep, Rebecca gasps across a space that is otherworldly.

The bear saunters through the village, then back into the forest. Rebecca calls frantically to the bear-child, but the apparition fails to acknowledge her presence. Her words transform into a strong wind, and the bear bends its massive head back over its shoulder as to thank the forces that bring new seasons, that offer ripe berries and the fat fleshy salmon.

Awakened suddenly, she sits up straight from her warm bed and gulps in deep, sustaining breaths. The apparition is gone. Outside her small cozy cabin the sky is deep silky-black and silent. She calls out for Dan.

1956–1966

Katherine's father was a quiet, serious man who spoke few words. His voice was thoughtful, as were his actions. He married late—Katherine came after he was in his late thirties. She was just a small girl when her father died from a fall while doing construction on a high-rise building in Seattle. Katherine's mother suddenly became her sole provider.

For some reason that nobody around her quite understood, Katherine held on to nearly every story her daddy ever told. She seldom forgot a single word or lesson. Her deceased father remained a living mentor. She remained proud of his legacy.

"My daddy was born in an Indian camp," she would brag to her girlfriends as they played on a deserted lot in south Seattle.

Katherine was nine. Her playmates would laugh at her. Tease her. That just cemented a sense of undaunted determination in the vivacious girl.

"Okay," she would say, her voice rising. "What did your daddy ever do that was great like that?" And when her young friends remained silent, she ascertained that her daddy had been *very* special. Someday, Katherine knew, she would live among the Native people. Katherine was proud. Already, she aimed high. If society disdained many of the Indigenous people and their values, Katherine choose a different path.

When Katherine was fourteen and in junior high, she wrote an essay about Native people living beside the Amazon River, deep in Brazil.

She remembered those people from a geography book that she had read in grade school. Now she spent a week gathering new material.

The essay depicted the struggle for survival that these Indigenous people faced in their daily lives. She became obsessed with their plight. Right then she pledged to do something about it.

Her middle schooling became a preparation (an obsession, really) for pursuing anthropology and environmental science. She wove together a symbiotic relationship between science and the natural ways of Native peoples. That included a smattering of spiritualism.

She excelled in all her studies, graduating as salutatorian from her high school class of three hundred.

As an adult, she reflected upon junior high and high school with a particular cynicism. As a young woman, Katherine remained introspective. Later, examining those formative years, she felt as if she had been treading water. Katherine was sure that she carried a sign board that read, "I'm different."

She remembered fondly two teachers who had been central to her education. Both had driven into her imagination a sense of purpose as well as a quest for excellence. They had recognized her gift.

One afternoon Katherine remained after class. Her English teacher, Emily Martin, told her, "Katherine, you have an inquisitive mind. Do you understand? This is a special gift! I want you to remember something for me: whenever you are in need, remember that there will always be a teacher. Some person will materialize with answers to your questions, answers aimed at your personal growth. What is important to a seeker is the pursuit of knowledge. The pursuit. Remember that. Please! You must go forward with courage."

Mrs. Martin had given her a copy of a recent article about a California Native American named Ishi. Ishi was the last of his tribe, the Yahi. The warrior had hidden from White civilization for over thirty years. His family and tribe had been driven into the wilderness and subsequently murdered. When he was discovered in 1911, Ishi was the last member of that tribe. The others had been annihilated. A bounty of twenty-five cents had been placed upon their heads. Katherine practically memorized the article by heart. The story gave her life mission a new meaning.

Afterwards, whenever Katherine doubted her strength and ability, she would fall back on Ishi, mirroring his plight and his determination. She would center on his strength, alone in the wilderness. She would forever think of Ishi's isolated wilderness as a garden, the Garden of Eden. Katherine figured that the Yahi had been chased from the garden. She wanted to recapture that universe.

CHAPTER SIX

Under a ghosting sky, three dreamers wake. Two are men, and one is a woman. The three are separated by many hard miles and a cloak of heavy snow. All three humans are held captive by deep, pivotal forces. Winter has become a catalyst in this dreamworld. Something as profound as love binds the three together, but none of the dreamers have answers yet to the puzzle that is their lives. As a new morning unfolds, dreams scatter. Only small fragments remain. No matter, their lives have already been changed. The pattern is indelible. There is no turning back. On the periphery, an eagle waits.

—Katherine Skinner-Patterson
Notes for a novel

Tom LaCross was knee-deep in snow, chasing a fading set of tracks, nearly invisible under a fresh cascade of snow. Like his departure from the dreamworld, only remnants of the trail remained. Sometimes he uncovered Dan's tracks from the faintest of traces as quicksilver light crisscrossed a fading landscape where heavy snow continued to fall. Sometimes he could only guess at the direction of the next footprint. Guess and wait. Discovery was a simple matter of patience and thinking like the pursued.

His thoughts were tormented by self-inflicting words, almost wounds.

Go home, part of him would say.

No. Damn it. I can't. I won't. He argued fruitlessly with himself.

His actions were as conflicted as a pair of boxers in a knock-down street fight.

Like a split personality, he argued interminably, plagued by a crucial mistake. Tree limbs, heavily laden with snow, muffled his private soliloquy and added a sense of frustration as his words folded in upon themselves.

"Even if I find him, how do I stop him? His advantage now. Damnation, man, I'm Tom LaCross. I was the best."

Was! The word stung him like a torrent. *How good is this other man, anyways? He is young, strong. Hell's fire, I trained him.*

Thoughts tumbled.

Tom plunged through more snow, immersed in the whiteness that covered all. Step. Breathe. Plunge. The air was frigid in the northern dawn. His body was covered with sweat, except where the skin exposed itself to the frigid air. There it froze on ten-day stubble, forming a white-bearded mask. White Bear knew all about masks. No Native celebration passed without an exhibition of the carved talismans. The masks represented a link to the other world, to the other side. His conflict remained simple: he was no longer certain who the man behind the icy mask was.

It is mighty cold, he thought. *Stinging cold.* This was the air that both gives and takes away life. This was killing frost.

He stepped through knee-deep snow. *Younger, stronger.*

His brain rattled out a private litany, waiting for an answer, and found him wanting. He had no place to hide. Suddenly, Tom was remembering the story of Dan and a grizzly bear. Dan had survived a mauling. Few men ever survived a close physical tussle with a Grizz.

"Thought him dead," Tom said, breaking the rigid silence of the winter world, tossing out words as if he was addressing the folks back in Kilnook. Grumbling, he was not aware of his voice, his Tsimshian accent. He would never admit that he was lonely.

"Came out alive after weeks in the wilderness. Injured but alive. That took some, alright. And he bushwhacks like a mountain goat." Words suddenly gushed out. Where had the words been hiding?

But in the end, his mine sauntered back to the present: this day, this wilderness, his chances for survival. And always, Danny Skinner.

Was he all that surprised? "That boy, he's grown. Grown tall."

Tom had trained the Skinner boy when he was nothing but a pup. Danny had been an apt student.

Tom thought about the Tsimshian word for "pathfinder." Figured it applied to Dan. The boy had evolved all right. *Can I find him? Find the pathfinder*?

He plunged forward. Snow greeted him. It wrapped around his calves and, at times, his thighs. He slipped into another waist-deep pit. He struggled to his feet.

And bringing him in?

That thought troubled Tom. Finding Dan would be hard enough. To stop him, he would have to kill him. And Tom wasn't all that sure he was capable of either.

Just then he remembered an expression his father had used frequently. "Got the h'ar of the b'ar."

Tom thought some about his father but found his mind wandering back to the boy, Danny Skinner. Back a decade or better.

"Not a boy now. He be plenty dangerous."

This was more talk than Tom had tendered in the last ten days. He was on a speaking binge now.

"What's he got to lose? Kill me and his chances are one hell of a lot better. Does he know I'm unarmed? Probably not. Makes him more dangerous. Desperate! Careful. Careful now."

He repeated the words like a benediction. "I'm okay. I'll get him."

The high mountain winds scattered Tom's words.

And again. "Why didn't I bring a rifle?"

Blame rekindled. So did guilt.

Like his thoughts, the snow continued to swirl and fall, a white dervish.

Courage—courage mattered here. Then it didn't. Winter might soon trump all. Trap a man's thoughts. Steal his breath away.

Here the forest was the stage and whiteness the backdrop.

Natural forces that the Natives referred to as "The Cold One" had transformed the wilderness into a life-and-death drama. Two men were at once participants and victims. One might die. Or two. The wilderness was patient. Nobody on this stage understood how patient. Nor would they until the curtain fell.

While different actors played their separate parts, Tom tracked the passage of his student—the pathfinder—across a powder of freshly fallen snow. The mountain receded. The thicket began to close around him. Anticipating trouble, he renewed his trapper's covenant: T*hink like a wolf. Mimic the courage of a wolverine. Move like a deer, light on your feet. Silently. Cautiously.*

Two applicable crafts wove an integral pattern through Tom's palette of skills. One was inherited from the Tsimshian peoples: t*hink like the four-legged ones*. The other was mountain man's lore, adopted from his father: *stay ahead of the pack*. He had grown into both. He was a master of each.

Tom's eyes saw where normal eyes failed. Faded as they were, Tom interpreted a nearly invisible set of tracks. He sized up their message, their seemingly indecipherable cartoons. He accurately guessed their ages. He instinctively calculated the speed and agility of the man who was making them. He understood when the man turned or bent or hesitated. Amazingly, Tom anticipated what Dan—or any other pursued man—might be thinking. The distance between the man's footsteps mattered. Any departure from the normal as well. What a broken branch might offer and finally, any new revelation or deformity in those tracks.

Was he rested? Was he exhausted? Tom's mind flooded with questions. He was more than cautious. Up ahead, Dan would be waiting. Death might be waiting too.

Tom took in all the sounds, or lack of sound. Silence waxed the greater message. When he was close enough to hear a man's voice, he was *too* close. By then he might easily be dispatched to the land of his ancestors.

Before the animals scattered, Tom's nose smelled the critters at a distance that would have startled the folks dining in Sally's Walton's café in Kilnook. If the four-legged ones were migrating, he estimated the relative time of their departure and their pending arrival. Was there a new scent in the air? Were the big mammals mating?

"Dig into your senses, son. You see that, don't you? You smell it now? Good boy!" The memories of his young student flooded back, tangled as they were.

Even as a child among the Tsimshian, White Bear dissected the different tracks of a deer (male or female), bear, or cat. By the age of twelve, all the smaller creatures as well. White man or Red—he knew them by the different ways they moved, their footprints and camp habits. A Native brave walked up on the toes of his thin moccasins. The White man walked heels first. Individual tracks left a signature that defined their purpose. Of the four-legged critters, he knew their sex, their size, and their relative age. Habits: he knew if they were mating, if they were hungry, angry, or injured. Tom sensed if they were grazing, hunting, or resting. He knew all the different species, by print, sound, and smell. He didn't have to see them, and they rarely saw him first. Above all else, he remained as stealthy as the animals he sought.

As a child he learned the smell of a White man, the Bostons, or the queen's men. To Tom, they were pretty much the same. Other than during the dead of winter when the Natives coated their bodies with bear grease to repel the cold, the Tsimshian people bathed frequently. The western pioneer might easily pass a month or more between baths. That was unheard of among the First Nations people.

More important than all these skills were Tom's senses, particularly his sixth sense. There was a sixth sense, alright, and it had saved his life more than once, and would again, most likely. Unless—he thought of Dan once more and shored up his concentration—unless he got sloppy.

Tom often predicted trouble before the event occurred. He knew when to cache and when to run. At the moment, that was a major problem. He knew he should be heading home, but, as he painfully remembered, he had lost his true home many years before.

He had no rifle. The weather was on a killing spree. His supplies were scant, and the man before him was a skilled trapper, a pathfinder. Stopping him would require the top of Tom's craft, and a measure of luck.

Beyond the sixth sense was his imagination. To take that from Tom would be like stealing his faith.

The dreamworld and the real world coexisted for Tom. There was no sharp delineation. He walked with a foot in both.

Tom had chosen forward momentum. He predicted trouble when the time to face the folks back in Kilnook without having caught or killed Dan Skinner. Tom was not the only man with relatives, and he was further motivated by an earlier incident, one long before Dan had hurled the boulder at his head.

Long ago in the one jailhouse for hundreds of miles, two Mounties were heckling Tom. Dan stood apart from the three men.

"Look at the man's hair. Don't he look like a woman?" Such was the indictment of the first lawman.

"Well, yeah," the second Mountie offered. "But he's Injun, or half. Just a breed. Don't belong to no one."

"You know this man, Skinner? People talk. Say you're tight. Old friends."

Dan stood apart from the hecklers and opposite Tom. Stood silently, like a deer studying a hunter from the shelter of a thick copse. He spoke not a word in defense of his old mentor. Just lowered his eyes and shuffled his feet.

Tom didn't react to the provocations. Though he was capable of striking hard and deadly, he held back. Retaliation just might get him hanged. He turned and left the two lawmen smiling at their mischief. The third man, Dan, looked as wounded as a mink caught in a trap.

All that still stung. Still caused Tom's blood to boil. And now the long-ago incident tracked him while he tracked his student, the pathfinder. And hauntingly, he remembered his own words, delivered years before to the boy. He no longer remembered the incursion: "Be careful what you take on, son. Might not be able to let it go."

Tom figured that Dan had half a day's start on him. Tom suspected that he might be walking into a trap. Inner monologue continued to play on irascibly.

You, crazy half-breed, go home. Make a fire. Disappear into the bush. They'll never find you."

His tongue had slipped easily into Native vernacular. He spoke to himself in the Tsimshian language.

Tom was not only speaking to himself but also to his relatives. He knew loved ones waited for him in the spirit world. One thought persisted: *If I'm not careful, I might be joining them sooner than expected.*

He would not permit himself to turn back, no matter what. A code of honor bound him. Even if the turn of events might cost him his life, fierce pride dictated. He had to see the job through.

The thought of death held no great threat for him. He had spoken to the other world since childhood. He put certain trust into the inescapable.

Spirits called to him even now, just as the landscape did. Here the winter song played out a natural adagio. The four-legged ones rustled and scampered deep within the thicket. Spring buds encased inside an icy crust of silver thaw dreamed of bursting out from the icy-encrusted grip. In the wilderness, nature displayed certain ambiguities.

He plowed dutifully on through the snow. Step, plunge, step. Plunge, step, plunge. Rest. Then again. All was as it should be. White Bear was a warrior of distinction. He was the best. He had always been sure of that. Then he would think of the man ahead of him, and his doubts would fly.

Dan woke to falling snow. It was still hours ahead of the dawn, but Dan knew his way back to the stream. The early opportunity gave him another head start. *My advantage.* Dan knew he needed every single one. Twenty yards away, a hare in its winter coat rattled its icy compound. Dan heard, but the small animal remained invisible. Had Dan known its whereabouts, the would have grieved at the lost opportunity. Hunger continued to growl inside his empty stomach.

Throughout the forest, windfalls of ice-caked limbs lay broken from the weight of snow and ice. This would be one of the coldest winters that any of the old-timers in Kilnook might remember. But those men were warm and dry before a hearth and fire or around the cast-iron stove in the mercantile, sharing tall tales.

A jay cut short its pre-dawn preamble as the man lurched from the sanctuary at the base of a fire-etched cedar. Dan stood and shook his arms vigorously. His muscles were cold and stiff. His back ached. Still, after a night's sleep, he sensed new energy. He tried to fit together pieces of the dream which were scattering with each waking breath. What did they matter, those fractured reflections? What did they matter, after all?

Dan gathered his blanket and rucksack. He chewed on a bite of smoke-dried meat and sheathed his knife, his single weapon against man and wilderness other than his undaunted courage and keen mountain skills. He rubbed the scar that burrowed beneath his leather capote. The garment sagged around his shoulders. That single deterrent against wind and weather was torn and filthy. After years the bear scars still festered, and cold wrestled there like a slow burn. *Well,* he thought, *I survived that one, survived a bear fight.* He wondered if his chances were any better now or even as good. He figured it was time to move. The day was getting on.

If man or beast had been watching, only the sharpest eyes would have detected Dan's furtive movements as he gathered up his body and slipped stealthily into the snow-covered landscape.

And if that same observer had ears as keen as his eyes, he might have captured Dan's final departing words. "Today," he whispered, "Today I set a snare. Today I'll catch the Tsimshian."

Soon he was back in the stream. The water had begun as a gurgle. Now it burst forth, a river in the making.

The only sensible route left for Dan was the water path. Part of his mind was set on that course. Another part—based on experience—harangued him. *Well, no sensible pilgrim would subject himself to more of this slow torture. But of course, I will. Tom will expect it.*

He played with different options but only one settled well. His choice was the hard choice: the river course.

The best chance a man might have against the likes of Tom LaCross was to wade that doggone river once again. There—and the chance was a long shot—a woodsman might lose the Tsimshian. That was if either the tracker or the pursued was able to endure the bone-chilling cold. Well, Dan reasoned, it didn't matter all that much. *Doesn't matter anyhow.* Tom would pick up the trail sooner or later. At some point Dan knew he had to leave the water. The scout would never miss that. On such an assumption, Dan would have bet the farm.

Tom would find him, surely, but Dan wanted to pick *his* place. He sought first advantage.

He reasoned that he could move Tom along by leaving a trail of clues. For sure, Tom would find his campsite. Tom would easily guess how recently the campfire had cooled. He would estimate the length of the lead that his student had forged. Warmth might hover there, hidden in the bowels of the lightning-scarred cedar. There would be no hesitation. No rest. Tom would move ahead, move against Dan, step by step.

Dan was playing a chess game with a master. Too many clues might alert Tom to Dan's purpose, his new purpose. *Be natural,* Dan thought. *Run light, fast, scared. If he wants you, he will find you.*

Quickly enough, Dan recognized the good sense in his decision.

He was searching for a place to set a trap. Today, snow was on his side. He would use the powdery cover to his advantage. *Advantage not taken is advantage lost.* Who had told him that? Had that been Tom?

No matter; the words made sense.

Dan reasoned that he had a several-hour head start on his mentor, maybe half a day. Just as snow disguised his tracks, that same covering would go far toward camouflaging his ambush.

Dan had survived starvation in the wilderness by snaring animals. Some of those critters were bigger and meaner than Tom. But smarter? Or as wary?

He pushed forward. Every exposed strand of his hair and face was covered with ice. His body was sheathed in snow. He took another full step. Hesitated.

Would he be able to trap Tom? Well, a man might die in any number of encounters in this wilderness. That being true, he might as well die fighting.

The plan enlarged. Tom figured that Tom was too good a tracker to miss an obvious trick.

Stay cagey, he reasoned. *Don't give anything away.*

Don't serve it to him on a platter. Don't startle him. Don't get him edgy.

Finally, Dan did what came easily. He played himself. He stayed elusive. He moved fast. He was sly. He would tire the old man out.

Dan spotted a wolf slinking inside a nest of trees. The animal suddenly stopped and turned and then stared intently at the pathfinder. The big male's eyes were dark and foreboding, with flecks of a golden-yellow.

Suddenly, Dan remembered pieces of the dream from the night before. Hadn't he seen this wolf before?

No. He kicked the strange thought aside. *No*!

Dan wasn't so sure just who had startled whom.

He studied the wolf again. Under the weaving, dancing flutter of snow, he wasn't sure if the creature was animal or spirit. Dan turned his head for just a second. When he swung back, the apparition was gone. *Gone*! He didn't understand how the animal had disappeared so suddenly. Dan was shaken by the surreal image and a sense of foreboding. One thought struck him: whether animal or apparition, he had better move like that creature. He had better stay invisible.

For several hours Dan waded the icy stream. The water bullied his legs and lower body. After a full night's sleep, he might have pretended that the previous day's ordeal had been overplayed, that his imagination was teasing him. That was not to be.

"Today will be better," he said, inherently knowing the lie behind his thoughts. Well, a man had to stay positive.

Soon, the river's icy fingers piggybacked on the previous day's bleakest memories.

He waded forward, always aware of the man who tracked him. Always seeking any advantage that might favor him, Daniel Abbott Skinner, student of that very Tsimshian master, Tom LaCross, or, among his own people, White Bear.

Dan committed himself to the turgid water, knowing that somewhere just ahead, he would need every second of advantage. Maybe today was the day he would even the account. If not, then what? He didn't like the options.

Good God Almighty! *It's so cold. Time to finish this thing. No reason to draw the affair out.*

That very day he would settle the score with his one-time mentor turned enemy. He thought again about André. Remembered his beloved Rebecca. Each of those thoughts steeled his resolve.

The winter solstice had passed, but the northern daylight was short, and the shades of the fragile light, unpredictable. As the sun dropped in the northern sky, Dan began to look for the place where he might lay his trap. He spotted it from the water, a natural outcropping of rock and timber.

Perfect.

He said a quick prayer of thanks for his good luck, for a rare twist of fate. In the subdued afternoon light, Dan had found his ambush spot. A wry smile scribed his face.

An animal trail led through a cache of rock and timber. The path led from the riverbank, then paralleled a small creek before circling back in an arc like a bent bow from west to north. Along the way it passed through an outcropping of tall, sheer rock. It was a natural shelter, protected from the wind. A nest of sorts, one formed out of basalt, eons ago.

The rock buttress would hide a fire. Heavy falling snow, a persistent veil of cloud cover, and nightfall would cover the smoke. Steep cliffs on three sides made it a natural hiding place, a refuge of sorts against storm and prying eyes. Even now, racing clouds threatened. Animal or man would choose to avoid an approach from the rear. The rock wall was too steep and noisy with loose scree, even for the likes of Tom. Even for a wolf. It would be a dark, go-to-hell night. Dan applauded his luck. In that spot he would lay his ambush.

Dan was not sure that he had gained much time on Tom. As tired as he was—as cold as he was—he didn't dare rest. God knew he would have loved a fire to warm his cold bones, but that came later. Later, that was, if Tom didn't bushwhack him first.

Dan took a rope from his rucksack and set it aside. He then cut an armload of the wide, flat boughs, heavy with needles from a hemlock deeper in the trees. He began to dig a pit, all the while planning how to lay out the lure. He figured to use himself as bait.

Dan worked in a fury. With both his knife and a rough cedar blade that he had fashioned quickly with his knife, he began to dig a pit. He saved the cedar shavings for the fire, a fire that he could already feel in the marrow of his bones.

"Waste not, want not." He considered the tinder-dry shavings while he remembered his mother's words.

He settled his knife carefully back into its leather case. Aside from the weapon, Dan always carried a leather purse with flint and steel. The purse hung by a leather strap around his neck. The articles flapped on his chest if he moved quickly. Lately, it had gotten a lot of practice.

A leather belt fastened the Green River knife and its sheath to his waist. He had carried the weapon for years. He glanced down at the ornate leatherwork, at the blue and red trade beads, an intricate pattern. Tom had given him the gift when Dan was a young man. At the time, Dan had been unaware of just how much the prize represented.

Unofficially, Dan had just passed the trapper's initiation. The knife and beaded sheath had been a reward for completing his master's in wilderness education. The sheath had been given to White Bear by the chief of the Eagle clan, a Tsimshian. The chief was dead two years later, a victim of smallpox. Tom had passed on his treasured weapon to his apprentice. Whether by White or Native standards, the gesture was huge.

Under the Tsimshian's tutelage, Dan hoped to become a famous pathfinder. Someday, he just might equal his master. Tom had never taken on an apprentice. Dan was his first and only. The scout never translated his pleasure over the boy's skills into words. No need—the Tsimshian was proud. Any greenhorn could sense that. Could see the approval glistening in the man's dark eyes.

In this wilderness, fire was as vital as food. Dan had been subjected to cold, sleepless nights many times before. Every instinct he had gathered over the years was screaming at him now. He knew there was no avoiding the luxury of rest. But the fire simply had to wait. He would need every advantage to best the Tsimshian. Tom wouldn't light a fire either; Dan could wager on that. Tom was too busy stalking him. The scout had a job to do, and he would remain as invisible as possible. Besides, any tracker could smell campfire smoke from a safe distance. Stealth would remain fundamental to Tom's plan. Tom would suffer long before he gave himself away. That thought brought a glint of satisfaction to Dan's eyes.

He smiled to himself and let his expectations run wild. In another hour, he could light a fire. Dan could already feel the heat swelling into the cold night air. He thought about the rabbit from earlier in the day. *God, wasn't that a century ago?* He could imagine animal flesh browning over an open campfire. He could taste the meat and charred fat. He turned the thought aside. No time for lollygagging. Leastways, not now.

He dropped his eyes once more toward the knife sheath. Oddly, he felt the harassment of conflicting emotions. No time to get sentimental.

Besides, after another day on the river, he felt as cold as a frozen animal carcass. Tom would be feeling the same. *He is human after all, isn't he*?

Dan had a momentary vision of a gutted deer suspended from a high, strong bough, dangling out of reach from the forest critters. He thought of a carcass devoid of life. In the wind the carcass turned slowly, back and forth. *Well, life often dangles like that, don't it?* He allowed himself a fleeting thought of Rebecca but let it go quickly. He was aware that exhaustion and hunger were working against him.

But the image of the deer drifted in and out of his thoughts. He wondered if the deer had a soul. *Well, that's Indian stuff.* He knew Tom believed in that brand of magic, an animal to soul transformation. Maybe Tom was right. Maybe even the animals possessed some higher gift. Dan stopped then. Stopped and stared at the naked trees as if they, too, anticipated incoming darkness.

Dan choose the location for the trap in a small clearing that opened between the evergreen trees. A natural path passed through the middle. He guessed this was an ancient animal trail. It remained the only clear opening through the trees. Over time animal traipsing had forced back the saplings and brush. Frequent use continued to keep it clear. He knew it would be short of impossible for Tom to choose another route. The woods were too thick, the night too dark. Too easy to break a branch, to stir up unnatural noises. It would take a measure beyond Tom's abilities to stalk quietly through the evergreen maze.

The weather was colder now. He realized that he had better get his work done. After his trap was set, he would light a fire. The expectation stimulated him. He had hardly finished the last thought when his mind shifted again. Dan was seeing another carcass. He was imagining his brother's body, broken and frozen at the bottom of the granite cliff.

After that, he dug like a man possessed.

Tom would choose to utilize surprise. Dan figured the Tsimshian would creep right down the middle of the path, as silent as snow falling.

He dug the pit deep and wide. Along the bottom he buried sharpened stakes, all pointing skyward. He carved them quickly from green saplings that grew alongside the creek. The points were as sharp as arrows. When he finished lining the pit, he trellised the top with flat, needle-backed limbs, these from the hemlock tree.

Dan sprinkled a thin layer of dirt and detritus across the boughs, hoping to camouflage the trap. Thousands of years of fallen needles had formed a thick black loam, and he was grateful for the ease which it surrendered to his efforts. Over the top of all this, he sprinkled some freshly fallen snow.

He was getting plenty of help from the sky. The snowflakes were falling heavily and covering the earth's surface with a thick white sheet of frozen crystals.

Finally, he scattered any remaining dirt back into the forest, out of view, leaving the ground around the pit as flat and as natural as possible. With the last broad bough of hemlock, he swept over and around the periphery of the pit. Snow continued to fall heavily. Dan felt blessed. Within the hour, a thick blanket of snow covered his tracks and any evidence of the pit. It was a neat job.

Dan turned his eyes skyward. Partway up a spruce tree, he saw what he wanted. He climbed up into the large conifer. Aided by a length of hemp rope—the same one that had tied the brothers together on the steep cliff—he pulled back a long, flexible limb. The appendage reached nearly forty feet into the air. By pulling with all his strength on the rope, he twisted the branch into a taut position. It was now cocked like a Native bow. He pinioned the branch by the same rope, securing the limb by wedging a spruce stake into a natural chink in the massive trunk. He looped the rope three times around the spike and drew the remaining length of rope from the stake back to the spot where he planned to light a campfire. From there he hoped to strike.

Finally, he dangled the last of the rope from the end of the bent spruce limb. The rope snaked down to the ground, circling a wide area directly in front of the pit. The loop surrounded an area big enough for a man to step into and be snared—well, that was Dan's hope anyway. If his plan went awry, Tom would shoot him. Survival depended on his trap and more than a little bit of luck.

Dan buried the looped rope under a few inches of newly fallen snow, then swept the entire area surrounding the pit one last time. All traces of the rope were well hidden. Snow continued to fall. In the failing light, all signs of the trap would soon become invisible. Only an animal with night-seeing eyes might perceive the trap. He hoped Tom was no more perceptive than himself. Tom wouldn't have the luxury of daylight or the aid of a torch. Dan liked his odds.

One mighty tug on the second rope, and the branch would jump free; the snaring rope would tighten and lift, closing around Tom. With luck he would hang in the air defenselessly. Then, as sure as sunrise, Dan would have him.

"I'll get him for you, little brother. I'll even the score."

Dan's anger penetrated the small clearing. If anything, it had intensified. A subtle tightness tugged across Dan's face and reshaped his lips and facial muscles. To the casual observer, his emotions remained invisible, his motions fluid and predictable. But what did it matter? No man saw him now. But from a hundred yards above, an eagle watched.

Three hours had passed since he began constructing the snare. Dan was feeling the burden of intense exhaustion, an accumulation of loss and fatigue. It felt like forever since he had left Rebecca standing on the porch of their small cabin. He had crossed the meadow behind the farm with his brother, not daring to look back. Although he knew better than to pine after her—he needed to concentrate on Tom—Dan began to count back the days from their separation until the numbers stopped at eleven. Or was it twelve. Dan had lost track of time.

Cold swirled around him. Wind moved across the treetops speaking a language that only the beleaguered fully understood. *Damn it,* he thought. *I'm cold and tired, and I miss you so*. Anticipation swarmed around the grove like a cadre of songbirds. An involuntary shudder chased up and down Dan's spine. He knew the necessity of discipline. Once again he pushed his fatigue aside. He knew better than to let exhaustion dominate his actions. He needed to stay alert. Methodically, he turned to his next chore, and this one brought him pleasure.

Dan lit a small fire from the cedar shavings and dried spruce tinder he had set aside earlier. For good measure, he added a gob of pitch. He already felt the small flames swelling warmth into his aching joints and stiff muscles.

Then came a surprise. As he dug down through the snow to clear a hearth for the fire, he found a small, neat cairn of rock. Startled, he realized that another man had created a pit and built a fire before him. From the looks of the fire bed, he conjectured that this had happened more than once and not so long ago. "I'll be go to hell," he said. Surprise swirled around the pathfinder.

His strong voice was small there, so deep in a hostile wilderness, trapped between the weight of the falling snow and the last traces of daylight. In the grove it was darker yet. What light remained in the sky would be the last for the next fourteen hours.

As if to clear his thoughts, he shook his head. "I'll go to hell," he repeated. Those words echoed hard off the high buttress of rock that swept upwards behind him for nearly a hundred feet.

Flint and steel found flame. Dan pondered the stone cairn as the fire began to swell. He built a mattress from remaining boughs, ate the last of his jerky, and then settled into an assassin's position to wait for Tom. He was certain that the scout wasn't far behind. Dan was thankful that he had accomplished his tasks before nightfall.

His dirty Hudson's Bay blanket warmed his limbs. The fire's heat was a blessing. Dan was prepared to wait out the night, prone but sleepless. Would Tom come? He lay motionless but perched to let fly the web he had laid for the Tsimshian scout.

Lastly, Dan carefully placed his Green River knife under his left hand. His right hand rested tautly against the rough hemp rope. Dan was ready.

1956–1958

At age eight, Katherine was reading adult books. At age ten, she began to memorize sections of those same books. She loved words and paragraphs, chapters and clever phrases. She loved the adventure of a well-crafted story. But mostly, she was inspired by the great authors and their messages. She felt empowered by their words.

CHAPTER SEVEN

Happenstance. Choice. Karma. Good luck. Bad luck. Weather had its own agenda. Human beings had to respect that. Hard weather was the equalizer, death its distant cousin. A man must come to respect the Great Force. The Creator. No human was ever safe from the Grim Reaper, from the forces that spoke to God. From God!

—Katherine Skinner-Patterson
Notes for her novel

While the last threads of daylight faded, Tom waded down the frozen stream. He was numb up to his waist, still keen in his senses but losing his sharp reflexes as the icy water pummeled him. He knew he must stay alert for any unnatural departure of footprints leading away from the water—stay alert for discovery or ambush.

At dusk, Tom stumbled upon Dan's tracks as they led out of the large stream and up a small creek toward a rock cache nestled behind a nest of tall evergreens. Because of the restricted light—and Dan's stealth—Tom almost missed the prints. He thanked his relatives for his good fortune; crept into a small stand of trees and gave himself time to think out a plan.

Just yards from the river, Tom lay hidden. After calculating his strategy, he decided on a midnight ambush. Carefully, he memorized the lay of the land. Darkness was pummeling down on the valley. Dan's tracks were barely discernible. They were only hours old, but already the snow had nearly camouflaged them under a new layer of drift. Even now, snowfall raked the wilderness like a great steel sickle.

All the while, Tom was scheming. He was troubled. He reviewed Dan's steps. One thought continued to bother him: why had Dan sought shelter so early in the day? *Cold and tired*, he answered himself. Dan had endured too much. *Sure enough!*

Tom could relate. He felt bitten to the bone from the winter exposure. He lay quivering with fatigue, not sure that he had ever felt so exhausted or so cold. Trouble was, he didn't dare start a fire. He wouldn't expose himself that way. Even so, he worried about his concentration. While hypothermia teased him, he played with several thoughts, exposing plans inside of plans. Stealth, he remembered, was his best weapon.

Suddenly, he smelled smoke. That startled him. Well, at least his suspicions were confirmed: Dan was waiting just ahead. That was fine, but the physical suggestion of fire and heat—of any basic comfort—teased his frozen fingers and toes, the taut skin across his forehead, and his chilled body muscles.

Forget it, he thought, his mind hunkering down and scheming how he might surprise his wily student.

No rifle. Once again, he cursed that decision. At least both men were even on that score. Questions grew into a litany of unresolved answers. Would Dan be asleep? Would he be waiting? Tom knew better than to rule out anything.

Again, he wondered why Dan had cached so early in the day. Sure, there were several predictable answers. They just didn't quite add up.

Dan sought out his relatives and queried them with the same question. No answer came.

He began to lay out a plan. Once he had settled on the design, he reviewed his decisions as carefully as if they represented the lay of the land itself. He walked across the mental landscape, foot by foot. But he remained bothered. *Forget it,* he thought. *Just be* ready.

Tom was uneasy. "Engager," he whispered in French to himself, his voice hushed by the harsh weather. *I'll move like a wolverine. He'll not see me, by God. I'll sneak in there. I'll get 'em.*

And he thought once more about his people, his Tsimshian, his legacy, his father's, a spirit now in the otherworld. His thoughts churned like heavy surf scrubbing a weather-beaten beach. *Younger. Stronger*. The words harangued him.

There was one final preparation. He began his death chant.

Just before darkness, Tom saw an eagle circling above the cache where he expected Dan to be waiting. Even to Tom's keen eyes, the raptor was nearly invisible in the graying sky. He pondered on the raptor. Was it a spirit bird? Did not the eagle represent his clan? *Eagle find me. Eagle save me. Hey mana naka say. Ho mana naka so.*

He repeated the chant over and over in his head. By now, he guessed that the eagle was a spirit bird.

The sky deepened quickly. Snow clouds raced across the high mountain valley. Night came on, moonless, cold, and penetrating. The snow continued to fall in dense swaths. The wind shifted. Was there any mercy to the weather? He pulled himself into a tight ball. Covered himself with his tattered wool blanket. White flakes continued to skirt across the landscape in slow pirouettes. Tom was too cold to care. He was no longer watching. His single perspective was fastened on Dan and upon his own survival.

Tom knew that he had the patience of the Creator. He had to be sure that Dan was asleep. He had to wait for the deepest part of the night. Trouble was, he felt so cold he just didn't know if he could endure the weather much longer. Snow and ice might kill a man. Here, there were plenty of both.

He prayed to his ancestors. "Give me strength," he pleaded. A small chant escaped his lips. He imagined an eagle sweeping past. "Eagles protect me," he whispered again in an ancient coastal dialect. "Eagles find me. Hey mana naka say. Ho mana naka so." Inadvertently, his eyes swept across the sky.

As the wind hurled down from the mountains, his words were quickly scattered.

Moonless, the deepest hour of the night approached. The forest settled into a lull, the errant wind subsiding. Tom began to shuffle silently up the trail, one foot at a time, each movement calculated. And each step awakened the numbness that aggravated his appendages. It felt good to move. The souls of his leather moccasins fell silently on the snowy trail. Cold penetrated his heels through two layers of leather.

His feet slid rhythmically into soft, silent steps, mimicking earth sounds, the rattle wind made when skittering through the flat delicate limbs of a hemlock or cedar. The earth voice was a melodic voice.

Tom's father had taught him the art of stalking. Tsimshian warriors employed similar techniques with uncanny skill. Tom had mastered the mountain craft from both cultures. His moves unfolded naturally now. After decades of practice, he didn't need to pay much attention to their design. His knowledge unfurled with conditioned ease.

As he crept up the path, he was thinking only of his student, pondering the man's skills. He remained apprehensive: *younger, stronger*.

Tom was confident but cautious. He remained circumspect. *Eagles protect me. Hey mana naka say*. Was that eagle a spirit helper? He needed all the help he could muster.

He took another step. Moved another yard closer to his student, the pathfinder.

The wind renewed its tirade, whipping the treetops with renewed vigor. He heard the forest music now, the night sounds. The wilderness cacophony settled his apprehension and covered his approach.

He moved deeper into the cache. His keen ears read the silence. Dark Tsimshian eyes pierced through the night screen. Those eyes were as cunning as any forest animal. Tom was reading the glade like the pages of a book, one written in Tsimshian.

The sharp skinning knife in his right hand would gladly have reflected moonlight if the yellow orb had shined its bright face down upon the honed steel blade. But no moonlight tinctured the grove. Tom moved on alone, invisible and stealthy. All nights should remain so dark, so quiet, so deep. His knife was ready to fly. The bone hilt rested in his fingers.

Deep night unfurled, moonless. In the end, Tom wasn't alone. Spirit helpers walked beside him. Above, the eagle waited.

She woke four hours after midnight and wandered her own house like a stranger. Even in a plain flannel robe, the outline of her lovely body telegraphed across the small space of her cabin. She was not a young woman, but Rebecca Skinner was striking. The labor of farm life had kept her body firm. Sunlight tanned her complexion and colored her strong forearms. Her face was attractive, strong and soft, reflecting her Nordic disposition. All the while her intelligent eyes traipsed across the small cabin's interior with a gaze that was disarming.

Only the house cat watched. Rebecca pranced nervously across the top of the wooden floor, her toes scooting over the even-grained planks like a ghost dancer. Her movements were lithe, but the pattern of her steps telegraphed anxiety. Her face said more, exposing pain and speaking of private desperation. Rebecca had worried herself into a corner. She was a strong woman, but there was no hiding the reality of her husband's quandary—her quandary. Worry lines broadcast a plaintive message: she couldn't take much more. Rebecca needed to know of his whereabouts. Whether her husband was dead or alive, she just had to know. She was sure that a posse was pursuing Dan and his brother. That news had traveled quickly through the community and up the valley. She feared she might never see either of the Skinner brothers again.

The house cat sidled up to her, seeking a soft lap. It sensed more than most humans might expect. Rebecca loved the touch of its soft fur against her skin. She loved the detached way it would sidle past her legs, rubbing her fair skin and then retreating, too temperamental to willingly commit true love on its first pass through.

"Come here, baby." She picked up the cat, stroking its silky ebony fur. "I can't help it, Jack. I just can't help it." The cat struggled in her arms. She relinquished her grip.

Then she cried, but her voice wouldn't let out more than small, restrained sounds. These were the hushed sounds of her private world, the same private language she might have bestowed on Dan while making love, a bridling of emotion as if she worried that others might hear or judge. She was a proud and private woman.

Rebecca continued to pace back and forth, speaking to the cat but talking to herself. She began to sing a Civil War song that her daddy had taught her when she was just a slip of a child. But she wasn't remembering her father. Her thoughts were all for her husband. She thought that she would do anything for Dan. Just then, she didn't know what or how.

Soon she stopped her pacing. The time had come when her pain no longer supported the bounty of her tears or the repetition of her steps.

She stood straight up on her toes, leaning from one leg to the other. Her hands came up to her face, touching randomly on her soft skin. She wiped away the telltale trail of tears and then ran her fingers through her lovely, thick hair. She shook her head side to side. Her auburn hair fanned and waved in the cold air of the kitchen as the yellow rays from a kerosene lantern backlit her tresses.

Rebecca scooted across the kitchen floor and began to sing again. Her sweet voice explored the sorrowful cabin air as if seeking an isolated cache of comfort. The cat watched her suspiciously, feeling her desperation. Then, as if coming to some mental conclusion, Rebecca said out loud or maybe to the cat, "I need someone to talk to. Sorry, Jack. I need someone who can talk back."

She stroked the cat and stoked the kitchen fire. "Busy hands are happy hands, Jack."

The words were spoken half in a mumble and half as a salve to her mounting anxiety. *Tomorrow morning—this morning*—she thought, *I'll find some help.*

"A friend in need is a friend indeed. No going back to bed now."

Rebecca was used to early risings. She knew it would be hours before light found its way through the small glass panes of her wooden house. It was nearly the end of February, but the nights this far north held forth like the grip of a wolverine. Rebecca had animals to tend to. She would be in the barn by 5:30.

Later, after a breakfast of eggs, whole-wheat toast (yesterday's oven-baked), and coffee, she saddled the big mare and began the five-mile trek into town. A frozen crust of snow broke under the weight of horse and rider. The echo of the mare's hooves clattered off the frozen earth. Cold air stung Rebecca's mouth and throat, but she sang another song anyway. This was the only diversion she knew for her pain. *Keep moving,* she thought. *Keep the mind busy.*

She sang on—stopped—then said out loud, "Let 'em know I'm coming," and then sang some more childhood songs, all the while thinking how the music robbed the forest of its natural solitude.

But Rebecca loved the comfort of her sweet, high voice. The forest would have to allow her that. Gently shaking the reins while nudging the animal with her heels, Rebecca spurred the mare into a slow canter.

There was not a hell of a lot to miss in the winter village of Kilnook. Paint a picture of nearly any northern coastal outpost of a hundred or so mixed Caucasian and Native people in the last decade of the 19th century, and one drew a familiar pattern: general store with post office, one boarding house (served three full meals a day), stable, blacksmith's shop, tavern (Kilnook had two), jail, and a Mounties' office. These were the Royal Canadian Mounted Police. The lawmen were all dead, and that would soon cause the largest scuffle of grief and retribution since the Big Drowning of '75. During the storm that spring, most of the sailing fleet capsized in a sudden ocean gale that rallied out of the northwest on the first day of the salmon season. Forty-one men under sail drowned. Nearly as many families felt the weight of the loss as it spiraled into their future lives.

Scattered randomly throughout the village was a café, a boat works, a fishing dock, a large smattering of fishing dories, fewer cedar canoes (Haisla and Tsimshian design, all older vintages), and about forty cedar-sided houses, some Native, some White. Some full, some deserted. These vestiges of frontier life spilled along the main street before punctuating the banks of the Kilnook River and a narrow beach that fronted the ocean. Upriver were a handful of small farms, one of which the Skinners owned and worked.

Two white churches countered the taverns. A small wooden schoolhouse stood prim and proper on the easterly end of town. Graveyards: White men. Red men. White pickets surrounded the former. Totems with wings and sharp-beaked faces scattered through the latter, a few bright with primary colors, the others fading into obscurity.

Finally, there remained a shuffling of nondescript wooden buildings: sheds and smokehouses, outhouses, split cedar-shake lean-tos for firewood storage. A pioneer had to keep his wood dry. The winters were long, wet, and cold. Just inland, big snow resided through most of the long, harsh winters.

Little to no landscaping enhanced the village. When the giant trees came down, they stayed down or got bucked or trimmed into firewood. Some were burned on the spot to make way for new farms and homesteads. Often the downed trees rotted. There was almost no price for cedar near the turn of the century. Sometimes they were taken down because they were in the way. That was how it was—few humans with white faces objected.

No rainbow oasis here. The landscape and buildings were clad in the cloying gray garments of winter. The only colors that distinguished themselves above that meld of winter monotone were small wooden signs proclaiming local businesses or a few white-trimmed windowsills. Or the schoolhouse painted white on three sides. Paint had run short

Fog, rain, and ocean mist often camouflaged even those few buildings punctuated by fresh paint. The environment was stark. The mingling of warm ocean air and colder mountain currents aided that fundamental weather pattern: long wet winters and overcast spring days.

Frost was common. There were no flowers and there wouldn't be any until June. Most of those would be daffodils that the pioneer wives planted to ward off the deep winter malaise.

Along the wharf two dozen Haisla shanties stood derelict in the early morning light. Only a generation earlier, the old town had been all Native. Three to four hundred Indigenous people had resided comfortably in that small pocket of habitable land.

Rebecca rode boldly up to the single café. She hitched the mare and put on a firm, determined face. Inside, her belly was in turmoil. Most of the town had already shut her out. She patted the horse affectionately, then walked into human silence as chilling as the winter frost outside. She stepped through the café's red-painted door, the only brightly painted door along the main street.

She pretended not to notice the undercurrent of hostility. The local burghers pretended not to notice her. Several patrons quickly exited. Sensing a change in the air, Sally Walton strutted from the kitchen, saw Rebecca, then hurried toward her. Sally wrapped her big body around the smaller woman as if to demonstrate to the entire village her affection toward her special friend.

Sally was impatient with the social games so frequently and maliciously displayed by the inhabitants of Kilnook or—as far as that went—most social outposts north of Victoria. Gossip was standard ammunition.

The woman hid her disdain for those norms but not her genuine affection for her best friend. Big-boned, tall, and imposing, she spoke the truth as she saw it. Her words trajected power. For a moment at least, she held herself back.

"Hi honey," she said, then hugged Rebecca again, this time for herself. They were tight. They had been for years.

Nobody in town—man or woman—would stand up to Sally or to her vernacular. Her body language proclaimed, "No nonsense." Her penetrating voice conveyed more. That morning she was more demonstrative than ever. Several male patrons (there was no cooking like Sally's until one reached the Panhandle in Alaska) began to leave. They retreated sullenly into the icy street without acknowledgment or protest.

Like coyotes sulking, Sally thought. *Nothing but the paper-thin whine of a varmint or a pack of 'em*. Her wide mouth tightened at the corners.

Sally stood back at arm's length from Rebecca and surveyed her friend. Reading the haggard lines on her face, she hugged Rebecca tightly for a third time. "You okay, honey?"

"Yeah! Yeah, I guess so." Her voice was hesitant.

Sally knew better. It was silly to even ask. Chagrined, she grasped her friend's hand a little too fast. Both women stood awkwardly, smiling the plaintive, half-hearted grimace of the lost, hungry, or disenfranchised. Together they disappeared into the kitchen. The last local swallowed a final mouthful of lukewarm coffee, then followed the retreat of the others.

"Talk to me, Sally. Jeez, I'm so lonely. When Dan isn't around the farm . . . sitting out there all alone, well, it gives me the chills."

"Honey, I don't know what to say. Hell's fire, what can we do?"

Bolstered by Sally's use of the word, "we," Rebecca pressed her troubles forward, scratching out her worst fears. She had little to lose. She had nowhere else to turn and only the horse listened. And as winter closed in, he only became further impatient.

"What if Tom and those deputies bring Dan and André back . . . back . . . well, back . . . Dead? What if—"

"Shhh. Don't now. Don't you dare think that way!"

Rebecca was close to tears. "Dan had nothing to do with that accident. You know that! The whole darn town knows that."

The desperation of the last several days pierced her natural confidence.

"Yes, dear. Yes." Sally placated her friend, smothering Rebecca with more love. "André has brought you nothing but trouble, Rebecca. Why did he go with him? Dan, I mean. Why did he go off with André, anyways?"

"Oh, God, I don't entirely know. Brother stuff. You know Dan. Loyalty above all else. And jeez . . . he loves André! And I guess . . . so do I."

Rebecca was crying now, stuttering between her words. But that wouldn't do. She was a pioneer woman, after all. She was used to adversity. She pulled herself together and wiped away some tears. "I'm sorry. I shouldn't . . . It's just that Dan was gone before I even said goodbye." Then the tears started to fall all over again.

Snow flurries began in earnest. Volleys blew down the street in austere gusts, in whorls of wet white flakes, settling and listing against the lee sides of the wooden buildings as if seeking shelter from the angry gale. The coastal highway—that nearly infinite body of ocean—brought the wind home nearly every day. A person might as well count on it, almost figure the peaks and valleys of the storms by the confluence of the tides, the thrust of the ebb and flood. By the full moon.

Beaches and spruce glades were shaped by daunting winds, by the hounding rain and sleet. Mountains that lay easterly behind the lower beaches of shifting sands—behind the dunes, the sheltered harbors, and the hushed thick forest—ordained that civilized life should seek that last westerly margin of livability. Both the ancient villages of the Native Americans and the more recent pioneer settlements hunkered along this shoreline as tentatively as a strand of cobalt trade beads clung to a Native woman's throat, held in place by a mere string of dried deer gut.

Inland travel was by boat. The inside passages ran for hundreds of miles. Saltwater and freshwater avenues flowed down the thousands of waterways and natural canals. Beyond that it was snowshoe country, a bushwhacking outback. Most of the land rose up into granite plateaus, thousands of feet above sea level, or into craggy mountain peaks, majestic with snow-covered crowns.

The inland passages were stunning with translucent water that might turn a celadon green or, after heavy rain, into a dirty coffee brown slurry. But no matter what the color, the water and the land beckoned. Nature called to the sensitive side of man or woman. If the wilderness remained inhospitable to these early trappers and pioneers, the vista was beautiful, wild, and inspiring.

If a pioneer handled the winters, summertime was paradise, even if lasting for only a few short months. During the short respite, folks couldn't get enough of the mild weather. Unfortunately, the land was seldom lenient toward the careless, the lost, or the unskilled. Summer or winter, pioneers had to watch their step.

Back at the café, a long pause interrupted the conversation between the two women.

Then, as if she had a fresh allotment of breath, Rebecca spurted out, "I've got to find him, Sally. If I have to, I'll go into those mountains by myself." She dropped her arms to her sides and balled her fists.

"Honey," her friend replied, inhaling a mixture of fresh air and a dose of astonishment. "Don't you talk that way. I mean honestly, don't be silly, Rebecca. Listen . . .there's no telling . . .well, he could . . .he could be anywhere."

"No, I'm serious."

"That's what worries me, silly girl. Mm-hmm! You just can't run off into nowhere."

"Not now. I mean . . . Later, I might . . . Sally, I've seen him in my dreams. I'm gonna go. Listen to me. As soon as I'm sure."

"And how the hell will you know that, for crying out loud?"

"I'll just know; that's all."

"Lord Jesus, protect us."

For a few seconds, Sally held her friend at arm's length, then she pulled Rebecca's body into her own. If anything, the tears fell harder now. Slid silently down both their faces, only to be absorbed into their wool clothing.

"What will we do now, Sally?"

Sally chewed some on that. She really hadn't a clue.

Wind and snow whistled down the dirt street. The ground remained frozen. Kilnook lay prostrated by the unmitigated assault of one more winter storm. The two women inside the café were oblivious to the onslaught. They were dealing with their own private devils.

"Rebecca, we gotta wait. And pray. And that's all there is to it. You hearin' me, honey? I won't have you talking such foolishness. Dan knows what he's doing. There ain't no better woodsman in these parts unless it's that damn Indian who's trackin' him."

Those inopportune words stopped Sally short. She wished to draw her words back. She took a deep breath and scurried on.

"Listen, Rebecca, when your honey shakes free of that posse, some dark night he'll be knocking on your door. You know that's the truth, don't you?"

Rebecca was hearing but not listening. She kept imagining her man. Kept remembering him as he departed from the farm, half-running as the two brothers scurried out of her life. Just once Dan had stopped and turned. Although he stood at a distance that distorted keen visibility, Rebecca swore she sensed his gray eyes locking onto hers. She imagined the sturdy way Dan always stood, feet splayed, hands on hips. But he hadn't raised his hand. Hadn't even waved.

Still, she had felt his love. Felt it all the way across the farmyard. She felt it now, too, by God, pulling her along. Pulling her into those snow-covered mountains. If he wasn't back by spring, she would go find her man. And nobody—not even Sally Walton, not an army of town folks—would stop her.

Rebecca looked up at her friend. Sally's words exploded, nail-driving hard. She liked the big woman for her conviction, for her courage. Beyond that, Rebecca knew she had a friend she could count on. Right now she needed that more than anything. Except, of course, her Dan.

Winter 1953

"Mommy," she would say, "tell me more about my daddy."

Katherine and her mother were snuggled together under layers of blankets. The bedroom was cold. It was winter in Seattle, wet and everlasting gray. Dankness settled around them, penetrating the paper-thin walls of their humble cottage. Penetrating their psyche. Winter struck hard in the Northwest that year—most years—if only for the pervasive lack of color and incessant dishwater-gray rain. But like most Northwesterners, Margaret and Katherine had come to accept the weather, to prefer the nocturnal moods that tarnished the green landscape. Others ventured into sun-drenched vistas. Dealt with the smog and the overpopulated urban centers; dealt with the soaring crime rates that inflicted other cities farther south. Mother and daughter were bound by the pithy silver-gray patina that painted the long cold winters days with dull, somber hues. But in the Pacific Northwest the air was clean and frequently scrubbed by the heavy rains.

In between rain squalls were those treasured days when the sun rebounded down the alleyways from Queen Anne to Elliott Bay, and when no city was more appealing than Seattle.

Supporting a daughter by herself had never been easy, not then and not later. For years after her husband died, mother and daughter shared the same double bed. The small rental had but one bedroom. A good job was still difficult for a single woman to corner in the late 1950s.

After Katherine's question, her mother would go quiet. She gathered up the best memories, prioritizing the loveliest moments. After the interlude, she would say, "Which story do you want this time, honey?" Already, she knew the answer.

"Mom, tell me about when you first met Daddy."

"Honey, I told you that one a thousand times. You know that story by heart."

"Just one more time, please? Just for me. Please, Mommy."

And Katherine's mother would drop her eyes upon her little girl, squeeze out a smile, and sigh. "Just one more time then. I met your daddy at a dance in Ballard. A union dance. He had rhythm, alright. A cutter. Everyone in the place spotted that right away. He tapped the shoulder of my partner and swung me out onto the dance floor.

“I wasn’t half-bad myself. I was real pretty, honey. I always got asked to dance. Almost never sat down, if you must know the truth. After a few minutes, I looked around and was shocked to see we were alone on the dance floor. Everyone else was just watching. A few clapped. Others encouraged us on. The dancers had formed a circle. Your daddy was catching fire. I just held my breath and hung on for the ride. Felt like I was skating on ice.

“We danced nonstop for nearly half an hour. Mostly, it was the swing. To tell the truth, I wasn’t counting time. After that, the first thing I asked was, ‘Where you learn to dance like that, cowboy?’ Well, he just smiled that mischievous grin of his and said, ‘Old Indian taught me. Any Tsimshian can dance any White boy into the dirt.’ Well, I figured I had touched a raw nerve. Turned out to be God’s truth. Your daddy didn’t look Native. He didn’t have no Indian blood. But he had the heart of a chief. He saw himself that way. His heart was tied to the Native culture. Apparently, he had lived around them. Up North somewhere. Sorry Honey, I don’t know much more. My God, he was handsome. Can’t tell you exactly why, but I fell for him right there. Fell for him hard.”

CHAPTER EIGHT

Something bigger had brought them together; something mysterious that was part eagle and part man, or maybe something bigger than that—one of God's mysteries: the way prayers can plummet like falling stars or ascend into pearl-glazed moons. Call that the human quilt. Call that the intangible!

—Katherine Skinner-Patterson

Notes for a novel

Doubts rankled Tom all day. That same intuition shadowed him even now, up the trail where Dan waited. A creeping sense of failure wouldn't leave him be. Like the Sisiutl, the double-headed serpent of Tsimshian lore—a shape changer—a phalanx of doubt tracked him from two directions at once. Maybe the warnings were the utterances of the newly dead or the relatives of the lawmen. Such spirits haunted a man. Tom held steadfastly to that ancient Tsimshian belief.

In a moment of clarity, he deciphered the pattern: here was a story waiting to be told. Part of the story had already happened. The next chapter dipped into the future. The two were as intertwined as the marriage of a deuce of mountain streams, both feeding a deep wilderness lake. A gathering place. A rendezvous of big water. Well, that lake was his life.

As he trudged up the darkened trail, all four directions of the Tsimshian compass remained invisible. He felt as if he had lost his bearings.

Nothing made sense to him. He was lonely, cold, and fatigued. Everything he held as steady had turned as soft as quicksand. Everything except for the knowledge that he still possessed his skills. Foremost, Tom was a tracker and a woodsman, par excellence. Not for the last time, he shook off doubt and trudged ahead.

The very whiteness that had crowned the wilderness during the short afternoon now receded, tumbling, an inky-black curtain.

Tom stalked the nightland, his plan of attack playing out like a fisherman feeding line into the deep dark ocean. Back and forth his thinking went, surging, halting, retreating, and then bursting forth again.

He would pounce upon the next clue and then move ahead. If doubt continued to haunt him, he simply wouldn't back down. Still, caution screamed at him like the high-pitched protest of a Steller's jay.

The tracker moved slowly. A disciplined man didn't rush these things. But as he closed upon his prey, other memories unfurled. Tom was suddenly remembering another time and place and a young man named Danny Skinner.

Tom watched from a thick grove of trees as the youngster, maybe fourteen winters that year, struggling to set a trapline. He knew the boy. Two years before, Tom had appeared suddenly before the unwary newcomer, startling him speechless.

The boy was just a shadow of the man he would quickly become. He wore britches that had been cut off at the ankles. That was a survival trick utilized by cautious loggers as they sprinted away from the giant conifers as the trees toppled unceremoniously to the ground. A man couldn't afford to get his pants tangled up in the briers while escaping a large, falling conifer, a two-hundred foot tree that could crush a logger instantly.

The sawed-off pants were hand-me-downs that had been modified to fit the boy. That day, Danny was also wearing a faded flannel shirt. Red suspenders anchored his pants to his shoulders. His hat was fashioned from the skin of a raccoon. It hunkered comically onto the top of his head.

That made Tom smile. He remembered a similar coonskin hat and his first attempts at skinning and tanning.

That day and often thereafter, Tom would stumble upon the boy as the youngster tracked through the forest or explored the big river as it tumbled from the mountains. Often the boy wandered a half-day or better from the security of his home, from the village once known as "Salmon Town" by the Natives.

As the months progressed, the boy wandered farther and farther afield. Tom liked the boy's tenor. Tom exposed the boy's desire to learn the trapper's craft, to become a *homme des bois*, a man of the woods. Tom's father was known as a *coureur de bois*, a French-Canadian trapper.

The boy was more than eager to learn. Danny had a wild spirit about him, a trapper's persona. Tom was instinctively drawn to the boy and spent hours teaching him his trapper's bag of tricks.

Watching from the evergreens that day, Tom saw that Danny had been crying. The skin around the boy's eyes was swollen like a bee sting, and his nose was red.

Tom was going up country where he would spend the spring trapping beaver, marten, and otter. That was the crux of the problem. It didn't take a genius to conjure up the reasons behind the young man's tears. The boy wanted to go along. Tom had only to ask a couple of questions, and Danny let his disappointment spill out.

Earlier that week, Tom had suggested that Danny might like to accompany him. Danny had just asked his dad. The invitation was a huge compliment, but Danny's father's negative response had been expected.

"Son, don't 'spect that makes sense a' tall For Christ's sake, boy, Ya won't never fish with me, your own father."

Danny suffered mightily from seasickness and would rather have eaten slugs than subject himself to the willful moods of the Pacific Ocean.

"T' hell with that, I say. He's just a no-good. Gol-danged crazy talk, you ask me, boy. No, son. No."

And that was as far as the talk went. No amount of prodding from either Danny or his mother moved the father, hell bent as he was on preserving his authority.

Against his father's wishes, Danny had come this far, right to the edge where backyard became wilderness. Anxious to rendezvous with his mentor, he had only tears to offer. And maybe that was a small relief for Tom. He remained skittish about his feelings toward the youngster. Tom didn't fancy becoming intimate with anybody, particularly a White anybody. He had already suffered enough emotional wounds from the Boston men to last him a lifetime. And he didn't plan to cut it short.

Creeping through the pithy darkness, Tom continued to be harangued by internal monologue. He stopped momentarily and drew in a few deep breaths. He knew better than to lollygag.

Cold air stung his throat and lungs. He knew he had to concentrate. Dan was waiting ahead. Under any circumstance, the man was dangerous. Right now, well, there just was no telling.

A scout had to stay flexible. He had to be ready for surprises. And the relatives had finally gathered about him. Unfortunately, that only created more confusion. Abruptly, Tom remembered a similar audience—that same wave of humanity—he had once observed during a small rodeo thrown by the Whites in a large meadow at Port Hardy. The audience was animated and, at times, slightly hysterical. There had been plenty of liquor about. Well, he related that spontaneity to the potlatch, to the dancing frenzy that happened during the extended Native celebration when lack of sleep, abundant food, and a kindling of near-magical powers erupted. Unfortunately, there were no potlatches anymore. The government had seen to that. But even the law couldn't outlaw spirit helpers. Not for the last time, Tom wished that the ancient ones would break the silence and advise him about what lay ahead.

No actual voices here—as the dark hours and another layer of snow draped across the moonless sky—but a spirit of kinship endured. The dead ones, his ancestors, surrounded him at once, spirit helpers whirling in a midnight dervish. Had the voices been clear, Tom might have overheard several dialects. Many of the relatives were ancient. Others were familiar. All the spirits were invisible, but their presence reverberated like the ricochet of rifle fire through the steep canyons of the Kilnook Valley. A man might only catch those spirits in the deep inner recesses of his mind, only imagine their bodily shapes and voices.

He took another step. The woods remained as still as a downed animal, a deer or elk, their breath torn away by a lead slug or an arrow.

His feet squeaked out a shuffling sound.

He remembered home, his first home. How he ached for that village. But there was no going back; those early chapters were closed forever.

Years before, on a small tributary of the Kilnook River, a waterway known as Broken-Paw Creek, Tom had stolen through the woods. Just as silently, he crossed the bear meadow until he stood just feet behind the young boy. Danny was oblivious to the Tsimshian. He was busy setting a trap.

"Howdy, son,"

Danny jumped nearly two feet high and turned as white as the snow-capped mountains that sprouted above the wilderness that surrounded him. He stood chagrined before the trapper. *Never, never drop your guard.*

The words spun silently through the young boy's mind, shaming him. The words belonged to the Tsimshian, the man standing just behind him. He had shared the lessons with Danny many times before.

"It's okay, son. You're not the first man I've surprised in the wild. Some of them was skilled woodsmen. But a word to the wise, now: don't never turn your back from a possible ambush. Don't drop your guard. You'll learn that right soon. You're plenty smart, boy."

The words were kind and flattered the young man. Danny's head rose a notch.

"Let me show you a thing or two about them traps." Silently, Tom applauded the boy's initiative but held his praise in check. There were lessons to learn first. An accident or mistake might cost the boy his life. "First things, first." And Tom began the trapper's litany, his checklist of survival techniques. "A man traps dawn and dusk in the low light. No shadow, you see. Stay in the trees when you can. Stay hidden.

"A pilgrim traps spring and fall for the fattest fur. The plew gotta be silky and thick for a good price. The fur be better then. You got to hide your smell, son. Hide any scent. That beaver, he be a wary critter. Did you ever try the bark of the devil's club? You peel it just like this." He reached nearby for the thorny plant.

With a razor-sharp knife, Tom demonstrated. He scraped off the thorns, then peeled back the bark. He rubbed the inside of the bark onto his forearms. "Hides your smell, son. Try it now. Rub it on your neck and arms.

"The depth of the water, the length of the chain—here is right, and here be wrong. Let me show you now. You followin' me?

"Look for sign. Beavers like young cottonwood and alder. Find where they been eating. Where they been sleeping. Where they move to at night. See that hut yonder? That's a beaver's home. They enter it from below, from beneath the water.

"Never, never turn your back on an enemy, where you think he might come from. Imagine how he might surprise you. Think ahead. You gotta figure he's just behind you. Always! Out here, that can be true of a bear or a cat. It's a feeling thing, your nerves set all day for surprise."

Every time Tom said it, Danny would steal his glance over his shoulder, as if suspecting anything, animal or man, might choose to jump him. The one time later that Dan forgot Tom's lesson, it nearly cost Dan his life.

Tom had a phrase for a bad trapper or an inexperienced woodsman. Probably he had inherited it from his dad. He called a man of this distinction "a *mangeur de lard*," a pork eater. Danny was sure he would never be caught off guard again. No man would dare accuse him of "eatin' no pork." The woods were still full of wild game. He was learning how to find them. How to shoot and skin the hides. How to cut up a large animal.

"No waste. Use every part." Tom hated waste. Many times, the Tsimshian had experienced lean times. Starvin' times.

Healthy respect for Tom's words bolstered the boy's attention to detail. Thereafter, Dan became ever more cautious, covering his backside as he moved in the wilderness.

"Here's how you take scent from a beaver. How you spread it onto this here float stick. Where do you set the stick? Show me.

"See that sign down yonder? Fresh or old? Tell me, otter slide or beaver? Tell me, son. That's easy now, ain't it?"

There was no end to the lessons. And the boy sucked it up like a pup lapping milk from a clay bowl.

With excruciating care, Tom crept along. Three hundred yards up the path he spotted the calling card of a campfire. The grove began to lighten perceptively. He knew an enemy was waiting ahead. He silenced his apprehension and his inner voices.

Then he altered his already delicate step. Not even the night critters heard him now.

As a wolf slinks in the wild, so did White Bear. His footfall glided across the snowy path, mimicking the stealth of a four-legged predator, the wolf in particular, the most cautious of animals. Indeed, the scout had wrapped the wolf's soft hide—leather side out—around his feet. The moccasins were a lie-saving essential. He had chosen a dense winter pelt. Together, man and animal had traveled far from Kilnook.

With every step that Tom took, his moccasins caressed the frozen snow. Each footfall brought him closer to Dan Skinner. Beyond that, the fur warmed his feet, his only relief from the winter frost. The man needed ever bit of that: any shred of warmth.

Tom could smell the smoke rolling off the fire, could anticipate the life-sustaining warmth. *Attention White Bear*, he repeated to himself. *Come on man. Concentrate. Death may be waiting just ahead.*

In time, the boy learned the bigger animals: how to trap them, how to skin them, and—most importantly—when and where to avoid them. Danny learned how to set a trapline with all the skills of a master woodsman. Tom LaCross was his mentor, and his lore had been passed down from father to son all the way from the earliest French-Canadian trappers. And by way of the skillful Tsimshian peoples. Those skills had been honed long before recent memories had played out.

Tom taught him how to stalk properly, how to decipher the sex of an animal by a simple footprint. How to shoot straight and true and when to shoot and when to hold up. How and when to use a knife, both as a tool or as a weapon. Soon, Danny was stalking through the woods as stealthily as his teacher.

At age fifteen, he spent his first week alone in the wilderness. That was followed by others. Soon his forays became constant. Danny's father was dead now. Drowned at sea. Danny had to choose his own way. With the loss of the family patriarch, he felt a new sense of freedom—and responsibility. Both emotions came at a cost. After his father's death, Danny continued to feel pangs of guilt over his personal emancipation, over that undefined rebelliousness that frequently draws a line between father and son. Tom usurped some of that paternal bond. The Scandinavian boy and the scout became tight. Everyone in the village saw that. Generally, they disapproved.

The young man soon duplicated the scout's cunning. When Danny reappeared from the wilderness, he packed a bale of prime pelts. Plew (a mountain man's word for furs) measured a trapper's success, his worth. Danny's bales measured as thick and as lush as the best of the woodsmen. Soon, the boy moved on. Precocious, by eighteen he was a legitimate free trapper. In between he served as a tracker for the Mounties, still shadowed by his mentor, Tom LaCross.

Danny was seventeen when Tom gave him a Bowie knife with the beaded sheath. The beads were Russian, the sheath an heirloom. A woman had crafted the sheath for her husband, a chief called Big Bear. The gift was the Tsimshian's most prized possession.

The kid had surmounted the rites of manhood. That was clear enough to see. Danny had demonstrated passage into that private fraternity of woodsmen, a true *coureur de bois*.

Alone now, following Dan's trail, Tom was remembering all that but cursing his stupidity. He knew that all his teaching might turn ruthlessly against him. "Why did I do it?" he mumbled. "Why did I let him in?" Truth be known, he would have done it all over again. Dan Skinner was the son Tom never had, the boyhood he had forfeited.

The last fifty yards took nearly a half hour to cover. Tom was standing less than a yard from the first snare, two yards from the center of the pit. Ahead of him, apparently asleep, lay Dan Skinner, his back toward the stone pinnacle, his eyes facing Tom but closed to the night land. No mountain man ever would have turned his back on an enemy. Tom trusted that but wondered why Dan was sleeping so soundly. *Well,* he thought, *if I ever lay this weary body down, I'll sleep like a stone, myself.*

A small fire blazed between the two men, and even at twenty yards, the heat beckoned.

Watching the younger man asleep and susceptible Tom wondered if he might take him alive. *They would just hang him anyway,* he thought. *Better to finish the job, here and now.* And then he wasn't so sure. Tom knew that indecision was a formula for disaster. He drew a deep breath, steeled his mind, and stepped forward.

Tom was a Tsimshian warrior. Each muscle was poised for a decisive strike. Four feet down, at the bottom of the pit, sharpened stakes anticipated his demise. The spear-shaped tips waited for the famous scout, prepared to impale and maim.

For twenty minutes, Dan had been aware of Tom's presence—ever since he had heard the tiny bark of one of the scout's moccasins as it broke through a thin sheet of ice. The noise was slight, but Dan missed nothing.

He hardly dared to breathe or stir. He besieged the winter Gods. *Please! May the snare trip up the scout.* If not, he would have to trust the pit. Tom might anticipate a trap, so Dan had crafted two. Over and over, Dan prayed that one would stop his mentor. If not, a bullet would likely bring him down. Armed with only his knife and his wits, he was no match for Tom and his rifle.

Dan gripped the knife concealed under his blanket. Felt the cold bite of steel and bone. If the trap failed, there was still the knife. Dan believed that Tom had a rifle. Sufficiently armed, he wondered why the scout was so cautious. Why did he move so slowly? What if Tom just shot him where he lay? Why not? Dan was a sitting duck. He was also responsible for the death of three lawmen. With a well-thrown boulder, he had nearly dispatched Tom to the other side. *He must want me dead!*

Even now he imagined Tom squeezing off a shot. He envisioned the scout's finger curling around the steel trigger. But Dan was certain that the Tsimshian warrior had more honor than that. Indeed, he was betting his life on it. Tom wouldn't shoot a sleeping man. Wouldn't shoot his old apprentice, would he? Dan remembered André, gunned down on the cliff. Right then, Dan feared that his supposition had gone astray. Any second now, he might be just one more dead man. Down the winter trail, Dan felt the wind stir. Even across the fire, the chill smote him, and he thought, *This is no place to die.*

Again, he remembered his wife, the curl of her ample smile, her soft penetrating eyes. He shook the thought aside. This was not the time for lollygagging. If he ever wanted to see his beloved wife again, he darn well better pay attention. *Never, never, drop your guard.* The adage rattled in his mind. The man coming down the trail was sure to remember those words. A hundred times he had repeated that specific lesson to his apprentice.

Dan steeled himself and thought, *This is not a good day to die.*

Winter, 1972
A poem by Katherine Skinner-Patterson

Streambank

Piercing
Avian whistles
Colored birds flitting through
Stark winter limbs

Winter stream
Swollen and angry
Jumps the riverbank
Tears and scurries
And scatters
Evening song

Oh!
Spring rain
How you taunt
Hard cold love

CHAPTER NINE

"The world isn't that easily turned upside down," Haida replied. "It's people who are turned upside down."

—Haruki Murakami

Tom didn't like the fact that Dan was lying so still. Didn't like that his instincts were shouting caution. He consulted his relatives. They weren't talking. Besides, he had come too far to turn back. The sky was as dark as sable fur. Snow fell, but it was thin and inconsistent. Tom would have appreciated more cover. He cursed his luck. Nothing was working well for him. He shuffled forward, poised on his toes, balancing like a cat.

For the second time in as many minutes, his foot pushed through a thin crust of ice. He didn't know it, but the film of frozen snow covered Dan's footprints. The crust rattled just barely, but even the slightest sound was too clear an announcement for the likes of Dan Skinner.

Damnation, Tom thought. *Don't wake the man. Damn it to hell.* Things weren't going as planned.

Just then, Dan took a gamble and rolled ever so slightly, higher onto his side, like a dreaming man making an unconscious adaptation to the daunting voices of the badlands.

The motion seemed natural, just a sleeper's adjustment. Tom liked the tenor of the movement. He felt the jangle of his nerves settle. His breathing slowed. He took another step. Suddenly—mysteriously—he sensed the snare. Had one of the fur-lined moccasins contacted the buried hemp rope? Had his relatives broken the rules of the dreamworld and warned him of an impending danger? Whatever the cause, his instincts reacted lightning quick.

But muscle betrayed the tracker. Everything flew at once. Flew forward like a night owl scurrying toward a mouse dinner—an Arctic owl, pure-white with a beak as sharp as a spear point, and an eyesight to match.

Poised all day for one decisive thrust, Tom found himself jumping beyond the snare. There, the trail collapsed under him. He landed squarely in the center of the pit. He was betrayed by his speed, by the inertia of the jump. He had not suspected the second trap. His keen instincts had failed him.

Tom fell fast and hard. Surprise pinioned him. Then and there, the shaved stakes sang their war cry, tearing through skin and muscle and into bone.

Like a man lost in a long fall into the underworld, Tom's world churned topsy turvy and then turned black.

Dan crouched in a fighter's position. He moved with blinding speed, prepared to stick either one of his weapons into the chest of his mentor. But the sharpened cedar stakes had already pinioned Tom. He lay unconscious, bleeding heavily. Dan lifted the long pointed spear in his right hand. From a distance he appeared poised for a deadly thrust, but something held him back. His arm tensed. Tom's muscles remained cocked and trigger sure, but there and then, Dan's arm fell slack. He was stymied. He couldn't kill his teacher. Dan wasn't the only man smitten by honor.

Beneath his feet, his enemy lay broken and silent. Dan thought of his brother, gunned down at the summit of the cliff at the pinnacle of his short life. At that, he nearly threw the weapon.

But then Dan envisioned his wife, and his whole persona softened. The icy wind whisked him a message. Like the gong of a brass bell, Rebecca's voice rang out softly. It spoke of clemency. Dan held up.

Death waited many long seconds before Dan plunged the spear through the crust of snow that continued to accumulate next to the pit. He couldn't kill an unconscious man. That was the law of the land. After all, Tom hadn't shot him as he lay defenseless beside the fire.

It was then that Dan noticed Tom had no rifle. He cursed himself for an oversight he could never have anticipated. He praised the man before him for his bravery. Who else but Tom LaCross would have sought him long and hard through this wilderness? Sought him unarmed or practically so? Dan had to question why.

Tom had moved so cautiously, so skillfully. Dan remembered how much he respected his mentor's skills. Revenge stirred, then faded, his mind stumbling between André's death and his wife's kindness and her Christian brand of forgiveness. He studied the man lying unconscious before him.

In a convoluted way, Dan was as helpless as Tom. Memories of André's death garroted his compassion but Rebecca's spirit of kindness trumped his strongest convictions. They argued for forgiveness. Conflicting thoughts remained prisoners in a strange twist of fate.

The relatives clamored. Neither man heard. The spirits would remain in the other world, the province of the dead. Tom was close to joining them. Dan was feeling hopeless but not destitute. Maybe, he figured, he might now sneak back to his wife. There were no lawmen left alive, or hardly alive. Tom was the last, and he was incapable of traveling.

Dan forced out a deep breath. What to do with Tom? He couldn't leave him there. Abandon his old mentor. But if he mended him, how long might that take? Even if Tom was healed and bound, what could Dan do with him? Dan was at a crossroad and he didn't know which way to turn. He thought about simply walking away.

Dan stood up tall and straight and listened intently to the night sounds. To the lack of sound. To that hollow place in between. He heard the pounding of his heart, felt the strong, pulsing message of clemency. Nothing offered him comfort or answers. What should he do?

He let out a solitary curse. The forest answered with silence, but the stalemate was brief. Other sounds were afoot.

The winter storm's fury descended again. Night winds unleashed a determined swath through the alleyways of spruce and cedar. The snow continued to fall harder now, covering the frozen earth. Gusts of wind teased the high, thick boughs, the giant evergreens, most, hundreds of years old.

Then and there, ten Native men stepped wraithlike into the firelight. These were not spirits. These were warriors of actual skin and bone. They surrounded Dan like apparitions rising from the dead. There was no hiding it. Dan heard the gasp of his own breath.

In their hands were ten bows and arrows. The arrows were notched and the bows drawn. Ten obsidian arrow points, razor sharp, pointed at his body. Each lance was capable of crippling him, of taking his life.

The Natives' eyes were steady and foreboding. One made a hand signal that indicated that Dan should forfeit his weapon. Dan dropped his knife and stood as still as the tall trees, resolute and leafless in the winter grove that surrounded him. The forest leaned toward him. The wind had suddenly dropped, but the night land remained grim and unforgiving. Deep in the thicket, Dan heard the call of a single wolf. Against his own volition, he shuddered.

"Come with us now," a large, muscular man said, speaking the queen's clear English.

The warrior was dressed in winter furs of the highest quality. The furs glistened in the firelight. Skin leggings ascended all the way to his knees. He wore a robe of sleek bear fur that covered his torso. A bear's head, still intact, covered the greater part of the man's cranium like a hood, and the ferocious animal's snout and teeth greeted the pathfinder with a cunning grimace. Dan was dumbstruck.

Wind skirted through the leafless alder trees. The winter land appeared suddenly supernatural. No longer was Dan able to make out the trees from the night. Exhaustion struck him like a disgruntled slap to the face. His body sagged. His single reality was that a hostile band of Native men had just materialized before him. Materialized like a hat trick, like a bit of magic. Tom's famous warning remained forever present and haunting. Though the man lay still and bleeding before him, Dan remembered his words as if the unconscious man was uttering them again. *Never, never, drop your guard.*

Dan's brain spun. *Wait a damn minute,* he thought. *This isn't the old West. This is 1896.*

Defenseless and subject to circumstances that had shadowed him to this very point of chance or fate, he turned and faced each of his captors as sternly as he could muster. Again, a wicked winter wind struck him. He shuddered, but his eyes remained steady.

On first impression, the Indian faces reflected sternness but quickly acquiesced into masks as impassive as a winter sleep. Dan was stumped. Like the hard storms that blanketed the wilderness around him, he realized with striking clarity that the Natives held the upper hand—the only hand. A moonless night closed around him and the ten warriors. Searching their faces for any sign of their intention, he lifted his head and focused on his captors. Another gust of wind reared up, carrying along the lone wolf's austere cry. From their impassive faces, Dan read nothing. And nothing had ever startled him more than the warrior's four clear words, "Come with us now."

The Native village nestled into the stone-faced mountains like a bird in a nest. On the perimeter of the large encampment stood four spears of granite that appeared natural but were situated so evenly that the pattern appeared oddly fantastical. The stone buttresses settled into the direction of the four compass points. First Peoples respected these points as the home of the four sacred winds. The Natives believed that wind emanated from those same directions. From there the dead would return to these spiritual beginnings. That was if their spirits were true and their intentions noble.

His captors led him through a narrow opening and into the interior of a large plank house. He was overwhelmed with doubt. The sudden appearance of a large gathering of Native people only confused him more.

The village was surrounded by dense forest. Nestled into a deep valley, the enclave appeared secreted away. It didn't take a pathfinder to appreciate the cleverness of the location. To find this cache, a man would have to stumble upon it. Well, maybe the Natives had beaten Dan to the punch. They had found him first. Now he was their prisoner. Prisoner—the word stung him. Just then his home and his wife seemed impossibly distant. In the trees overhead, a Steller's jay spirited out a severe admonition. Dan felt the chastisement.

Frequently, he would remember Tom. Not fewer than a half dozen times did he query, "Where is the man I left in the pit?" His captors refused to answer.

Dan wasn't sure how many of his captors spoke English. Certainly, one did, the one with the bear-skin robe.

Would these men just leave Tom for dead? There were but six traveling with him now. Where were the other four? And did he really care? Inevitably, his thoughts threaded down the silver valley toward Rebecca and their farm.

Though Dan was surprised by the rock pinnacles, his gaze was fleeting. Moving ahead of him, his eyes mounted the sheer mountains and ridges that surrounded the valley. Sheltered it. As it was, the four pinnacles only reminded him of the pattern of corner block houses erected for protection against the "savages." These were typical log fortifications, common along the Northwest Coast until the late 1870s. After that the tribes had been subdued. Near the end of the nineteenth century, the structures had nearly passed into obscurity. Hostility had been bled out of the Native population, or at least severely subdued.

Dan had come to believe that. To expect it. Instead, shadows from the past had loomed out of the night. He had been blindfolded and tied, his arms secured behind his back, then firmly coaxed over miles of rugged terrain. Hours later, they had arrived at this village, leaving him exhausted and confused.

As the men entered the village, the Natives released Dan's blindfold. Above the mountain buttress, daylight was beginning to unfold. He was pushed inside a massive cedar lodge and secured with stout leather thongs to a thick wooden post. The plank longhouse was not dissimilar from those he had seen up and down the coast as a young boy, but he knew immediately that this building was newly constructed and of fine craftsmanship. And the lodge was warm and dry. Dan could only thank his lucky star for that.

Hours passed. Seemingly indifferent to his plight, his captors and their families came and went. He caught the covert stares. Some of the Natives appeared simply curious. Other faces telegraphed anger and retribution. Was that pain he detected behind their human masks? He shrugged. Dan had his own problems without worrying about the emotions of a bunch of "Indians." Mostly, he was left alone to contemplate his fate. Pinned helplessly against the pole, his thoughts jumped erratically.

Dan had seen plenty of the cedar longhouses before. Had seen a large colony at Village Island and another at Port Alberni. More than once he had traveled down the Inside Passage with his father. Without appreciating the long heredity and accomplishments of these Native peoples, he had passed by many deserted villages without comment or curiosity.

This one was larger than most. It had been constructed by fine craftsmen. Any man who worked wood could see that. He was impressed first by the four large carved totems that cradled two huge cedar beams that ran across the front and back of the plank house. These, in turn, supported the long roof joists that ran east and west. Dan figured they must exceed seventy feet. The roof was laced with thick cedar planks. Positioned between the two frontal totems, a man-sized entrance extended westerly, facing forest and sky where normally an ocean might have waited. No one had to explain to Dan that there was no ocean nearby. Why, he wondered—and not for the last time—was the village there at all? Why was it hidden so deeply in this inhospitable wilderness? How long had it been there? Questions continued to careen through his mind.

He pitched his gaze around the rectangular hall and across the packed earth floor. Vertical posts formed the four corners of the cedar lodge. Stout beams supported the roof. Dan was startled by the size. This was a major achievement. Just moving these huge timbers had taken ingenuity and arduous labor. Again he wondered at the strange nature of the village and contemplated the circumstances that had lured him to it.

He scraped his foot across the earthen floor and darted his gaze deeper into the gloom that penetrated the windowless structure. Through the natural fissures in the plank walls, stabs of light streamed through. One large, sunken firebox was positioned centrally in a rectangular earthen pit. That space lay below ground level, and a dozen others, smaller in dimension, lay scattered throughout the lodge. This smattering of cooking fires blazed with soft radiating light. The longhouse had two levels. He was tied to a pole that extended above his head through the upper level and into the plank ceiling. Wide wooden platforms were raised above the floor and extended out from the outer walls. On these platforms, living spaces resembled small bedrooms. They wrapped around the perimeter of the longhouse. A dozen or more families inhabited the spaces.

The lodge was well lived in. Dried foods hung high above the fires, punctuating the ceiling like smoke-dried confetti. Elsewhere were articles that spoke to daily rituals: wooden boxes for storing food, wooden dishes, some filled with eulachon grease, a gathering of cooking utensils, mostly conscripted from alder wood and a few from animal horns, wooden bowls and brightly painted bentwood chests for the storage of blankets, clothing, furs, masks, and other ritual items. Dan was surprised. The space was orderly, putting his barn to shame.

Settees constructed from split cedar planks were carved with beautiful, sharp-edged designs representing the animals of Native mythology. Dan was reminded of Tlingit design.

He conceded that the interior space was both handsome and practical. Occasionally, Dan had admired the richness of the Native design, particularly the magical quality of the totems. But the spiritual aspects of their symbolism perplexed him. Like most Whites, he had never bothered to understand the stories or the history that lay behind the carved and painted images that defined their culture. And why should he? *These are just Indians, anyhow,* he thought. *Mostly, they live by superstition. They have lived on this land for a thousand years and never done a damn thing with it. Just squatters.* Self-justification and wrath continued to usurp his better judgment. More than anything, he was extremely confused and frightened.

The space was warm. A woman brought him a bowl of fish soup with chunks of dried salmon floating in the broth. Fed from her hand, the soup invigorated him. Dan came to the sudden conclusion that he was being treated graciously, and that surprised him. He wondered how long the courtesy might last, what they might do to him. He also remembered stories of Native cannibalism. How the heart of a captured whaler was extracted and eaten. It was rumored that the victors believed if they ate the organ, they would inherit the captive's power. The thought stopped him. Truth or fiction? Dan refused to guess.

Smoke agitated his eyes, but that wouldn't kill a man. All in all, Dan felt lucky to be alive.

Later in the afternoon, Dan watched the approach of a silver-haired man and his companion. The older gentleman was being guided by a younger man down a dirt aisle that stretched the length of the longhouse. His hair reached nearly to his waist. He walked with a tentative gate, as if he had trouble seeing. *An elder*, Dan thought.

Dan watched the two approach but then let his eyes wander off, studying instead a thin cloud of smoke as it ascended through an opening in the cedar-plank roof. There, the light of day backed down the smoke hole, forming a bright rectangular pattern on the floor. Through the hole he saw intermittent falling snow.

His eyes smarted from the steady bath of wood smoke. Much of it remained in the longhouse. Tied securely to the post with stout cedar twine, he shut his eyes but continued to see a small square of cranberry light that colored the world behind his eyelids.

When he returned his gaze to the old man, he realized it had taken the two an inordinate amount of time to reach him. With a start, Dan realized that the elder was indeed blind. He also recognized the guide as the same warrior who had been dressed in rich furs the night before. It was the same warrior who had spoken those four brief words. Now he stood before him. In a distinctly different environment, Dan found the man's appearance to be far less frightening. Had the darkness and the trauma of the night overwhelmed his perception?

"Grandfather wish to say hello. He welcome you to our village."

As the younger man spoke, Dan gazed suspiciously at his captors, his gray brooding eyes settling warily on their strong faces.

"Grandfather asks me to tell you that you will find no harm while you stay here."

Dan couldn't help himself. he blurted out several quick words like birds of prey. "Why then must I be bound?"

"Please, you must be patient."

"Can your grandfather speak with me?"

Dan had interrupted. Both Natives remained patient.

"He speaks Native tongue," the younger man replied.

"And that is?'

"Haida and Kwak'wala. Some Haisla."

"Where did you learn your language?"

"Which language?"

"Boston tongue."

"At residential school. Port Alberni."

"You learned well."

"Thank you. It was not good time. The worst in my life."

Dan went quiet. He reviewed his surroundings again, mindful that there was much to learn. He thought about what had just been said. Both Natives appeared patient, their mannerisms courteous. That waylaid some of his apprehension. He swiveled his eyes back to the guide. Before speaking again, Dan steadied his emotions and thrust out a question. "How many people live here?"

"Hundred or more. Maybe hundred fifty."

"You're hidden here?"

The younger man didn't answer the question but turned toward the elder. The old man was studying Dan, seemingly, hanging onto his every word. He had deep brown eyes, almost black, like the fur of an otter. The elder's stature resonated with unusual patience and strength. Although short, he stood bolt upright and fixated his blind eyes on the trapper from beyond.

"Does he understand some of this?"

"Yes, but he is blind. Yes. Grandfather very perceptive."

"I don't fully understand. You said he doesn't understand English." Dan felt his attention shifting back toward the elder. "What's his name?"

"Black Wing. Grandfather is called Black Wing."

The old man reached to his guide, then placed his mouth close to the young man's ear.

"What does he ask?"

"Grandfather says your words run fast like a swift river." The younger man grinned.

Dan reddened, then changed the subject. He was not about to be intimidated. "What's your name?"

"My name is Charlie. Grandfather says you ask many, many questions."

Dan knew he was being rude, but he ignored his normally good manners. "Am I your prisoner, Charlie?"

The young man turned to the elder and spoke privately in his Native tongue. The conversation between the two was brief but animated. Charlie turned back to Dan. "Grandfather says you have little to fear, but you must stay here in village."

Dan had already heard that piece of information, and he didn't like the options at all. He turned to the old man. The elder's face continued to display little emotion. It appeared to Dan that the old man was lost in an inner meditation.

"Grandfather says no man's spirit should be held prisoner. He says he is sorry for this. Sorry for you. Your thoughts are free, he says. He says to remind you that others—your people—still hold many of our people as prisoners. The Boston men have broken the spirit of the tribes who once lived freely on these lands. Lived for untold centuries. This was our land!"

"I don't understand much of that," Dan replied.

"Grandfather thinks you do. In time, he says, you will come to understand it much better."

"I wish to leave soon," Dan said.

"I'm sorry. You must stay. Must be patient." Charlie's voice quivered with an angry resonance. He was fighting for composure. Dan realized he had struck a tender nerve. The old man again whispered into his grandson's ear. Charlie was grasping at straws. "Grandfather says we must go. We talk later."

Dan feigned indifference, but then blurted out a question that was pregnant in his thoughts. "That other man, half-White, Tsimshian?" Dan spoke with a quavering voice, suddenly swollen with emotion.

Now it was his turn to wrestle over words. As he spoke of Tom, he felt a tightness seize his throat and noticed that the elder turned his blind eyes toward him, seemingly, concentrating on Dan's every word.

The old man swiveled suddenly and began to walk away without the aid of his guide. He obviously sensed the direction. Maybe he identified with the miasma of light at the far end of the lodge, kind of a screen of rectangular light. The younger man rose awkwardly, his eyes following the elder's retreat. Charlie took two tentative steps, then stopped and turned back. "We go now. Grandfather say you very brave. Grandfather see you on the cliff. Grandfather says he is sorry about the brother." Then the young warrior hurried on, leaving Dan's next words hanging in the smoky air.

"What . . . I . . . " Dan's breathing quickened, his heart racing.

The young warrior quickly departed, closing the gap between himself and the silver-haired elder.

Spellbound, Dan watched as Charlie took the old man's arm. The elder walked with such composure that Dan felt forced to follow each movement as if it were a study in quiet dignity. Both passed between the two massive house posts, through the entrance and out into the sunlight. Already the sun was disappearing behind the mountains.

Dan craned his head toward the smoke hole in the roof. The snow appeared to have slowed its descent, and he figured the return of cold weather was imminent. When he gazed again at the entrance of the plank house, the two men were gone. For a moment, two bluish auras surrounded their fading images.

Dan's eyes remained glued on the lodge entrance. His gaze was vacant, his mind galloping. He kept hearing Charlie's last pronouncement, "Grandfather see you on the cliff."

For crying out loud, he thought, *that old badger must be a holy man.* Try as he might, Dan couldn't unravel the implication of the elder's last words. "For God's sake, the old man is blind," he muttered.

Dan felt terribly tired and lost. He thought again about Rebecca and saw her standing in the late-afternoon dusk as he and André scurried through the forest. He had turned just once, just before they scampered out of sight, his eyes glued on hers. But just as quickly, the farm was gone, and so was Rebecca.

He thought about André, but the old Indian's words kept crowding back into his mind, usurping all other memories. "Grandfather says you very brave. Grandfather see you on the cliff."

From the lodge's entrance, two pairs of huge, carved eagles glared back at the trapper. They held him in their grip. But it was the eyes of the blind elder that settled like a target into his mind. He simply couldn't get away from their spell.

Long after light fell, Dan continued to brood over the blind man's words. Although the elder had not spoken to him directly, it was clear that there had been a silent communication between them. Dan was sure: he had never encountered anyone quite like him.

He thought about the ministers he had come across through the Anglican Church. Their words hadn't excited or inspired him. He wondered who this elder was and what powers he wielded.

Dan was exhausted. He felt his eyes close, an involuntary reaction to the last two weeks, exhaustion, and the cloying smoke that stung his eyes. In a near slumber, he envisioned a sail unfurling. The image woke him abruptly. What had he just seen? What did the vision represent?

"Gol darn," he mumbled under his breath. "I'll be go to hell." In his mind's eye, he continued to envision the elder's penetrating gaze.

1963

Katherine read the poem over and over. Who was this man, this poet? Was he her muse? There were many poems in the short paperback by William Carlos Williams. Katherine liked the short ones. One struck her hard. It was called, "Locus Tree in Flower." Oh, how she loved that poem.

Among
of
green

stiff
old
bright

broken
branch
come

white
sweet
May

again

She thought of her daddy. Hadn't he been a poet of the forest, a nature poet of sorts? Didn't his words bring pleasant images to her mind? His speech had been so careful, so simply articulated. Yet strong. Dignified. He spoke with a rhythm that reminded her of the freedom of his infamous dancing.

Katherine walked up to a nearby park and ambled under the tall cedars and Douglas firs. Could she put words on paper that others might read? Would others take solace in her brand of expression? A song, perhaps? Or words braided together. She walked on, lost in thought.

Right then and there, Katherine made a promise to herself: someday her words would inspire others.

It began to rain. Just as quickly, the sun broke through. There was a fragile beauty all around her. A soothing sound swept through the tall evergreens. She just had to learn to slow down and use her eyes and ears. Slow down to hear the music. To touch it. To wrap it around her mind, her being. She would learn to shape the right words. She just would. She was sure. She would make a difference.

CHAPTER TEN

One can't see the forest for the trees.

—English proverb

Three days passed, filled with revelations. On the afternoon of the fourth day, Dan was fed from a carved wooden bowl shaped like a sea otter. It was filled with chunks of venison, savory roots, and a pungent, hot broth. *Christ*, he thought. *Has anything ever tasted so good?* His great hunger felt suddenly satisfied, at least temporarily.

The leather thongs that bound his chest and legs to the lodge pole were removed. His hands remained tied behind his back and he was still tethered to the post by a length of the pliant, woven cord, but the additional movement brought great relief.

A small Native girl, of perhaps thirteen years, with kind, dark eyes and a smooth, round face, hand-fed soup into Dan's hungry mouth.

Odd, he thought. She appeared sympathetic to his physical constraints. He didn't know what to appreciate more: the warmth of the broth or the girl's company. Her presence made him happy, and that surprised him. Whatever lay behind her quiet disposition, Dan couldn't begin to guess. She appeared well mannered and curious. Her eyes, full moons of deep sable, revealed no clues. He didn't know what to think. Although Dan didn't know it, her demeanor was typical of her people.

Much to his surprise, Dan found these Native people to be both mindful and caring. They communicated with soft-spoken words and bestowed kindness toward their prisoner. Dan's vision of being served as a dinner entrée began to fade.

Two more days passed. Without much else to do than observe, Dan had taken in plenty. He noticed that there was a lot of laughter inside the longhouse. Fathers and grandfathers spoke in lengthy dialogue with the youth. Mothers and grandmothers schooled their daughters and granddaughters. There was thoughtfulness in their communication. The children listened. He never once saw a child beaten, and the parents seldom raised their voices. A father could be firm without causing a ruckus, and the kids hung on to the adults' words. There didn't appear to be much hard discipline.

Too soon to judge that, he thought, inadvertently moving his memory back to the pair of taverns located side by side on the main street of Kilnook. Fat chance of passing a Saturday night without a fistfight in either one. Without a brawl.

He shrugged it off. The vision hit too close to home. His mind tripped to the festering loss of his wife and brother. *If only a few things had been different.*

He cogitated about André's drinking problem and was suddenly struck by a revelation. It dawned on him that there was no alcohol in this village.

Dan looked around the lodge one more time. He had come to a conclusion: the people appeared happy. The living space reflected a particular peace of mind. But Dan couldn't begin to justify the loss that waited downriver. He missed the small accomplishments that he had scratched out each day on the farm. He missed his pioneer life. He missed home.

Dan surprised himself. He found his mind exploring the social aspects of these people. He noticed that food was shared and distributed equally. Apparently, in this society, a hunter was entitled to the liver and heart of a deer or elk, maybe the tenderloin. The rest of the animal was community property. The infirm received first portions. The elders were elevated to a position of high esteem. Anyone with longevity was honored as "grandmother" or "grandfather." Any neighbor of middle age was a "cousin," "aunt," or "uncle." Families lived together there. Family meant everything to these First Peoples.

Children not only listened to the seniors but also appeared to respect them. Their response bordered on a deep-seated reverence—at least that was Dan's early impression. He had never seen the likes. Dan projected that when hard times descended, the tribe suffered together. Good times or bad times, the tribe stood as one. The revelation startled him. Admiration disrupted his natural cynicism. He had been raised to condemn these Native people. Were these typical? *Wait and see*, he thought.

On the sixth day of Dan's captivity, Black Wing and his guide, who Dan learned was his nephew, returned. As before, the elder spoke through Charlie. "Grandfather ask how you are today."

"Oh, just fine," Dan replied, rather sardonically, wondering privately about his rude behavior. Deep down, he was thankful to have visitors, and the old man fascinated him.

"By the way, you say, 'grandfather.'"

"Yes, that common term for an elder. Black Wing my uncle."

"Oh!"

Charlie eyed Dan skeptically but made no reply.

Dan was obviously perplexed over his internment and by the fact that such a village even existed. Why, after all, were these people even there? Why was he there? The year was 1896. Nobody knew this band existed. Not the government. Not the locals in Kilnook. And what were their plans for him, anyway? Questions volleyed inside his head.

He eyed the two men suspiciously. Questions flooded in. What had happened to Tom? Had they added to his injuries or aided him in his recovery? Was he friend or foe? Was he even alive? Perhaps Tom's people were natural enemies of this tribe. Was there one or many?

Dan could hardly help himself. His mind was harangued with unanswered questions, none of which harassed him more than the most vital question of all: would they eventually free him? His temper rose, smothering his good manners. Dan was overreacting. His two visitors were the natural culprits. He felt overwrought. Thinking it over, he figured that he would have to make his escape and make it soon.

"Will you tell me a few things?"

"At a later time. Now, just eat. Rest. We must go. Come back later."

"Wait a second, you just got here!"

"Perhaps you don't want visitors today?"

Charlie was subtly letting Dan know that he didn't appreciate his bout of sarcasm.

"I'm sorry." Dan blurted the words out. He felt panicky and slowed his breathing, attempting to gather his wits about him. He privately cursed his sassy mouth. The two Natives stood patiently, neither speaking nor moving.

A minute passed before Dan succumbed to his higher emotions. "How is Black Wing today?"

Charlie eyed Dan skeptically but then turned to his uncle and repeated the question. Black Wing understood what Dan was saying without the aid of his interpreter. It appeared that the elder intuitively picked up the gist of Dan's conversations as well as the tenor of his feelings. The elder turned and spoke several carefully measured words into his guide's ear. Charlie then turned and answered Dan. "Grandfather is fine today. He explains to me many times that he loves his home here. This village. His ancestors lived here many, many moons. Many lodges come and go. He is happy man. He say you learn too. Learn much happiness in this village."

"But I don't wish to stay."

"Soon, you understand. Be patient. Grandfather reminds me to tell you that you not try to escape. We wish to show no force. If you run, we bring you back. You will be punished severely."

Dan figured he knew which way that stick floated. He changed the subject. He needed to gather as much information as possible. "You stay hidden here, don't you? The village stays hidden from others? From the Whites?"

Neither man answered. They stared straight ahead, their faces impassive.

But Dan could tell that Charlie was annoyed by his questions, his prying. Anger flashed briefly across the warrior's large, sturdy face. His eyes squeezed together. Still, Charlie's response placated some of the warrior's tensions. Well, Dan thought, any man needs to let go occasionally.

The old man turned his head and cast a blind eye on his nephew, as if he was sending a silent admonition through the smoky air.

Dan took a deep, slow breath. He was not prepared for Charlie's next reply.

"If you run, escape, and tell others about us—tell the lawmen—we no longer safe here. No longer have our home, this village. Many die the same as we see elsewhere. White man take our religion. Bring diseases we not imagine. You Whites trample everything that comes before you."

Furrows on bronze—definite pain etched across Charlie's pouty face. The man needed to vent. He couldn't hide that. One didn't have to be a history professor to understand the truth in what Charlie was saying. The last several decades had devastated these tribes. Everyone knew that, even those in denial.

Dan just nodded. After all, he wasn't in any position to disagree. He was aware that no Native had ever put it to him quite that way. He changed the subject. "I can't ever leave then, can I, Charlie?"

Charlie chewed on Dan's question before answering. "No. No, you can't. Well, I can't read the future . . ."

Charlie turned a sideways glance at the elder and then went silent, as if he was protecting a secret.

Dan had many questions, and he was impatient for the answers. One stood out. In the last couple of days, his mind had endlessly pondered Charlie's departing statement.

Talking to Charlie, but pitching his words toward the blind elder, Dan asked, "Please, how could Black Wing watch me on the cliff? He is blind."

Charlie's face remained impassive. He turned first to the old man, but the elder's blind eyes staring straight ahead as if to say, *You're on your own now.*

Charlie turned back, facing Dan. "Grandfather is blind but travel far. Maybe he borrow eagle's eyes? Eagle see you, not Black Wing."

"Eagle! How's that? Far, you say. Black Wing is blind. He can't . . ."

"Grandfather knows much that eyes cannot see. There are many things that sight not teach. He says eagle find you on the cliff. Grandfather, he wait several moons. Later, Grandfather tells our warriors about you and the Tsimshian. I was with them that night. Listen! Grandfather knows much that I cannot explain."

Charlie turned to the elder. Dan hardly felt placated. "Is he a seer? And the eagle, I don't understand."

"Later, talk more. Must go now. Grandfather tells me to say to you . . . Grandfather, he repeat, 'Don't run.' He says he likes this White man, this Boston who is very brave. You must stay. Very important to Grandfather. Please, you remember."

"Thank him for me."

"Yes. We must go now. Soon you see other man."

"What?" Surprise was in Dan's corner again. "You mean Tom LaCross?"

"Yes. Half-White. Tsimshian. One called White Bear. Yes, him."

"White Bear? LaCross? When? He's alive?"

"Yes. Soon now. Yes, White Bear."

Watching the two men retreat, Dan felt a surge of unmitigated anger and then something else. Was it relief?

The drone of his ancestors woke Tom. Pain smothered him. Before he opened his eyes or made any discernible movement, he let his sixth sense travel around a manmade shelter that contained heat, light, and—yes—another human body.

The seated person repositioned himself. It was a man. Tom sensed that. He appeared to be waiting for Tom to awake. The space contained old smoke. Even with his eyes closed, Tom felt the residue from burned alder wood. The space reeked of smoked salmon.

Tom found that queer. The smell was months old and thick. He ascertained the man beside him was Native and that the shelter must be a smokehouse.

Tom repeated a Tsimshian chant to himself, gathered his spirit helpers about him, and prepared himself in the warrior's way. He felt the bonds that tied his hands together. Cedar rope. Marks scathed his wrists and left his hands numb and achy. His legs felt bandaged and splinted and smelled of herbs. A clay poultice had been layered over many of the lacerations, over the deep wounds that penetrated his legs and chest. Spruce pitch covered several of the smaller wounds. Again, the pungent aroma of plants greeted him. This was good medicine. This was the medicine of his people.

Faintly, he remembered the pit. Remembered falling. After that? Well, just shadows. *What the hell is going on? Where am I?*

One side of his chest jumped in pain when he breathed. Broken ribs for sure. He pondered the medicine packs over his wounds and wondered who might have dressed a wound in such a fashion. The answer startled him. He knew these people. They were old neighbors.

Once, the different tribes had been enemies. More recently, they had amalgamated. They had become hospitable with each other. Had patched up many of the old rivalries. What choice did they have? *My God—they should have done that eons ago—that would have been a fighting force.* With his eyes still tightly closed, he thought about how his world had changed, so rapidly, so radically.

Revenge against the Whites was out of the question. There were hardly enough of his people left to organize a potlatch, and even that was deemed illegal. In 1857, the queen's people passed a law called the "Gradual Civilization Act." A decade later, a ban on public ceremonies criminalized potlatches and organized authorities to "seize, sell, and destroy regalia."

There would be no more wars between the Native tribes, or, as far as that went, against the Whites. Again, Tom wondered what would have happened years before if the disparate tribes had "joined hands."

From his bound position—curled on a cedar mat on a dirt floor—Tom pondered whether the man before him was Kwakwala'wakw or from another tribe. Maybe Haisla or Heiltsuk. Right then he realized these Native people—whoever they were—had just saved his life. *Allies,* he concluded. Lying there, bound and wounded, he was also pondering Dan's fate and the strange string of events.

"Welcome back, brother."

A deep gravelly voice pushed aside the smoke and crept across the earthen floor and into Tom's ears. The voice hushed the clamor of his spirit helpers. Its voice appeared kindly and thoughtful but also big and firm. Tom knew the language behind the voice. His guess had been close. This man was Haisla. Tom spoke the language haltingly. He did not use the lingo frequently, even in Old Kilnook where it was common among the survivors of smallpox and influenza. Besides, he preferred the Xenaksiala derivation. Tom had chosen to live apart. He was Tsimshian and proud of it.

LaCross continued to lie motionless. The pain in his body was excruciating. He felt nauseous and faint.

Pain or no pain, it was time to stop pretending. He wondered if his ancestors were listening.

Intentionally, in Tsimshian rather than Haisla, he replied, "Brother from the River of Eagles—my brother from the People of the Snow—may we share water?"

Tom wished to conceal his knowledge of Haisla. First, he needed a few answers, and he didn't want to tip his hand.

His eyes sprang open then, his gaze plunging through the dim light. His vision was greeted by pain. Smarting, his eyes swam through it all, circling the rectangular room built from cedar planks that quarantined the smoke, the smells, and himself, each captive in their own distinct way. All but the Native guard. He was free to come and go. He was a free man.

Tom's eyes skirted every detail until they landed on the Haisla's rugged, weather-worn face. They rested there uneasily, not sure what to expect.

"Have you water to share?"

"I have always shared with my Tsimshian brothers," the guard answered, speaking Tom's language fluently.

That startled Tom. He had quickly reached the conclusion that the guard would brook no quarter. Was his kindness a contradiction? This was a big man with a husky voice that resonated with confidence and strength.

The man rose and moved across the small room, light on his feet, and then returned with a wooden ladle filled with water. He slowly spooned the liquid into the prisoner's mouth.

Parched, Tom drank gratefully. The water slipped down his throat, fur soft. "Thank you, brother."

The attendant answered again in Tsimshian, pleasing Tom. "We are one family."

Well, that said a lot. Tom felt the tightness in his chest subside.

Again, in Tsimshian, Tom asked, "Where am I?"

And in Tsimshian the guard answered, "In a smokehouse belonging to our people. This house was built to preserve the flesh of our cousins, the swimmers."

"I am grateful, my brother."

The drone of relatives subsided. Outside the building, Tom heard a cacophony of sounds: children's laughter, songbirds, the ancient marriage of wind and forest, fat spruce limbs waving softly in the cold steady breeze, subdued, just now, under the solid weight of snowfall. But the children's laughter startled him. It had been years since he remembered hearing such joy and spontaneity. *Where have they brought me?* he thought. *And who are they?*

Outside, a spry, wily raven with a coal-black body danced limb to limb. In a bird-voice thick with audacity, the raptor chastised the laughing children and the adults who moved quietly about. Snow fell randomly throughout the short afternoon. The frozen landscape gathered the flakes in, one by one, until they were transformed into a winter cloak. Outside the smokehouse, the village rested at peace.

Inside the great lodge, Dan, his hands still bound, was released from his tether. He stood and shook his shoulders and head with a great sense of relief.

He was then escorted from the longhouse, out and across the same patch of earth that was gathering up the snowflakes. Three men crossed the village wordlessly. Two braves, positioned on either side of their ward, firmly pinioned the Boston man's arms. They led him through a low door and into small rectangular building that appeared to be a smokehouse. Dan's eyes sorted through pale light and the palpable weight of old smoke and then reacted wildly as he recognized Tom's form lying prone on the floor. Dan attempted to lurch forward, but four strong hands held him fast. His tied hands balled into fists. Words that the Tsimshian and Kwakiutl had not added to their vocabulary sprang through his angry flushed lips.

Tom turned his head and studied Dan. The Tsimshian lay silently and let his gaze linger on his prized student. Strangely, he did not react like a surprised man. Nor was there hatred in his eyes.

Over the village, snow began to fall harder, silencing the happy sounds of the children. Confusion and surprise filled the smokehouse. In a tall spruce tree, the raven croaked. "Attention. Attention," it repeated in private raptor language. Nightfall fell upon the village.

Fall 1967

The United States was engaged in a war in Southeast Asia. Katherine saw it for what it was. Saw it as huge mistake. Like other students in the 1960s, she took a stance.

She attended lectures and demonstrations. She handed out flyers and marched steadfastly. At a protest rally at the University of Washington, she met a short, black-haired protestor with dark smoky eyes, a beard, and a proclivity for activism. Paul Hanson was a fine speaker and organizer. Though short, he was also handsome. At five foot seven, he stood a couple of inches taller than Katherine. She was attracted to the strong-talking man. Katherine was in her freshman year. He was a senior.

Katherine was nineteen years old that fall. She relished the atmosphere of the university and quickly made new friends, mostly women. When not studying, they loitered along a street that the students called the "Ave." Together they ate Chinese food, ice cream, and Mexican burritos. Constantly, they talked about the war in Vietnam and the politics that shaped it.

She met Paul along the "Ave." By the end of the fall term, they frequented a café famous for Texas ribs, imported beer, loud raucous music, and an appetite for protest. Katherine often found herself staying later than her roommates. As her companions departed, she was left in the company of the dark-bearded activist. They talked together like conspirators, their heads pushed together, closer and closer.

Katherine was bashful around men. Losing her father at a young age had stifled her outgoing nature, at least toward the opposite sex. In relationships she was cautious. She called her mother frequently. Had dinner with her nearly every Sunday night. She sought her mother's advice. Her mother remained her best friend.

Katherine was not a great beauty, nor was she unattractive. Her body was firm and shapely. Simply put, intensity amplified her persona. Her deep, questioning eyes drew a steady bead on whomever she encountered and then held firmly, as tenaciously as a wolverine.

With a group of her peers, she organized a major march through downtown Seattle. The protest was free of violence. Paul gave an impassioned speech that lasted nearly fifteen minutes. Katherine had seldom felt such a sweeping sense of euphoria, such mission or purpose. She had begun to believe that an organized populace *could* change the politicians' minds, that students *could* inform and shape an apathetic public. She believed that political change was possible but only if a larger community stayed committed to a cause, in this case ending the war in Vietnam. She was certain she would do her part. Surely, change would come.

In 1968, Lyndon Johnson announced that he would not seek a second term of office as the president of the United States. Katherine felt elated. But she had come to realize that commitment had a price. Everywhere there were bruises. A wedge of political partisanship was dividing the nation.

In the span of a few years, Katherine watched tearfully as national television played and replayed the assassination of two of her heroes: Martin Luther King and Robert Kennedy. Riots ensued. Buildings were burned. Soldiers patrolled the streets.

Only a few months after the peace demonstration in Seattle, Katherine moved in with her bearded lover. They became inseparable.

Katherine and Paul helped galvanize the student community, but they were just beginning to learn the price of commitment. Hard days lay ahead.

CHAPTER ELEVEN

"To attempt to describe the condition of these tribes on my arrival would be but to produce a dark and revolting picture of human depravity. The dark mantle of degrading superstition enveloped them all, and their savage spirits, swayed by pride, jealousy and revenge were ever hurrying them to deeds of blood. Thus, their history was little else than a chapter of crime and misery."

—Anglican William Duncan, 1857

Rebecca saddled the mare and then steadied the animal against a snowstorm. Harsh weather had subdued the big animal's feisty character. Tugging on the worn leather reins, Rebecca turned the mare's head. The horse whinnied in protest, then, sensing appropriate direction, lowered her great mane and dutifully trudged toward the village of Kilnook.

The tangle of thick hair along the animal's broad neck was swept before the storm. The frigid wind continued to blow steadily off the sea. Snow blew full force and then lapsed into intermittent flurries, only to strike back with even greater vengeance.

The mare steadied her velvety brown eyes against the gale. Where she rode, silence ensued. Small, furry animals sulked in their burrows.

Rebecca and her steed passed slowly through the forest. The worn path to town widened. Soon she could make out the outline of the village. The horse moved down the main street. Months of accumulated mud had frozen in place. The mare's shod hooves offered up a laconic sound that was immediately silenced by the harsh weather.

Rebecca remembered her grocery list and reined in the mare. *Better stock up before leaving town. Long ride back.*

She coaxed her animal forward.

The mare submitted to Rebecca's prodding without protest. Secured to the hitching post, the big animal hunkered her massive head into the lee side of her chilled flank, avoiding the wind's direct attack. Nothing helped. The animal stood mute and dejected. Rebecca kicked her leg from the stirrup, and up and across the animal's broad rump. No sidesaddle here—this was pants weather, two pairs with long johns. Besides, Rebecca had never much taken to the frilly dress style of the day. This was the north country, and in the countryside, women adapted to different rules than the ladies in Victoria and Vancouver. She walked up the steps to the mercantile.

Rebecca shook her head, once, twice, pretending that the motion might ward off the accumulation of the heavy snow. The motion cleared her mind.

The snow spiriting around her. Rebecca stood before a pair of double-hung doors. They beckoned—or the warmth awaiting inside did—but the impression was fleeting.

Once inside, the women—shopping but mostly gossiping—broke their talk, turned, and pretended not to see her. Rebecca quickly became invisible. One woman sneered repugnantly at her. Rebecca had been friendly with these women for years.

A clerk offered assistance, but the conversation was stilted and unnatural. "Good day, Mrs. Dan," he said. The store clerk had always used "Rebecca" before. His words were stiff and stuck together like balls of wet bread dough. She left quickly with some sugar, oats, and a pound of coffee. Distracted by the snubs, Rebecca had forgotten to read from her list. As she exited, the women's conversation resumed. Her neighbors' rancor stung her like a slap to the face. Rebecca was apparently as guilty as her brother-in-law and her husband.

Outside, Rebecca felt the weight of pain and worry. She wondered how long her money might hold out now that Dan was gone. She wondered if anyone would give her a job. She answered her own question dejectedly. Even Sally had to depend on the locals, and there was barely enough business in her small café to sustain one woman. For a moment, Rebecca despaired. Anger rose in her then, converting into a tough obstinacy.

Let them think what they want. She knew who she was. And that went for Dan too. She knew her man, always had. Always would.

She would get by. *Damn right.*

She untied the mare and headed out of town, thankful that the wind was at her back, that she didn't have to face any more "good neighbors." The cold was intense, but she preferred the frigidity of the storm to the human equivalent. Both cut through her psyche like an iron wedge splitting firewood. Her thoughts were reeling.

An unlikely thought persisted, crazy perhaps, but Rebecca had nothing left to lose. Recently, she had mulled over this pregnant, if improbable idea. Mulled it over and over, like unfurling seasons. Indecisive perhaps—she knew the real reason for riding into Kilnook.

Abruptly she reined in her mount, turned, and headed back through town. Again, the mare protested as the wind bludgeoned the animal's large, strong face. By then the horse was totally confused.

Horse and rider headed toward a cluster of Native shanties in Old Kilnook, a string of buildings built along the edge of the ocean. A bitter ocean wind stung, pressing hail pellets the size of buckshot into the exposed faces of horse and rider. The mare neighed in protest.

"Easy, baby. Easy now."

Rebecca pulled the wool scarf tightly across her cheeks and nose. The mare scuffled along. Perhaps the big animal was dreaming of a warm barn and a bale of hay or, better yet, a crisp red apple. "No apples today, Liz," Rebecca mumbled, as if reading the animals mind. They plodded on.

Rebecca was seeking help but wasn't entirely sure what she wanted or how she might find it. Hadn't the village rejected her? To her way of thinking, even her best friend thought she had slipped a cog. Rebecca was desperate. An unwelcome thought persisted: Sally might be right.

She leaned her hopes toward the Haisla village on the western edge of town and then spurred the mare into a trot. Rebecca was hoping to find a Native man who might guide her into the wilderness—a scout who might help her find Dan. On the surface the thought was preposterous. But she had nowhere else to turn. Not a single White man for a hundred miles would even consider her request.

Between another round of heavy snowfall, the old village finally appeared. The gray weathered shapes of the longhouses and a few stick-built shanties snuck out of the storm-riddled landscape like a herd of giant caribou lost in a blizzard.

Rebecca tied her horse in front of the first house she came to. She remembered that once a Queen's agent had lived there and that the man was long gone. *Not enough Indians left to bother with.* Most of the Natives had fled to major enclaves such as Port Hardy, Alert Bay, or Skidegate in the Queen Charlottes. There, larger concentrations of the disparate tribes hoped to find social and economic opportunities. They hoped to find any opportunity. The Natives were fighting to preserve their old ways, or what was left of them. And they were fighting to survive. Dilapidated longhouses were further evidence of that fall.

Rebecca was neither overtly aware of their problems nor particularly sympathetic toward them. Like most White women who inhabited such pioneer settlements, she was uncomfortable around the Natives. She shared a common bias, a disdain. However, she was chewing on a new idea. Just possibly, she thought, somebody in the Old Village might help her find Dan.

She figured these Natives knew the Big Country. Knew how to survive there. Her thoughts kept returning to Dan. Well, she had to take the chance.

She screwed up her courage, dismounted, and then stepped toward the first longhouse, positioned as it was along the line of weather-beaten cedar-plank lodges that paralleled the shoreline.

During milder weather, the Natives sat along the waterfront and whittled away the hours. Local logic prevailed: the Whites thought the Indians lazy. Rebecca thought of them that way herself.

Native patience translated into a different mobility. After their fishing, hunting, and gathering had been decimated, the Natives appeared stunned and broken. Their hunting-gathering ways had been replaced by a welfare state. Alcohol only aggravated the problem. Destitution and apathy surrounded the once-proud people.

Even the otter were gone, trapped out of existence, or nearly so. And the mighty trees that the Natives had so carefully preserved were being plundered, acre by acre. One of the few jobs left for the Natives was to fall their own timber. The major lumber companies paid them small tokens, then sold the old growth for fortunes.

And logging remained one of the most dangerous jobs in the world.

Riding the mare into their village, Rebecca realized she didn't understand the people she was about to encounter. Now she'd stand before them, hands clasped across her abdomen, seeking a favor.

That winter day, the Natives of Old Kilnook huddled inside their cedar lodges, sheltered out of the reach of the tormenting northern winds.

A few of the structures were carpenter-built, tongue-and-groove homes that the queen's government supplied. Perhaps the government's intention was to buy European normality, or to assuage their personal guilt.

The Natives' only defense in the face of these Arctic salvos was the warmth elicited from a few small fires banked with driftwood and bark. The cedar longhouses were cavernous. Under normal conditions, heating remained an arduous task. Against the frontal assault of this storm, all they could do was huddle inside under their Hudson Bay blankets and dream of better times.

The ancestral forests closest to the village had been decimated and with them the best source of firewood. The Natives seldom felled living conifers for their lodge fires. Instead, they gathered deadwood, drift logs, and bark swept downstream by water torrents or deposited along ocean beaches by storm and tide. The great groves that had been the ancestral forests of the Kwakiutl, Tsimshian, and Haisla had been quickly devastated by the new settlers and their steel saws.

The retreating parameters of virgin timber now lay far beyond easy accessibility. Besides, the government controlled those stands, selling the logging rights to timber barons for just pennies on the dollar. The Natives were left out entirely. There was no recompense. From coast to coast, Native peoples coveted their old ways. Their lands. Their forests and the rivers and animals that inhabited them. Summarily, they were being ripped away.

Rebecca entered the first longhouse without knocking. There was no other way to announce her arrival. An elk skin hung over the entrance. As her eyes slowly adapted to the pall of smoke, she saw the outline of a Native woman. Out of a smoky haze, the woman emerged. Rebecca was stumped. What would she say?

The woman was short without seeming so and had serious brown eyes that leapt at Rebecca. Her arms remained bare and exposed, as were her legs. Her round, handsome face appeared unfriendly. She wore a short-sleeved cotton-calico dress with a faded white lace collar. The garment struck Rebecca as incongruous. After all, Rebecca was dressed in thick pants and a heavy wool coat. The woman's garment offered little protection against the gale that swept across the village. Instead of the traditional cedar shawl, the Native woman had modified a wool blanket. It covered her shoulders and chest. Time and the infusion of the European culture had changed the habits of these First Peoples. As with the pioneer dress, those changes hung awkwardly on the Native culture.

The woman stood directly before Rebecca but chose not to speak. Rebecca broke the silence with, "Good day."

The Haisla woman chopped her hand across the air horizontally. "No Speak Boston."

A half dozen men, women, and children remained scattered throughout the longhouse. Nobody offered any verbal remedy against the awkward silence. Rebecca tried to think of something to say, but words failed her. Embarrassed, she turned and fled, thinking that the experience echoed the reception she had just received at the general store.

The next two encounters went much the way of the first. At each lodge she attempted to explain her problem—she needed a guide. She needed a tracker. She needed help, plain and simple. Rebecca thought they might as well have said, "You're a White woman. Not welcome here."

And why was that any surprise? After all, the Natives were not welcomed into the homes of the Whites, into their businesses or schools. Was this all so strange? These were their homes. This was Indian property, *their* property. There was so little left, and they clung fastidiously to what remained.

Rebecca was ready to quit, struck by the absurdity of her mission.

She hesitated before the entrance of one last house. It had a wooden door, but like the others, it seemed stamped by poverty. She nearly turned away, but then she pounded on the wooden frame. A minute passed. She counted the seconds on her cold breath as wisps of vapor clouded the air. Just before she turned and walked away, the door opened several inches. A pair of dark, penetrating eyes peered out from the dim space within. Rebecca said hello as evenly as she knew how.

A voice within repeated the salutation. The words hung in the wind like identical twins.

"You speak English."

"Little, yes," returned a man, calmly.

He had a strong, intelligent face. As he opened the door wider, Rebecca calculated that he must be about thirty years of age, of medium build, strong muscled, and nearly Dan's height, six feet plus. *Tall for an Indian*, she thought.

The Native had an open expression on his face. His gaze remained kindly. Behind him—around a stone fireplace pit—sat his wife and his children: two beautiful girls and a smaller boy. An older couple, his parents or in-laws, squatted near the three children.

The entire family appeared puzzled by the sudden appearance of the White woman. Although their eyes stared warily at Rebecca, their curiosity was invasive.

"Come in," he said a bit reluctantly, swinging the door open for her to enter.

As Rebecca stepped through, the young man closed the door behind her. That motion corralled what little heat remained in the lodge. Rebecca felt vulnerable, as if the closed door cut off her retreat.

Like the Natives in the last several longhouses, the young man waited for her to speak. Rebecca realized suddenly that the tardy reply was probably Native protocol. *Good manners*, she thought, feeling slightly abashed.

"I need a guide to take me upriver," she blurted out.

"Excuse me. I'm not sure what . . ." He paused, his bronze face illuminated in the soft firelight, his thick brows crinkling into furrows that highlighted a high, flat forehead.

"Guide. Track. Find my husband." She pointed a finger to her chest as if to display her need.

He replied succinctly. "I am not . . . guide."

"Can you help me find a guide? A tracker. I need an Indian who . . ."

He didn't like the word "Indian," and his face hardened. Rebecca read that look, alright. She scrambled to recover lost ground. *Rebecca,* she screamed to herself. *Use your head.*

"I am Haisla."

"I'm sorry. I didn't mean—"

"Okay," he said, his face softening slightly.

Rebecca was feeling frantic. She lifted her arms in a beseeching way. "Please help me find my husband!"

"My name is Richard Washington. Spirit Runner. You are?"

"Rebecca Skinner."

"You live?"

"Five miles—last farm—out of Kilnook. On the river. Cedar house with split-rail fence. Elk antlers over the gate. Look, I can pay . . ."

The last words were besmirched by the dense air inside the lodge and the large empty space. She grappled with her words, unsure of her next move. But it was the Native who broke the silence. "Your husband is Dan Skinner? I know Dan Skinner. Your husband is in trouble? Have I not heard something?"

"Yes, he is."

Rude or not, Rebecca turned her gaze directly into his. "I need help to find him. He is a good man. I promise you."

The Native studied her intently, translating the worry lines that etched her face.

"Yes," he said. "I met him before. Trapping the Skeena. He shared fire, food. The weather very cold. We told stories around campfire."

"You did? You know Dan?"

For the first time in days, her face brightened. But the expression didn't last long, and soon twisted into long worry lines. "Please! Will you help me? I . . . I don't know what else to do." Her eyes anticipated tears but held back. She knew that she had to be strong.

The man fell quiet again. He considered her request in earnest. Time crept by. Rebecca felt the passage as never before. She was reminded of the same deep fissures that time exaggerates when all a person can do is worry. But she would have sworn there was a caring look in his eyes. That surprised her. She managed to project a glimmer of hope. Then his next words startled her. "Tell me the story," he said. "Tell me all."

And Rebecca did. Then she waited, her heart beating rapidly.

After a long consideration, he finally spoke. "Okay, I come. I come later. I bring guide. Very cold now. Come later, this spring. Listen, the guide, he need money. Sorry. You say you can pay?"

"Yes. Will you come soon, please. Please!"

"Yes, okay. In thirty days. Maybe before."

She felt stymied by their cultural differences. Rebecca turned quickly to leave, avoiding his eyes. He stood in the doorway, a beacon of hope. She turned once and waved. He studied her intently but didn't repeat the gesture.

As Rebecca mounted the mare, she chanced one final glance at the ancient village. Still standing at the entrance of his plank house was the Indian. Haisla, she reminded herself. "Haisla!" The man was called Richard Washington. His eyes followed her every move. Awkwardly, she waved once again, but only a lift of his brows acknowledged her departure.

She gently kicked the mare, turning toward her farm, hers and Dan's. That thought caught her. She turned his name over in her mouth, letting it slip through her lips like water spilling. The horse needed no prodding now. In a strong canter, the mare moved swiftly back through town, back upriver. The streets were deserted and deep with snow. The wind unleashed itself in torrents. Rebecca passed up the street unobserved. That was just fine with her. She had had enough of Kilnook and its fair citizens for one day.

Soon, she was riding upriver. As the familiar landmarks drew her closer to home, she felt a sense of relief along with a bout of emotional exhaustion. Loneliness and desperation began to tighten around her like a snare. She shuddered at the thought of another night alone. Inevitably, Rebecca began to cross-examine her recent decision, her agreement with . . . *Yes,*

Richard Washington. Spirit, what? What was that last name? Runner. Spirit Runner. That's it! Well, what other choice do I have?

Snow flurries stung her face. She readjusted the muffler tightly about her neck and chin, aware that any new tears would freeze in place.

As darkness settled in, Rebecca found herself in the barn with the mare, watering and feeding the horse and rubbing down its thick fur. She set out the oats and threw down an armful of dried straw. As she wiped down the animal's lathered hide, the horse turned its large head and nuzzled its cold, soft nose into Rebecca's chest. Rebecca was appreciative of any affection, human or animal. Her mare's large brown eyes mitigated her pain. Did the animal understand the depth of her destitution? It had been Dan's horse. She rubbed her hands across the long strong bridge on the mare's face. Patted its forehead. "Thanks, Liz," she whispered. "You're the best."

Rebecca finished her barnyard chores and then headed for the cabin. She revived the fire and lit the kerosene lamps. She laid out the groceries, not a lot to show for a half-day's ride.

Though she hadn't eaten since breakfast, she had little appetite, but Rebecca knew she had to eat something. She had to keep her strength up. She also knew that it was best to stay busy. *Bacon and beans,* she thought. *That will give me something to do.*

Rebecca turned to her chores but was startled moments later to hear the whinny of another horse and overjoyed when the deep baritone voice of Sally Walton announced her entrance like a bugle call in the night.

1968

The year became a turning point. The convention in Chicago and later the killings at Kent State sent the country into a tailspin. The war expanded. The deaths in Vietnam mounted up. There was no easy solution. No end to the long conflict.

Paul and Katherine remained committed to the cause of peace, but the country became increasingly fractured.

On a dreamy evening in Seattle, they celebrated the anniversary of their first real date. They ate a fine dinner at a restaurant called *Place Pigalle.* From an open window high above Elliot Bay, they watched the ferries come and go. They pushed their chairs together, held hands, and kissed. It didn't matter who watched. They were deeply in love. Katherine had never looked so pretty. She wore a summer dress that revealed her shapely body. Her smile remained as committed as the clear azure sky over the city, an uncommon apparition. By then Katherine was considered a master student. Her GPA was a straight 4.0. She was on speaking terms with the college president.

Paul had become the go-to-guy for activism. His speaking skills excelled. As the power of protest swept the country, he was in demand.

With the sun setting over Elliot Bay, they talked of love and commitment. The ferries crossed the silky evening water. They skirted talk about marriage. "Not yet," Paul said. "The war will grind down. Let me get my diploma. Settle into a job. Let's get through this year. Plenty of time, and nothing is going to tarnish our love."

They toasted with a glass of Northwest wine, a cabernet from eastern Washington. Gulls circled the harbor, squawking their protests and begging for leftovers. A sea lion crooned out its message. Like a trumpet call, the mammal's bark reverberated into the soft twilight. Dusk fell, and the city lights stretched far and wide. The couple walked up the steep streets that wove through "Rain City," as content as lovers can be.

CHAPTER TWELVE

The earth is the mother of all people, and all people should have equal rights upon it.

—Hin-mah-too-yah-lat-kekt
Chief Joseph

The forest smelled of spring. Buds were sprouting from the alder trees. The wet, decaying odors of winter had been replaced by spring's sweet aromas, by new birth. The land was drying out. Hope burnished the forest and the souls of the humans who traveled through.

Up behind the village, Black Wing nestled beside a small campfire. A swift mountain stream rushed by, tumbling as it raced downhill. The chilly water was dappled with sunlight.

The sky was steely-blue, unusual for the time of year. Black Wing had just risen from the river. There, he had repeatedly plunged his body into the icy waters, only to rise and sing. His music was a joyous recital. Shuffling onto the gravel streambed while shaking off the river water like a wet duck, he rubbed his body vigorously with the flat evergreen boughs of a hemlock tree. He scrubbed until his body stung. He then covered himself with a cedar cape and leggings and slipped a conical cedar hat back onto his head. A warm fire awaited.

Nurtured by meditation and prayer, the elder sat cross-legged before the small fire. Around him, camouflaged by the evergreen canopy, many of the forest animals were awakening. Nightfall was their grazing time. They didn't have long to wait.

The fire soothed the cold water's stinging bite. Joyously, the elder's voice rang out. The song was as ancient as the stones that lay about him. The first star had already risen above the horizon. More began to rise in the east. Black Wing said a prayer to the departed. The old man suspected that he would be joining them soon. He reminded himself: *Not even the rocks live forever*.

Black Wing's voice rose higher and higher until it appeared to fill the great void itself. Then his voice fell mute.

A circle of round river stones lay before him. Inside the ring, a fire burned down into hot, glowing coals. Night followed then, as did the tiny dancing lights from the embers, each one a beacon. A prayer.

Black Wing stirred and thrust a fan of eagle feathers back and forth across the flame, spreading the heat and the smoke across his chest and face. He threw a pinch of Indian tobacco, *Kinnikinnick*, onto the pyre. Pungent scent possessed the space where he sat, cross-legged and still. He loved the smell of burning sweetgrass and tobacco. Part of him—the spirit walker—followed the smoke. Before him, firelight danced and shimmied. Black Wing heard the tiny sounds tumbling toward him from the depths of the fire. He waved the fan across the coals one more time. A cacophony of ancient voices touched him anew like a birthing.

He continued his song in a high, ethereal voice. The words whisked through the twilight, mixing with the smoke, lifting higher and higher until they disappeared into the miasma humans call space.

He sat as still as the round river stones. The elder was in the clutch of a vision quest. He followed the smoke as it flooded over his beloved valley. Black Wing had a mission. That evening he was seeking answers about two men: one, a Boston man; the other, Tsimshian. His mind was flying now, whisking through the night air as weightless as a wraith, or as an eagle.

He found the two men entrapped in the house of smoke where the salmon were cured.

The situation caused the elder to chuckle but only briefly. Suddenly, his thoughts turned deeply serious. The space inside the stockade remained hateful. Rancor greeted the two men as surely as a steel trap grasps the forefoot of an animal. Black Wing knew that hate was a killer. In his many years, he had witnessed such hostility frequently. He called that spiteful space, "The House of Many Fears."

And now he flew high above the village.

His blind piercing eyes penetrated the space where a village lay, docile in the evening twilight. From high, Black Wing saw smoke rising from the lodges. He watched the Natives' movements, their reunions, their joyous spontaneity and intimate romances, their trials and tribulations, and the ever-present fear of discovery.

The elder knew these people. He had lived among them and their ancestors for years untold. This tribe was not the first in his memory. Over many moons he had watched others, a steady confluence of Native peoples lost to the memory of the living: Tsimshian, Haisla, and Kwakiutl. Ancestral bands. The Tlingit and Haida. Stories relegated to legend—Black Wing remembered them well. Part of their continuing chapters had frequently erupted into suffering. Internal strife had broken more than one civilization. Wars had scattered remnants of greatness like shards from cloven arrowheads, each broken, discarded, or lost.

"Rebecca," Sally proclaimed, plowing unceremoniously through the front door. Outside, the chilly blue air danced and parried. "Honey, I just couldn't leave you alone tonight. Just couldn't do it. God, it's frozen in here. Don't you have a fire going? Listen, girl, I brought some eggs and bacon. Flour for griddle cakes. We're going to have a party. Mm-hmm."

"Whoa. Slow down, Sally. I just got in myself. Why don't you take Jessie to the barn? I'll feed the fire. Make some coffee."

They both turned in opposite directions, each leaning toward different chores. Sally's hand was on the doorknob when Rebecca turned, her voice finding her friend. "Thanks, Sally. This means a lot to me. You coming."

Sally stared at her friend, winked, then headed for the barn. "Get that coffee going, sweetie. And a fire. I'm freezing."

The split cedar crackled and spit as the wood ignited. Rebecca loved the rich wood smell. An incense, the smell swept across the room and lifted her spirits. Soon the coffee was percolating in the blue-and-white enameled pot, and the aroma was every bit as rich as the cedar smoke. The two smells made her happy. She was more than ready for that.

Rebecca heard her friend coming across the meadow from the stable, her feet crunching the frozen snow. Sally was singing in a clear soprano voice. Rebecca considered how much she loved the woman.

They feasted on the bacon and griddle cakes. Rebecca threw fresh chicken eggs into a cast-iron skillet. Bacon grease sizzled around the whites, singeing the edges, each yolk brighter than the pale winter sun. She toasted some of her homemade bread over the wood stove. Spread the tops with butter and homemade blackberry jam. The women sweetened their coffee with raw brown sugar. Poured in cream from Helen the cow, the same liquid that was transformed into butter. This was a feast worthy of Thanksgiving. Then Rebecca remembered what was missing. Her face drew up tautly in the corners.

"Thinking of him again, huh?"

"Sorry."

"It's okay, honey. How can you help it?"

"Sally?"

"Yes, dear?"

"Thanks for coming."

"Wouldn't have it any other way."

"Sally," Rebecca said, hesitancy in her voice. "I don't want to hurt your business."

"Shhh. Don't worry about those things. I'm a big girl."

"But Sally . . ."

"Rebecca, to hell with those people. Dan Skinner is as fine a man as I've ever known. He was just helping his brother. Why, I wouldn't have done no different."

Rebecca pulled her close and gave her a hug. "I don't deserve you."

"You got no choice, honey."

Between hugs, they giggled, and the sounds soothed Rebecca.

After dinner, the women cleaned the dishes, and then sat together at the round oak table. Rebecca retrieved a neglected bottle of rye from Dan's meager cache. The women poured double shots of the whiskey. Soon they were both giddy. A kerosene lamp hung over the table and threw soft shadows across the room.

"You stay tonight?"

"Sure thing. Mm-hmm. Got to head back to town early though. You know, breakfast at the café. Those old duffers would hang me if I was five minutes late."

"You mind sharing the bed? It's that or a blanket on the floor. Actually, you can have the bed."

"Wouldn't think of it. Can you handle a fat girl? We can share."

"Sally, you're not fat."

"No, just big."

"Sally, don't talk that way."

The two cuddled up under a pile of wool blankets. They talked a little longer, but exhaustion hit Rebecca hard. She didn't quite get around to telling Sally about the visit with the Native—with Richard Washington. She was afraid to spill her story. No yet, she thought. She had to hold on to her secret for a while. Besides, she justified to herself, the whole thing was a long shot.

I probably won't see that nice Native man again. Reluctantly, she chewed over the conversation. W*hat else can I do? Where else can I go for help? No*, she reasoned, *he will come. He must come. He must!* Her apprehensions would not let her be.

The last thing Rebecca felt before she fell asleep were Sally's large, strong arms wrapping around her from behind, just the way Dan did. She leaned into the woman. Bent her knees and tucked close like a baby curling inside a warm womb. Outside, scattered snow flurries scudded like the flight of a million butterflies, blanketing the landscape without as much as a murmur.

Rebecca slept more soundly than on any night since she had watched Dan and André disappear up the river trail. That had been nearly two weeks before.

Dreams followed, but by the next morning they had vanished as surely as the dun-colored earth that lay fallow under mounds of snow. The morning began as silently as the flight of an eagle.

Sally slept later than she intended. Without waking Rebecca, she slipped from the security of the warm blankets and into the brisk air of the unheated cabin. The wood fire had burned out hours before, leaving the two-room cabin with a lace of cold that cut to the bone. Sally dressed quickly and relit the fire. Rebecca slept like a woman cast in a spell.

"Thank God," Sally intoned, speaking in a low, hushed voice while she affectionately studied the sleeping silhouette of her friend.

Then she slipped out the front door. The silky pearl hues of pre-dawn greeted her.

Spring is coming, Sally thought as she secured the saddle onto the back of her roan. Even before hard light illuminated the landscape, a Steller's jay barked out a "shack-shack-shack" into the brisk morning air, scolding the world at large. Then a raven: "kla wok, kla wok," as adamant as an evangelical preacher.

She rode her big roan up the river trail heading west into Kilnook. The trail broke through the forest into an occasional clearings as the path bent, running parallel to the river, and then away. At times, the passage dropped down off high clay ramparts and traversed across gravel spits that were nothing more than the gathering place for the smooth river stones. Then the trail would amble away from the water, and she would ride back into the forest.

She loved the way first light unraveled with unencumbered rays of sunshine, a meld of peach and canary and a hundred hues, an undefinable blend of colors breaking through the forest on that rare, clear morning. As she rode on, her thoughts kept returning to her friend. The air projected a clean, fresh feeling. That soothing quality refreshed Sally and wrapped about her with a special brand of contentment.

Sally loved the force of the water, the sound it made as it raced closer and closer on its drive to the ocean. She loved this time of day, the crossover between night and dawn. She closed her eyes and let the cacophony of sounds come to her: the birds, the river, the forest, and its many creatures. The small rustle the wind played out, as if just awakened. A downy woodpecker struck with fervor at a decaying alder tree that stood forlornly amid a sea of evergreens. The chiseled sound pleased her.

Again, the piercing chatter of a Steller's jay rattled off the cold river stones. Sally turned her mind back to her best friend.

She sang a song then, in a high-spirited voice, and the music blended with the forest sounds as naturally as breathing. Sally was a happy woman. Long ago she had settled into the fact that she liked who she was. She would remain content until the right man happened along—if he happened along. She would insist on a man who would not disrupt her spirit, a gentleman who would complement her personality. Sally would not sell herself short for anyone or anything.

Riding along the river trail, she thought some more about Rebecca and realized what a special place the woman held in her life. She treasured that rich feeling of companionship. For a moment she pondered the word "love." She thought she understood the word and its many faces. She laughed then. Wasn't all this—this exquisite morning, her friendship—just right without having to define or defend it? On such a morning, it was enough to be lost in awe; lost to mother nature and her ever changing alure.

The roan's hooves scattered metallic sounds, the ricochet of its horseshoes tripping off the round granite stones. The echo wove through the spruce and cedar trees that lined the riverbed. The sound was muffled by the thickness of the fat evergreens. Sally urged her horse into a trot. Two miles ahead she spotted a clear-cut. Ahead of that was the village of Kilnook.

On that winter morning, 1896, Sally felt better than she had in years. But as she entered town, her euphoria was shattered as abruptly as the windows in her café. She started to cry. Caught herself. Quickly, she firmed up. She would not allow any man to catch her crying.

It was obvious to Sally that the violence was no accident. Certainly, the windows had been shattered by her neighbors. It didn't much matter when or by whom. As she surveyed the destruction, nausea overwhelmed her best intentions, and a deep loathing subverted her natural goodwill.

She tied the roan to the hitching post and entered the café through the locked front door. The door's window was smashed like the other two on either side of the entrance. Once inside she saw that the broken glass was the largest extent of the damage. That did not account for her emotions.

Again, she felt a welling of tears. She bit her lip and went for the broom. *I won't break,* she thought. *I don't work that way.* Instead, she took her temper next door to the mercantile.

It was early yet, but Isaac Stamp was sweeping the floor of the store. After Sally hammered on the hard oak door, Isaac unlocked it. It swung inward with a clatter. The sound of Sally's fists boomeranged down the street like the bleating sound of a wounded lamb.

He's up mighty early, Sally reasoned. *Likely, Isaac is waiting for me.*

The merchant stepped back from behind the front counter, feigning surprise.

"God damn it, Isaac, what's all this about?" Sally spoke in the firmest voice she could muster, but it was cracking on the edges. Right then, Sally was not so sure of herself, but she realized that a show of strength might fool Isaac Stamp. On the surface, Isaac appeared to be a timid man.

The merchant stood there like a trapped animal. He was a tall, gangly man, mild-mannered and balding. His face was bare of facial hair. Wire-rimmed glasses wrapped around his face. Sally always thought of Ichabod Crane.

Isaac leaned toward Sally with two eyes that appeared small and shallowly set. His face was thin and elongated. He cowered before her angry words, but like many of the lesser-endowed creatures from the animal kingdom, he fostered far more courage than what might meet the eye.

"I don't rightly know what you mean, Sally."

"Come on, Isaac. You saw the front of my place. Don't play innocent with me."

Isaac lived above his store, but said he hadn't heard a thing, at least not during the previous night. His eyes met hers then, a dark chocolate-brown like a cowbird. Around town there were few who dared sidle up to Sally's brand of determination. Few who would face her down. But Isaac Stamp housed his private brand of courage.

Isaac hadn't missed the vandalism. He knew what was going on, but he wasn't about to let Sally bulldog him into a confession. He would tell the story in his own time.

Isaac fiddled with his cash register. He opened and closed the sliding drawer twice before coming around to the front of the counter where Sally waited, her eyes set like a wolf on easy prey. Then Isaac walked to the front door and pulled down the shade. He turned cautiously toward her.

"Listen, Sally. After dark, two Indians come from upriver with some bad news. They found canoes, then the bodies of four men. The dead were too broken up to easily identify. Animals had picked 'em apart. From the scraps, the bodies appeared to be those of William Casey and his two deputies. From their clothes—what was left—well, you get the picture. Apparently, they had been climbing. Don't ask me about that.

"The other body most likely was the younger Skinner boy. All fell a heck of a long way. God knows what they were doing on such a cliff. Only one man was shot up, the boy apparently. The others had more bruises than a man can count. And a cartload of broken bones, to boot. The Haisla buried 'em along the water's edge. Brought back some of their possessions and two good canoes. William Casey's badge was there. Apparently, the critters don't enjoy a diet of pot metal. Town got pretty riled up last night, Sally. Riled up plenty, alrighty."

"Dan Skinner?"

"They didn't think he was among them. Neither was the breed, Tom LaCross. Not unless the animals carried 'em away. Not likely though.

"Sally, you shouldn't be hanging around with that woman. Might darn well affect your business."

"That is my choice, Isaac. And Rebecca didn't have anything to do with any of this, anyhow."

"You know people around here, Sally."

"Afraid I do. Mm-hmm. Too well at that."

"None of my business, mind you, but if I were you, I'd lay low for a few days. Listen, I'll see that Jim Long boards up those windows. Replaces the glass when we get a mild day. Jim's always thirsty. I'll buy him a bottle. Sally, I'm awfully sorry. I like Rebecca. Appreciate it if you give her my regards. Word to the wise though: keep her out of town for a few days. Okay?"

Sally knew a kind offer when she heard one. She always warmed up to Isaac. She leaned into him and gave him a hug and then a peck on the cheek.

The storekeeper took it all in, tall and steady.

"Isaac, I need another favor. A big one. Can I borrow your buggy? I'll get it back to you tonight. Leave it in the back of the store. I'll make sure nobody sees me going."

"It's out back already. Put some provisions in her. Hook up your roan but keep this to yourself. Don't worry none about paying me back. Heck, you been my best customer for years."

"I love you, Isaac," Sally blurted out.

Isaac leveled his eyes on his friend, never blinking, and offered a final salutation. "You be careful now. You be mighty careful."

Sally harnessed the horse and then emptied a cache of supplies from the café into the buckboard. She was out of town in half an hour, riding hard for the Skinner farm. The sun was cresting above the mountain peaks as the buckboard shimmied up the river trail. She saw a lone eagle circling high in the sky and stopped the buggy. Shading her eyes with her right hand, she gazed heavenward.

"It's a good sign, Jessie," she said, addressing the horse, or perhaps anyone in range of her baritone voice. "Did you ever see an eagle that big? My. My, oh my!"

Autumn 1967

Katherine's lover was drafted into the army in the autumn of 1967. Like so many of his fellow protestors, Paul refused to leave his country. He would not choose a life in Canada. He had promised his parents that he would not go to jail as an act of defiance, that he wouldn't endanger his future with a felony conviction. After Paul was inducted, he stayed committed to his promise.

"Listen," he reasoned with her, "I'll become a medic. I'll help the wounded. I'll take care and be home soon. The hard part will be missing you!"

That soothed her feelings, but it did little for the pain that spoke of an extended separation. Nor did it really address the danger.

Nothing could damage their love.

Paul did three months of basic training in Georgia. He applied for and was lucky enough to receive an assignment in the Medical Corps. As always, he was an inspiration to those around him. He worked hard. He was intelligent. And he continued to be vehemently opposed to the war. By then the tide had just begun to turn on U.S. involvement in Vietnam. Many of the recruits objected to the engagement. Quietly—efficiently—Paul organized the opposition. But few of his protests went unnoticed by his superiors. Paul faced a load of abuse.

He was threatened with a court martial and spent a week in jail on a trumped-up charge. He preached to the inmates. One of the guards hit him, a hard sucker punch to the belly, and followed by a second round. Still, Paul refused to equivocate. The war was a terrible mistake. He knew that in his mind and heart.

After boot camp, Paul was one of the first of the new recruits to be shipped overseas.

Before leaving the States, Paul called Katherine twice a week. She hung onto his voice—his message of abiding love—as if each of his words had been carved on a stone tablet. She was so lonely. Paul felt much the same. He kept telling her that it would be alright. That he would come home soon.

He never told her that the Viet Cong shot corpsmen, that the enemy had learned what effect the loss of a medic had on the morale of the fighting infantrymen.

Within weeks Paul was sent north toward the DMZ. Katherine moved into an apartment with a friend and waited. At first, Paul sent word regularly. But the messages became less frequent and more troubled. Like most foot soldiers, Paul never could have predicted the hopelessness and fear of combat. He soon carried a rifle, hiding the fact that he was a corpsman. Medics were a specific target of the Viet Cong. It was one more way of demoralizing the American troops. There was a long list of others.

Letters became infrequent. Katherine guessed that Paul was troubled. There was no avoiding the inevitable consequences of combat. Well, she figured, somehow, they would ride it out.

Three months into his tour of duty, the messages stopped altogether.

Early in the winter of 1968, a letter came from Paul's mother. Paul had been killed while evacuating the wounded outside of Quang Tri.

The region's name meant little to Katherine—another outpost lost in the glossary of American combat. Here was one more killing field. Here was one of many misjustices leveled upon young men by politicians and a warring society.

Katherine was inconsolable.

She moved back in with her mother and dropped out of school. Pain continued to harangue her every move.

"Give it time, honey," her mother would say, over and over.

But time was torture. Katherine knew she would never forget Paul. Her mother and friends prayed that Katherine would adapt quickly to the loss, but they didn't really expect that to happen. Everyone knew that the healing would take a mountain of time. The couple had been so tight.

Two months later, Katherine joined the Peace Corps. As an adjunct to her newly found commitment, she began to write a diary. She also added her mother's maiden name to her father's.

She continued to mourn her lover. She always would.

CHAPTER THIRTEEN

I see no reason why mankind should have waited until recent times to produce minds of the caliber of a Plato or an Einstein. Already over two or three hundred thousand years ago, there were probably men of similar capacity, who were, of course, not applying their intelligence to the solution of the same problems as these more recent thinkers.

—Claude Levi-Strauss

Three interminable days passed in a house of smoke. The stench of hatred wafted above the thick, oily smell of smoked fish.

Dan had forgiven nothing. His brother was dead. Rebecca was unreachable, likely gone forever. If anything, Dan's wrath had intensified. That took fierce determination.

On the other hand, it was hard for Tom to hold a grudge against his prize student. In the Tsimshian culture, elders were essential teachers, and fathers supported their children from a calculated distance.

Smallpox had robbed Tom of that sacred privilege. Dan had stumbled into his world, and Tom had filled a void. How could Dan forget all that? How could Tom? Confusion tore at them both.

The way Tom reasoned, he had just been doing his job. Well, that was his justification, anyway. But deep in his heart, he knew better. As the weeks wore on—as the fugitive eluded the pursuer—tensions intensified. Justifications stirred. He had forgotten more than most of the villagers remembered about his relationship with Dan. He kept dropping back to the incident in the jail, his mind rallying around the fact that Dan had stood silently by as the two Mounties harassed him. Tom had felt abandoned.

And then Tom would let it all go. Let his anger untangle.

Often Tom felt flummoxed. The wily student had impressed the scout. As the boy grew into a man—seemingly overnight—he developed and employed an impressive set of skills. Perhaps Tom had loved the boy once. And now? Answers clung to him like tattered clothing.

With his wounds bandaged and splinted, Tom just wanted to heal and to be left alone in his private world. He was sick and full of pain from the deep wounds. He didn't have the extra energy to dispense on an angry man, least of all this one, who, until recently, had remained more than his friend.

Dan and Tom were pinioned firmly inside the smokehouse. Two guards kept close watch on both men. The same shy Haisla girl who had cared for Dan in the big lodge, brought food twice daily. He had come to look forward to her visits. She did far more for him than just break the monotony. She soothed his suffering, and her kindness softened some of the anger that twisted his body and soul.

Each afternoon after his meal, the guards escorted Dan around the village. With the guards hovering nearby, he wandered for an hour or more. He had never been imprisoned before. The confinement tormented him. After the guards loosened his bonds, he would rub the welts around his wrists and imagine his escape. He imagined his strong legs breaking trail. He tasted his freedom.

Dan schemed constantly, thinking about how he might overpower the guards. But his captors were armed with bows and arrows, and their body language indicated alertness. These were big, quick, strong men. Dan understood the reality of reprisal and remained cautious, his instincts alert. Black Wing had warned him a number of times. Dan would have to remain patient.

On his escorted walks, Dan memorized the village setting and the lay of the land. He discovered trailheads. Imagined a path unraveling as he fled.

He formed educated guesses as to the general direction and termination of those trails. From the sun, Dan estimated the compass points. He paid attention to the hunters: the direction of their departure, the length of time they were away, how and when they returned. He committed to memory the mountain peaks, the narrow, craggy passes where a man might squeeze through and avoid the high mountain snow. Avoid the imposing cold and suffering.

All this would be vital when he attempted his escape, and Dan was clear on that one intention. He remained confident. By moving at night and hiding during the day, he would sneak back to Rebecca. He figured he would need just enough time to secretly meet with her and secure a rendezvous. They would start life over then. Find a safe place far away from Kilnook. Maybe they might rendezvous in Seattle or move east into the Rocky Mountains. Or south into California. He thought about San Francisco. A city of that size would swallow them both up.

Like a spider laying a web, his plan expanded day after day. In the mountains a man learned to bide his time. He would wait. Dan had learned patience from the man lying wounded on the earthen floor just a few feet away. The man whose body lay crumpled up on a dirt floor, his breathing still fractured, his wounds still seeping. In the end, Dan was wracked by contradicting emotions, the sharpest of those was guilt.

Dan was clear on one front. He would find the way back to Rebecca. Dan had a plan. He would have to avoid the traditional routes. He would find his way if only he avoided two dangers. One, a band of warriors from a handful of disparate tribes. The second, a posse of lawmen. And he intended to avoid any more cliffs. Dan had seen enough of those.

It struck him then. What would he do if Rebecca wasn't at the farm? What if she had fled? Everything depended on a certain degree of mountain luck. Thinking him dead, Dan conjectured that Rebecca might leave the area. He knew the locals would put big pressure on her. They would isolate her. *Damn it*, he thought. *They will punish her for my sins*. The thought angered him, fitfully peppering his thoughts during the long nights. He prayed it was not so. Prayed she would wait for him. But the thought of losing her clouded his waking hours. He did not have much else to do but think and plan. Time metamorphosed into slow torture.

On a cloudless winter afternoon, Black Wing and Charlie approached Dan. The two guards were escorting him around the village. It was the first clear day of the new moon. High in the mountains, the temperature remained cold, even in the direct sun—even now, during a late winter midday. But the air was exhilarating. It was a perfect bluebird day.

All three squatted on the bare earth, still chilly from the hoarfrost that penetrated deep into the soil. A small fire blazed between them. While the guards wandered, the three men sat in a circle with their legs crossed. Dan had spent years in the wilderness squatting around campfires and preferred the position.

When Black Wing offered a handsome carved pipe to the trapper, Dan had enough mountain savvy to graciously accept the tobacco offering. Black Wing had borrowed the custom from somewhere. Maybe from the trappers, or perhaps the custom was Native, a way of showing gratitude. Either way, Dan saw that Black Wing enjoyed his tobacco.

Dan wasn't much of a smoker, but he knew better than to turn down a kind offer.

The pipe was passed slowly from man to man. Each inhaled deeply and then released the smoke into the pure mountain air. It circled above the men like a talisman of goodwill. The deep, rich smell reminded Dan of his father who smoked a pipe.

Charlie broke the silence first. Speaking in his best English, his voice cascaded so softly that the words dodged wistfully through the mountain air with all the stealth of the furry marten. The message shocked Dan.

"Grandfather had a dream about you and grandfather bear. Big fight, he say. He say you got plenty courage. That you have strong medicine."

Again, the pipe was passed around the circle. Silence floated in the same space where the smoke had hung only seconds before. Inside, Dan was shaken. He could decipher many things from a faded set of tracks, from a variety of clues that nature exposed, but he couldn't read minds or foretell the future. In his lifetime he had never met anyone like this elder. Dan was not the kind of man who put much stock in magic. To be sure, he hadn't given the topic a lot of thought. But something strange was going on inside the shaman's head—or in his—and Dan couldn't put his finger on it. Nor was he able to decipher what was attracting him toward the old man.

Was this a gift? Most likely. Dan was rattled, but he listened intently, and now—several weeks into his captivity—with unreserved respect.

"Grandfather say you are meant to find this bear. That was your test. The bear honored you."

"That bear nearly killed me!"

"Yes. Nearly."

"Gol dang, how could he know?"

Black Wing was staring intently at Dan. His blind eyes penetrated right through the trapper. Dan felt naked and exposed. He turned his head away from the blind man and spoke to Charlie.

"Black Wing is a medicine man?"

"Yes."

"He is different from others, from you and me?"

Charlie was a little perplexed by that question. Pondering it for many seconds, he answered haltingly. "Grandfather is more than . . . than normal man. He has belonged to many tribes and adopted many teachings. You right. He is much more. Black Wing has traveled far. Many lives, perhaps. Some of our people believe that a man comes back many times from the land of the dead.

"But he is also one with us, our clan. I am Haisla. He, Haida and Haisla and Tsimshian. He says we all have this . . . this gift. Only a few learn to use it correctly. Few can see or feel it, though it sleeps deep inside all of us. Often, Grandfather, he say that this gift is abused or maybe, just not realized."

"What do you mean when you say that Black Wing is more?"

"Grandfather speaks many tongues. He has lived long. Many tribes have honored him."

"How can that be? Has he traveled the coast? And who honors him now?"

"No more. Most tribes gone, scattered like, uh . . . leaves . . . leaves floating on fast winter river. Or grass seeds blown far on summer winds."

"Didn't know you were a poet, Charlie."

"Excuse me?"

"Nothing. Nothing. Listen! Help me out. I—"

"Wait. Please hold your tongue. You talk so much. Today, Grandfather asks me to bring you message. He say White Bear, the Tsimshian, he not the enemy you think. He say you destroy yourself with hate. You good man, Grandfather say. But hate burns you. He say, 'Stop. Stop now, while you can.'"

Dan's first reaction was anger, but he quickly sought a retort. "Has your grandfather no enemies?"

Dan stole a glance at Black Wing. On the elder's face was a half-smile. Dan felt an intimate connection, like an eclipse, not of the sun and moon but something passing undefinably between humans. The old man's eyes were blind. Dan's were farseeing. Yet here, Dan keen eyes begged to see.

Dan sensed much of this intuitively. Sensed that the elder was exploring his soul. With a jolt, he realized that Black Wing was at peace with himself, at peace with the earth. "Mother Earth." Hadn't Black Wing called it that? Here was a brand of contentment—a stability—that Dan had seldom realized. Well, more than that. He had trouble even visualizing the concept. Such gifts rarely visited his neighborhood. The realization shook him, and Dan shifted his gaze away from the elder.

At that very moment, Dan realized that since his brother's death, he had gone as blind as the old man. Maybe—just maybe—this strange elder had a gift that extended beyond the range of Dan's reasoning, beyond his pioneer experiences. Maybe—and the realization shook him—Dan had something to learn. At that very moment, some of the hatred inside his mind receded. He felt something like a redistribution of weight or a cleansing. *Holy Mother*, he thought. *I'll be go to hell.* Dan had no doubt: the old man was gifted.

Diverting Black Wing's blind eyes, Dan shrugged. Even as he avoided the elder's gaze, he felt the elder's eyes penetrating his. Dan contemplated the range of the elder's divining powers.

The next words from Charlie—his final words of the day—turned Dan's world inside out, all over again. The old man leaned toward his nephew and spoke in Haisla. Charlie turned to Dan and translated. "Grandfather says you should ask the Tsimshian why he not let the lawman shoot you when you hang from the top of that cliff. Shoot you when the sheriff had his chance. Grandfather say the lawman was fine marksman. He might have killed you. Ask the Tsimshian. He know answer."

Tom lay straddled on his side on a dirt floor inside the empty smokehouse. His body remained crippled by pain, but the constant ache was subsiding. Indeed, he no longer felt hamstrung by his injuries. *Things looking up*, he reasoned. His captors and the strange circumstance of his internment confused him. They were treating him kindly, more than he might have expected. Even Dan's temper had moderated. Silently, Tom praised this reversal of fortune.

He realized that his attempt to ambush Dan had been foolish. He must have thought that all along but had lost his focus. A man's pride got in the way sometimes. Pride goaded him into Dan's trap. Tom smiled inwardly at himself, a reaction born of pain. *Foolish, alright. But under such conditions . . .* Even a condemned man was allowed an occasional miscue. Even White Bear.

He knew he shouldn't have let Dan run. He should have encouraged the sheriff to get off another long shot. He felt the brunt of his misjudgment keenly. Tom was not the kind of man who beat up on himself, particularly over past mistakes. On the other hand, he had never made one so costly. After all, the decision had nearly cost him his life. And he wasn't exactly in the clear yet. There was still more forest than blue sky. At that very moment, he was sorting out his options, and they weren't particularly attractive. He rolled onto his side. New pain broke up and down his chest and leg and scampered into his buttocks. Wounds that had cauterized squeezed open. Blood and secretion oozed from a few of the deeper wounds.

He didn't utter a sound.

White Bear was too proud for that. The guards had left with Dan. Lucky man—at least he could walk. The guards knew that Tom wasn't going away anytime soon. Besides, he was tethered to a post with his hands bound behind his back. Most of the time now, his hands were left free, but not when he was left alone.

For a moment he set his problems aside and let his senses focus on the activities that were happening outside the smokehouse. The voices and sounds spoke of social mingling, of children's play and adult routine. The sounds spoke of chores and lessons, of hunting, fishing, and gathering. They reminded him that he was a prisoner, reminded him of the *other* world outside his internment. Like Dan, Tom despised his confinement.

The sounds emanating through the cedar walls added weight to the physical space that caged his body. He ached not only with the pain from his injuries but also with longing for his freedom.

He understood the necessity of patience. In applying patience, a man learned acceptance. One fed the other. The attributes were like brothers. Hadn't his uncle explained that many years before? There was little value in negativity—Tom knew the truth behind that thought. And berating oneself wasn't the warrior's way. What happened couldn't be reversed. He had done his best. He knew he would have to live with his decisions and their consequences. That was the warrior's way.

Tom listened intently and let his senses wander out and about the village. His home had been called Raven Town. He thought about the Tsimshian word for "freedom." It was defined differently than the White man's word. The Native interpretation was delineated by the element of acceptance. A warrior had to roll with his fate, good or bad. Some of the spirits were tricksters. Others were spirit helpers. A warrior had to overcome obstacles as they rose before him. He had to ask the ancestors for their assistance. Later, a warrior could offer his gratitude. Through those choices a man might obtain freedom. But freedom meant nothing without honor.

Outside, Tom liked what he was hearing. He caught the happy sounds of children's laughter, the scattering of their high-pitched voices. He heard the low, insistent drone of the adults, working, teaching, and remonstrating. Old lessons took on new meanings. The children listened, then failed to listen. Joy abounded just outside the smokehouse walls.

The inspiration sent him spiraling back to his village along the sandy shore of the great sea. He was a boy of eleven. His father had recently died.

Tom remembered waking to the drumming of the surf. If a boy listened closely, he could focus on the hollow sound that lay inside the belly of an ocean comber. That sound was the call of something larger and inexplicably holy.

That deep sound was followed by the deafening crash of surf as it rushed upon the beach and broke over the shallows. Tom heard the sound distant water made, a music replete with a deep sense of solitude.

Daydreaming from the dirt floor of the smokehouse, he realized how he longed for that distant place, a village of elders and family.

The ocean had been his front yard. A fine, wide beach led like a gentle sloping meadow from the lodge to the water's edge. Along the beach rested dozens of carved cedar canoes, vessels of all sizes and shapes. Canoes had different purposes: fishing, raiding, and gathering. There were river canoes, ocean canoes, and war canoes. One canoe extended nearly sixty feet, a show-your-wealth canoe. The chief owned the largest lodge in the village. Sixty family members and a half dozen slaves shared that house. Tom wasn't proud of the slave-trade legacy. He had learned the price of human imprisonment well enough. But that was the way it had been for a thousand years. No civilization had all the right answers, and Tom couldn't change the past. *Still,* he thought, *no man should be bound to another.*

He thought again about the wealthy chief. Two years later in a village celebration, he had given away most of his wealth. Tom thought again about the canoes, how they were carved from the finest cedar trees, from the tallest, straightest trunks. Frequently, the trunks rose forty or fifty feet in the air without a single limb. That made for perfect carving.

The giant cedar was a cultural icon and a talisman for his people. So much came from the tree: straight magnificent planks and lodgepoles for their lodges; benches, boxes, and furniture crafted from the straight, strong fiber; arrow shanks for shooting.

The cedar's inner bark was stripped and woven into ropes, fishing lines, nets, and paraphernalia for every conceivable job. Clothing—hats, shawls, dresses, and costumes—all came from the trees. Musical instruments and children's toys were also fashioned from the fragrant wood.

Skilled carvings transformed cedar bolts into the awesome masks that decorated the Tsimshian dancers during religious ceremonies. Above all else—higher and mightier—cedar totems rose to physical and spiritual heights, lauding their magical forms before the villagers with images representing legends and gods, family crests, historical events, and always, some degree of power.

The finest carvers of the soft, strong woods were as respected as any of the tribe's honored warriors or powerful leaders, man or woman.

As a child, White Bear began to assist his mother in her daily chores. He helped her to gather essentials from the forest and the many rivers that laced the land. By his sixth year, he followed Blue Shell everywhere, traveling on his thin, bowed legs. All in good sport, the old men smiled their broken-tooth smiles and kidded the young man about his crooked walk. "That boy, he must have gotten those legs from his Boston father, or, interjected one of the elders, from a grandfather grizzly." They chided White Bear and laughed uproarishly.

At age nine, White Bear sought early independence. Blue Shell's son traveled freely with the older boys through the forests and along the waterways that punctuated the Pacific Coast.

Like the White man's religion, the Natives honored the one Creator that gave and took away life. The animals that inhabited woods and shoreline were the life-sustaining helpers of the First Peoples. Their images were carved and painted on nearly every free surface. Without the official recognition of the Whites, Native art and the images it projected were as powerful as any of the art objects from disparate cultures from around the world.

On White Bear's eleventh birthday, Blue Shell's brother, Man Fishes Alone, took his nephew on his first ocean voyage. In a canoe that his uncle had carved with his own hands from a great red cedar, the two ventured through the white-capped surf and into the Pacific Ocean.

Westerly of the Haida Gwaii—beyond the homeland of the fierce fighting Haida—there was no visible landmass for as far as a sailor could see or imagine. The idea of paddling westerly far beyond the offshore islands was seldom entertained.

Looking east, White Bear watched the mainland slipping away. First went the low beaches, war canoes, fishing canoes, the paraphernalia that Whites called tackle: cedar boxes, cedar nets, and cedar gear. The drying racks with splayed salmon and halibut and the delicate herring roe—these all disappeared from eyesight as the canoe sped west.

White Bear watched the handsome lodges and the families who inhabited them sink below the horizon. The last to go were the carved totems, some fifty and sixty-feet tall. A few even taller. The shorter mortuary poles disappeared first, then the ceremonial poles. Finally, one stood alone. The highest totem along the beach displayed White Bear's family crest, the eagle crest. The pole rose majestically above all others. It rose proudly under the shadow of the coastal mountains, the backdrop of the Tsimshian world.

As uncle and nephew paddled west, all that was left was sky and ocean, the broad Pacific horizon sweeping as far as White Bear could see.

His uncle fished the deep water for halibut. On a fishing line of braided cedar twine, he tied a cedar fishing float. From there dangled a fish hook shaped of spruce root with strips of bait filleted from the sides of whitefish. Often the hook was baited with herring or anchovy. An ivory barb was pegged and secured to the wooden hook by sinew or gut. The baitfish was extracted from the ocean by way of a cedar rake, barbed with sharp wooden tines. The bait was then lowered as close to the sandy ocean bottom as possible. The halibut is a bottom fish. Ranging in the hundreds of pounds, a large fish became a feast for many families that resided in the longhouses, each ringing the half-moon beaches from British Columbia to Alaska.

On a cloudless day on the immense ocean, White Bear and his uncle caught four large fish. The gifts from the ocean were copious indeed, and White Bear and his uncle offered thanks.

Surfing the waves back into shore, the splendor that was the young man's village rose before him like a phoenix. Driving for the sandy beach, the shapely canoe's bow sliced through the water. Behind them, the combers broke and split. The dash through the surf was invigorating.

For most of the fishing trip, White Bear had felt a certain queasiness that fishermen associate with motion sickness. Now he shook his misery aside. Rushing through the combers in a handsome canoe full of great, white-fleshed fish made White Bear feel like a conquering hero.

His mother and other villagers received the young man with quiet pride. His uncle smiled proudly to himself. This was how it was. This was how it had always been for as long as anyone remembered, since the time of Raven's first visit, when the Curious One pried open the clamshell, and the First People spilled out.

Two years later, smallpox ravaged the village. Before the disease had finished its cycle of destruction, White Bear had lost his mother, his uncle, and over half of the tribe. He lost nearly every member of his immediate family. White Bear had fallen for a lovely Tsimshian princess, a youthful infatuation. He lost her too. He lost his grandmother and grandfather. Gone were two chiefs from the four clans, storytellers and carvers, the shaman, and the majority of elders.

As massive common graves were unceremoniously stuffed with the dead, the young Tsimshian stood shaken and bereaved. Suddenly, he was alone. White Bear's grief was penetrated by an anger that he would soon level against the new order. Along the northwest coast from the Columbia River all the way into Alaska, the locus of power had changed. The dominating new world order was there to stay. Its face was white.

Three years later, the disease ravaged again. Soon after came a new sickness the Whites called measles. Then influenza. All killed savagely. The remaining Tsimshian of White Bear's clan moved to Port Hardy where they gathered with other survivors from other tribes. As the canoes passed west through the surf and then south down the coast, the boy watched his village slip away. He would never return. Without looking back, White Bear began his evolution as Tom LaCross, the Tsimshian of half-blood whom the Whites called "Breed."

1968

The months galloped by. Thousands more troops were deployed to Vietnam. At home the country split wide open. Katherine focused on an image of an iron mallet splitting firewood, the two sections flying in opposite directions. Katherine was called a "hippie" but never defined just what that meant. Confusion reigned.

The Democratic Convention in Chicago captivated the nation. The police tactics enraged a good part of the citizenry, dissenters and protesters. There were huge demonstrations in Lincoln Park. The police beat the demonstrators to a pulp. As a candidate, Eugene McCarthy was discouraged from attending the convention. His voice was lost in the uproar. Hubert Humphrey won the nomination in turmoil. It was a fiasco. Katherine watched spellbound. What was happening? The world was on fire.

CHAPTER FOURTEEN

Give me the splendid, silent sun with all his beams full—dazzling

—Walt Whitman

Dan was escorted out and around the village. For an imprisoned man, the walk was invigorating.

After he came back, lay down, and drifted into sleep, Tom suddenly awakened. The Tsimshian had been dreaming, but any recollections of those dreams quickly evaporated. He thought some more about the history of his people—as they were now and as they had been. He thought about this strange village nestled so secretly, deep in the Canadian wilderness, in what had been Native land. He knew the village shouldn't exist. He knew it represented another time, a better time.

His thoughts flowed backwards to the Tsimshian's celebrations and potlatches, to his people before the disease, before the Whites brought the pox, influenza, measles, and with them, insurmountable deaths. He thought how he had loved the dances, the pageantry, the shadow and light that emanated from the bonfires. Excitement careened across the lodge as the participants turned joyous with the rising crescendo of the music, and with the high-stepping movements of dance and drums.

Often the celebrations lasted for days. Before the low throbbing flames of the wood fires, dancers with fantastical masks intertwined in half-shadow, half-light explosions of pageantry. Cedar drums with skin heads and rattles and whistles carved from wood and bone cast a mood of euphoria and comradeship. The tribe danced and sang far into the night, into a second night, and often a third—danced until they became exhausted. The tribe feasted for days. The potlatch might revolve around marriage, death, a display or shift of power, a young man's coming of age, or a princess's first menstruation and her formal passage into womanhood. White Bear loved every ritual.

But those ceremonies disappeared too. They were banished. The provincial government of British Columbia proclaimed the potlatch illegal. If discovered, the practice of ancient ceremonies meant certain imprisonment. With the Northwest tribes often reduced to ten percent or less of their historical populations, it was hard enough to get together a major hunting party. Still, in the stealth of the night—in the deep groves out of sight from prying eyes—the Natives gathered to keep alive many of the disappearing pieces of their once-proud and powerful culture.

Tom had heard stories of the Kwakiutl legend, Chief Mungo Martin, who reestablished much of the lore and heritage of his people. How the chief held secret ceremonies deep in the evergreen forests. How he taught the younger people to carve traditional art, and to put to memory the songs and stories of their ancestors. All was done under cover and out of sight from the prying eyes of the Canadian government.

Of all the losses, the largest sacrifice was the defacing of Native pride. The demise of self-confidence. Their honor.

In this village hidden deep in the mountains, Tom felt the same ancient self-worth that had once flowered among the Tsimshian. He deciphered that spontaneous joy with his ears even as he lay broken and bruised on the dirt floor of the abandoned smokehouse. One thought continued to ring true. Something reminiscent of his past was happening in this isolated village, and he wanted to be a part of it.

As his mind wound down and sleep approached, Tom felt the return of his ancestors. He imagined their faces caught up in the freedom of music and dance. He imagined a sense of awe as his relatives praised the

Creator for His generosity and abundance. In the pitch-black night, Tom resurrected images of his mother. He remembered her loving nature. He imagined her cradling him when he was an infant.

"Come!" she would shout to the young boy. "Come home. Come out of the woods. Time to eat."

Blue Shell died a young woman, not yet thirty winters. Pox.

As Tom began his meditation, he felt something as tangible as his mother's sweet breath touch him through the invisible space of time. He began an audible chant. In the room of smoke, the guard stirred. The guard knew a Tsimshian prayer when he heard one. He liked this man, the famous scout who was the talk of the village. Everyone in the camp knew his reputation. That knowledge would have startled Tom. The guard hoped White Bear would not attempt an escape. That way he would not have to chase him down and kill him. Of this the guard was clear: no man would be allowed to freely spread word of the secret village.

But then the big man wondered. White Bear was mighty closed-mouthed. Though he worked with the Whites, he also disdained them. Would he keep their secret? The big guard thought so. White Bird reeked of honor.

Shortly after midnight, Tom fell into a deep sleep. His dreams radiated with color. The same intense lights he had seen dancing in the northern winter skies, a rainbow spectrum called the aurora borealis, electrified his vision.

In his dream, the dancers step forward. They dance in cedar leggings, woven bark skirts, the softest of animal pelts. They dance in painted draperies of primary colors wrapping about their shoulders and upper bodies like a bodice. Music corrals them all. Light and shadows ricochet off the carved masks in the firelight. The dancers become one. One form, one motion. Tom thinks of the flight of the sandpipers: hundreds of wings tipping in unison, the sparkle of sunlight twisting off their tiny, feathered bodies, all flutter and scurry.

He remains stranded in the dreamworld. He is cast in a spell. But suddenly, his vision rivets upon the exaggerated faces of fierce, masked dancers. Perched on the stocky bodies like riders on horses, an army of wolves materializes, their features both grotesque and fearsome. The next thing he sees in this unfolding drama is the glint of hundreds of yellow eyes framed by hairy faces and fangs, their ivory teeth gnashing. Out of each mouth tumbles a kaleidoscope of colors, each drawn by the north wind.

Sweaty and agitated, Tom woke with a start.

In the early dawn, he realized that only two men remained in the smokehouse. Staring at him from across the room was the alert face of Dan Skinner. The other was himself, White Bear, the Tsimshian,

For a second, Tom thought he was back in the spirit world. But no! Just he and his old student. He realized the guard had left the smokehouse—left the two men to themselves. Both men were tied and secured. Across the dim space, the faint light of dawn paired night and day. Neither man was comfortable with the other's hard gaze. Tom expected the worst. Instead of confronting the pathfinder, he turned his attention upon dawn's earliest songbirds, centering his concentration on their sweet orchestration.

Dan's words reached him anyway. Tom braced for the worst.

"LaCross, tell me something."

Tom didn't respond immediately but looked Dan directly in the eyes. As improbable as it seemed, Tom suspected that the relationship between them had miraculously improved.

"Why didn't you shoot me first? You had me in your sights. If you had got me, André would have been easy pickings. André never would have made it up that cliff alone."

Before speaking, Tom turned his full attention toward his apprentice, reflecting on the sternness of the younger man's face and the intensity of his words. For many moments, Tom chewed on Dan's question, grappling with the current behind his words. Tom was a careful man, as thrifty with his thoughts as he was with his speech.

Dan shifted impatiently before Tom answered his question. "Never had much problem with you, son. No good reason to kill you."

Dan's next words surged from his lips like an explosion of cascading water. "Why my brother, then?" There was a deadly edge to his voice now.

More silence wrapped the smokehouse before Tom spoke. He chose his next words carefully, as if his survival depended upon the very nuance of his explanation. "First place, didn't have no rifle. Second: William Casey made that shot. No talking him out of it."

Another long silence settled between the two men. Tom broke the spell. "Casey had the only rifle. Long shot. Not much time. And . . . well . . . well, reasoning between the lines… I'm saying that André being your brother… I figured you would protect him at any cost. Casey figured that too. He wanted to put an end to the affair. Wanted to go home. Can you blame him? And two of his deputies was dead.

"Everyone in Kilnook knows how you doted on André. How close you was. Well, I reckoned that *you* didn't stir up any of that trouble in the first place. Couldn't see any good reason to shoot *you* for your brother's sins. You didn't murder Driscol; André did. And Driscol wasn't much of a man, anyhow. Tell you, though, Casey was mad—stompin' mad—when I called him off. Thought for a minute he might turn that rifle on me."

Tom stopped again. Maybe he wished to grab a quick breath before he doled out any more words. Maybe he was just searching for the right sequence. With so much talk after so many days of stingy silence, he felt uncomfortable. But as suddenly as he had stopped, Tom began again. "Sorry to say, that was my mistake. Mine, all mine. Cost William Casey his life. Mine nearly. Sure, I'm alive, but no help from you. All that anger in you. Ever think I might have a righteous beef, myself? You tried to kill me. Have you wondered why I didn't just pack it up and go home? That boulder narrowly missed me. I was damn lucky. And mad as hell! That's one of the reasons I climbed on. Believe me, there were others."

"And just what might those be?"

Tom sat as still as a fence post, his tongue probing the inside of his cheek. "Tell the truth, Dan, I never quite forgave you for abandoning me in the jailhouse the day those young Mounties crossed me. And you crossed me too. I always came to your defense. Always. Where was you that day?"

Dan sat quietly off to one side, his mouth twisting like he was chewing on a piece of elk gristle. "Bothered me for years. You're right, Tom. Dead right! Listen, I was new to the law and needed the job. Didn't want to buck those boys. Hell, I was sowing my oats. Just a young pup. But I was dead wrong. I knew it then, and it has haunted me ever since. Sorry, Tom. Should have said it years ago. It cost me our friendship. I owed you so much. I'm sorry. My apology comes from my heart. Should have come out years ago."

Tom sat there for several minutes, mulling over Dan's confession. There was not much that Dan could read from the scout's facial expression. Tom had the perfect poker face, and he had already poured out more than his usual allotment of words. That was about as long an oration as anyone had ever heard from Tom LaCross, or, for that matter, the man the Tsimshian people called White Bear, an introverted leader even among his own people. Now the tracker was dead quiet, introspective, sullen, or maybe just fuming. The scout's words had petered out. It was as if he had stored up a barrel of thoughts over the long winter, and now they were all spent.

Dan was quiet too. But thoughts were rattling his brain like raindrops striking still water. "I loved my brother."

This provoked the tracker. His expression changed. His face turned ruddy and bright. He spoke now in an ireful voice. The careful reflection that Tom prided himself on had just disappeared. "Well, Dan, I loved my mother and my uncle just the same as you keened on that troubled brother of yours. Pox killed 'em both. White men brought that on. Spread it on blankets—or so I been told. Never got condolences from your people. Never got nothing but a boatload of grief. White men killed my whole family, destroyed our nation. Conquered us! Then you bastards stripped us of what little pride remained. The only way I survived was working for your government, adopting your ways. I hate your laws. White man's laws! They're all one-sided."

"You're half-White."

"Not in my heart I ain't. I'm Tsimshian. My people gave me plenty of reason to be proud."

"What about your father?"

"Son of a bitch."

Again, silence descended between the men. Each of them was lost to memories. Dan had hardly known his father, and his mother died young. The brothers raised themselves from an early age. Before André reached his mid-teens, they were on their own. Dan felt the loss of his kid brother keenly, but the blame for his death was shifting away from Tom.

Dan was cogitating on Black Wing's last words, his pronouncement from the afternoon before. He resurrected the old man's eyes, his blind eyes, and his humane message. Yeah, André was no saint. Sure, he made a certain amount of trouble, but that was no reason…

"Your brother murdered a man."

The words cut through the thick air like an owl on the wing, its talons ready to rip and maim. Dan went dead quiet. New currents singed the air. Dan was mulling over Tom's last words. Over earlier ones. Maybe, just maybe, André had brought some of that trouble down upon his own head. His brother *had* killed a man. Dan hadn't liked that man. The big logger had been a troublemaker and a bully to boot. But André had killed him as sure as rain falls on a northwest forest.

"Tell me about the killing. 'Murder,' you call it. I only got my brother's side of the story."

Tom thought about the question, rolled the words around the inside of his cheek like a wad of chewing tobacco. The tongue reached, then extended the skin on the right side of his face, next to his deep-black mustache. Above, a fresh scar etched his face. Tom's mouth was exaggerated by his large round lips. When he made a face, his mouth appeared even more pronounced.

He answered slowly. "Your brother lost his temper. We all seen plenty of that. Hit Stan James with his big fist. Hit him hard. They both had been drinking plenty. Arguing over cards. Something was said about you. Bad words.

"André struck first. Jabbed Stan in the throat. Was a mean punch, a bull's-eye. You know how fast your brother was, how strong. Crushed Driscoll's Adam's apple. Fell without a word, curling his hands around the wound. Stan never come up from the floor."

"André said he was provoked. Said Stan accused me of being more like a Red man than a White. That I hung out with the likes of you. Sorry. Sorry to say that. I apologize. We always defended each other. André made a terrible mistake."

"Law won't let you kill a man for bullying."

"André never handled name calling."

Tom shrugged, then answered slowly and clearly. "Good thing he weren't Tsimshian. If we acted that way, we'd all been lynched. Plenty were anyhow. Outright murdered."

Dan thought some. He had to admit there was a wagonload of truth behind Tom's statement. He spoke again, as if he was talking to himself. "Do anything for that kid."

Tom acknowledged the statement with a flicker of his eyelids.

"Had to replace Ma and Pa. Kind of brought him up myself."

Tom's face showed little to no response. He had gone back into himself. Were old injuries, mental and physical, kicking up again? Or maybe he was thinking about his own childhood, weighing out another pain, like counting out a bale of beaver furs.

Light was flitting through the slats in the cedar plank wall. It was cold outside. A surly wind raged across the valley. A slow drizzle was smothering the landscape, coating it like a layer of campfire ash. Evergreen was transformed to sepia.

The village was stirring. Women began their morning chores, refreshing the previous night's embers into cooking fires, gathering dried armloads of firewood. Men were priming for the hunt. Young boys were emulating their fathers. Together they strung the gut bowstrings. The boys were anxious to assume the mantle of a warrior. They rubbed animal grease along the finely tapered bow ends, along the grains of the coveted yew wood. Mothers and daughters were preparing food. Tom tasted the smoke in the air. He smelled food cooking. For the first time in days, hunger knotted his belly.

That morning, Tom planned to talk with the guards. Rain or no rain, he wished to sit in the open. He wanted to breathe fresh air. He didn't care about the weather. He wanted outdoors and would take it anyway it came.

He remained reflective as his mind began to spin out a litany of questions and answers. He mulled over his predicament. Thought hard about the village he had left as a youth. Gone!

He had nothing to draw him back to Old Kilnook. No relatives or friends. No family. The only people waiting for him would be angry townsfolk. Right then—and the thought came as a revelation—he realized that he didn't have to go back. The life he sought was right here in this village.

Right before his eyes. Well, he would chew on that, alright. He had plenty of time on his hands.

Dan was of a different frame of mind. Rebecca wasn't in the village; it was as simple as that.

At the thought of Rebecca, Dan felt a recurring ache. Felt it acutely. Sitting upright in the dim smokehouse, his mind chased the thin rays of morning light as they squeezed through the occasional openings between the uneven cedar planks. He envisioned Rebecca just as Sally was seeing her at that very moment. He saw her face cast in sleep, peaceful in the repose of their bed. *Jesus,* he thought, *I've got to blow out of here. I've got to find her soon.*

He turned toward Tom, his thoughts stirring back to his brother. His old mentor had a legitimate beef. As Dan's eyes settled again on Tom, he saw the brushstrokes of truth painted across the scout's dark face.

Dan had one last thing to share. "By the way, Tom, I could have finished you off in the pit. These Indians helped pull you through, alright. I'm not taking a thing from them, but . . . just want you to know, I had my chance. I could have killed you."

Tom turned and eyed Dan. Dan knew he was incapable of defining that look. Slowly, very slowly, new words passed the Tsimshian's thick lips. "Yeah," he said. "I figured as much. Why didn't you then?"

Words peppered the oily air, moving in a truncated, slow-motion soliloquy.

"I kept thinking about your kindness toward André and me when we was kids. Remembered how you took me under your wing. Taught me mountain ways. You helped me plenty. Just maybe, you saved me. My turn now."

Peace Corps, 1971

The Peace Corps sent Katherine to a small village, a "no place" along a deserted coastline where she hoped to assist the native Hondurans with their fisheries, or the lack of them. That was a strange call for her. She had never gone fishing in her life—knew nothing about it. She didn't like the smell or the feel of fish flesh, but she did know Spanish, and she certainly had mastered the many complexities of a foreign language. She was a brainchild.

She loved her new neighbors and delighted in their lifestyle. She was charmed. Sure, by US standards, they were unproductive, but, as it turned out, Uncle Sam didn't have all the answers.

The Peace Corps requisitioned a bunch of electronic equipment all designed for ocean trawlers. The technical marvels arrived in large wooden crates. Talk about primitives—the Peace Corps took the cake. Not only did the practicality of all that equipment go right over the locals' heads, but Katherine didn't even know what to do with the stuff. She barely got it out of the crates. And, of course, there were no sea trawlers, no large boats to employ the equipment. And nobody had ever heard of three-phase electricity. The Natives fished from dugout canoes. A few had antiquated outboard engines.

She buried the new equipment in the back of a tin-roofed warehouse that lacked even an electrical outlet. Then she settled into a routine of watch and wait. That took weeks.

Katherine read books. She wrote in her diary and penned out poetry. She had plenty of time on her hands. While tanning herself on the pearly white beach—book or pencil in hand—she quietly studied the Hondurans. Initially, they were indifferent. Secretly, they respected her intelligent and open manner. The woman was highly likable and, in their hearts, the locals knew that Katherine had come to help.

Her first mission was simple enough: assist these people in developing a sustainable economy. The second was harder: forget Paul.

But she wasn't capable of leaving his memory alone.

The days wore on. The crystal-clear skies cleansed her. She soaked listlessly in the turquoise sea while she listened to a scattering of conversations, all in local Spanish. She watched with steady, inquisitive eyes and followed up with the villagers. Katherine took advantage of every opportunity to visit and learn their ways. All the while she was organizing a plan, an economic framework. She knew that she would never forget her lover but realized soon enough that she might survive without him. Here was an opportunity to heal herself. Katherine focused every ounce of energy on the two goals.

The villagers went about their fishing as they had for centuries; it was every man for himself. When the Natives got into a bumper crop of fish, they took it all. Often the fish just rotted on the beaches or in their boats. They had no refrigeration to speak of, no market to sell their wares. *Feast or famine,* Katherine thought. She might fix that. She formed a plan. She was optimistic.

Katherine began to organize the Natives into teams. She designed a new direction.

The villagers listened respectfully. The Hondurans knew how to fish. Their craft extended back into ancient history. Katherine simply added a measure of strategy.

Everything took time, lots of time. Together, they became more effective. Katherine garnered their trust. She delved into the art of fishing, into the practicality of success. She read everything about fishing that she got her hands on. She wrote letters. She listened. And then she sprang her first coup. She convinced the village to form a collective. In a simple, kindly way, she introduced them to ecology. She told them, "Take only what you need, and then there will be more fish the next time around.

"Share the bounty with your neighbors. Help yourself, but don't take too much. Those words were her father's words.

"You must not fish on weekends. Those fish need a couple of days to breed and move upriver. Let some escape."

She reminded them that Jesus didn't work on the Sabbath. Then she extended their rest to a second day. They adhered to their own brand of Catholicism. She charmed them with her style of amicability. Her voice was kind but strong, her language nearly perfect. She slowly adopted local jargon.

The Natives began to trust the woman from the States. Three months passed. Finally, she was able to pull her trump card.

Katherine helped them build a fine smokehouse, one large enough for the whole village, large enough to smoke all the leftover fish. It was designed after a North Coast smokehouse she had studied from photographs at the library of the University of Washington. Her mom sent her photocopies and a book full of recipes.

The Natives worked on the structure from dawn to dusk, each Saturday and Sunday. The point was, they weren't fishing on the weekends. They were conserving. They were building their future.

The fish had to be brined first. She and the villagers struggled to find the right balance of salt and water. They wrestled with that for days. Katherine even conquered her squeamishness for fish carcasses. Soon they had it down pat.

Katherine enlisted the women. She found a few small markets for the smoked fish in a nearby inland city. The Natives loved their newfound responsibility. The women were eager to participate. She taught them accounting. They were quick learners. The villagers split the profits.

The times, they were a-changin'. For the first time in months, Katherine felt the return of hope.

Katherine Skinner-Patterson had scored one for the Peace Corps and scored another one for her father. And the bleeding over Paul began to abate.

CHAPTER FIFTEEN

The Bella Bella thought the first Whites (the seamen were Italians) to be incarnations of chum salmon because of their hooked noses. During mating, salmon amass a hook in their extended jaw. The Natives thought this physical sign to be a good omen. The Bella Bella brought the foreigners two great tyee (legend claims ninety pounds each) and fed the foreigners like princes. But the Caucasians weren't interested in fish. The Whites traded for furs, sleek sea otter, marten, and beaver. The White man's appetite was insatiable. They traded until the animals were gone. After that, all that was left to trade was the very soul of the Native culture. Little by little, even that was carved away.

—Katherine Skinner-Patterson

Diary notes

The great eagle flew west, its awesome plumage spread wide, its movements silky and graceful. The raptor's huge wings were painted like the face of winter itself: smoky gray and sable black, ancient strokes of charcoal like those used by the First Peoples to paint their ancient images in caves and on rock walls. Then a blaze of white, as pure as first snow. The raptor jostled the wind the way a canoe paddle stirs the smooth surface of a mountain lake. Even at a fair distance, an observer felt the promise of wild and liberating freedom.

In a gust of wind, the bird would glide, easy and free. Suspended above the cold, thin air, the raptor appeared to be nearly motionless. But the eagle was floating on wind currents at speeds that were deceiving. High above the tall granite mountains, above the celadon-colored river, the eagle soared. It raced down from the high country guided by instinct and a visual trail defined by the ribbon of the river below. The raptor moved silently under the burnished glitter of sunrise.

The raptor saw distant things with a precision that would have startled many humans. On this clear spring day, the giant bird glided effortlessly through sky the color of a spring iris.

When the eagle arrived at the coast, it turned north and flew along a coastline that had been home to Native peoples for uncounted generations. Of course, the Natives didn't own the land. They simply occupied it. They shared the wilderness along with the long list of creatures that the Creator had ordained as partners in His movable drama. To the Native way of thinking, all the birds, fish, and mammals were of one spirit. Unlike the European cultures, these Natives didn't place themselves above any of the other animals in the chain of God's abundant creations. They were all joined together like two hands clasping.

Below, the land had taken on a different shape. Pioneer towns no longer hugged the landscape the way the Native villages had. The towns spread capriciously across a vast new territory, a least in the eyes of the newcomers. Around the homes, timber had been shorn like the hides of the White man's wooly sheep. Land had been domesticated. Not just a cedar or spruce tree dropped randomly—not a small rectangular patch carefully cut from the bark of an ancient tree to be used for baskets, weaving, or clothing. No, the forest were dropped with impunity. The north coast Natives treated the timber as a respected ancestor. The new culture helped themselves to everything. Gratitude was not a mainstay in their vocabulary.

If the Natives needed planks for a lodge, they split out three or four from a single tree, leaving the giants to grow and survive.

Under the new order, every tree was cut, burned, or sold. The cedar was often wasted entirely. There were so many of the wooden giants that the great trees lacked value in a saturated timber market. The sacrifice of the tree was something the Natives of the northwest coast never understood. The Haida and Tsimshian—most of the Northwest tribes—believed that to unceremoniously kill a tree brought out angry spirits, predicating wrath from the forest. They considered the forest sacred. Few Whites could stomach such an impractical philosophy. "Superstition," they said. And who could argue with the new kid on the block, the one with all the power and prosperity?

The new order's logging practices were simple. The first trees were selected for easiest access. They were felled close to the water, then floated downstream in great timber rafts. If the streams ran shallow, a splash dam was constructed downstream from the fallen timber. When the winter rains came—when the river rose exponentially—huge rafts of old growth accumulated in the murky water. As winter rains swelled the streams, and the timber backed up behind the dams, the massive wooden structures were dynamited. The rush of timber gouged and stripped the streambed of its natural flora and fauna. Along with the fallen trees, tons of detritus was swept downstream before settling into the decimated watershed. The damage to the fish and the forest that surrounded the riparian zone was devastating. With the complete removal of the trees—a classic clear-cut—mudslides from the steep terrain further ravaged the stream bottom, covering the round river stones and salmon nests called redds. Tons of the thick runoff also suffocated the salmon eggs. With the eggs lost, runs of the salmonoids were diminished or destroyed in a single generation.

If the splash dams and the mud didn't stop the salmon, the few remaining minnows or smolts were carried away by the freshets. The giant trees no longer absorbed the water, no longer cushioned the impact of heavy torrents of rain. As cedar and salmon—mainstays of the Native culture—were diminished, the ways of the First Peoples were completely and irrevocably jeopardized.

The eagle saw all this. He watched the canneries and fish traps spring up inside every major coastal bay, blockading the inlets to the great salmon runs. Within three to five years (the salmon's natural lifecycle), entire populations of the fish were eradicated. Suddenly, there were great wheezing steam engines that fueled the iron machines, which ran the boats, canneries and mills and subsequently aided in the deforestation of a thousand generations of evergreen forests.

The mechanical marvel of the new century, the Iron Chink, methodically stripped flesh from the salmon. The discarded carcasses were hurled unceremoniously back into the inlets and crystal-clear waters.

The eagle watched the steel-toothed saws fall the ancient trees, clearing patches many miles square, leaving them naked and spiritless.

The ancient lands of the Haisla, Kwakiutl, and Tsimshian filled in with White man's homes, farms, and businesses. Settlements sprang up. Domestic livestock came north.

The Natives had never imagined the likes. There had always been enough food to feed the families. The Creator provided. Now, even as Native populations were devastated by the introduction of European diseases, the few remaining Indigenous people starved.

The Bostons continued to inundate the landscape. There was no stopping the migration. Conversely, there were fewer Native peoples to compete with the flood of pioneers.

The eagle continued out over the ocean that separated the homeland of the Haida from the mainland of British Columbia. That chain of islands had been impacted as radically as the rest of the west coast of British Columbia.

Far down the west side of the islands, the eagle flew. A great sadness pervaded his spirit. He knew the Haida Gwaii from the old times. He remembered the old ways.

Just over a hundred years before, the first European sailing ship had anchored in an obscure Haida inlet. The Native people experienced all the fear and anticipation that accompanied the mysterious arrival. Like an apparition, the giant vessels rode the tides with fluttering canvas sails that jostled Native superstitions with images of departed spirits or ghosts. Great spruce masts reached high into the sky. The Haida described the ships as giant canoes with trees growing out of the deck. A tri-colored flag unfurled gallantly in the stiff northwest wind.

Initially, the Native people were covetous of the European trade goods. They quickly succumbed to the allure of the manufactured offerings. Rifles shot straight and true. Copper was malleable. Glass beads were bright and alluring.

Metal cooking pots and iron tools saved hours of arduous labor. Cotton cloth was pretty, and Native women didn't have to spend days curing animal hides. Many of the objects appeared to simplify their lives. With few exceptions, Native cultures glorified in these objects created by sophisticated European technology. But from that simple exchange came the downfall of every single Native American tribe.

The English had successfully applied a divide and conquer strategy to colonies all around the world. Upon the Native peoples of British Columbia, it was easier than ever. The transfer of power was a cakewalk. Disease and alcohol were the icing on the cake.

On the Queen Charlotte Islands, known to the tribes as the Haida Gwaii, half-moon harbors and protected beaches were buttressed by igneous rock. With their narrow openings, the inlets provided protection from powerful storms that galloped over the ocean from the west. Over millennia, awesome waves of, twenty, thirty and forty feet had shaped and reshaped the landscape.

The Haida were the greatest sailors since the Vikings. As far as San Francisco, canoes, often fifty feet or better, sailed, traded, and raided. Before the Europeans invaded their shores, the Haida had few equals. They were warriors of distinction.

As he turned to the north, the eagle's keen eyes recorded the changes. In a sickle of craggy, rock-faced beachheads rested the cedar remains of deserted longhouses and deteriorated totems. For centuries, ancient villages had nestled into ancient groves of giant evergreens: spruce and hemlock and cedar. Under overcast skies, the structures appeared wraith-like and broken. In just a few years, wind, rain, and decay had taken them back. A weld of gray swarmed across the landscape. A civilization built of old-growth timber had fallen. The duff and dust of decomposition swallowed the mighty timbers. Beds of moss inundated, burying history under a blanket of floral-green vegetation.

Above the ground, mortuary poles listed. Many already lay face down. The bones of the deceased had been scattered. The knock-cluck of Raven, forever present, sounded hollow and eerie. Gone was the laughter of the children, the lessons of the elders, and the voice of the living. Only the cacophony of winter storms abounded.

Trees jostled by winter storms croaked and groaned as the westerly winds wove through the ancient groves. Only the raven heard. The First Peoples had departed.

And here was the relic of an ancient village, one among many that the eagle remembered. One he had known intimately.

Before him a high embankment rose steadily above the surf. A finger of land extended seaward like a green thumb, isolated but secure on its rock foundation. A new forest had seeded naturally and now extended evenly down the outcropping. The high incline of a mountain reached toward the heavens, its peak rising several hundred feet. To reach the pinnacle, most men had to bushwhack through an onslaught of bramble. If only they could fly like an eagle!

Scattered through the forest like forlorn sentinels, totems that had honored Native families now sank back into the earth. Families were interred here, as forgotten as the decayed grave houses and mortuary totems that held their bones. Here were the family crests of the Raven and Eagle clans. The carvings of two other clans—whale and grizzly mortuaries—had decomposed into dust. A hard crust covered a beaver crest. The horizontal memorial pole of a frog lay like one asleep. Moon hawk, goat, sea bear, black bear, grizzly—all the carvings languished like so much forgotten laughter.

The eagle saw the remains of the waste-food-house where, to preserve the salmon runs, a Haida chief once scattered the bones and entrails of hundreds of salmon. If the Whites found the rituals superstitious, Native populations reveled in the power of prayer and ceremony.

Before smallpox, twenty lodges stood there. Nearly four hundred people. Scattered about were the remains of more memorial totems: salmon, cormorant, and dogfish. Dilapidated six-beam houses were consecrated by moss, salal, and loam. Before the six beams, two-beam longhouses. Before that, no living person remembered.

The carvings were long unattended. Silver-gray patina impregnated the cedar faces, spoke of the same color values that so frequently waxed the northwest. Gone were the bright primary colors that the artists had painted on the carvings. All that remained was the dignity of the artwork and the legacy of spirits.

Toward the back of the grove, three mortuary totems remained standing, but the human remains had been spilled. Long ago, the animals had foraged their bones. Scattered them.

One day soon the remaining poles would be gone too. Like the bones of many ancestors, the totems would dissolve into the soil or decay along the sandy beaches. Duff would be blown or decamped. The ocean would sanctify their remains.

The eagle did not have to read the future to understand that the old ways of these people were in great jeopardy. There might be no way forward, no redemption. The thought festered.

From above, perched on the carved eagle crown of a family totem, the eagle watched the ebb and flow of the surging breakers. A low, diffused light dappled the tops of the ocean swells as they unfurled rhythmically onto the shore. The hypnotic sound that the waves made was the foundation of the land—where the sands began, where the ocean relinquished its power. The eagle was thinking about beginnings. He was thinking that without solid bedrock, any culture could easily become lost.

He listened intently to the sound of the surf. Farther out, the ocean surged with a bass resonance. The music reminded him of distant drums.

Like the woven cedar cloaks of the Haida, ocean music wrapped around the eagle's feathered body. He felt the Creator's spirit touch him. He felt huge, as if he were a universe unto himself. Then, almost simultaneously, the eagle felt like a tiny spot of energy twisting as a single delicate feather might, tossed to and fro upon sturdy winds. The eagle let the swirl of forces pull him heavenward. He was at peace with himself. His spirit soared. He was free.

A single guard and the young Haisla girl returned to the smokehouse early the next morning carrying a breakfast of dried fish and boiled goose eggs. A tea had been steeped from salal leaves. The pleasant aroma drifted through the house of smoke.

The guard was back and did not appear surprised at the marked transformation between the two men. He seldom seemed surprised by much of anything. His life had been constantly shuffled between dramatic forces. A slight twitch lifted the corner of his thin black mustache. Tom noticed but said nothing. Was that a smirk or the hint of a smile? He figured the latter.

Dan was struck by an aberrant thought and turned cautiously toward Tom, shaping his question in a kindly voice. "Heard you speak a little with the guard. How much of his language do you know?"

In his typically taciturn way, Tom chewed slowly on the question. He stared straight past the men and the young girl as if they were invisible. Only then did he turn his dark eyes upon his old student.

At the same moment, the guard was studying the two prisoners. The big man figured that changes were happening in the house of smoke. The civility between the prisoners was clearly noticeable.

"Enough to get me by," Tom stated matter-of-factly.

Dan took in a deep breath. Let it out slowly. "Ask the girl her name, would you?"

Tom was thinking through several translations when the girl with the silky raven hair startled both prisoners by answering the question herself. "My name is Yellow Bird Singing. Uncle speak your English. Teach me. Two years in a residency school added more but nearly kill me."

"Well, I'll be go to hell," Dan said, startled. His words fluttered across the closed space like a wounded bird. "What happened? How did you get here?"

"I ran away. Uncle hid me and brought me here. It was a long journey."

As quiet as a ghost, Tom scanned the room again, lost in private thought. Over his shoulder, Dan slyly eyed the Tsimshian. Tom was also contemplating Dan's play on words. Three languages were competing inside the small wooden enclosure.

Was Tom lollygagging, his imagination dream-walking into the bright bluebird dawn? Dan refused to guess. Among the Tsimshian, the right choice of words exemplified a man's control, his status as a leader. Tom was as cautious as a mother deer guarding her fawn.

Dan turned toward Yellow Bird Singing, but it was she who asked the first question. "I'll be go to hell. What does that mean?"

"Ah, just some barroom talk. I'm sorry. Don't mean a thing. You spoke your name in English?"

"Yes, many here speak both tongues."

"Many?"

"Yes. Black Wing has Charlie and others teach us Boston tongue. And many of the young people were forced into residency schools. Kidnapped and forced to learn English. This easier for children. They learn quickly or get punished. Many die! Many disappear!"

Now it was Dan's turn to feel flummoxed. He watched the girl's reactions carefully. All the while she continued to avoid eye contact. Dan couldn't help himself. He was touched by her mannerisms and her gentle demeanor. *Lord*, he thought, *she is lovely. And so bashful.* He thought suddenly about Rebecca, about their lack of children. Hadn't they dreamed of a girl-child many times before?

Tom studied the young Haisla and Dan with his sharp hawk eyes. His gaze was noncommittal, but inside, his mind was racing. The guard was silent but alert. The men shuffled their feet over the dirt floor. Everyone in the room lowered their eyes. Each had run out of words. The smokehouse was as quiet as a cave.

Dan turned suddenly toward Yellow Bird Singing and broke the silence. "Does he speak English, too?" He pointed his finger at the big Haisla. The guard answered the question himself.

"Little Boston."

"And Black Wing?"

"Talk to Black Wing yourself. I not speak for him."

"Jesus," Dan said, shaking his head in confusion.

Everyone pondered his last word. Each stalled separately, as if in moody reflection. Using Jesus as Godhead and religious wedge, the clergy and missionaries shredded Native teachings and their spiritual beliefs.

Yellow Bird Singing spoke out again. "Someday, you will tell me about this man, this Jesus?"

"Well," Dan said, "if you teach me some of your words, we'll work out a deal."

"Deal?"

Tom finally broke his silence and translated the word into Haisla. He had learned that word in a half dozen dialects from his father. In the fur trade, "deal" was more than an important word. It was a survival technique.

Yellow Bird Singing spoke again. "We trade." Her voice was ebullient. Dan felt happy, perhaps for one of a handful of times since his capture.

In that brief encounter, Dan had forgotten about his mission to outwit his guards and run for his life. Unconsciously, he felt the noose loosen.

The guard and the girl were leaving the smokehouse. Dan's reverie broke. More to himself than for the others, he turned and spoke. It was as if he was finally able to digest the strange turn of events. "I'll be go to hell."

"You can say that again," Tom replied, and for a moment, laughter pealed between the two men, the first in many moons.

Dan liked her name, Yellow Bird Singing. As the days sped by, he anticipated her arrival. Dan had always wanted a daughter, and she was young enough to be his. His imagination played out. Even as he cogitated on her name, his thoughts drifted from the smokehouse to the worn footpath that bordered the farm. He was remembering the speckled yellow songbirds that flitted so gracefully through the copse of evergreens beside the river; how the wild canaries bolted when he and Rebecca walked along the river path. He imagined holding Rebecca's hand. He imagined the rich sweet songs, their allusive character. He loved the way their music patterned itself into the warm spring air. A Chinook wind they called it.

Spring returned to the high country. On the river, ice was breaking up. Chocolate lilies and wild paintbrush burst into bloom. Their arrival signaled the promise of a wild harvest to come.

The Natives called this rich alluvial field, the "Bear Meadow," and from these lands the Haisla harvested dozens of edible plants, such as the rice-root flower, which generated a starchy, grain-like kernel relished by the First Peoples.

After months of hibernation, the grizzlies were back. In those gathering places, alive with so many edible plants and berries, Native women moved cautiously. They did not want to stray into the haunts of the thick-furred giants.

In the springtime, female bears were known to attack savagely when careless wanderers got trapped between a sow and her cub. Often warriors would accompany the women and their daughters on their treks into the tall grassy flatlands. The law of the land spoke of caution.

But incidents were infrequent. The Haisla trained their youth to never run from the giants but to stand firm or retreat carefully. One must solicit courage from the Creator, the elders warned. Grandfathers admonished the children, "Be brave. It is normal to be fearful, but to panic, that is inexcusable."

Dan listened to the vast flocks of geese moving north. The sound always flooded his thoughts with fond memories. Generally, he attempted to count the birds. Often the task became impossible—the numbers were simply off-putting. But the sounds and movement of their flight always gladdened him.

The union that Dan felt with the geese had more to do with a kinship with the bird's spirit than with the practical act of shooting and eating them. Something about their call struck him deeply, something about their intelligence and lifelong mating habits. The great northern wilderness had always been Dan's first love. Hunting and exploring was the catalyst that had bound the Skinner brothers together. A youthful passion for the outdoors glued their relationship.

Dan could clearly recall the day when he and André set off to hunt ducks in a cattail marsh separated from the ocean by a long ridge of low frontal dunes. Rising waters had been trapped behind the mounds of sand. The buttress had developed over decades into a freshwater sanctuary favored by waterfowl. The marsh was filled with the withered trunks of stunted dead snags, ghost-like images of the once-proud conifers.

There was only one accessible spot adaptable for clear shooting. When the boys arrived an hour before sunrise, they were disappointed to find Tom LaCross already settled into the solitary cattail blind.

"Come in, boys," he said. "If you don't mind sharing with an old man." Graciously, the Tsimshian made room for the brothers inside the camouflaged shelter. It was tight. Even then—a few years before Dan was lucky enough to indulge into the scout's secrets—Tom silently held court.

Fortunately for the boys, there wasn't much time for gossiping. Swarming through the first dull light, the waterfowl broke upon them, twisting and turning with dramatic bursts of speed. A strong west wind blew that day—a storm brewing off the ocean—and the mallards, geese and pintail sought shelter inland from the northwest winds and wild tides. The boys were soon sore from their shotguns' kick as the gun bruised their respective shoulders. The brothers were shooting but not hitting. Most of the waterfowl in the blind were the result of Tom's fine marksmanship. He had twelve, the boys three. The brothers were embarrassed. Tom remained quiet, his taciturn nature further prompting the boys' unease.

Finally, in a lull, Tom said, "Want to shoot ducks, you got to learn to properly lead the birds. You boys got no swing. You just point that shotgun. Jab, then shoot. Bam, bam. You got to follow through. Watch me now. Watch the end of the barrel. Watch the swing."

He demonstrated on his next few pass shots as his count rose to fifteen.

Later, he said, "My old man could shoot the eyes out of a running coyote. He was a true deadeye. Never saw better. The old man said, 'Forget the rules.' He said that shooting was a 'feelin' thing.' Listen, boys," he said, drawing his shotgun smoothly through the air. "Imagine the duck's speed. Swing your barrel through them birds as you move past their heads. Pick just one. Lead by five, six, or seven lengths of the bird's body, dependin' on its speed or the strength of the wind. Mallard, he faster than a widgeon. The sprig faster than either. It's a feelin' thing—remember? But no man should ponder pulling that trigger. Ought to just happen naturally. When the moment's right, just squeeze it off. Other than the kick of the shotgun, you won't even be aware that you've taken the shot."

For the rest of the day, Tom spoke few words, but the boys shot better, and in time, they became keen marksmen.

The brothers hunted with Tom many times after that. There was seldom a formal invitation. The Native man and the two brothers seemed to just happen upon each other. Perhaps they preferred the same spots. Did Tom in his unpretentious way allow the encounters to take place? No matter. He was a fine teacher. Later, there would be chance meetings in the woods and rivers and other wilderness environs that surrounded Kilnook. But it was in that duck blind that a kinship blossomed.

The following year, the boys' father drowned. The brief times they spent with Tom couldn't alter the loss of a father and would never fully replace him. Still, Dan and André felt something irrevocable in the developing bond between themselves and the scout, something far beyond just an occasional encounter with the quiet, confident man. Dan plied Tom with questions about the trapper's lore, the mountain man's craft.

"Boy, you sure full of questions. Well now, how about this here answer?"

Time cleaved out a strong attachment. Over the next decade, the two men of different cultures worked closely together. Dan became a temporary deputy, Tom, the lawmen's eyes and ears. The working relationship bound them, but to the casual eye the relationship appeared mostly on a professional level. And perhaps it was. A bad one-time encounter seriously damaged the relationship, causing a keen friendship to slip away.

Through a crack in the smokehouse wall, Dan watched as sunrays streamed through a thick wedge of dirty-dishwater clouds. Maybe some of that earlier bonding with Tom was beginning to filter through in much of the same way that the winter light crisscrossed the room. Dan thought some more about what Black Wing had prophesied. Perhaps he would give his mentor another chance. Just maybe, he might give himself and his vendetta a little space to heal.

Peace Corps, 1972

Katherine lay on a simple cot in a grass hut. The setting didn't matter to her now. She was red-hot with fever. She was delirious. Back in America, nobody knew she was sick. No coworkers were expected for several weeks. None of the medicines she had brought worked. Katherine didn't even know what was killing her. And even if she had, she had no way to communicate it to the outside world. Her radio had been dismantled. Letters took a week to get out. Traditional medical care was unreachable. Katherine was close to falling into a coma.

Her Honduran friends brought in a woman from a tiny village—a few thatched huts—that was buried deep in the jungle. The woman, a shaman, brought indigenous medicines with her. She covered Katherine's chest with a poultice concocted from jungle plants pounded with a mortar and pestle. All night a bonfire burned outside the hut. Katherine's new friends gathered as she lingered, her face flushing beet red as her temperature soared.

In a deep hallucination, Katherine envisioned a soldier in camouflage fatigues. He was slinking through the jungle. Perhaps, she thought, the soldier was searching for someone or something that lay beyond her field of perception. Or perhaps from the vista of her dreamworld, the soldier appeared to be hiding from danger.

His bearded face has been shaved, and his short dark hair is covered with a steel helmet. His handsome face smeared with black grease that reminds her of war paint. Katherine realizes that the soldier is Paul and that he is searching for her. She knows instinctively two enemies are stalking her lover. One is her own government. Her nation is exposing him to deadly danger. They are separating him from her. The second enemy is the Viet Cong. In the darkest of jungle nights, they are hunting her lover. And, like the Americans, they are a very capable and disciplined army. Unlike the Americans, they are protecting their homeland. Their ante remains high.

His eyes ghost back and forth, moving frantically until they settle upon her. She remembers suddenly how his steely eyes attracted her. She hears Paul's words then, his voice penetrating through the miasma of the dreamworld.

"There are no governments, really. Just people in flux. Politicians can't stop the committed. Only fear can. Often men are guided by ignorance or prejudice. Many times they can't recognize their weaknesses. Nations are no different."

Suddenly, instead of the soldier, a young boy is standing before her. Katherine realizes that the apparition is still her Paul. And then that disappears as well, replaced by jungle, thick and lush and dark. Her lover has disappeared.

Katherine's mind tripped back to the hut. Her hearing was amplified. Every one of her senses seemed amplified. She was sure that she was being baptized in an abstract cloud of brilliant colors—a kaleidoscope of colors. The medicine woman continued to sing in an intoxicating timbre. The woman chanted deep into the night, into the early morning. A nocturnal landscape filled with jeweled stars and constellations thicker and more vibrant than Katherine ever remembered.

The woman placed large oval leaves over Katherine's eyes and, with a needle dipped in a blood-red liquid, drew a long thin incision along the loin of Katherine's feverish leg. When she finished, the old woman danced and sang and chanted in a beautiful, intoxicating voice that lingered in the hut like steaming tea. Her sweet soprano voice sounded like a nighthawk. Outside, the villagers heard a high, piercing wail followed by an extended silence. During that lull, the medicine woman prayed.

In the morning the air carried the scent of flowers. Katherine rose from her bed as if she had been awakened from a rapturous sleep. She walked across the beach, entered the sapphire-colored ocean, and bathed in the salty water. She felt as if she was levitating. She spread her hair across the water surface, a veil of gold surrounding her head. She floated on her back. The water touched her as if the liquid was possessed with a million tiny fingers, each one caressing. She felt as if she was being seduced.

Katherine glided back to the hut unaware of her footfall. The water that had anointed her rolled down her legs and drew rivulets onto the white beach sand.

Later, the villagers put together a feast of fruit, rice, nuts, and smoked fish. The woman who saved her life was gone.

Katherine never saw her again. Never even got to say, "Thank you."

CHAPTER SIXTEEN

I am trying to save the knowledge that the forest and this planet are alive and give it back to you who have lost the understanding.

—Paiakan, contemporary Kayapo

Along the coast, springtime emerged, first in dabbles and daubs of rich color to offset winter's gray face and then in broad, dominant brushstrokes. The Haisla people called this time of year "green up." Those swathes of vibrant color were most noticeable on the alder trees that lined both banks of the Kilnook River. The limbs were tinged with dabs of color that spoke to the fine, ruddy feathers on the head of a male canvasback duck. The hardwood trees had endured another long winter. So had Rebecca Skinner.

The mountain snow was melting, freshets stirring, cold water racing. Near the mouth of the Kilnook River, celadon-hued glacier water galloped across ancient stones, always heading downstream to the great mother of all waters, the Pacific Ocean. The sprouting leaves on the bare limbs would soon turn again, tinting the forest with a rich phthalic-green.

In deep river currents, muddy water spiraled across broken boulders and fist-sized stones, then eddied into soft pirouettes, flowing into deep, platinum-colored basins. The river drew shallow, then deepened, always prepared to fill whatever void waited around the next corner. Still high from the mountain runoff, the water charged hard. Shrill above the aqueous rustle came the bugle call of the jay, a resounding "shock, shack-shack-shack" that intonated the arrival of a rebirth, of optimism and warm bright days. Spring was fleshing out.

The color and smell of the new season was an emancipation after the long months of ice and cold. The four-legged ones felt it at once and stirred eagerly from their earthen dens.

Rising before dawn, Rebecca savored the change. She was warmed by the sensuous touch of spring air carried along by a soft ocean breeze that swept off the ocean and up the river. She smelled sweetness in the air and the sensuous bouquet gladdened her.

As she went about her chores, she thought about her solicitation with the Native in Old Kilnook. She reasoned, however, that most likely, nothing would materialize from the encounter. Still, she refused to give up hope. Rebecca held to the promise but plotted alternatives. Her mind was constantly scheming. Each day she anticipated deliverance. No matter how fragile her expectation, hope swelled. Where was Dan? Certainly, he was alive. Certainly! Would he suddenly appear like the long-abandoned prodigal son, reunited once again? Rebecca was a strong woman who believed in the power of prayer, and, as of late, there had been an abundance of that around the Skinner household.

The sun rose brightly out of the east, across the buttress of magenta-colored mountains that shadowed the wilderness beyond the farm. As the rising sun elevated, Rebecca's instincts soared. She sensed unnatural movement along the river trail.

She stalled, pitchfork in hand. Silage tumbled from the steel tines. Quickly, her eyes experienced a subtle motion, an unexpected stir in the trees—no more—but she was sure that someone was approaching the farm through the arbor of conifers that bordered the river. Perhaps, she reflected, the motion was only the stir of songbirds or a larger animal. Maybe a mother deer with her fawn. But by then her instincts were shouting caution, or perhaps, deliverance. Rebecca was a woman who trusted her instincts. After all, she had spent a decade around Dan. His wilderness savvy forecast a sixth sense, a trapper's intuition.

Yes, she thought, something was afoot in the grove, and as she contemplated furtive movements, another small flurry of shadow and light bolstered her expectation. These were no songbirds. A flutter constricted into a jolt in her abdomen. She heard Dan preaching his mountain mantra, his overt caution. She had no reason to anticipate friend or foe, but she prayed for allies. Other than Sally, Rebecca didn't have many friends left in the small coastal town. Briefly, she considered that the commotion might be her female friend, then remembered that Sally was asleep in Rebecca's own bed. *Silly me*, she thought. Besides, stealth was not one of her faithful companion's attributes.

As her eyes adapted to the shadow, she made out the feeble outlines of two men. Her heart thumped harder as she realized that the men were watching her. She could distinguish the silhouettes of their bodies now, a nimbus of darker shades against a boundary of brambles and evergreens. The shapes stirred. She supposed they realized that they, too, were being watched.

The birds somersaulted from the thick huckleberry and salmonberry bushes, charging across the field in an audible scramble of fluttering feathers and birdsong.

The two men stepped forward, and her heart raced even faster. These were the Haisla. Immediately, she recognized one of the two as the man she had hoped to persuade to be her scout. Had that been just the month before? Suddenly, time seemed to move in slow motion.

She searched her head for a remembrance of his name. She had spoken it just days before—finally confessing her visit and her intentions to Sally—and she felt silly about her lack of memory. She felt anxious and a bit rattled. She remembered the Native's sensitive eyes and strong face, his muscular body and the steadiness of his gaze. A mixture of emotions swelled in her chest, but mostly, she felt hopeful. The farmyard spun in a haze as she stepped forward to greet them.

Richard Washington—she remembered then—and spoke the name to herself. Then she remembered the rest: Spirit Runner. She repeated his name out loud, running the words through her dry lips. She repeated it twice more, hoping not to forget. As if she might. Yes, she was excited. Rebecca realized her hands were quivering.

Unaware of her own footfall, Rebecca crossed the remaining distance between herself and the two Natives. The two men stood awkwardly before her, appearing far more uncomfortable than she imagined herself to be. Rebecca reached her hand across the several feet of crisp spring air, all that divided her from the two copper-skinned men. Her mind applauded her action. She had just crossed that invisible line drawn between White and Red. At that moment she was very conscious of the distances that segregated the two cultures. She felt a heap of emotion and had no idea how to sort it all out.

"Hello," she said, plain and simple.

The two men nodded and smiled but offered no words. Their smiles appeared genuine, if not a bit bashful. Their faces reflected strength through their clear dark eyes. As the sun rose over the mountaintops, they squinted, their eyelids folding into narrow slits. Rebecca felt instantly warmed by the depth of their wordless greetings. It occurred to her that they might feel apprehensive standing before a White woman.

"Welcome," she said.

More silence. More smiles. The men stood steady and straight, but no stance could disguise their awkwardness.

"Will you please come in? Come into my home?"

She led them across the field and onto the cabin's wooden porch. She knocked on the door three times, then grasped the handle. It felt awkward in her hand. The echo of her fist on the weathered fir paneling bled across the valley, reminding her of the resonance of a flicker, its audible, hard-headed clapping.

The Natives looked at each other and raised their eyebrows as if to say, "Why does she knock on the door of her own house?"

Rebecca perceived their furtive looks and felt a bit foolish. "Sally!" she shouted, hoping to prepare her friend for the unexpected visitors and, likewise, send a clue to the strangers.

Sally had been watching the reunion from the window. From the porch Rebecca heard the sound of Sally returning the .30-30 to its position against the kitchen wall. Then she heard her friend's footsteps as she moved toward the front door. A moment later the door opened with a laconic crack, and Sally stepped through. The door shut behind her. Sally stood tentatively before Rebecca and the two Natives, her back pressing into the solid wooden frame for support. Rebecca recognized the covert look in her friend's eyes and rushed out a message, trying to sound reassuring. "Sally, this is Richard Washington . . . Spirit Runner. Maybe you remember . . . remember me telling you about my visit a month ago."

"Oh yeah," Sally said, as warmly as she could muster. "Please come in. Coffee's on."

Those were Sally's first words to the Natives. Her voice stumbled out, hard off the tongue. A little too hard.

However subtle the inflection was, the Natives felt tension in the air. The strain was like an old song, a verse that won't go away: *Red man, red skin, red savage. Red, red, red.* They knew the color. It didn't look anything like the skin on their faces. The Natives remembered who they were. They were Haisla, and they were proud.

Sally entered first. The two Haisla followed reluctantly. They had never been invited into the home of a White woman. Never. They moved expectantly into the kitchen where Sally pulled out two chairs and motioned for them to sit. Her gesture was stiff.

Both men glanced at the .30-30 where it rested against the wall. Their eyes fastened onto each other. Spirit Runner's mouth revealed a slight twist, a look that was hard to read. Neither man felt endangered. But the rifle reminded them of conflicts between the two cultures.

"Please," Sally implored, her voice softening suddenly, as if she'd just realized that her manners needed an adjustment.

It was quiet while the coffee was served.

Rebecca finally broke the silence. "Thank you for coming," she said. Her voice revealed strain. A month to prepare for this rendezvous, but now she felt that her best intentions had abandoned her.

Overhead, the geese were moving north. *Already,* she thought. Her concentration was interrupted by the cries of the great birds. She wondered where her Dan was at that very moment. Knew that if he were nearby, he would be listening to the high-pitched cackling, nature's proclamation that seasonal change was on the way.

Gathering herself, she turned and gestured toward Sally. "This is my friend, Sally Walton. She has stayed with me this month while . . . well . . . while Dan has been gone. I haven't met . . . "

In a maladroit manner, she reached out her hand toward the second Native. She assumed the other man was the tracker whom Spirit Runner had promised to locate.

"This is Man Hides Good. My friend. Yes, we know about Dan Skinner. Even in our village. That is why we come. I not forget you. Not forget your husband or my promise. Man Hides Good a fine scout. He know the wilderness like nobody else in our clan."

"Well, thank you. I was hoping . . . " Rebecca reached for her coffee then, feeling a compulsion to move her hands, to steady herself. All the while she was groping for direction. When Rebecca didn't find the right words, she broke open the conversation in a rush of sentiment that belied her fears. "You have come to help me find Dan?" Although the words were abrupt, they helped her collar her courage.

The two Haisla studied her intently but offered no additional thoughts.

Rebecca glanced sideways at Sally. Her friend winked in support.

Man Hides Good poured an extra two heaping teaspoons of sugar into the black coffee, then added a shot of cream. Most of the North Coast tribes preferred their coffee laced with ample doses of sugar. Cream was dessert. The Haisla were no exception.

Man Hides Good held the silver spoon delicately in his callused hand as if it were hot or a foreign object. Traditional Haisla eating utensils were carved from fine-grained alder or from the roots of the spruce tree. The most coveted ladles, however, were shaped from the horns of a mountain goat, the rarest of four-legged creatures.

The teaspoon circled the cup four then five times as if it had a mind of its own. Man Hides Good poured more cream into the coffee. The cream came from Helen the cow. The drag of the spoon cut a trail through the liquid, and a soft creamy wake followed behind. He appeared fascinated by the motion.

Much like a child, Rebecca thought.

The trail drawn from the cream in the coffee reminded Man Hides Good of the deep eddies swirling down the Kilnook River during the spring freshet, when the river was high and muddy from silt and debris.

He appeared deep in thought. Man Hides Good had never owned or used a cup and saucer. As far as that went, he had never owned a pocket watch or any one of the fancy timepieces that the Bostons constantly referred to. Man Hides Good was driven by the sun and the stars, by tides and natural forces. He remained perplexed by the constant motion of the Whites, their lack of patience.

Rebecca was patient now. She restrained her heartfelt emotions but couldn't ignore the strong rapid beat of her heart.

Man Hides Good picked up the thin-skinned porcelain cup and cautiously held it between his thumb and forefinger, imitating the women. Watching the scout out of the corner of her eye, Rebecca realized he was examining the cup's intricate details. Rebecca owned four such China cups. They had belonged to her mother.

Suddenly, Man Hides Good turned his gaze upon Rebecca. Slowly, as if he were choosing each word individually, he spoke. "Yes, we come to help. We find Dan Skinner. You trust us. We come help. Sorry now, we need talk about money. Sorry."

"How much money?" Rebecca's voice revealed a shade of suspicion.

"Twenty dollars."

That was a lot of money to Rebecca, particularly since her ability to gather it had run as dry as tinder.

Before she answered, Sally poked in. "I've got it. That's fine. Tell me, though, what have you in mind? I mean, how will you find one man in all that wilderness?"

"With the help of the Creator."

The answer agitated Sally. She rocked her body in the chair and shook her head. The Haisla watched her without comment.

Man Hides Good continued. "If possible, we find Dan Skinner. We work very hard. This land I know well. If clues are left, I spot them. If Dan Skinner leaves trail, I find!"

The tracker turned to the taller, raven-haired man sitting next to him. "Spirit Runner, he come with me. Good together. We find your man. Dead or alive. We find. No find, no money."

"When?"

"Later. Thirty days. Ice gone."

"How do we go?"

"We?"

Sally's last words took the Natives aback. Their eyes shifted warily like a cagey salmon skirting suddenly from the shallows into a deep river pool, scattering at the earliest sighting of foreign shadow or something more dominating, a predator on two legs or four.

Sally interrupted their covert glances, her words leveling. "You can bet on that. Mm-hmm. Rebecca goes for sure. We'll see about me, but y'all can probably count on it."

Man Hides Good shifted his eyes back to his friend. Spirit Runner nodded as if to say that Rebecca was to be trusted. Her friend as well. The Natives didn't have to say it out loud; two women would likely encumber their speed and perhaps whatever chance they had of finding the White man. Finding him alive.

Spirit Runner answered Sally's earlier question for his friend. "River canoe, using paddles and poles. Maybe sometimes on foot. Pull canoe with rope."

His eyes drew a steady bead, moving from one woman to the other. "Thirty days, then. When snow and ice melt. Allow safe passage."

Man Hides Good nodded in affirmation. "Be here at farm thirty days, one moon. You are ready, please. Must pack food, bedding, and warm clothes. How your man say. 'Possibles?'"

Sally rose and went into the bedroom. When she returned, she was carrying ten silver dollars.

"Down payment," she said, then began to divide the coins into two even piles, laying the silver on the table. Oddly, she thought about Judas Iscariot and the thirty pieces of silver.

Man Hides Good took the dollars and rose. He smiled at the two women, backed away from the table, and moved awkwardly toward the door. The door squeaked on its hinges, and then he was gone.

Spirit Runner sat a little longer. His eyes settled on both women. He nodded and then smiled. Rubbed his chin between his callused forefinger and thumb. His hands said fisherman. Said nets, cold water, salmon. They were working hands. Because of the color of his skin, his options were limited in the White world of employment.

Both women were comfortable with strong hands and hard backs. They knew the look. Rebecca had married a working man. Most of Sally's customers were loggers and fishermen. It was rumored that she had lost a lover to the war and had fled north as a young woman. But who was to say? On this subject, Sally remained mute.

"We find your man," Spirit Runner said with finality. "We return in one month."

He was a man who spoke without embellishment. Neither Rebecca nor Sally realized this was a custom of his people. They should have understood that English was a second language, one born out of necessity. This verbal shorthand was their awkward way of communicating with the outside world. But his simple words had a sheen of truth to them. Both women sensed that.

Spirit Runner rose. Like Man Hides Good before him, he moved quickly out the door.

Sally's eyebrows lifted as her eyes settled on her friend. "You thinking about what all this means?"

Rebecca faced her friend's concerned gaze. The question was a bit ridiculous to her. It was *all* she had been thinking about for months. "Damn it, Sally, of course! I think constantly about Dan. And how to get there, wherever that is. And when to start, to say nothing about whether we can trust our new friends, though I believe we can. Something tells me."

Sally interjected. "Hope you're right, Dear."

Rebecca was testy, but she knew where Sally was coming from. "Sorry, I keep rolling all this over in my mind, in and out of my sleep. Fitful, I guess you'd call it. Keep sorting out parcels of problems. Won't let me be. Instead of resolving something, the list just keeps growing. Only thing I know for sure is that I must find him—Dan—or what's left of him."

She bit her lip then. Let her eyes drop toward the fir-plank floor.

Sally felt the potential of her friend's tears again. "I'm coming with you, honey."

The thought of Sally heading into the wilderness to search for her husband caught Rebecca off-guard. An impossibility, she reasoned. Rebecca had never considered this course of action. "No. Absolutely not." Her teary face turned taut with conviction. Rebecca was vehement. For a moment she set aside her sadness. Her foot thumped on the fir flooring. "If you think I'm going to risk both of our lives, you've got—"

"Whoa, Nellie," Sally interrupted. "Just how in the hell you think you're going to roll out of here without me?"

"Sally, I'm warning you."

"Listen to me, Rebecca Skinner. We're in this together. I haven't got any other place to go. No family. No friends. Not even a man. Rebecca, whatever happens after this is finished, we're gonna leave this mule-headed town. You, me, and Dan. You hearing me, lady? You'll have to leave your farm. Me, my business. I'm not going back. I've had it up to here with Kilnook." Sally raised her finger horizontally and whipped it across her throat.

Against her better judgment, Rebecca grinned, realizing what a powerful ally she had in her best friend.

"Those good citizens of Kilnook can get by quite well without me," Sally continued. "They can cook their own gol' dang food. You better count on me, Rebecca Skinner."

Sally took a deep breath and composed her thoughts. Her face was flushed. Rebecca saw that her friend's insistence was driven by concern and a steady pulse of affection.

"Honey," Sally added, "you ever thought that if Dan is . . . still alive . . . he might find his way back here?"

"Sure. Think about it all the time. Keep wondering why he hasn't. Maybe . . . no. We will find him! Or he'll find us. I believe that. I've seen it in my dreams."

Sally lifted her eyebrows, askance.

As the two friends paused their conversation, a blaze of sunlight lifted above the eastern mountains, across the meadow, and into the ancient grove of spruce and alder. From high branches the airborne melody of dozens of tiny juncos rang out like the jangle of brass horse bells. The sound skipped along the trail and down over the river. Just outside the quiet of the kitchen, the sharp throaty music of another bird, a red-winged blackbird, banked its sharp melodious cry above the sharp crackle of burning kindling in the firebox. But Rebecca heard none of it. Her thoughts were far away from the farm.

Rebecca's mind was scheming. The two Natives had just disappeared back into the woods along the river trail that led downstream to the Haisla village. In thirty days, hopefully, they would be back. In thirty days, the four improbable players would be following Dan's cold trail. Unless Dan mysteriously reappeared. Unless. How many times had Rebecca prayed for that?

Silence fell around Rebecca like a shroud.

In the grove, the songbirds settled, their music suddenly restrained. As Rebecca moved across the kitchen, the only sound in the cabin was the squeak of the floorboards. As if she had just arrived at a decision, Rebecca inhaled deeply. Breaking the lull, she turned toward Sally, who had taken on a pensive mien, an unusual circumstance for the big, blustery woman.

Rebecca's voice interrupted her thoughts. "Guess we'd better get packing. You ever pushed a cedar canoe against a swollen river?"

"No, honey, but I'm one tough cookie."

Knowing the truth behind those words, Rebecca smiled. *Maybe*, she thought, *more obstinate than tough*. Secretly, she liked the idea of traveling with her best friend. She always enjoyed Sally's company.

"An adventure, Sally. Let's pray it ends well."

Sally's smile was as bright as all the daylight flooding through the cabin's small glass windows.

Dan was a free man—free as long as he didn't attempt to escape. Free if his good manners continued. Free if his captors didn't change their minds and imprison or injure him. Dan refused to think beyond that.

His shackles were removed. He felt liberated and ready—more than ready—to move about the village.

He reviewed the irony of his position. The Natives might expect their captive to run. *If only*, Dan thought. *I shall. And I will. And soon*. He set his jaw determinedly.

His captors appeared oddly relaxed about his movements and Dan found the circumstances peculiar. On that overcast morning, sitting in a secret village many miles from his home, he was chewing over a bushel full of questions. Black Wing continued to caution. *Well, I know which way that sticks float.* Blind or not, Black Wing appeared to fathom the gyrations of Dan's mind. *Uncanny,* he thought again, and not for the last time. The elder somehow anticipated his moves, jumping two steps ahead of his every question. Dan was stumped.

Before a breakfast of salmonberries and eulachon grease and one goose egg—before the sunrise broke above the eastern sky—Dan found himself wandering along the village's northern perimeter. He moved higher into a valley that cradled a small creek. The waterway fed a larger stream the Natives called "Big Trout River." Dan felt his captors' steady eyes following his every move.

As he ambled through lush evergreen forest, he was struck by an undulating cushion of moist air. A cool mist had woven a wraithlike blanket through the flat cedar branches, tinting the landscape as if a magician had covered everything with a magical spell.

He headed uphill. The forest was unusually quiet. The mood of the misty air deadened nature's song: the tiny songbirds, small and large mammals, and the invisible, cushioned movements of underground critters. Dan reasoned that he had spooked the creatures. Generally, he was too cautious for that to happen. Under his practiced shuffle, a twig snapped abruptly. The sharp crack stirred the sleepy forest and startled the trapper. He stopped and adjusted his step. Maybe, he thought, it was time to begin wearing moccasins again. He glanced down at his bedraggled leather boots.

He had nothing to hide that morning—he wasn't hunting or being hunted—but like many other animals that applied a diet of stealth to their daily activities, Dan was a creature of carefully nurtured habit. He preferred to move as the critters moved. *Never, never, give yourself away. Never drop your guard.* For the thousandth time, Dan repeated the scout's mantra.

He moved deeper into the forest, following the trail as it rose above the stream. As Dan crested a steep ridge, he was startled to find Black Wing below, knee-deep in the cold mountain stream. The blind man was facing sunrise, his back turned toward Dan.

Black Wing's arms were drawn high above his head in what appeared to be a salutation, or perhaps some form of a chant or prayer. The elder appeared to be offering thanks to the mother sun. Her unfurling rays were already dissolving the morning mist. Black Wing was speaking in a language that Dan had never heard before. Unknown to him, Black Wing was praying in Kunghit, a Haida dialect from the most southerly of the Haida clans. The tribe was nearly extinct.

Dan posted up as still as the great trees. A ruffed grouse settled onto a hemlock bough just yards over his head. The bird was unaware of Dan's presence. Dan's concentration remained on Black Wing. There was a poetry-like cadence to the elder's words. His movements were slow and precise.

It became clear to Dan that Black Wing was praying. What force or power the prayers attended, Dan could not divine. He reasoned that both men from radically different cultures were drawn to a similar God. Dan felt bound to Black Wing through their common love of nature.

As he watched the elder, Dan found himself drawn into the old man's litany. He felt a dislocation, a detachment between his body and his mind, and then—inexplicably—he felt lightheaded, and then lighter yet. The sensation was frightening.

Black Wing's chant rolled on. The elder's words ricocheted inside Dan's head and left no room for his own thoughts. They were temporarily replaced by an inner vison. He saw a cavern where sounds bounced off cold stone walls, becoming a music that flooded back in upon itself. And then, he felt his body rocking and swaying and lifting. He was aware of momentary fear and then of letting his anxiety fly away. As he let go, he became lighter than air, aware suddenly that his spirit soared high above the tall, virgin trees that dominated the valley. Dan ascended like a raven. As he rose in the cold air, a faraway music flooded through his head. He felt at one with the elder and with a greater undefinable force. And then everything went dark.

Dan jolted awake. Black Wing had come up from the stream and was standing directly before him, face to face. That was the first surprise. The second came when the elder began to speak. The elder's eyes were blind, but Dan realized that somehow, they were seeing him as nobody had ever seen him before, not even Rebecca. Dan was consumed by wonder.

Black Wing's eyes pierced his psyche, that part of Dan that remained foreign, even to himself. Still lightheaded, Dan listened as the elder spoke in a language that was Dan's own but impassioned with mesmerizing grace. Until the day before, Dan had no reason to suspect that the elder was even capable of speaking the "queen's" language. Now Black Wing's words hung in the mountain air and swirled around Dan like campfire smoke.

"My father walked me every morning of my youth to the seashore where we prayed before the ocean and the rising sun," Black Wing continued to speak in English, and somehow, none of that came as a surprise. All this and the last two months were finally beginning to make sense. "My father prayed daily to the Creator. That Spirit, he believed, rested in all things: plant, animal, and rock. That same energy washes freely in the sky, even now as we speak. It dashes against the beach. We breathe in that same spirit. It is in the air around us and offers grace to our person. And it floats mysteriously above the ocean waters. But then you know this!"

As if gathering in pieces of the sky, Black Wing lifted his hands heavenward, his palms open. Dan was stunned by the elegance of the elder's words. How was this possible? Not even the occasional politician or the circuit minister could begin to match the elder's eloquence.

"My father gave thanks every morning to the Creator. He offered me this gift. Some call it prayer. We would stand before God, before the Creator. We would reach out and a great force fell upon us, surrounded us. My father opened the door to the other side. That journey is so simple, yet so many people from both our cultures never find the trail. I can tell you, Dan Skinner, the value of this gift. It is a great treasure, the richest that the Great Spirit can bestow on any human being. I continue my father's quest. Just minutes ago you found me offering thanksgiving just as my father did and his father before him. I've done this all my life."

With the forefinger of his right hand, Black Wing reached out and touched Dan on the forehead. Dan felt his lightheadedness lift. Never in his life had he experienced such a sublime feeling. He shuddered from a surge of emotion. He wanted her then. He wished Rebecca could experience the old man and his spiritual gift. He wondered if he would be able to explain the depth of the elder's power. That was of course, if their rendezvous ever took place.

"You wonder why I have deceived you? Why I have not spoken to you in your own tongue, in the queen's language? There is a time and order to all things. I did not believe you were ready to hear me, and I stayed distant. You must believe me when I tell you that I never intended to trick you. Now, each day, we become closer. We now come together as brothers from different cultures. Trust me, Dan Skinner. I am your friend."

Dan was silent. He was mesmerized, his mouth dry.

"Again, I must warn you. Do not run from our village. I tell you this would be a fatal mistake. I tell you that because I care for you. You must see this by now.

"Come with me and give thanks. Pray with me for our one family, yours and mine. I have need now for your eyes. Mine have left me once again."

"But you found me here," Dan stammered, his words sounding awkward in the mountain air.

"No," Black Wing replied, "you called to me. Do you not remember? You greeted me from high above. At first I thought it was Raven. No, I . . ." Black Wing hesitated, choosing his words with infinite care. "Come," he said in a calmer voice. "Lead me now. We will talk of this later."

Dan took Black Wing's arm. The sun broke higher over the valley. It reared above the great cathedral tops of the ancient cedar, then plummeted upon the two men in rays of golden light. Dan felt baptized in wonder.

Both men stood in an ancient valley. Dan was struck by the *oneness* of the mountains and the forest. He felt whole and quiet and free, and empowered by his affection for the elder. He wondered why such a sentiment had remained so distant, particularly when the feeling was so natural. So joyful.

"Where have you come from, Grandfather? Where was your home before you found this valley?"

The elder answered him warmly. "I come from the islands far west of here. I was born to the Haida nation under the eagle crest, born to the Kunghit Haida."

In a shift as deft as a gambler's hand, Dan detected sadness in the elder's voice.

"They are gone now. My family. My friends. They are all gone. My village is deserted. Only few old men live in Skidigate, farther to the north."

Black Wing went quiet, obviously saddened by his own declaration. He slipped into a gentle reverie. The birds were back again, their melodic voices awakened. As the sun rose, waves of warmth washed around Dan like an embrace.

Black Wing's eyes squeezed shut. Dan thought the elder had slipped away into old memories. Memories and pain. One followed the other like shadow followed light. Dan waited patiently for the elder to speak.

"Before this tribe there were many others."

The old man stood so still and erect. His words confused Dan. Black Wing's eyes remained closed.

"I don't understand."

"That may come later."

"And all the languages? Where did you learn those?"

"I have learned different languages by listening to the speakers. By sitting still and opening my heart to the spirits of these many different voices."

"Can you show me how to do that?"

"No. You can only learn by yourself. But I can teach you the beginning of the path."

High above the valley, disguised in the thick evergreens, Dan caught the movement of a human. He realized he was being watched. His captors were taking precautions. He would not be allowed to escape the village easily.

Dan set all that aside. For the moment, he was living in a life that he had never imagined. He had been handed a gift. There was no running from that.

The two men turned then, one seeing, the other blind, and together they began the trek down the trail that led back to the village. Though the elder was old in body, Dan found Black Wing to be a spry, if bowlegged, companion. He chuckled at the way the old man walked.

Black Wing picked up on the gist of Dan's amusement. Rocking back and forth like a drunk seaman, he hammed it up. With Dan guiding, the shaman tottered along, listing left and then right. Black Wing was full of surprises. If Dan had learned little else, he now felt better prepared for the unexpected.

The two men cleared another ridge and followed the trail back into the village.

As they entered, Dan spotted Charlie trotting up the trail toward them. Dan figured he was looking for Black Wing, but Charlie showed no surprise in finding Dan leading his uncle.

In Haisla, Charlie asked, "You had a good meditation, Grandfather?"

Black Wing nodded, then broke into a smile that stretched across his entire face. His teeth glittered in the sunlight. By then the rising sun had broken through the mist. Morning clouds were dispersing at a gallop. The day was turning warm. "Yes, nephew, I have found a new friend." Black Wing turned to Dan and spoke in English. "You join us, now?"

"I'm working on it."

"That is very good, Dan Skinner. Very good."

To Dan, Black Wing's smile was as bright and refreshing as the morning sun itself.

The eagle soared down the great breach that divided the granite mountains and shaped the great valley below. It flew above the river where ice had gouged a slow but persistent path for tens of millions of years and beyond.

It was the time of year that the Southern Kwakiutl, Haisla and Tsimshian netted copious quantities of the candlefish they called the *eulachon*. They netted the slender fish by the millions. They ate them fresh, boiled them, and processed the rich oil as a condiment and preservative for salmon and berries, for the long, cold winters when meat was often unattainable. They covered roots and berries with the rich oil or traded the "grease" to other coastal tribes.

For the Boston people, the condiment took some getting used to. That was being kind. Certainly, that was the reaction Dan's displayed on his face during his first tasting. His mouth puckered with protest. But the Natives prized the grease. The fish oil was exchanged for handsome trade goods up and down the northwest coast. As with so many other customs, Dan adapted slowly.

When the ice departed in the early spring, the Haisla wandered down the Kilnook River, seeking the delicacy. Fishing camps interrupted the slumber of winter's solitude, the long months when the land was inundated with snow and ice.

As the eagle slipped across the south wind, it saw few visible reminders of the people whose seasonal gathering and feasting had been the keystone of the Native culture for generations beyond memory. Only as his flight drew him closer to the river's mouth did he spot a few Natives in their traditional gathering places. The sightings made his heart soar.

Soon, the eagle was over the Skinner ranch. From a vista high in the air, he circled the farm in a slow, widening circle, searching for any glimpse of human activity.

As the eagle watched, two Native men stepped from the Skinner porch, leaving the cabin and crossing the farmyard. Both turned and watched the bird, lifting their hands in a sign of greeting toward the great raptor. Both were startled by the eagle's size. As the men disappeared downriver toward Kilnook, the eagle's keen eyes followed them until they entered the woods and slipped into shadow.

The eagle lifted a wing and fell away with the wind. He circled the farm two or three more times. On the final loop, he saw Rebecca step onto the porch and gaze downriver, her eyes watching as the two Haisla faded into the trees. The eagle dropped lower and let out a cry, shrill and clear in the spring air. The woman shaded her eyes with her right hand and looked up at the eagle.

"Sally!" she called excitedly. "Hurry out here. There's this eagle, the biggest I ever saw. It's a sign, Sally. A sign for sure."

The eagle rose effortlessly on an updraft and then disappeared upriver into the granite fjord that had been a pathway for his people for thousands of years.

Early Values

Katherine's mother taught her right from wrong. She raised Katherine to be a responsible woman. Often Katherine remembered those lessons and thought about the rules that bound her to the society of the twentieth century, and, at the same time, offered a crossroad, a retreat into her mother's world, an older world with different perspectives. Like every new generation, she wrangled with both sets of values.

"The meek shall inherit." How often had her mother offered up those words?

Katherine repeated the phrase out loud. In her formable years she had explored many of society's established rules. They were clearly intonated: work hard, get good grades, meet a nice man, get married, buy a home in the suburbs, raise children, and above all else, remember a woman's place.

Well, it hadn't worked out that way. Right or wrong, she was different. Aside from a few preordained rules, her mother was responsible for much of her independence. Her father too. There had never been a church. If anything, for her parents—especially her father—church was the deep woods and the snow-capped mountains, particularly Mt. Rainier, which he called Tahoma, and the wild, undulating waters that flooded from its steep, snowy flanks. Of course, Katherine didn't directly remember much of what her father believed—he had died so young—but, thankfully, her mom had preserved much of his philosophy. Hardly a day passed that Katherine didn't think of him, mentally reciting his stories and lessons and imitating his passions.

And now, standing on a distant beach, Katherine was remembering a discussion she'd had with a Native woman only a few weeks before. The woman compared her own experience of raising children to that of her daughters. The mother was a full-blooded Honduran woman.

"The young mothers today, they just say 'no' to their kids, over and over. They say, 'No. Go away now, I'm too busy.' When I raised my children, I did it differently. I said, 'You can't do that because . . . I explain everything. We explain the difference between right and wrong. Father and I, we let the kids know why we punish them. We didn't just say, 'No.' If they did not listen the first time, then we repeated the lesson until it became clear. We believed in discipline."

Sometimes it burned in Katherine like shame: she had no man and no children and wasn't sure she ever would. Paul had changed that—or ended it. She wasn't clear about all of the far-ranging consequences. Yes, things were always changing. But for now Katherine was interested in finding herself, finding her way forward. Love might just have to wait.

CHAPTER SEVENTEEN

The valley spirit never dies;
it is the woman, primal mother.
Her gateway is the root of heaven and earth.
It is like a veil barely seen.
Use it; it will never fail.

—Lao Tzu
Tao Te Ching

In the soft, flickering firelight, the wolf's yellow eyes found him. Like an arrow heading for the heart of a bull elk, a penetrating gaze riveted into Dan's face and held steady. And the row of bright bone teeth—well, they were fully capable of shredding a man's skin. At least in real life. And then the wolf retreated. Another human with a cedar face danced before him, and then another. Each represented an animal. Each told a story. Dan had never before been invited into the inner sanctum of the Native world of dance, fire, and celebration.

The ceremony fascinated him, stirring deep emotions in his mind that were at once primordial but ultimately rich and exotic. Dan had never been a man to get caught up in a crossfire over religious values, never pitted one belief against another. That night he was curious. He was witnessing a spectacle. His fortunes remained good. He had a front-row seat.

Dan was determined to keep an open mind, and he was captivated. He was too much of a rebel to fall for anyone's dogma, whether that be Christian, Buddhist, Native American or any other. Much as a man might enjoy watching a theater production or a ball game, he was observing a ritual, one both rich and fascinating. Tonight, the hometown crowd was putting on quite a show.

As his eyes accustomed to the dim light, Dan picked out the figure of Tom LaCross—White Bear—sitting by himself on the far side of the long, spacious lodge. Dan couldn't help but notice how the scout had healed rapidly. With the support of the guards, the Tsimshian now hobbled about the village.

Tom spent hours watching or participating in the tribe's activities. He was intrigued by the rituals. The daily activities in the village filled an emotional void, but Dan only guessed at the whole story.

Tom loved to play with the children. Likely, he was massaging an old wound that had festered since his aborted childhood among the Tsimshian. In return, the children heaped him with affection. Smiles were abundant. Lessons were imparted. Games were won and lost, lost and won.

Tom taught the children much that he had put to rest long ago. He may have believed that all his youthful sentiments had died with the scattering of his people, with the pox. But here, deep in the mountains, he was rediscovering his lost youth and, just maybe, remnants of those forgotten years.

On that spring evening as the sky filled with a flurry of stars, Tom was caught up in the ceremony. Like Dan, he was bewitched.

The ceremony was a dance of thanksgiving, of sharing and feasting. The ceremony preceded memory. Most winters, Native diet consisted predominantly of dried and stored supplies. Now the rivers were alive with the "swimmers," the great Tyee. And the forest was budding with edible riches. A person had to remain thankful. Bounty surrounded the tribe. The Creator was generous.

Dan chose his dinner from intricate woven baskets or from carved cedar bowls filled with salmonberries, roots, and wild legumes. Others contained fresh game and fish. After months of eating everything dried or coated in eulachon grease, he reveled in this new menu like a kid eating his first stick of hard candy. Roots that had been buried under deep snow during the long winter months now abounded. Women and children from the village gathered edible rhizomes, the roots of the clover and fireweed, shoots from delectable sprouts such as cow parsnip, wild rhubarb, and salmonberries.

As the ice broke up, the cagey steelhead and the succulent sea trout were caught in large numbers. Fishermen from the village watched as massive sheets of ice and snow disappeared into shrinking vortexes of spinning and melting islands.

Here was the salmon's final destination, a culmination that had led them—three, four, and five years earlier—into the ocean and back, following some primordial scent like a wilderness map all the way back to the mother stream. On this last leg of their final journey, the hens would lay their eggs by the thousands into stone nests called redds. The male—bucks or cocks—would fertilize them. Then the pair would die. Afterwards, the flesh and bones of their decayed bodies would release proteins into the same tributaries that spawned their young. To the Haisla, the cycle was holy. To most of the pioneers downriver, the abundance of the red-flesh salmon translated into cash.

This was how it had always been. Dan couldn't begin to imagine the ecological implications of nature's gyre. He couldn't understand how a wilderness such as this might ever become endangered. Over the last several years, his largest chore had consisted of slashing, clearing, and burning the great trees that populated his farm like unwelcome squatters.

When the salmon were prepared and brought before him, all he thought of was how good the flesh tasted. As far as Dan's inclination went—and scores of pioneers before and after him—the forests and rivers would always offer a never-ending supply of food, timber, and profit.

Dan was not sure how many of the fish were caught or how many had been traded. After several months among the Natives, he realized there must be an exchange or barter system among the disparate tribes living along the coast, or, perhaps, deeper inland. One night he was served whale blubber, another, seal flesh. Obviously, there was a link to the ocean. Dan assumed this was all done with untold stealth. It was best not to ask too many questions.

Once again a dancer appeared. A carved and painted mask of a black-eyed raven hovered before him. The head rested high on the dancer's forehead, but as the dancer spun, the beak sprang open. From inside the protruding bill, a second face of an otter man appeared, emerging much like a wooden puppet being pulled from a trap hidden behind a stage. Behind the second mask were two human eyes, and from the deep cavern of the mask, the man's gaze appeared feral and mysterious.

Dan thought about his church—thought about a religion he had never adopted. After his father's death, every Sunday morning his mother had dragged the two brothers down to the white-painted chapel. The boys spent hours on their knees praying to a deity they didn't pretend to understand. To these boys who coveted the call of the wild—the deep north woods—the ceremony was long and torturous. Once, during an hour-long communion service, André fainted. Kneeling in a protracted position for an extended time was too much for the boys. Even their mother was appalled. After that, the boys generally stayed clear of the Episcopalians.

Dan's memories drifted to a schoolteacher who read *Tom Sawyer* to his students. The brothers emulated the errant hero. As they grew, so did their adventures. The surrounding wilderness was the lure. They pursued their craving for the wilderness, hook, line, and sinker.

As near as Dan remembered, his spiritual connection began in the forest with the primal light at daybreak. The wild called to him in ways that were still beyond the reach of any explanation. He was at home there, and so was André. And wasn't that enough?

The dancer wore a traditional skirt of woven cedar bark, shredded cedar leggings, moccasins, capes, and red and black paint concocted from natural dyes: charcoal and colored clays and berries. The paint covered the man's torso and thighs.

A dancer gyrated before Dan and then spun away into a larger circle. Then, one by one, colorful and mythological masks careened before him. As each one folded into the shadows, another dancer would appear. Dan felt intoxicated by the freedom of the dance and the aura of celebration. But along with the festive nature of the dance, there was also an expression of thanksgiving.

Dan was having a flashback. Sitting in the lodge that represented another time and place, he remembered how, as a young man, he had emulated Tom LaCross. How, one day, oh, so long ago, he had promised himself that he would become a scout worthy of the Tsimshian, a man true to his craft. He wondered if he had attained that pinnacle, or if he ever would.

Black Wing sat on a raised dais toward the back of the darkened lodge. In the shallow light, his face appeared to be etched with joy. With two intricately carved rattles, he was keeping time with the music and following the motions of the dancers. He chanted in the language of the Haida. But through a haze of smoke and dancers, his blind eyes remained fixated on Dan Skinner.

Another dancer appeared, supporting a huge mask of a killer whale. The dancer's silhouette cut off Dan's view of Black Wing. A hand reached out, beckoning. Dan rose and followed.

Bashful at first, he stood alone. The man in the whale mask retreated until Dan was left in the middle of a human circle. A primal sound rose to his ears, rolling and pounding and reverberating with a deep bass resonance.

Out of the dancers came the young girl, Yellow Bird Singing, and Dan could no longer justify his reluctance to join in the celebration. With great patience, she led him through several dance steps until the rhythm of the music began to jangle in his head. Confidence smote him as his legs adjusted to the dancers' cadence. As the minutes swept by, he felt further at ease. The tempo of the music melded him naturally into the family of performers.

From his dais, Black Wing continued to watch Dan, a smile tattooed across the elder's face.

Across the floor, Tom was also watching. The scout's face reflected a tinge of amusement, followed by a glint of approval.

As Black Wing turned his blind eyes between White Bear and Dan, he couldn't help but to notice the growing bond between the two men. He imagined a renewed friendship. The thought dangled in front of him like a flame he sensed but couldn't touch. His mind danced back and forth.

As a sense of jubilation penetrated the room, the dancers stepped high and whirled like a pod of whales frolicking in the ocean's depths. The rhythmic beat of the rattle, drum, and whistle swelled from cedar wall to cedar wall. The dancers' bodies moved in unison to some genetic language, a current as old as humankind. Like the swell of an ocean wave, their arms and legs lifted and fell naturally. *Holy*, Dan thought. *Kind of holy.*

The rhythmic frenzy grew until the dance and the music coalesced into a pulse that reverberated down the lodge's long central corridor and then scampered out and into the night. A full moon brandished its yellow shadowed face down upon the village.

1971

In my dreams, midnight seas fed voraciously
On blues and violets of distant horizons.
I believe we were alone in that boat, just you and me
With a map to anywhere.

Katherine Skinner-Patterson—A poem for Paul

CHAPTER EIGHTEEN

Every one of us is, in the cosmic perspective, precious.

—Carl Sagan

The sky was already hinting at sunset as Dan sat alone, eating a dinner of boiled roots and venison steaming in a rich broth. The fresh meat was succulent and tender in his mouth.

Springtime had arrived, and the larger game animals had shuffled higher into the mountains. Game was far more abundant and Dan felt gladdened.

For the last several days, the weather had been warm and clear. The sky was a soft, mottled blue. Dappled into the field of blue were transparent flecks of pink and mother-of-pearl. Unusual, Dan thought, to have several such perfect days during a season that was usually wet and gray. But Dan wasn't complaining. Nor were his captors.

Tom wasn't complaining either. Dan had seen him hobbling around the village with the help of a wooden crutch. His hair had grown longer, hearkening back to his youth. His mustache shone otter-black and softened his stern, round face.

"Howdy."

Dan was startled by the greeting—startled to look up from his dinner and see Tom standing in front of him like a friendly spaniel. He couldn't remember the last time the scout had offered such a pleasant salutation, brief as it was. Dan lowered the cedar bowl and looked directly at him. "Care to sit?"

"Thanks. This leg still hurts some."

As he studied the man's injury, Dan felt a sudden sense of guilt.

Tom—his gaze quick and perceptive—seemed to gauge the meaning behind the furtive expression that crossed the White man's brow. "Listen, I'm long past the place of holding a grudge over this leg—or any other wound, far as that goes. I'd have done what you did.

"I'm shooting straight with you, Dan. I've liked you ever since you was a kid pup. Probably never showed as much as I felt.

"I like this village. Like it a lot. Takes me back some. Place shouldn't be here, but it is. Suspect you can determine the cut of things. The old man juggles the pieces. Your guess is as good as mine just how he does it."

Tom shifted from leg to leg. The sky was darkening. Dan's bowl of stew was cooling. "Three tribes here. Enemies once. He brought 'em together, bound 'em into one family. Don't have to tell you about old feuds . . . well, things change."

He drew a deep breath and thought some about his message before plowing ahead. "Don't suspect it can hold together. People can't hide here forever, even ones this crafty. Somebody will stumble onto this place. We did. Well, nearly.

"I'd like to stay and be part of it. So long as I can, that is. This here is about the closest thing I've had to a family since I was a kid."

Dan dipped into his stew and chewed on a hunk of meat—chewing over the scout's words at the same time. Was the gesture rude? Dan didn't care. He was hungry, and Tom was lost in thought. Both men were.

After the mouthful settled, Dan acknowledged Tom with a slight nod that said, "I'm listening."

The pain and exhaustion Dan felt as a result of his brother's death were not as acute as they had been. Long months had passed since André's demise, and that time had allowed healing to take place.

Dan shook himself from his thoughts and looked up. As their eyes met, Tom's face suddenly tensed, his lips pressing tightly together. Dan was baffled. He didn't fathom the expression. When Tom began talking again, there was anger in his voice. "I've carried bad memories for years, hard memories. The Tsimshian treated me far better than your people. They treated me like a son.

"Sorry to talk this way. But you Whites took away everything worth a damn. It's been hard. Hard on me for many years."

Hadn't Tom spelled out the same story just ten days before? But he was talking and Dan was listening. That was positive change, by God. Dan figured he would allow Tom his palaver, allow him to clear his mind.

But after a minute or two, Dan wasn't so sure. As Tom talked, Dan felt the tracker's anger winding up like a rattler. He felt the jangle of his temper. What he couldn't see was the pain brooding behind Tom's words.

"Finally, there wasn't anything to hold the tribe together. Weren't but a few of us left. My village was gone, my home, my only family. I drifted, found occasional work. Tried to blend in."

Tom was talking out his story as much for himself as for Dan's ears. He had already spoken plenty, much more than his usual allotment. Then, as if he had suddenly run out of words, he stopped talking and began remembering.

He was thinking about a White woman named Ruth Anne McCauley. A woman he had loved. He couldn't tell that story to just anyone. Particularly to a *White* anybody. The fact that he was speaking to Dan at all revealed an unusual allotment of trust.

Tom had met the trim, pretty woman while working a cannery job at Albert Bay. He had family there, an aunt and uncle. Best an Indian hoped for was cannery work or fishing for *the company*. He was grateful enough for that.

What stopped him were the woman's beautiful blue eyes. They were his mother's eyes, the translucent blue of the coveted blue trade beads. The young woman captivated him. Her persona grabbed him like a trap—quiet, reflective, and penetrating. He had never met a White woman like her. Stranded in memory—standing long ago on the thick Douglas fir planking of a cannery floor—Tom felt an emotion that he had long before set aside.

All this happened several years after the Canadian authorities dragged him from the small village of Tasska, far up the Kilnook Valley and placed him in a residential school at Port Alberni. He was thirteen years old. There, he was beaten ragged for the smallest infraction. Tom wasn't allowed to speak his own tongue. He didn't know what he had done wrong. He only knew that he got whipped every day. Got whipped in front of all the other boys: Kwakiutl, Haida, Salish, Nuu-chah-nulth, Tlingit, and Nuxalt. A hundred or better all hunkered in a circle around him and his best friend, Johnny Johns. The other young Natives likely were relieved that the beatings were allocated to the two Tsimshian boys rather than to themselves. Of course plenty of the pain got passed around.

He and Johnny were the only Tsimshian. The other boys spoke only small pieces of Tom and Johnny's tongue. The best exchange was a little sign language and a bit of the universal trade language, Chinook jargon. The boys felt the full burden of isolation.

It was weeks later that Tom discovered that they were being punished for speaking their Native tongue. Of course, that was the only language they knew. After that they pretended to speak English, quickly assimilating as many words as possible. The foreign language scratched at Tom's throat and burned his ego. He felt conquered.

Always together, the two boys leaned toward the old language whenever they could. They spoke it secretly, identifying each other by their Native names. Under a shroud of stealth, the beatings slowed.

Johnny spat into his hand. Tom followed. The boys rubbed their palms together and swore never to forfeit their culture or their friendship.

Months later, the headmaster—a Christian minister—attempted to rape Tom. Tom hit the pastor hard in the face and ran. Even to this day, he saw blood and rage swirling across the churchman's face. He could hear the man's dirty benediction as it followed him out the long hall and into daylight. No one had to translate the sting of those words. The message held the same bitter inflection in any culture. So much for the honor of the Christian medicine man and his church. So much for the spiritual education of Tom LaCross.

Even before the incident, Tom knew which way the river flowed. After he left the agency, he just kept moving. He had a destination in mind. He moved north, taking on enough work to feed his lean body. Five years passed quickly.

Tom stared absently at Dan. He had gone deep inside himself.

Dan studied the scout curiously. He waited for Tom to continue. After all, hardly a smattering of civil words had passed between the two men over the last several years. At the moment, they were not doing so badly. He stuck another chunk of meat into his mouth, relishing the taste. He chewed slowly and waited. The venison tasted wonderful.

Tom mulled over his private thoughts. Maybe he was holding court with some lost spirit. Or maybe one of his relatives. Or perhaps he had gone loco. Whatever was motivating his actions, Dan couldn't begin to guess. One thing was certain: Tom was lost in an ocean of reflection.

In his mind, Tom was reciting a chronicle he had stored away as unreachable for several decades. Now he faced an unexpected urge to get it out—to tell it to someone. It had been years since he had recalled the details of an incident that had etched such a deep scar.

The authorities never caught the young Haisla, which was a good thing. If they had, he would have been severely beaten, more likely maimed or murdered. Many of those stories got whispered about.

Picking up lame jobs as he leapfrogged up the coast, Tom slowly gravitated toward home. Home was the village of Tasska, which was his second home, his aunt's village. This was where his people had relocated after being forced from their ancient lodgings.

It had been a time of suffering. A rage of influenza had recently wracked his village, dispensing another maelstrom of death. Protestant and Catholic missionaries came into their lives and burned many of their totems. Burned heaps of artifacts, many considered sacred to his clan. Worse yet, the church of Jesus Christ kidnapped their children and sent them to residential schools across Canada. Many never returned. There was never an explanation or an apology.

One overwrought "man of God" destroyed most of his family's possessions, any obvious "heathen artifact." Anything that proclaimed "Red man" without a Jesus Christ disclaimer stamped on the cover. The government of Canada sanctioned the theft.

For years afterwards, his aunt claimed she saw the smoke billowing above the burning village of Tasska. Said the smoke never left her alone, neither the smell nor the pallor of gray ash rising into the evening sky.

The smoke engorged the summer light, the burnt umber reflections at sundown. The loss haunted his aunt for the rest of her life.

Tom stood in silence as Dan watched and chewed on another hunk of deer meat. The scout's memories were wafting through his head like the ashes that had billowed above the village of Tasska. The memories were like the hard, long winters that the Cold One brings. The Tsimshian called that force "Cold Maker."

Still deep in thought, Tom drifted to the memory of a White woman, the first Boston he had ever trusted. She, in turn, had never trusted a Native man.

At first she shied away from him. Him being Native—well, half—meant he looked plenty threatening. *Indian through and through.* Handsome as he was, his face had a haggard, defeated look. The missionary school had engraved that. A person didn't have to be a detective to fathom the look of dejection and pain.

For a change, time became his friend. Tom and the White woman worked closely together. A row of fillet tables dictated that. Close encounters happened naturally. Soon, he was talking with her and she with him. Initially, Tom radiated an anger that wasn't particularly approachable. But as the weeks leapfrogged, their relationship grew closer and closer, and his grief softened. They exchanged small talk, ideas, and then confidences. It was green-up time in the mountains, and Tom was beginning to blossom too. In Ruth Anne McCauley, he found a refuge from the empty years of sorrow that had tagged him since his youth.

Little by little, the fear and distrust between them was replaced with a tentative trust. Soon, it came to a point where Tom believed Red and White might live together. Still, it was hard to define a current that a person couldn't see or touch.

In Albert Bay he chose to live the White man's way. Tom changed his habits: shaved, barbered, and dressed in Boston clothes. Cotton and flannel, not skins. She was worth it. With his hair and beard cut, he almost looked White.

They had fun together, natural and easy. Ultimately, she fell for him, fell deeply. Dreamed some then—the two of them together—how their lives might be if only . . .

Finally, after two years, he asked her to marry. She smiled, choking a little, shy-like, as was her way. "Yes," she replied, plain and simple. Her mouth had a funny twist to it as if her lips were caught between irony and mystery, between wanting and not knowing when to trust or just how much. Then her lips parted. Her words were direct. "Will you have me, Tom?" Her eyes flushed with joy.

Her question threw him. Turned everything topsy-turvy.

"Yes," he answered, gulping involuntarily but never so sure about anything before, never so happy. They hugged. Made love. Night shrouded them with a curtain of happiness and certainty. The smoke and ashes rising above Tasska dissipated.

Even now, years later, he remembered every detail of their lovemaking: the soft, creamy radiance of her skin, the excited flush that flooded her face and naked body in a pink glow, the way her breasts rose and fell in the hot passion of their embrace.

He remembered the delicate caress of her cascading hair as it fell upon him, glossy-brown and feathered with faint streaks of red, gossamer threads sheaved in rich afternoon light. They lay on a bed of soft green moss. He remembered how sunlight had baptized them in hope and passion. And always there was that tender look in her eyes.

Dan eyed Tom's face. Not a word passed between them. Tom squatted and sat cross-legged on the ground. His eyes spoke to a faraway place.

He went to see her father. That was the Tsimshian way, to ask permission of a respected elder. The honorable way. McCauley was his name. Butler McCauley.

In his house of glass windows, Tom said, "I wish to take your daughter for my bride. Will you honor me with her hand?"

He had practiced the words, and now, standing in front of Ruth Anne's father, eye to eye, he felt confident.

Straight up the father said, "No. Won't have no Indian son-in-law."

That smarted Tom.

He looked the father directly in the eye one more time. "I'm sorry," he said. "Don't think I heard you right. I'm asking for your daughter's hand. I love her. I want to spend my life with her. I promise you, I will be good to her. Mighty good."

"Won't have any fuckin' Indian son-in-law. You hearin' me this time? 'Spect you'd better leave my house and my daughter now."

Tom picked McCauley up, right off the floor. Tom was a strong young man. Working a cannery job twelve hours a day required endurance and strength. He held her father at arm's length and repeated his words. "I want your daughter for my wife."

McCauley answered as before, word for word, adding a sneer that cut like a fillet knife.

Tom released his hold on Ruth Anne's father and turned to her with pleading eyes. "Ruth, will you spend your life with me? I'll love you forever. You know you can trust me. Will you walk with me?"

But Ruth Anne leaned toward her old man. Natural, he thought. She being just seventeen. He was her father, after all. It startled him though. Startled the Tsimshian out of being White. Pretending that he was. Startled him more than he could ever say. Ever forget.

Ruth Anne had made her choice. She loved Tom, but she was leaning toward her old man.

Tom turned his face, disguising his pain. Turned away from them both.

I'll not share my hurt with any White man. He was bleeding inside, but his pride was taking over. Without another word, he left the White man's house and left his lover standing beside her father, tears in her eyes.

A week after the incident with her father, Tom saw Ruth Anne standing alone on the cannery dock. He had just given notice. Under the huge planks, the water was ebbing. He watched the currents, hoping perhaps that they carried an answer for his loss.

Standing before her now as a broken man, he gathered up his wounded pride and spoke. "I'll be gone for five years. Don't look for me. Don't worry about me."

"But I love you," she whispered.

Trouble was, he was mad. He was proud. Tom turned and walked away.

Ruth Anne just stood there and shook her head back and forth, unbelieving. Tears fell hard in a silence broken by the soft muster of wind and the faint songs of distant birds. Her long hair danced gracefully on the wind.

Moving away from her, Tom felt as though all that birdsong was wrapped in deep sorrow and aimed squarely at him.

Five years passed. They weren't happy years. For a while, Tom found the bottle. Then, on the streets of Vancouver, he gave it up. He simply couldn't stand the shame. It was the hardest thing he had ever done—well, nearly. Pain and suffering engraved his spirit like a steel rasp etching designs on a Haida silver bracelet.

A few years later, Tom was back in Albert Bay. Two letters were waiting for him. His aunt hadn't dared to open them. "Bad spirits," she said.

He opened both, holding the dry yellowed paper in a steady hand. His grasp was sure, but inside he was shaking.

The first letter sprawled out a sad story. "I'm carrying your child."

He wanted to stop there. It had been several years since he had cried over the White woman. He held back the tears.

The second letter continued like a straight stretch of a wild river that refuses to bend. "You have a daughter. My father has threatened to kill the baby if he ever sees you and me together. He won't let me keep the child. I have given her up for adoption. Yes, a sweet little girl. I love our child. I love you. I'm sorry. You don't know how sorry. Forgive me. I've given the child to a minister and his wife. They will love the baby like their own. Give her a good life."

Tom's aunt said that Ruth Anne left town after she gave the baby away. He imagined what it would be like for a White woman to live with a mixed-race baby in the small outpost. He didn't wish that on her or their child.

At that moment he was too broken to care. He thought of his beautiful daughter. No shaking off the loss.

"Got married later to a sailor," his aunt said. "Never had another child. Least never heard of such. Turned barren maybe. Pain can do that."

As she talked on, Tom was hearing but not hearing. His aunt didn't know where the baby had gone. Didn't know where Ruth Anne was. Even if Tom had known of her whereabouts, he would not have had the willpower to look her up. He carried enough pain for one lifetime, maybe for two or three. He was twenty-six years old that year, and heartache would stalk him for the remainder of his life.

As the memory faded away, Tom looked past Dan and saw wisps of flesh-pink clouds stirring above the horizon. The sun was nearly down. He smelled the rich broth from the wild meat wafting in the mountain air. He remembered that he was hungry. He swallowed into a dry throat. Hadn't eaten all day. He ignored the sensation. Before taking another breath, he looked into the eyes of the man sitting in front of him, young Danny, his student of old. *Give me back those years*, he thought.

Leaning forward, he remembered why he had come. "Friends, again?"

Tom extended his hand. Dan hadn't seen that coming.

Even as he extended his hand, Tom felt the weight of both worlds: Red and White, past and present. *Maybe it's time to write a new story*, he thought. He had found her again, at least in memory. *This is good.* More than anything else, Tom wanted peace in his life.

Dan felt something indefinable in the air, something he couldn't grasp. Tom's hand was there, five fingers reaching for his.

Once again, it was Tom who broke the silence. "Our trail together has stretched over many moons. I want it like it was once before. When you was a kid. You remember that, don't you? Trapping the lower river. The Skeena? Outback Creek? Learnin' the old man's tricks? You were a fine student."

"Not as good as the teacher," Dan replied, his mouth firm in its expression.

Dan extended his hand.

The village was quiet. Two hands touched.

Twilight flooded in like the grasp of their hands. Both men let their eyes drift away. The sunset had faded into a metallic luster. Dan found himself thinking about Rebecca, then oddly, found his thoughts drifting back to Yellow Bird Singing.

He squared up and looked his old teacher in the eye. The scout's expression held steady. There was patience there, and wisdom, but a different brand than the old shaman's. *Trail tested*, Dan thought, wondering suddenly about his own life, all those hard lessons stacking up, year after year. To his surprise, he saw strong traces of emotion on the copper-colored skin of his mentor's face.

Dan's next words raced out. "That young girl, Yellow Bird Singing, she taught me a lot of Haisla and Kwak'wala and some trade language, Chinook jargon. Truth could talk, I always wanted a daughter. Wanted one powerfully. She's filled in some missing pieces. Rebecca and I can't have children. Rebecca is all I have, and now I ain't even got that. I feel powerful lonely, missing her. I guess you understand loneliness aplenty. I'm sorry that I don't know more about your history, the suffering of your people."

"Yes," Tom replied in a whisper.

He turned away from Dan. His face was drawn. Emotions scudded across his face and eyes. Suddenly, Dan felt stumped for words.

Minutes gamed along, as twisted as a shank of cedar rope. Dan's voice sought the proper words. Sought explanation. He spoke now, his voice flinty and deep. "Keep thinking this tribe is different from my people back home. Just my prejudice, I suppose."

Tom remained quiet, embarrassed by his show of emotion. He remained as still as a fence post while Dan talked on.

"You know, Tom . . ."

The name hung in the air, familiar, warm, and personal.

"That young girl, she taught me more than language. All these people here, they've shared a brand of peace that I never felt before. Taught me about family and sharing, about community. And something more. Something hard to put into words."

Tom watched Dan closely. He studied the cast of Dan's eyes and face as if they were a petroglyph etched in stone. A minute raced by and then two. Finally, Tom broke the silence. "With my people, the Tsimshian, daily life was much the same as you see in this here village. It was later—after the diseases—when all that changed. The rules got riled up. I guess there's no going back, anyhow. My world—the world I grew up in—well, it just seems gone for good.

"But here, these people move like the Tsimshian did before the pox. They pay attention to old ways, to their children and family. The pace, the chores, the way people talk and share—I remember all this. They make their easy choices slow, the hard ones fast. Big difference I remember is this: among the original coast people there was much warfare. Lots of savage fighting. Grandfather, he and my uncle told many stories about raiding parties. Nootka and A-y-chants. Bella Coola warring on the Kwakiutl, Haida against all comers. One always battling another. The tribes traded in slaves. A few of the rituals were bloodcurdling. No, we was a long way from perfect.

"Well, smallpox changed everything, changed it right quick. We joined hands. Tribes should have come together long before. Even in the clans, there was always petty stuff. Always one family in a feud with another. One chief showing off, proving his worth by giving away most of his wealth. Giving away more than he could afford. Still, most bragging rights happened after Bostons and Queen's Men offered all those trade goods to our people. Seemed like an Indian got rich on furs. For a while, anyway. Well, that fell apart. Soon weren't any otter left. So, none of my people was ever perfect, but what society is? Better here in this village. Better than I ever saw it."

The sun was down now. Nightfall began to penetrate the landscape around the two men. Tom, now a mere silhouette against the dark, back-lit sky, continued talking.

"The old man holds it together. I never met anyone who teaches like him, and, in my time, I knew plenty of elders and chiefs. A shaman or two to boot. Tell you to your face, Dan, I want to stay. Maybe you can understand that?"

He was speaking to Dan but convincing himself, as if his thoughts needed a verbal confirmation. The words were coming fast. Faster in English than anyone might remember from the taciturn man.

"Your nation never suffered like ours. Our pain never ended. After the pestilence, tribes clung together by a thin strand of sinew. There were few survivors. We held on to what we could, but there wasn't much hope, believe you me."

The silence that settled between Tom's words spoke just as loudly as his voice. A deeper meaning lay there, both seen and unseen, in the same way a fish or otter sent rings expanding gently across the surface of a still morning lake. Old, unspoken memories were surfacing and circling from the depths of their silence, from the pool of their souls.

Tom had one more thing to say. "I lost more than brothers and sisters. My people lost their songs and dances, the old stories and legends. Our elders' voices disappeared overnight. Here, in this village, well, it's like going back forty years for me."

The silence settled in again, seeming almost normal by then. Dan turned his eyes away from Tom. Found his mind skittering back to the beginning of their conversation. Now it was his turn to speak. "Listen, Tom, you got a point, alright. It's long past time to bury my brother, to bury the hatchet. I've come 'round some too. I like it here. I like these people. I see why you might choose to stay.

"But listen, my wife's back at the farm, at least I pray so, and that's what keeps pestering me. Can't shake it off. I miss her terribly. Long as I stay here, I'm a prisoner, and she can't know if I'm dead or alive. All she can do is worry. And if I don't find her soon, she might pull out of town. Rebecca is sure to feel pressure from town folks. Maybe she's already caved in, though God knows she's a mighty tough woman. Soon, I got to take my chances. Pull out of here. I think I can make it."

"Good a chance as any man. Way you move, probably better. Think you passed me by, son. You've learned the trappers' ways, damn sure."

Dan let the compliment sink in. The words left him energized. But then Tom added another thought, and Dan felt his elation evaporating.

"But think plenty hard on that—on trying to run. I mean, ever figure why they can't let us go?

"Sure. Government or the Mounties would have some small army up here quicker than smoke followin' fire. This village would be gone in ten minutes."

"That's about right. They can't let you run, Dan. Too much at stake."

"What would you do if you were in my shoes, Tom? If you had another life waiting for you, a woman you loved more than God?"

Tom thought immediately of Ruth Anne. Felt his emotions well up again. But he didn't have to chew on Dan's last question. He was remembering that he had chosen not to follow Ruth Anne, not to follow his one true love. Worse, he had lost her forever. There was no retrieving the past. His answer to Dan's question was as clear as a summer sky.

"I'd do what you gonna do. I'd run hard. Run all the way back to her. But I'll tell you, Dan, I don't believe you'll get far."

"You won't talk?"

"Oh, no. I owe you that much. I won't forget that you let me live, lying unconscious as good as dead in that pit. Listen to me, will you?"

He paused for several moments and let his dark eyes settle on those of his newly incarnated ally. "Be careful, son. Be mighty careful. I don't want to lose you now. Not again."

Central America 1973

Dawn crept peacefully over the beaches in Honduras. The cackling serenade of a parrot stirred Katherine from her dreams. Already the sun was radiating waves of heat off the sparkling white sand. A blanket of heat fell hard on the village, distorting the shape of the harbor, the shape of the soft lapping waves. For a second, Katherine thought she was hallucinating again—thought her fever had returned.

After she recovered from her sudden illness, Katherine figured she had as much to learn from the local people as she might offer them in return. But there was a difference between the two offerings. It wasn't as if either lesson had more value—not hers, not theirs. It was as if there were two kinds of learning and both were *good medicine.*

In an odd sort of way, she was a technocrat. Katherine possessed skills that the United States industrial culture had perfected over the last three centuries. Most of those skills were unheard of in this backwater, and many were unnecessary or extreme. Katherine was trained to think efficiently, to think technically. There was little doubt in her mind that what she had to offer was of great importance to these people. Only later would she reflect on some of the consequences.

Still, she reasoned, something was going on in the background of this Native culture that she needed to understand. Even so, she knew there was much about the culture that she would never fully grasp—things more important than her country's GNP. She needed answers to a few of her spiritual questions. She needed to penetrate the inner language of these Native people. She wanted to know the full extent of their beliefs.

She had begun to discover the presence of spirituality, its slow-burning mysteries. She wanted to explore the roots. An old crone of a woman had just saved her life. Her medicines and spirituality were unknown to modern culture. The old lady's magic would be written off by many stateside as "voodoo medicine." There was much to be shared between two cultures, but an invisible wall divided them. Katherine realized that the wall had to be scaled. She was determined to climb over it.

In the next twelve months, Katherine turned her energies toward penetrating that mystique. Although she never found the lady who saved her life, she did find a medicine man who lived in a nearby village, a thoughtful, wizened healer with plenty of knowledge to share.

The man was standoffish at first. Resolutely, he guarded his craft. But Katherine had the patience of a saint.

She visited the shaman frequently and spent untold hours building up his trust. Asking few questions initially, she simply hung out. She was fascinated by his indigenous skills and insights and was excited by the prospect of becoming his friend. Slowly, the old man softened, and Katherine deciphered many pieces of his knowledge. In time, he showed her many of the local medicinal plants and shared his knowledge of healing. And she respected him, realizing perhaps that healing manifested itself through the simple act of faith. The aboriginal medicine worked for the old man and those he served. She saw it happen repeatedly. Katherine thought she was expanding her perimeters, but all the while she was finding herself.

As time and events crisscrossed her life, Katherine developed a deep respect for the Indigenous peoples and their ways. In time, she would defend the rights and lifestyles of these people with the same fervency with which she had developed in opposing the Vietnam War. Katherine had found the heart of her father.

CHAPTER NINETEEN

The whales turn and glisten, plunge
and sound and rise again,
Hanging over subtly darkening deeps
Flowing like breathing planets
in the sparkling whorls of
living light—

—Gary Snyder
From *Mother Earth: Her Whales*

Rebecca fed the farm animals at first light. As she returned to the cabin, she remained alert for any unusual sounds—or lack of sound—the flitting and skittering of birds, their sudden and evasive movements, and telltale signs of change. She understood what others might miss. Her life with Dan had conditioned her. Part of her mind thought like a trapper. *Never, never drop your guard.* How keenly she remembered those words. Dan's words. No, those words belonged to Tom LaCross.

A volley of songbirds darted through the fractured rays of sunrise. The light was thick and golden. The sweet song of the birds swept Rebecca into her life before Dan. For a moment she felt girlish again, innocent, happy, and free.

She knew the songs of the robin and the blackbird. But the dwarfish warblers and golden-crowned sparrows charged so fast through the spruce trees and then across the meadow that she could scarcely decipher their individual markings. That morning the world was sprouting sedges and grasses, cow parsnip and chocolate lily. This she knew: the country was warming up in the crisp spring air, and so were the animals that lived there. For the first morning in months, she felt a flush of exhilaration.

Coastal tribes marked this budding time as the start of a new year. "Green up," they said, explaining the change as their moods turned festive.

The wild rhubarb and the tightly bound fiddlehead of the bracken fern was coveted by the First Peoples. The women gathered the bounty in beautifully crafted baskets woven from local grasses, reeds, and roots. They wove the fibers together with a skill and dexterity that was the backbone of their ancestral heritage.

That year, spring came late to the valley of the Killnook. After an extended winter, spring had finally arrived, and few, if any, appreciated its arrival more than Rebecca.

The air was thick with the sappy smell of budding cottonwoods. Natural colors, as rich as a painter's palette, daubed the tips of the alder branches, bushes and plants and grasses.

That morning, the delicate branches twined an intricate lace that became tangled with the morning light. A dozen varieties of ferns unfurled cautiously from the chilly winter earth.

The valley had entered a time of rebirth. The songbirds greeted each change with a symphonic chorus. The Chinook wind blew down the river, delivering a warm sensual touch.

Rebecca sensed something else stirring in the morning air. Although she didn't see or smell it, she felt the presence of the two Haisla long before they broke free of the evergreen grove that separated the farm from the river.

Their sudden appearance was a vivid reminder of her dire circumstance. Rebecca's heartbeat quickened, and her nerves quivered with excitement and perhaps, more than a little apprehension.

She turned and started for the cabin. *Best warn Sally*, she figured. *Best start some coffee*. In the blue enamel bucket under her arm nestled a dozen chicken eggs. She knew such luxury would soon enough disappear, that is—the thought came upon her suddenly—unless they gathered goose and duck eggs during their upriver trip into the mountains.

Across the barnyard a bright sun lifted, brighter now than the yellow yolks she envisioned simmering in a skillet, coated with bacon grease. Even the sun was brightening up. She imagined Dan sitting in the kitchen, sopping up the yolks with a piece of her whole-wheat toast, a recipe passed on from her mother. Life had remained so simple then, their future bright.

The two Natives had started their canoe journey well before first light. They moved silently up the Kilnook Valley, following an easterly wind while bucking strong river currents. Propelled by two finely honed cedar paddles and the surge of incoming tide, the men made good progress.

When Spirit Runner and Man Hides Good sensed the nearness of the Skinner farm, they slid their canoe into a natural opening under the riverbank, covered the cedar vessel with the flat, broad branches of a hemlock tree, and approached the farm nearly as adroitly as the flight of the songbirds that Rebecca observed skirting through the evergreens.

Thirty days had passed since the Natives' last contact with Rebecca. Perhaps she had come to doubt their word. But when their footfalls rattled across the porch, her heart raced, and she felt gladdened.

As Rebecca led the men into the kitchen, cedar kindling crackled in the stove, and the fresh smell of bacon and coffee wafted through the cabin. After she poured the coffee, Sally dropped several more eggs into the cast-iron skillet. The whites sizzled in the bacon grease. She sprinkled the eggs with salt and cracked pepper and flipped a pan of fried potatoes. "Mm-hmm," she murmured.

The men ate in silence, taking in every detail of the room with keen eyes. Piled next to the door were enough provisions to survive a month in the northern wilderness. Rebecca had not been idle.

She offered small talk, feeling strangely at a loss as to how she should shape her thoughts. The Haisla sat quietly. Sally broke the stalemate. "Ready to go, boys?" Her voice had swagger.

But the Natives weren't ready to go. Man Hides Good hunkered down in his chair and answered Sally's bravado with carefully chosen words. "We go tonight. For several days, we travel only by moonlight. Travel only under cover of darkness. This is good travel. Quiet time. Few eyes watching."

"How will we see?" Sally asked. Her voice wasn't so confident now. Sally didn't care for the dark northern nights. The river and its obstacles scared her. Traveling the big water in the light of day presented a parcel of problems. After sundown the difficulties became exaggerated, and Sally was a poor swimmer.

She addressed her concern, this time even more strongly. "We travel at night?"

The tone of her voice had lifted several octaves.

"Don't worry," Man Hides Good replied. "We see plenty. Spirit Runner and I find way, even in dark."

"Don't think you want all your neighbors to know where we go," Spirit Runner cut in.

"Sally," Rebecca said, "nighttime is a safe time. Dan taught me that. This evening will be fine with me. Besides, we have much to do. You can start by turning the animals loose in the pasture. Throw out all that winter silage. Scatter some feed for the chickens. Isaac will need to know that we're leaving. I'll hurry into town."

Isaac Walton had promised the women that he would keep an eye on the animals, but mostly, the critters would have to fend for themselves. There were no other options. Neither woman wanted to alert the locals of their pending departure. Only Isaac would know, and he had sworn himself to secrecy.

"Right time of year to leave the animals out. We'll spend the afternoon tying down loose ends. That okay with you, Sally?"

"Yeah, sure."

Sally wasn't so sure. Rebecca studied Sally's face expectantly. Rebecca knew she would come around.

Man Hides Good rose from his chair and turned to the two women. "We leave at dark."

Rebecca eyed Spirit Runner, as if seeking a confirmation.

"Yes, just after dark," he said.

"And our stuff?" Rebecca asked.

"We take that now. Load the canoe. Be back soon. Leave farm around midnight."

Under a half-cut moon, the canoe with four riders plied the dark, swift waters of the Kilnook River. A yellow moon glared down, ricocheting magically against the cupped and faceted side of each river swell. Sequins and glitter—the night remained still and bright.

"Weaver of baskets," Spirit Runner declared, eyeing the dark shape on the moon's face.

Rebecca followed the Native's eyes and studied the moon as if she had just discovered a new landscape. She deciphered the shape, alright. In the moon shadows was the weaver of baskets—a woman, not a man—and the revelation pleased her.

The canoe was cleaved from a straight-grained cedar tree, dropped and shaped by hand adz, chisel, fire, and a studied eye. The Natives who toppled it had blessed the tree. They told the cedar of its new purpose and its beautiful transformation. For twenty-four feet, the grain ran true. One and a half arm lengths from port to starboard. The vessel's interior had been gutted with a White man's steel adz and burned, ever so carefully, shaping the inside of the vessel to accommodate the travelers. The exterior of the vessel was honed with an steel adz, stone chisels, and finely sanded with sharkskin until smooth. When the sides were ordained the proper thickness, the cavity was filled with seawater, steamed with red-hot stones until the water boiled and the cedar turned pliable. Cedar thwarts swelled the pliant sides like a sealskin bladder filled with a hunter's breath. The Natives used wedges fashioned from heartwood. The canoe was considered a masterpiece of artisanship by both cultures, Native and White.

Compared to an ocean canoe, a river canoe was narrower, smaller, and shorter in length. The carving on the river vessel was not as ornate. Function propelled the smaller vessel. The canoe's design changed from tribe to tribe. Design became a calling card, a way of saying who you were and what you were doing. The painting, carving, and style spoke to short or long voyages, spoke of peace or war. Canoes could bring relatives or distant neighbors. Often they carried trade goods. Weddings and potlatches arrived on that same water path. A fine canoe was a statement of pride. But sometimes the canoes brought savage retribution. Warfare between the tribes was as ancient as the oldest stories, even older than some of the most ancient trees.

The vessel that Man Hides Good and Spirit Runner piloted was a river canoe. The canoe was an old one, the design refined over decades for the specific purpose of traveling through wily river currents. The bow protruded into a high tapered prow. The shape was both graceful and practical. No carvings or painting there. The canoe was designed by a master craftsman for speed and stealth, to blend into the natural setting. The sharp bowsprit sliced through the water. The cedar hull was as buoyant as an otter.

Under the cover of night, the narrow vessel swept gracefully along, creating only a small rustle on the river.

Already, Rebecca felt the security of her farm receding. Already, her anxieties swelled.

The canoe's movements were nearly silent. Only a small wake lapped onto the rocky shore. Even the cagiest of animals might miss the vessel's passage.

The two women sat and watched the miles glide by. The flood tide was with them once again, allowing the men to paddle the canoe easily upriver toward the place where Rebecca prayed they would find her husband. This was their assignment, and the four voyagers took their obligation seriously. Each was determined to find Dan and find him alive.

Would they have to travel all the way to the river source? No one in the canoe began to guess. Steadily and evenly, the paddles dipped into the river, stirring the moody water like a witch's brew.

Hardly a word was spoken between the voyageurs that entire evening. Rebecca sat forward of her friend and only occasionally chanced a backward glance. Both women were lost to the beauty of the night and the privacy of meditation. Curiosity strayed but quickly returned to the mission at hand.

Within hours they left the lower river and entered the world of deep-water channels and tall granite cliffs. The river favored them like a friendly companion. Still, the humans who shared the canoe knew that swift and dangerous water waited ahead.

At times the cliffs plunged directly into the river. There were no beaches or grassy meadows there. Ancient evergreens and dense brambles extended from precarious footholds, reaching out from the land's edge and fluttering over the water like delicate Japanese fans. It was the limit of the forest's reach, of its thick viridian hands.

Fifteen miles from the Skinner farm, the canoe sought rite of passage along a wide, deep channel.

Along that waterway and into the gentle night, the dark surge of water cradled the cedar vessel as comfortably as a baby in its mother's arms. Even at the end of April, snow clung tenaciously to the cliffs and steppes of the granite wilderness. Spring came late that year. The eagles—always drawn to northern rivers, alive with salmon and waterfowl—settled into the broken treetops in huge nests with their newborns. The raptors chose the tallest conifers along the waterways in that land of granite and snow.

Rebecca spotted an otter in the spangle of moonlight. Such sightings were rare now. She knew this was one of a few. Sea traders had exacted a heavy bounty on the sleek animals, so coveted for their luxurious fur by the Russians and Chinese. The playful animals had brought huge profits to the European explorers. Unfortunately, by the late nineteenth century, the once plentiful mammals were nearly extinct.

For longer than the elders remembered, pods of killer whales had plied these same waters, preying on the seals and salmon with the same ferocity that the warring Tlingit and Haida had once inflicted upon rivals during savage raids up and down the coast. Though an ocean mammal, they moved stealthily many miles upriver in the deep and dark waters seeking the silver swimmers during their annual migration.

In the deepest hours of the night, Rebecca heard a rush of exhalation as a pod of orcas simultaneously expelled explosive blasts of water vapor through their blowholes. The spray rose high into the night, singeing the pale air with sparks of effervescence. The river route was alive with the tender serenade of dozens of unseen creatures singing to the moon and stars.

Four-legged animals paused in their nightly ritual, first sensing and then hearing the stealthy motion of the cedar vessel. Their senses were keen, and darkness hid them as they scurried for cover. Hints of moonlight glinted in their eyes like distant stars. Rebecca was lost in wonder.

High above on the cliffs, mountain goats found tentative footholds on the narrowest of ledges, safe and secure from the water visitors far below. Although the goats appeared untouchable, Native people hunted them by climbing above the unsuspecting animals and dropping seal bladders filled with pea gravel onto the sure-footed mammals. As the gravel spilled over the precipice, the agile, white-furred beasts lost their footing and followed the tiny stones to their death. With relish, the First Peoples feasted on the goats' tender flesh. As with all bounty forfeited by Mother Earth, no food was procured without blessings. Nothing was taken for granted, The feast of a mountain goat remained particularly rare.

Man Hides Good and Spirit Runner steered the canoe as near to the shoreline as the shallow-hulled vessel would allow. No sense being discovered in open water. Even under the cover of darkness, they paddled steadily, stealthily.

The Natives' eyes were sharp. At all times, their movements emulated the wariest of animals. Their eyes were continuously scanning the shoreline, in search of a quick cache, should the need arise.

Just before dawn, a bear scampered out of the river and up a steep bank in full view of the canoe. The bear was enormous, perhaps six or seven hundred pounds. The women were terrified.

In contrast, the guides took the visit in stride. After all, this was the bear's home, and the travelers were only guests. The Natives had great respect for the cunning and determination of the grazing animals, whether black bear or the larger grizzly, or even the smaller sleek marten and the tree-eating beavers. One of the smallest animals, the wolverine, was the most ferocious. Spirit Runner had seen the critter attack a grizzly, grab and tear at the monster's nose, scrambling and slashing as the bear thrashed in pain. When the bear gathered its senses—losing a good part of its tender snout in the process—it smashed the smaller, feral-toothed fighter with a single swipe of its powerful paws and then turned and skulked away. Such was the way of nature.

Indeed, the wilderness was harsh. Neither of the two Haisla was startled by that revelation. The seasons came in fours. Each season had its moods. The First Peoples saw the disposition of the quarters as a natural but somewhat unpredictable evolution. Nature was moody. Animals were no different. The Creator was gracious, but his spirit embodied an element of tenacity. Many of the four-legged creatures could surprise a human and quickly maim or kill. In the canoe, Rebecca was once again remembering Dan' oft repeated warnings.

Spirit Runner felt honored to be in the presence of the giant, but wherever he went, he approached the bear's haunts with caution.

The tide turned at four in the morning. The Natives beached the canoe in a sheltered, rocky cove. For the second time that day, Spirit Runner and Man Hides Good covered the canoe with evergreen boughs. The four retreated into a forest that extended away from the water's edge.

"We go find game now," Spirit Runner proclaimed. "We gather dinner." He and Man Hides Good turned and disappeared into the thick copse, fading into the undergrowth so abruptly that Sally and Rebecca felt as if they had been deserted.

Dawn unfolded, a rich, pearly blanket with a mist of cold air covering the river. Along a valley shaped by ancient glaciers, first light pushed through a cold mountain dew.

Sally and Rebecca found themselves conversing in whispers. Even so, Sally's voice volleyed with considerable force. Her words were seldom missed. "Jes', that was something, honey. Mm-hmm."

"You mean last night?"

"Yeah. Did you ever?"

"No, breathtaking. A beautiful night. Special . . . the moon . . . night sounds. Did you hear the whales?"

"Hard to miss, sweetie. Hard to miss anything that beautiful."

Sally twisted her head in the direction where the Natives had disappeared. "When do you think they'll be back? My, they're a sneaky pair."

"Yes, they are. Dan's that way in the woods too. His senses are always on alert. I'm sure they'll be back after they find some game. Listen, Sally, won't be the breakfast you're used to. No bacon and eggs. No flapjacks. I suspect there won't be a fire today. You get my gist?"

"Yeah, raw!" Sally squinted her face into a crinkled, unpleasant mask. Rebecca grinned broadly.

"Likely. Listen, we'd better get comfortable and get some rest. I brought some apples along. Let's grab a couple. I'm hungry."

High above the shoreline, an eagle soared. Just as suddenly as it appeared, it was gone. A raven croaked in a nearby tree. Always the messenger, the raven piped its cry in a scolding, desultory manner.

Sticks knocking together, Rebecca thought. That was the sound, a gnashing sound, for sure. Strangely, the sound disturbed her. Rebecca stood as still as a tree, listening to their soliloquy. She gnawed on the apple. Mostly, she was thinking of Dan.

"Think he's trying to tell us something?" Sally asked.

"Sorry . . . he's trying . . . Oh! You mean the raven?"

"Yeah."

"Like, who are these two crazy women, traveling in a wooden canoe with two Indians in the middle of the night? Something like that?"

"Yeah, the two of us together. Here. Crazy, alright."

"Still time to find your way home, Sally."

"No thanks, honey. I'm in this for the long haul."

The two women nestled down, their backs pressed against the rough, scaly skin of a massive spruce tree, a grandfather better than twenty feet in circumference. Its dark limbs appeared huge in the early light. Lower on the trunk, a number of the limbs had died from lack of sunlight. They now hung limply, silhouetted like dangling appendages. Thin, phthalic-green moss covered the wooden appendages like a furry skin. The limbs appeared slightly grotesque and haunting in the chilly morning air.

"Hope they're not long," Sally blurted out, feeling suddenly self-conscious. "I'm no sissy, but this place gives me the creeps."

"Don't worry, Sally. We'll have a beautiful day. The sun will break through soon. You'll see. It's going to be a beautiful day."

A couple of hours passed. The women slumbered. True to Rebecca's prophecy, the rising sun began to evaporate the last wisps of fog, foreshadowing an unusually hot day for April. The women roused. The weather was too perfect for lollygagging.

Rebecca stretched, swinging her gaze out and around the valley. Quickly enough, her eyes settled on her friend. "Show you a trick, kid. One that Dan taught me. He learned it from Tom LaCross."

She thought suddenly about the scout, and the revelation struck her with all the shock of a sudden apparition. Had Tom trapped her husband? Had one of two fine woodsmen killed the other? Were they both dead?

Sally saw a cloud of doubt darken the face of her best friend. One didn't need to read minds to decode the message. Sally placed her arm behind Rebecca's back and gently moved her best friend toward the copse. "Show me, honey. Show me that trick. Mm hmm."

A grove of Sitka spruce with trunks thicker than a buckboard wagon rose high before them. The denseness of the growth was so thick that it nearly hid the morning sky. Under the green umbrella, Rebecca pointed to a plant disdained by the wary as "devil's club." It was tall and cane-like with a willowy stem and hundreds of tiny stinging barbs.

Rebecca unsheathed the blade of her knife, turned the steel parallel to the plant, and then scraped away the stickers that dominated the stalk. After several minutes of the tedious process, she cut the shaved stalk at both ends, hacking above and below the one-foot section that she had prepared.

With stalk in hand, she peeled away the exterior skin from the plant, gathered a handful of the pliable bark tying them together a thick bundle. "Soap, she said."

"What the heck?"

"The Indians refresh themselves with this. Hunters claim it hides human scent. Allows them to get closer to the animals. A natural perfume."

"What do I do with it?" Sally's nose pinched in anticipation.

"Rub it across your skin. Don't be scared, silly. Honest, it's refreshing."

Sally twisted her lips into another grimace. She held the plant in her hand as if it was rotten. Slowly, apprehensively, she rubbed the bundle across her arm, smelled it, then looked up at Rebecca with surprise. Rebecca's face had taken on a wry smile. She laughed, and Sally joined in. The laughter enlivened the two women. How long had it been since Rebecca had belly laughed?

Suddenly, she sensed motion. She spun quickly, alert for danger. Standing but a half dozen yards from the ladies were the two Haisla. Rebecca's grin turned sheepish. Dan's admonition shouted at her. She had been caught flat-footed.

Shaken from her revelry, Rebecca studied her guides' rugged faces. Spirit Runner was holding two slain beaver. Man Hides Good had an armful of what Rebecca recognized as cow parsnip. He lowered the armful of greens to the ground and showed Rebecca and Sally how to peel the plant's lower stalk. Once finished, he broke the stalk into bite-sized pieces and offered a sample to the women. To their surprise the plant tasted sweet and crispy, something like celery but sugary with a wild aftertaste that puckered their mouths. The taste left the women feeling refreshed.

After Spirit Runner skinned the beaver, he carefully cut the meat off the animal into thin, narrow strips. Rebecca had been wrong; there would be a fire. With flint and steel, Spirit Runner struck a flame by using some dead spruce twigs that were scattered on the forest floor. Then he collected pitch from the same tree that the women had rested against. Lastly, he gathered larger kindling and bark. The fire burned hot with virtually no smoke. Using trimmed green branches, the four roasted the strips of meat over the fire, eating as they went. Spirit Runner held back the tail. "Later," he said. "Best part of beaver. Make you sleepy after a long day of travel. Taste good. We eat when we stop next."

The men alternated the watch while the women ate. When everyone had eaten, Man Hides Good said, "Three sleep now. One stand guard. We switch every few hours. Move out at dark, after tide rises."

In the cool of the forest under the midday sun, three slept, and their dreams were filled with reunions.

As he stood watch, Spirit Runner spotted an eagle soaring overhead. He watched the mighty bird as it circled into a wide, graceful glide. The raptor rose higher and higher, then flew upriver into the mountains.

Spirit Runner had seen many eagles that day, but he sensed there was something different about this one, its size perhaps, or the deliberate way it flew. After it had gone, his thoughts returned to other matters.

The sunlight was intense now. Above the Kilnook Valley, the sky was tinted with a steel-blue patina. Silt in the water told Spirit Runner that the ice and snow were melting and flooding down from the mountains. The sultry weather warned him that the river would soon be rising dramatically. *Harder going this evening*, he thought. He was familiar with the signs.

Spirit Runner shifted his eyes upriver. Ahead lay the land of his ancestors, ancient villages built from straight-grained cedar. There, the remnants of burial grounds and totems remained, reminders of family and friends, of descendants with their stories of old. Spirit Runner was drawn there. To his way of thinking, he was coming home.

Well after the sun set, cool evening air sheathed the river runners in a light dew. After everyone was back in the canoe, Man Hides Good pushed the bow into the current. If the travelers had listened—if they had known the language—they might have heard the river singing their names. Water trilled a note. Wilderness drew them in, baptizing the travelers with an ancient song that only a few might decipher.

Seattle 1975

Back in the States, Katherine began to search for a new identity. She moved home to Seattle and went to work for a conservation organization. The environmental movement was new, and Katherine found herself on the ground floor. She worked hard. It was obvious to everybody on the staff that not only did she have skills, but that Katherine was also a potential leader. She moved from receptionist into a secretarial job with the vice-president of the organization. That didn't last long. Her talent was too obvious. Soon she became the director of economic development. In the two years she was there, the organization tripled in size, as did their sponsorships.

She moved back in with her mother. Their bond was as strong as ever, but her mother encouraged her to rent a place of her own, to find a man to replace Paul. Katherine wasn't all that interested in finding someone new. She wasn't sure that would ever happen.

Katherine secured an apartment and threw herself into her new job. Men respected her but steered away. She was aloof, a bit cold. When nobody asked her out, she pretended that she didn't care.

She took night classes at a junior college in South Seattle, studying environmental science and business. She excelled, but that was no longer a surprise. She knew as much about the subject as her professors. Katherine had a knack. She had ambition. But late at night, she felt the bitter sting of loneliness. She missed the Hondurans. She missed their lifestyle. But most of all, she missed Paul.

After three years, Katherine became the assistant to the president. The job didn't go as planned. There was division in the organization. She began to perceive that many of the players were more interested in a private power game than in the principles that governed the organization. Over the next several months, the rift widened. Katherine felt a pressure to take sides.

Two months later the executive director split from the organization. Katherine and five members of the conservancy followed.

CHAPTER TWENTY

"When men lack a sense of awe, there will be disaster."

—Lao Tzu,
Tao Te Ching

A solitary man ran through deep viridian forest. The understory was dense. Daylight remained a pale bloom, the sun only an hour high and hidden by a lush concentration of evergreen. He tailed little shadow.

Dan liked the rhythm of his legs. Dark, thick trees surrounded and hid him. Already his skin was slick with perspiration. Overhead, colored birds watched his flight from dense limbs that studded the ancient evergreen trees. The running man heard a cacophony of songbirds but did not see them. Like the birds, he intended to stay hidden.

The forest was a mat of brown and green. Fern and lichen were scattered along the forest floor. The evolution of the forest was ancient. Few, if any, humans had ever passed through there. The sword ferns were as tall as a man. *Living sculptures*, Dan thought. The birds were curious but silent when interrupted from their reverie.

Running with a steady, smooth gait, as another mile glided by, Dan let his mind wander, picking any point in his memory that diverted attention from the exhaustion that was spreading up his legs and into his arms and back. The ache began to settle into his chest and lungs. That ache amplified as the miles slid by. He had a headache, but that didn't matter. He believed he had a long head start on his pursuers. He knew he had to create distance between himself and them. Dan was certain that they would follow. Exhausted, he contemplated a rest. Instead, he spurred himself ahead.

Dan didn't know what his pursuers might do to him if he was captured. No need to worry about that. Still, none of the options spelled out anything acceptable. One expectation haunted him, however. He realized that his pursuers might kill him if he was caught.

Pandering to himself, Dan turned the negative thoughts away. Mostly, he thought about Rebecca, gathering emotional strength from memories.

There were only animal trails there. The forest floor was covered with nature's debris: generations of needles, broken ends of branches, duff, decaying ferns, and rotting cones. But mostly, the forest was tall and clear, giant evergreens creating a canopy that filtered out much of the sunlight, leaving open spaces for a man to run. The light—when it found its way down through the treetops—was soft and sensuous. Sunbeams bent into radiating pulses of gold, amber, and canary yellow. Not much grew down there under the forest canopy. Dan was mostly unencumbered.

Before leaving the village, he had decided on a general direction. Following the sun and the design of his plan, he steered away from what he perceived as the traditional travel routes. He aimed for the thicket, figuring it might cut down on his visibility. Intentionally, he avoided damp, loose dirt. *Leave no tracks. Break no branches. Move fast and silently.* He repeated old instructions in his head until they became a litany. The repetition gave him confidence, and he needed that more than anything. Dan could rely on his mountain skills. He trusted himself and his craft. Luck, well, he knew that only time would answer that question. Dan knew that he wouldn't survive without a bit of Lady Luck.

Dan reasoned that he couldn't run forever, that his legs would give out sooner or later. He figured on a plan that would help him most: run five or six miles in a straight line, then walk one. Run four, walk one. He would do that several times that day, then cache. Sleep three hours and walk through more of the pesty darkness. Tomorrow he would start all over again. Start his running. *Six and one. No tracks. Move fast.* If he got terribly tired, he would try three and one. And his walk was fast, almost a trot.

The Kilnook River had to be south to west. Had to be ahead of him. He followed the sun and the stars. On a wet day, there was always a tree map to follow. Moss clung to the north side of conifers. That was easy enough. Rain generally pressed from the northwest. Only that side of the tree would dampen. And Dan knew the stars. He was set.

He avoided the tributaries that ran closest to the village. Those would be searched first. Someone like Tom would follow but not at a fast pace. In those woods nobody tracked at night. Maybe Tom, but he was out of the picture. As the hours passed by, he kept repeating to himself, *Get ahead. Stay ahead. Remember, they can't afford to be seen either. There is a reason they stay hidden. Watch your step. Careful now.*

The bottom line was simple enough: if discovered, they became the hunted—they, this band of Native people hidden deep in the wilderness, away from the prying eyes of the queen's lawmen and their damning laws. Dan knew how that worked. He too was a fugitive. *More than one secret to protect in these woods.* The thought helped. He planned on getting to Rebecca in ten days. He imagined her face, her flushed skin when he held her in his arms. Her eyes wet with tears. Likely, his too.

A half day out of the village, the terrain turned unexpectedly rugged. The undergrowth was nearly as thick and sharp as porcupine quills. Briars tore his skin. The ground was craggy, lots of rock poking through the duff like stubble on a man's face, some with sharp edges. The lay of the land rose and plunged. Even Dan refused to run through the worst of it. He didn't think many animals would either, not quickly, not easily. Well, neither could a tracker. And the best one among them wouldn't be looking. Funny—he took the man at his word. *Tom,* he thought. *White Bear.* He chewed the new name over on his mind. Well, the scout deserved that respect.

He found himself bushwhacking, gravitating to a fast walk or a trot. Still, the brambles ripped at the rawhide fabric of his leather clothes, tore at his skin. That didn't panic him. He knew his pursuers were facing the same obstacles. But doubts continued to plague him. He shifted his concentration back to Rebecca. Saw her cooking an early breakfast in their cabin. He smelled the bacon. Heard the crackle of eggs in the cast-iron pan. He prayed that she had remained. That she hadn't deserted the farm. Hadn't deserted him. Well, no man would blame her.

He didn't stop to gather berries. Didn't want to chance leaving a sign for his pursuers. Easy to see where he picked those. But he did drink water. Dan was cautious there, warning himself at the same time, not to leave tracks in the soft ground at the water's edge. He found a small stream but steered away from it. Stayed wide, courting the dry duff that ran under the giant spruce and cedar. *Going fine,* he told himself. *Doing just fine.* He let his imagination play freely while ignoring his weary body.

He met her at a dance. It was a village celebration down on Vancouver Island, a town born out of thick woods with massive stands of old-growth timber practically growing down the middle of the street. Dan was bucking old growth for cash. He dreamed of acquiring a large piece of acreage back behind Kilnook. He had seen the land and fallen for its lush abundance. An opportunity for good fortune, however a man defined that. Building a farm—he and his brother. A man got acreage easily. Chop. Clear. Burn. Fifty acres for free. A hundred with a wife. Work the body into a frenzy—that was all a pioneer had to do. And André promised to contribute his fifty acres and his strong back.

Carve a farm from the forest. Topple the giant trees and not get crushed in the process. Burn the stumps. Fertile soil there, underneath. Ten thousand years of rich loam. Probably many more. Good dirt—that was why conifers grew into giants. That and the temperate climate. Seventy inches of rain annually aided the process, aided plenty. But a man got tolerably sick of all that moisture.

Rain and thick soil—a rich land for sure. And the relative accessibility to the forest. Abundance made a man's success attainable. But wielding a hand axe or a cross-cut saw, a man could only cut so fast. Those trees would last forever. A strong man would only make a dent in the wilderness. At least that was the conventional thinking.

No doubt, opportunity was waiting. It was a rich new land, and dancing before him was his future wife.

She was a young woman, just nineteen. She danced light on her feet, danced gracefully, if not just a little restrained, as if she wasn't quite sure of herself. Bashful, he thought. He would discover her determination later.

He loved the fact that she was shy—loved the fact that she dropped her eyes, embarrassed when this handsome man asked her for a dance. Her face dimpled pink on the cheeks. Her lashes were dark and thick, enhancing her lovely eyes the same way a black-laced Japanese fan might augment the ivory face of a fine lady.

He didn't know she had eyed him discreetly as he crossed the dance floor on nimble legs, or before, following him discreetly about town. She had seen the logger enough times to begin thinking about him, especially at night when she was alone in her candle-lit bedroom with nothing but a book. She daydreamed about him constantly. He was a handsome man, but she concentrated on the pride that clung like drapery to his person, a determination that etched his square jaw and penetrating eyes. His hands were steady and strong. His chin appeared as if cut from hard stone. And he moved gracefully on the street or across the dance floor. His shoulders were wide and his hands strong. And most importantly, he thought out his words. *Heavens*, she thought, *he's a smart one.*

Perhaps infatuation had found her first, but what did that matter? The chemistry was preordained. No matter how they had stumbled upon each other, they were a handsome pair. Everybody said that, as if everyone on the island spotted the bond right away.

After that first night on the dance floor, the couple became inseparable.

Dusk came early to the forest, a heavy mist enveloping the clear space between the cedars. The undergrowth cleared out. Tall conifers held back the sunlight. The earth carpet was mostly a mixture of needles and duff.

The late afternoon darkened, then darkened more, as air cooled and closed around Dan. He wondered if the landscape had a mind of its own. He wondered if nature might transform its dun-colored features with a change of costume. This one was soft and pewter-colored, like a tarnished brooch. Nightfall.

The birds scattered, vanishing into giant limbs at the tops of the towering evergreens, invisible, their music going dead as ghosts. Fog crept through the copse like the spirits of those ancient trees, the oldest of the old, dead and fallen now, turned to duff and dust.

The largest of the fallen giants might take hundreds of years before decaying into a chocolate-colored loam. Under the soil lay the bones of many animals, ones that had roamed through the forest long before the two-legged men came, before the ancient tribes, before legends were born and lost again.

In the fog, it became harder for Dan to pick his way, to hold on to that mental compass that offered a woodsman directions.

He trotted on, determined, even as tiny doubts began to obscure his quest, much the way too much drink seizes the keen edge of a man's thinking. Before a bottle of bad whiskey shreds common sense.

Dan wrote a letter to Rebecca's mother in the Midwest, asking permission to marry her daughter. Her father was gone now, dead and buried. He had barely survived Chancellorsville and the bitter aftermath of the Civil War. Dan and Rebecca were married in an unpainted clapboard church a few weeks later. Hadn't heard back from her mother yet, but they just couldn't wait. Dan's parents were both dead, his mother more recently, dying of loneliness, fatigue, and a broken heart. Dying young and embittered. In that wilderness, the weak didn't survive long. As far as that went, many of the stronger warriors were cut down early too.

Logging was the most dangerous occupation in the world. Fishing ran second. There weren't many options.

Running hard, Dan hoped the devil might pass him by, even as he sought her. Crying out loud, he just had to see her one more time. One more time at least. He was sure of that—as sure as rain.

His mind skipped back and forth like a lone fir in a heavy wind. Dan remembered working in the woods all that fall until the winter rains came, when oxen and the huge logging equipment mired down—when a strong man wallowed knee-deep in too much muck, exasperated. Clear-cut logging left square miles of forest terrain stark with devastation. Well, that was how it was done. Nobody thought much beyond the profits that came with the bounty, the valuable deadfall. The key words were, "Get 'em out." Get out those giant logs.

The bride and groom took a steamer to Kilnook. André met them at the wharf, his eyes shining with that charming, impish smile that women found irresistible. If heartbreak tended to follow, well, so be it. If anything, André was more handsome than Dan. He moved with pomp and swagger. If anyone else had seen his image in their mirror, they would have been proud. Or vain. Unfortunately, André and his fine looks and fast fists always found more trouble than comfort. Travail followed him like a faithful retriever.

Dan was exhausted from his day of flight. Night painted the grove the way thick, black coffee discolors the ivory belly of a porcelain cup. If there was a moon up there, the yellow orb refused to find a path through the monster trees, around their pitch-black silhouettes. Darkness made everything appear larger, amplifying his senses, his imagination. He realized the futility in going much farther and began to explore the surroundings for a cache to bed down in.

He found a spot hollowed out of a rock precipice just a mile or two deeper into the woods, a natural cave cradled in soft, igneous rock. The cave was high and protected, a mass of rock and shale poking above the earth landscape like a whale surfacing on a calm sea. He applauded his luck. He climbed easily up the six feet of stone, settling into the depression like a grizzly bear honing out a sleeping quarters for a long winter's nap. Well, what the heck! The space smelled of bear. Dan realized quickly enough that animals *had* used the cave before him, maybe recently. A musty smell pervaded the hollowness of the cave, a melding of aromas representing dirty socks and dead leaves—of animal sweat, dung, and gnarled old bones. Dankness pervaded the cave, enhancing the feeling of unannounced company. Bad company.

Rock has skin too, Dan thought as he rubbed the flat of his hand along the cave wall. Damp, he noticed. *Dank*. His hand came away wet, and a dirty odor touched his nose. He thought of the hollow tree where he had passed the night while running from Tom. That was a few months ago, now. He remembered that hollowness, that same protected feeling. He palpated the feeling of *hollow*, both from the physical presence of the rock cave and from the empty place he was feeling inside his gut. He understood the word, alright. "Hollow." He said it out loud. The word echoed along the rock corridor. He was dreadfully lonely, and the fog and the damp cave only intensified his foreboding, his sense of isolation. Protected sanctuary or not, he felt alone. And, yes, he was hungry.

Maybe he should get out of there, he thought, spend the night in the open. But Dan didn't like that proposition either. Too easy to get trapped. *Get some sleep. No man is going to catch me unawares. Not six feet in the air with my back against a wall.*

When he thought more about the animal smell, he thought bear, and the reality hit him square in the face. Bear! He was sure. Better not be one there. Not that night. He had enough experience with bears to last a lifetime, maybe a couple.

But the cave didn't appear deep. And with so much springtime in the air, the bears were back in the wild. Old Ephraim would be traipsing the forest, looking for food, eating as much fat as possible to hold him through the next long winter. *Just another grazing animal*, Dan thought, and chuckled, the first of the day. Again, he reacted to his hunger. Nothing to do about that, at least not now. Maybe tomorrow he might shave off a few minutes, grab some salmonberries or tender roots. He had learned a lot about wild edibles from his new Native friends.

Dan was sure he was safe. He would pass the night near the entrance. If anything stirred, he would beat it out of there.

He settled in. Tried to get comfortable. But he kept thinking about her, and the memories wouldn't let him be. *Stop,* he thought. *Might just be seeing her in a few days.*

Again, he felt the hard scratch of hunger. He figured he would have to ignore that gnawing sensation for at least a couple more days. It wasn't the first time. Surely, there would be more. Then he slept.

In between jobs, Dan took to clearing away the mighty trees that dominated their backyard. He was intent on fashioning a farm for Rebecca and himself. Logging was dangerous work. Dan and Rebecca wanted a family. They wanted the security of their cabin and property. Rebecca wanted a cat.

It took three years of strenuous work from sunrise to sunset, seven days a week, to clear the farm. The only interruption in that pattern was when Dan went trapping. Things moved according to the young couple's plan, with one exception. They hadn't had the child they longed for.

Rebecca got her kitten. Dan finished construction on a small cabin. André came out and pitched in with all his youthful vigor. The brothers bought rough-cut lumber from a mill on Clio Bay. The fir boards were straight-grained and true. They split the cedar shakes themselves, split them from huge, round cedar bolts they felled on the property. When Dan and Rebecca couldn't afford a couple of store-bought windows, André purchased them, wanting nothing in return. "Hell, Dan," he would say, "I'd just drink it up anyway. Think of it as a wedding gift."

And his eyes would twinkle.

One window faced out from the new kitchen where Rebecca watched Dan returning from the woods at night. A wood-burning stove with a deep oven was Rebecca's prized possession. She bought it from a Sears Roebuck catalog. Got shipped from Seattle. Dan was trapping marten and beaver, shuffling the profits back into the farm.

On weekends when André wasn't working at the mill, the brothers built a barn. With more trapping money, Dan bought their first livestock. Life settled into a routine. Life was good.

Rebecca made them leave several stands of cedar along the river. She had different ideas, alright, but both men loved her thinking. After months of hanging around Rebecca, André became infatuated with his sister-in-law. After a while he would do almost anything for her. Dan teased André about his puppy love. The prodding was playful. Rebecca saw it. The brothers were as tight as men could be, the finest of brothers. She didn't anticipate any trouble over that.

Months passed. They all began to wonder. Why didn't Rebecca conceive? Outside the confines of the bedroom, nothing was said, but the tension became palpable. Year three on the farm came and went. Things were shaping up: barn, cabin, a cleared meadow and garden, but no baby.

A couple of months later, an itinerant doctor came to town. Rebecca said she wanted a check-up. Nothing else needed to be said. Both brothers knew why she was going.

The doctor gave the answer they all dreaded. There would be no baby. The sawbones figured she was barren. Rebecca came home in tears. She cried off and on for several days. Dan kept a barrel-full of emotions packed deep inside. She needed his support. And what the hell might a man say? He worked hard on the farm, playing out his frustration on the big timber that constantly blocked his way. He trapped in the spring and fall. The large bales were profitable. But mostly, he lent support to Rebecca, who remained swollen with sadness.

Inside the cave, he dreams deeply. The sky is raven-black and moonless. In the dream there is a son. Dan's son. Rebecca's son. The son they never could have. In the dreamland he is a young man about fifteen years old. Dan has never seen a large city, but the boy is standing in an urban tunnel between tall brick buildings. He is staring high into a clear pocket of sky, an open space that crisscrosses the city, block after block, like a spider web. The streets run downhill until the cobblestones stop at the edge of a large saltwater bay where the docks, canneries, and warehouses begin. In front of the last buildings, a soft offshore wake laps around thick wooden pilings. From the dreamworld, Dan studies the calm, sheltered bay that rises and falls with the tides. A huge, snow-capped mountain stands sentinel behind and beyond the half-moon bay.

His vision shifts. The young man with Rebecca's high cheekbones and intense eyes is sailing away from the city. He is standing on the bow of a wooden schooner. A soft wind scuds the sails. The young man appears to be waving. Five fingers perch in the thick salt air as if caught in slow motion. The boy scans the horizon. Rebecca is there, too, beside her son.

Caught up in the night land, Dan feels the agony of their separation. Rebecca is older now, past middle age. She is still a lovely woman. Dan can't figure it. Can't figure where the boy fits in. Fear rifles through his belly. Perhaps he never found his way back to her. Perhaps he is still lost in the wilderness, lost or dead. But the boy?

In the dream, her radiant eyes never waver.

He is dumbstruck with longing. She is lovely but untouchable. And a son that he has never known, handsome, tall, and strong—how can that be? In his dreamworld, Dan is dumbstruck with awe.

Suddenly, there is no city, no wharf by the bay, no mountain beyond. The ship continues to sail toward the far horizon, out of Dan's reach. Infinite ocean is the only landscape. Offering only his intense gaze, the young man continues to scan the horizon. There is no wife, no Rebecca now. The son stands alone. Beyond, and rushing across the bucking sea, an immense Haida war canoe with the mask of an eagle carved high on the prow slices through lofty ocean combers. The canoe is superbly built. It can withstand time and storm. Dan surmises that the vessel must be magical. An aura of astonishment fills the air.

The eagle's carved wooden eyes scan the horizon like a living predator. The eagle is searching for Dan's son. Dan shouts a warning, but the boy cannot hear. The raptor's eyes are circled in thick black. Outside, one ring of ebony. Inside, one black dot surrounded by a yellow ring. Yellow turns to gold—pure, brilliant gold. The son stands unaware as the canoe rushes upon him. Dan can't reach him. Can't save his son.

Suddenly, the landscape fades. The world is empty but for four elements: water, sky, fire, and stone. The only sound is Dan's hard breathing.

The scene shifts one last time. A golden sun rises above a familiar horizon. The sea is deserted of friend or foe. Water, sky, fire, stone. Four elements. Four colors. Four directions. The Native map of the world.

Loneliness strikes Dan in his dreamland and seizes like ice covering a frozen mountain lake.

1976

Two books opened a new trajectory into the center of Katherine's life. The first was *Bury My Heart at Wounded Knee*. Her mother had recently read the book (first published in 1970) and shared it with Katherine. The second was a book about a sacred figure to the Siouan peoples. The seer was called Black Elk. His book, *Black Elk Speaks,* added a new dimension to Katherine's education.

America was slowly beginning to discover the truth about Native peoples and the abject poverty that had been cast upon them.

Katherine pondered new writings. She riveted in on recent events that were dramatically changing the world—her world—or at least significant parts of it. She understood Native people's dedication to the environment. Always, she remembered Ishi.

Time to get more involved, she thought. Opinions were changing regarding the war in Vietnam. Changing quickly. Was peace in sight? Were there new causes ahead of her? As she pondered, the world turned slowly. The Beatles' music stirred her. So did the Dalai Lama.

She threw herself at change and the evolution of a new ideology. John Lennon and his compatriots had started a revolution. Their music aimed directly at the younger generation. Katherine quickly climbed aboard. And then there was Dylan.

The times were a changin'.

CHAPTER TWENTY-ONE

Whose voice was first sounded on this land?
The voice of the red people who had but bows and arrows . . .
What has been done in my country I did not want,
did not ask for it; white people going through my country . . .
When the white man comes in my country, he leaves a trail
of blood behind him.

—Red Cloud of the Oglala Sioux

Dan rose in the middle of the night, propelled from a deep sleep that festered with dream fragments that he could no longer align. He had forgotten the son who wasn't to be. He had lost his wife once again.

Stretching his weary limbs, he lifted his stiff body off the cave's rocky floor, then scampered down the wall with his back to the forest. His chest raked the cold, wet granite. Still high up the wall, he heard the drum beat of a large raptor's wings. Suddenly, Dan felt the unexpected grasp of talons as they penetrated his shoulder. He shouted involuntarily and released his grip on the slick stone. He fell hard, butting the back of his head solidly on the rock buttress at the bottom of the wall. His world went blank as darkness enveloped him.

Hours bled by.

Later, he pondered a memory of wings, the sharp *womp, womp, womp* of air scattering.

Before his eyes opened, he sensed hard, fierce light. Half-conscious, he acclimated quickly to the verdant land around him. Of course, there was pain. Pain called out to him like his mother had done so many times in his youth when he and André escaped into the deep woods behind the house.

"Boys!" she would call. "Boys! Y'all get home for dinner, and I mean now! Before I give it to the possums. Before your pa gives you a whippin.'"

At least the fog was gone, that dense gray that imprinted a message of self-doubt on a man's mind. The pain twisted through the bright morning air—said "Good day," as tauntingly as a snake-oil man. There was plenty wrong with the picture before him. Above the pain, his other senses were sorting out what had happened in his world before he fell.

His body felt numb and cold. He realized with a shock that he was barefoot. Someone had sliced and removed his moccasins and his leggings. They lay in a heap. He reviewed all this suspiciously, angrily. Nothing made sense. Dan's mind felt as shredded as his leathers. Perhaps a person might be nearby. *Might be watching me now.* His mind somersaulted back to the night before. He had not been cautious when he left the cave. *Damnation*, he had not. Dan knew better. *I might be dead!*

Then Dan remembered the sound of wingbeats. He thought some more about that. After a while, he wasn't so sure. He must have been dreaming. And if not, how could he have prepared himself?

He opened one eye slightly. The outside world leaped in at him, a private world of head-splitting pain. *Stay calm. Stay calm.* He repeated his private litany in his head. He would not allow words or motion to alert his enemy. Private warnings continued to skitter along, like an insect that pesters a man.

One eye shifted into half focus, exploring the world of taunting light. His other eye remained closed, a cautionary reaction. *Is someone here*? *Is someone watching*? His inner eye, the one that never saw but felt and listened, waited patiently. It confronted the late-morning sounds, the sweet music of a copse thick with songbirds, the rustle the small wind makes, a choir, a wilderness strum. His mind wandered while his ears picked apart the different sounds, or lack of sounds. He allowed the forest to play out its natural rhythm. Normally, he would have been enchanted, but not today.

Time pressed upon him. He guessed he would leap to his feet and face his enemy. He would just have to stand and fight. He might run. Questions festered, but he was ready, as ready as he would ever be. He knew he could die. But why hadn't his attacker killed him already while he lay as helpless as a newborn?

He jumped up. The movement crippled him with pain, plunged him into near unconsciousness. He struggled to get upright. His head was on fire, feeling split like a round of firewood under an axe's iron head. He spun, both eyes wide open now.

Nobody was there! Nobody was waiting. *What's going on?* His mind screamed. The birds saw all and went mute. Then they scattered. Half in a fighter's position, half in a runner's, he groped about in search of a fight waiting to happen. Dan was prepared to strike out. Oddly, only a few remaining songbirds piped in.

"Where is the enemy?" he muttered to himself.

He thought some more. If there were men in the woods, the birds wouldn't be singing their tiny hearts out. *Wait a darn second.* He held himself cautiously, his muscles ready to fly. *Wait a gosh-darn second.* He was alone, as alone as the millennia of buried and rotten bones, so many secrets hidden under the forest floor. So much time passing.

His inner eye was seeking again, but the nerves in his feet reminded him of an earlier clue. *Barefoot*! He studied the ground where his body had lain for . . . well, he wasn't all that sure how long. But there were his moccasins, or what remained of them. They had been cut up, sliced into ribbons by a knife. No use now.

Then the thought struck him full force. *Talons.* The leather was shredded as if by a raptor's razor-edged talons. No knife would leave that pattern. He breathed deeply, sorting through a field of pain, through frustration and confusion. His heart was racing.

His leggings and moccasins had also been shredded. And the knife he had stolen and hidden many weeks before was gone. His only weapon! He wondered if the blade had flown away too. Flown away, like the wingbeats he imagined from the night before. Dan thought again about the eagle, distinctly remembering the torrent of air as the raptor spread its majestic wings and soared aloft. *Is any of this real*?

In the evergreen forest—alone, desperate, dejected—he felt as naked as on the day he was born. Not since he was attacked by the grizzly on the Skeena had he felt so vulnerable.

Then he saw it. Lying on the ground as plain as daylight was a single eagle feather of unusual size. "I'll be go to hell."

The eagle had left a calling card.

To survive, Dan knew he had no choice but to walk back to Black Wing's village. He knew the name of the village now. Black Wing had called it Wolf Haven, making a vague association with old memories and then moving on without further explanation. As usual, Dan was left with more questions than answers. Black Wing indicated that the name was ancient. Said his people descended from that place thousands of years before. Said it fell like many civilizations, broken by inner strife, by dissension, and, of course, by warring and invective. Common factors all. Well, for a change that explanation appeared ripe with possibilities.

The old civilization had been kept alive in legends. The stories were handed down from father to son, from generation to generation, growing in the hearts and spirits of the First Nations over millennia. *Well, those old stories are just shadows now. So much lost.*

He had listened respectfully to all that Black Wing had offered. If Dan was skeptical, he kept it to himself—no ignoring that man. And the stories were something, alright. Good palaver.

What about now? *What about my story*? Dan picked up the feather, his index finger pricking the spline. His mind was spinning. *Feather. Calling card. Eagle.*

"I'll be go to hell," he muttered, his voice discordant there, so deep in the wilderness.

Backtracking along the trail, he thought about the feather some more and limped another mile.

Burrs ripped into the exposed soles of his feet. When they collided, barbs and vines tore through his skin. The bugs were merciless. His skin was burning. So was his pride. Dan couldn't imagine what had happened.

He knew that if the warriors had caught him, most likely, he would have been maimed or killed. *This wasn't warriors. This was a warning.*

By then Dan suspected that he couldn't escape his fate, couldn't escape whatever the hell had happened *back there. Eagle*, he thought, his mind tired and confused. How could that be? Time to head back to Black Wing's home. The way things were going, it might become Dan's. That was, if they didn't kill him first.

Dan had nothing to do but cogitate, and he was doing plenty of that. Alone with his thoughts, he remembered how, once before, he had come out of the woods, badly maimed but alive. Once before, caught unawares.

It was early spring. He had been trapping the Skeena, a river rich in beaver. It had been a good day; he had retrieved eight. Dan was into a routine. He was pulling traps, shaking loose the drowned critters, resetting the steel teeth. With each set he would dip a stick into his cache of beaver candy, castoreum, and bait the trap. Stake and set it into the water on the long chain. He was making good time. The traps were full. The sun was shining. He was happy. He let his guard down.

The bear caught him midstream. There was nothing a grizzly loved more than beaver grease, and Dan's hands were covered with it. The giant most likely smelled the scent from a mile away.

Dan had just baited a trap when the bear rushed him. Perhaps they were both surprised. The big bear was famous for poor eyesight. Maybe Old Ephraim thought another animal was stealing his supper. Dan saw soon enough what was coming. He turned suddenly. Unsheathed his knife.

It wasn't a fair fight. The grizzly hit him four times for every time he struck the giant with the long blade. Four times to one, like the difference in their body weight.

When the knife plunged, it didn't seem to stick. Not a penetrating wound, *fer sure, eh*. The hide appeared impenetrable. The bear continued to bludgeon him. Dan tried to run. No luck. Then he attempted to swim for deeper water. He was bleeding badly. The bear bit into his leg and held on for what felt like an eternity. Seconds turned into hours. Pain screamed at him. The pain was like nothing Dan had ever felt before. Nothing!

Water began to fill his lungs. The grizzly's teeth and paws were tearing at his body. The bear would shake his head—Dan's leg was still attached to the bear's mouth—and Dan heard himself screaming in pain, yet he felt detached. He tasted water, blood, spittle. Right then he knew what a steel trap felt like, clamping onto the leg of a four-legged critter. Right then he thought that if the bear didn't eat him, he would surely drown. He kicked at the bear with all his might with his free leg. Hit the bear on its soft, vulnerable nose, about the only vulnerable spot on the massive body. The grizzly opened his mouth. Hollered like a man branded with a red-hot iron.

As the grizzly reared in protest, Dan broke free. That was the first miracle. From above a raven watched the battle with keen interest. Deep, shining eyes followed each altercation as if it were an invitation to dinner. The raven was always hungry, always inquisitive. He figured by nightfall he would have some flesh to gnaw on. The prankster was owed a favor or two by these strange human beings. The trickster had been foiled more than once. The story was old, but a raven never forgets.

The bear followed Dan into deep water and stood straight up. The current threw him off balance. It was only for a moment, but it was enough. Dan sank the knife deep into the animal's chest, aiming for the heart. He watched the water turn red with blood. A good strike, but that just slowed the furry monster down. The bear was in the flow of the river now and inconvenienced by the wound. It spun, once, twice, three times, thrashing as Dan struggled through waist-deep water toward shore. Even then, Dan knew his injuries might prove fatal.

He saw the rifle leaning against a tree next to his sack of possibles, loaded and cocked, begging Dan to grab it, to ignite its fury. On the wind was that old admonishment, "Never leave your rifle." That was the law of the land. Any tenderfoot would have known better. He had broken the golden rule, the motto of the free trappers. Dan knew he was lucky to be alive. But time favored the bear.

As he reached for the rifle, he felt the Grizz breathing up his back. He was praying that there would be enough time to get one shot off before the bear swatted him down. Getting off a shot would be lucky, more luck than he deserved.

He was fortunate. The gun was in his hands. He swung on the bear, the giant's face nearly touching the end of the barrel. Its paws raked the air, pressing at its victim. Rage filled the valley. Even the raven had scattered to higher ground. Dan pulled the trigger. Felt the bark of the rifle as the recoil tore painfully into his masticated shoulder. His whole body felt like an open wound, but he had no time for reflection. The bullet tore into the bear's throat. The grizzly stood up straight and bellowed in protest. Far up a grandfather tree, the raven froze, and then vaulted higher yet, into the deep violet sky.

The grizzly was thrown backwards by the bullet's impact, but the wound wasn't fatal, at least not immediately. Pulling erect, the monster gathered itself for one more charge. Dan was awestruck. *No,* he thought, *it can't possibly . . .*

The great animal lunged straight for Dan. Frantically, Dan pumped the steel lever. Still hot and smoking, a spent brass casing flew from the chamber, tinkling as it clattered across the smooth river stones.

Dan's movements fumbled into slow motion. He prayed as he pumped the next cartridge into the chamber and heard the bullet slide tightly into place. His finger jumped for the trigger. For once in his life, he didn't squeeze off the weapon. His reaction was frenetic.

There was a loud roar, but the trapper failed to tell whether it belonged to the rifle or was a final bellow from the bear. Maybe it was both. The weapon erupted within inches of the monster's face. The bear went down. Instinctively, Dan pumped another shell into the steel chamber. Thank God he had a new .30-30. Thank God he could fire the rifle without the handicap of reloading with powder, plug, and a round lead ball. Under ideal conditions, that action would have taken a fine assassin better than eight seconds.

Adrenaline was cascading through his body, as was a bucket of blood, racing from open wounds and onto the ground.

Weak and lightheaded, he stood above the bear. He saw that the bear was a goner, but the mighty animal was still breathing, still twitching. Dan slumped to the ground, his knees folding like wet parfleche. He had already lost interest in the bear. Dan's wound might well be fatal—the realization struck him as surely as the bear's paws. His mind faded into the world where dead men walk. Emotions and pain painted a collage, an abstraction that spoke to the next world, to his next life. He no longer deciphered if he was walking into or away from the land of the dead. One thing was for sure: his body was swimming in pain, and he saw a strange white light. *Is this, then, how it ends.*

Leaning on his rifle for support, he raised his body. In a stupor, he fired twice more into the bear's eye socket. It took all that to stop the Grizz. And still the great animal's fur quaked, the great heart refusing to stop pumping, its pulse grinding out those last moments of life. A minute sped by, then five. Seconds crept by like hours. Dan's breathing came in rasps. He was a grievously injured man. His world turned into a whorl of pain. The bear was dead, but Dan was barely alive.

He thought of Rebecca, but his thoughts were flighty. His mind shifted to her father, imagining John Stamp lying semi-conscious in a putrid pool of mud and blood at Chancellorsville, two Confederate bullets lodged in his arm, belly and thigh. A Yankee, his body on fire. Dan related. Just as quickly he pictured Rebecca again. He wondered when she might begin to miss him. Wondered if André would come looking. Checking his body, Dan wondered if he might last beyond a few minutes. Pain, nausea and a distant feeling of floating overwhelmed him. He felt suddenly out of his body. He was staring down at himself, staring from afar. Adrenaline was running like a pony galloping across an open meadow.

Somehow, he cared for the worst wounds, patching the shredded skin together. He had a pair of clean long underwear in his backpack. Frantically, he sliced the cotton and wrapped it around the big wounds. He covered the rags with some shredded rawhide that the bear had torn from his coat. No broken bones, he surmised. Thank God for that.

His movements felt wraith-like. He studied the dozen or so lacerations. He had lost so much blood. He didn't know how his leg had survived the bludgeoning with his bones intact. If he lived, he didn't know if he would be able to walk normally. That is, if anyone came to his rescue. The word "gangrene" kept bubbling through his mind like the pale bubbly froth seeping from the dead bear's throat.

He rubbed some pitch from nearby spruce trees over the lesser wounds. Dan knew his time was running out. Every second was urgent. He was so lightheaded, so dizzy. He stumbled back to the stream. Feeling nauseous, he threw up. The shaking intensified. *So cold.* No standing firmly—he was quaking like a treetop ravaged by the wind. Suddenly, he fainted, falling into the dreamworld of the near dead.

Hours later he rallied, waking, his life clinging by a thread. The long minutes danced by. His temperature swelled. He worried about infection. Had it set in? Most likely. He bled heavily every time he moved. He said a prayer of thanks that his gear had been nearby to aid his survival

When he awoke from fits of unconsciousness, the river was close. He drank deeply. The early spring weather stayed moderate, and more importantly, dry. If Dan had gotten drenched—if rain had found him, bleeding and susceptible—shock would have killed him. He slept once again on the razor's edge of a coma.

He woke many hours later, but it was hard to call the act waking. Hard to know how long he had been down. A Hudson Bay blanket had warmed him at night. That was a surprise. He'd thought he was burning up! Heat had replaced ice. Some of that was good. He wasn't going to die of shock, not right away, anyway. His skin was ablaze.

From under the blanket, he walked the faraway prairies of the dreamworld. His soul was back on the Skeena. His body near enough to hell that he was sure he felt the fires burning. The flame—the fever—razed his body and soul like a firebrand.

At least Dan didn't have to worry about a hostile attack from Native warriors. The Whites had taken care of that. Up there, most tribes had never been much of a problem. He had the whole territory to himself. *Too bad,* he thought, as the clarity of his vision was overcome by rising fever.

He prayed for anyone who might save his life. Any man, regardless of skin color.

The spirits of Native warriors remained in the valley. He clearly felt their presence. In his mind's eye, Dan wandered their forests and streams. He trapped. He fished. Apparitions haunted him, For once, the relationship between their disparate cultures remained symbiotic.

Dan succumbed to hallucinations. Native people waited on the periphery, just out of reach. In a stupor he envisioned their ghostlike faces. The images haunted him at night, and the night was everywhere. In the dreamworld, the Natives had a story to tell, but Dan couldn't decipher their words. They spoke in Native tongues, their facial expressions eroded by sorrow. Dan understood that, alright. He thought he might be joining them in the world of the dead.

After going without food for five days, he forced himself to cut some raw, fetid meat from the bear. He swallowed it greedily. Perhaps, he just might survive.

When Dan didn't return home, Rebecca did plenty of worrying. The good citizens of Kilnook were sure Dan was dead, that he had gone under.

"Too good a trapper to be lost."

"Weather's too mild."

"Trouble, Mrs. Dan. Bad trouble there."

Two good-hearted forays into the wilderness presented rescue parties with no victim, no signs or clues. They figured he had gone under. They should have been right. Alone now, André forged ahead, never losing faith. Rebecca clung to the same belief.

Still, no Dan.

When Dan hobbled out of the Skeena two weeks later, she and André were the only ones who were not totally surprised.

Dan had survived the grizzly, but now, years later, he found himself nearly naked and beaten by an unseen assailant, forced to convert a one-day run for freedom into a humiliating two-day retreat. He stumbled along.

Night turned cold, burning him with icy fingers. The sharp briars and needles that littered the forest floor cut into the soles of his feet. He tore leather patches from his britches. Wrapped the shreds around his feet. It helped a little. Sharp branches tore at his exposed skin. Still, he was not in any rush to return to the village. He was not anxious to face his captors. The weather stayed overcast and gray. He stopped and ate berries now.

He thought often about Rebecca. When that happened, he tried to divert his attention away from her memory. Heartache was more rugged than the terrain. More than ever before, he realized she might remain unreachable.

1973

Far up valley
A log truck
Down shifts
Engine sounds
Tumble
Gears snarling
Like cornered
Badger
Steel-trapped

In a copse
Rain will find us
When autumn is gone
When leaves fall

We wait now
Nothing certain
But river song

This close to God
Only the stones
Remain sure

—Katherine Skinner-Patterson

CHAPTER TWENTY-TWO

Lord protect me from my friends. I can take care of my enemies

—Voltaire

Dan crept into camp at about midday, four days after leaving the village. He was limping. Right away the young boys gathered around him. They let out a wail to raise the dead. The kids knew his story, alright. The Whiteman had been missing for days. He was a runaway. Their natural curiosity was driven by adult frustration. There would be a ruckus. Any man could palpate the tension that hung over the village like an eagle's extended and terrifying claws.

After the young braves sent the kids scurrying, the mood turned surly. Dan was taken by both arms and half led, half dragged toward the smokehouse that had been his jail during the first two months of his internment. Instead of being taken inside, he was shoved hard against the outside wall. His face scraped the hand-hewn sides of the wide cedar planks. He smelled the cedar's oily resin, felt sticky red blood as it careened from his nose and off his chin. The smoke was back, a blend of alder and dried fish. The sky had turned overcast. A storm was brewing. Dan was oblivious. He tried to remain calm but quickly raised his arms in defense when a young warrior struck him. Dan hit back hard, overreacting perhaps, and the brave staggered. Others backed away.

Dan crouched like a fighter, his fists balled. “Hi’kyusta!” he shouted in Kwakiutl. “Don’t touch me. I’ll not be your slave!”

His sudden use of Kwakiutl, a few words he had learned from Yellow Bird Singing, surprised and confused the Natives. For the moment at least, the pushing stopped. An elder entered the scene and tried to calm the vindictive ire of the younger men.

Rain clouds were racing in from the west.

Dan wiped blood from his nose with the back of his hand.

The gathering crowd grew angrier.

What was gnawing at them was the fact that they had spent the last several days searching for this man in vain. Far more important, his escape threatened their way of life, threatened their families and the tribe itself. Their pride was wounded because they could not claim to have found the wily pathfinder themselves. And they couldn’t enlist White Bear to help. “Leg not ready yet,” he confided.

A council started. Thirty men circled him. Charlie appeared, and an argument ensued. Nothing was going Dan’s way. Dan needed a friend more than ever. He was overjoyed to see the Haisla. He wondered how much Charlie’s brand of persuasiveness might help. Black Wing was nowhere in sight.

After months living with the Natives, Dan could glean enough Kwakiutl and Haisla to discern pieces of the argument. He knew they were arguing over the scale of his punishment. The rules were simple: attempt escape and forfeit your life. That took him back. Dan had hoped that things weren’t this bad. If he had, he probably would have continued his way back to Kilnook, naked or not. Eagle or no eagle. Better to die fighting. Better to die like a man.

Charlie stepped forward, arguing that Dan had walked back to camp on his volition. “He came back of his own free will. He stands here now in our village. Stands strong, a proud man. He is my friend, our friend!”

“What happened to his clothes?” someone asked.

Charlie didn’t rightly know, and that argument didn’t matter much. The runaway was back.

The argument continued. *Where the hell is Black Wing?* Dan wondered, his anxiety rising by the second.

He thought about the elder's warning. He knew this trouble was of his own making. He realized that Black Wing couldn't do much now, even if he wanted to. Rules were rules. Dan had broken the one that mattered most. Black Wing was allowing the council to make its own decision. That was the Native way. He would not attempt to overrule their verdict. There was nothing new about that. For a thousand years, decisions had been settled in council around a campfire. Charlie was likely acting as the elder's spokesman. Dan wondered if he should hold out hope. Without Charlie, he wouldn't have had a sinner's chance in hell. He thought again about running, but he knew he wouldn't get a hundred yards. He composed himself. *Better stay calm. Stay alert.*

Dan stood quietly and erect. Every time a brave spoke, he fastened his eyes on the speaker. *Stay proud*, he thought. *These men respect that above all else.* But he felt that his poker face had played out. He failed to follow all the details of their conversation. He didn't know that the decision was coming down to a punishment of a lesser degree, but even those alternatives would have scared most any man.

Several braves insisted that they break both of his legs with a club. They reasoned that would stop him from running for a while. It appeared that they were winning the argument. Charlie had a worried expression on his face. Dan's heart was beating wildly.

Again he thought of running, but once again he held back. At that point, any such decision was ridiculous. It would spell his fate. Wasn't this like facing down a Grizz? Standing tall and firm? Standing bravely before the warriors?

Dan tried to look relaxed, but his bravado fooled no one. His mouth was so dry he couldn't even spit. There was nothing to even swallow, other than fear and his pride. His stomach growled like a mountain lion. Dan was forced to admit the truth. He was frightened.

Several of the men took him by the arms again, pushing him toward the west end of the village. Two stout posts embedded into the earth for the purpose of hanging and curing game stood out starkly.

He struggled, but his resistance was of no use. A dozen men surrounded him, striking whenever he resisted. A horizontal beam crossed the two posts. A young warrior threw a rope over the beam while others raised and tied Skinner's hands together, lifting them as high over his head as possible. They raised him up until he dangled like a puppet. His toes barely touched the ground. This wasn't what he had expected. *Stay calm*, he pleaded to himself. *For God's sake, look brave*. Inside, his emotions raced. His survival was in their hands. *Not good*, he thought, his teeth chattering.

A large Native that Dan remembered by the name of He Walks Bold had a club, a long, tapered bat shaped from the root of a spruce tree. He approached the rack. It took everything Skinner had, but he remained steady. He swiveled his eyes pleadingly toward his executioner but found little sympathy. The huge man was preparing to swing the bat when Dan caught a blur of motion out of the corner of his eye.

A smaller man grabbed the club from He Walks Bold, and then threw the big man to one side. Another brief struggle ensued before Tom pushed himself in front of Dan's suspended figure and stood rock solid, a determined adversary.

In Tsimshian, he began to berate the men before him.

Dan caught the first words, the same as Charlie's: "This is my friend."

Slowly, Tom explained the history of how Dan had jeopardized his life to save his brother, about his courage on the cliff, his endurance and skill, and finally his honor. How he had left his wife and his farm to save his brother.

"This is an honorable man. He carry his courage like a grizzly bear. And he not kill me when I was trapped by his cunning. A fine woodsman. The finest. He defend our village, our people. I trust him to keep our secret."

His words bellowed out, carrying weight. "Which among you would have traveled so far, knowing that you were leaving your family behind? Which of you would have shown such courage and endurance?"

There was plenty of anger dancing through the crowd. There was also respect. Every man in the village venerated the Tsimshian. As far as that went, they also admired the trapper.

Tom promised that if they pardoned his friend, he would work out a deal with the pathfinder. He was sure that Dan would give his word not to attempt another escape. The Natives listened respectfully, their anger abating. After all, White Bear was a man who never twisted the truth.

Minutes fled by. Gunmetal clouds darkened the sky. Raindrops pressed upon the gathering. A quiet conversation ensued. Tom stood rigidly in front of his friend, his eyes steady and proud. Dan felt emotions tapering off. The truth was, the warriors liked Dan, and above all else, they respected his courage. They had come to trust him. After all, hadn't the White man returned to the village of his own free will? Suddenly, it was a turnabout world.

Charlie interrupted, backing up White Bear, but leaning toward Dan. "Listen to your heart," he urged the crowd. "This is good man."

Finally, the men agreed to give the White trapper another chance. But there was one condition: Dan would have to give his word that he wouldn't run, not ever again. The tribe couldn't chance that. Too many things could go wrong.

Tom explained the situation. Dan knew what the decision meant. He closed his eyes and let the reality sink in. He thought of the consequences of such a commitment, the bond of honor that passed between brothers. Last of all, he thought of Rebecca. He had to see her. He just had to. Dan swiveled his eyes toward his captives. Felt the return of mouth dryness and haunting fears. His face was ashen, as white as a White man could become without turning ghostly. Slowly, he spoke. "Can't promise that, Tom. Like to, believe you me. Just can't."

He just couldn't stay here forever. He would run at the first clear chance he got. He felt obliged to speak the truth. His self-respect demanded that much. Tom asked again, almost pleadingly. Dan responded with the same answer. "Tom," he said, his voice steady and proud, "I appreciate all this. Trouble is, just can't give you a promise I may not keep. You know I would never betray these people. But the problem is still my wife. I gotta find her. And I can't lie to you. Can't inflict another untruth upon these people. You know that, Tom, don't you? You understand?"

A great sadness flickered across the scout's face. Then the expression turned respectful. Tom stood proudly. His apprentice had just put his honor before all else.

Tom turned to the other men. Many had already figured which direction the White man was heading, which way the stick was floating. To the man, they admired his courage.

The Natives huddled together, one last time. After the brief council, Charlie spoke. "Hit him only once," he said. "You, White Bear, once across the leg. Hard. Break it."

The last two words hung like riprap.

Charlie turned and left, numbly pushing through the Native delegation, leaving the men standing like a gaggle of geese.

In Tsimshian, Tom asked for the club. He took the weapon, spinning it abjectly in his hands. He turned toward his old student, looking him steady in the eye. "I sorry, my friend. I respect your decision. I've always picked my friends carefully. I'm proud to say you're one of a few."

Tom lifted the bat over his head. With a smooth, powerful stroke, he brought it down across the bones in Dan's lower left leg. Before Dan fainted, he felt the large bone snap, followed by a stunning shock, nausea, and then blackness. He was left hanging from the crossbeam until dusk scuttled daylight. Until a hard rain fell.

A *Kwa Gulth* moon—the full blue moon—twisted through patches of dark-gray clouds. The rain was cold and thick, and it fell like stinging needles, silver in the moonlight.

Dan was carried gently into the great lodge. Several women waited, preparing natural medicines to care for his injury. The pain was excruciating, but he had felt worse. Movement intensified it. Even semi-delirious, he knew he could live with the wound. Sooner or later it would heal.

Later, lying prostrate on the earth floor and wrapped in an elk-skin robe, he listened to the night sounds. Other than two sentries at either end of the village, the camp slept. The rain lightened, natural sounds mingling with the soft mountain wind. He wished suddenly that he could tie a bowline knot around his thoughts. Slow them down. Tonight he was grappling with the price of honor.

Once again, the moon broke free from the clouds. He wondered about Black Wing, his absence. He thought some more about the eagle. Again he remembered *her* and let his mind sidle down the long, deep valley toward their farm, their life together. He imagined the spring sounds abounding throughout. Imagined birds trilling in the trees. The chickens and ducks. Helen the cow. Two goats, chewing their cud. The barn animals, he remembered. Their pathos—they were all familiar. And the river that swept past the farm. It too had its individual voice. The water thundered along or slowed to a trot, a song in constant transition.

Dan did something he hadn't done in years. Quietly, he mumbled a private prayer to the Christian God, to Jesus Christ.

The moon threw deep shadows between the lodges. Inside, empathy for the Boston man lingered like the sky dance that touched them all.

Too much pain to sleep. The ache in his leg throbbed insistently. For the hundredth time, he let his mind go silent, the way Black Wing had taught him. He let his mind flow out into the cool spring air. He reveled in the common respect that binds brothers together. Would he ever forget André? Of course not! But by now, Dan knew that he would learn to live with the loss.

His mind picked its way back down the granite corridors of the Kilnook Valley. Maybe love had a power of its own, a message separate from his broken body. The thought startled him. He turned his imagination loose. Dan was like a wolf on the trail of recent scent.

Suddenly, he confronted a surprise so overwhelming that he nearly lost the syntax of the vision. For just a second, he saw her. Well, maybe? He would never know for sure. Then his mind went blank, stunned into his old reality by the shock of such an intimate encounter. Dan had seen—or thought he had seen in that brief instant—a woman wrapped in moonlight. A woman sitting inside a cedar canoe.

The woman was listening to the breaching sounds of whales, and he was sure that the woman was his wife. Doubts invaded. *Rebecca in a canoe? Whales? How could that be?*

He cogitated, and after a while, wonder transformed logic. *Maybe*, he thought. *Just maybe.*

Then no canoe. No vision. The moon slid once again behind the clouds, and sleep took him fitfully.

1987

Katherine had never seen such destruction. Everywhere she turned, a cloud of smoke hung over denuded glades. The ground was charred. Like a graveyard, burned stumps rose above a sea of ashes that had once been a proud jungle, a rainforest. *Nubs*, she thought. *Corpses.* A proud, fallen army of trees reduced to corpses. Miles of Amazon jungle gone. It was slipping away faster than anyone comprehended. It was worse than Katherine had imagined. Worse than the scant newscasts. With it went the security of the Indigenous peoples, a lifestyle thousands of years old. And with it the planet slipped further and further into an environmental abyss.

She couldn't begin to determine how many plants, insects, and animals had disappeared along with the forest, how many had been burned into extinction. In the States she had read statistics on the speed of the demolition of this huge ecosystem, the largest of the remaining rainforests. At the time it hadn't seemed possible: one football field every sixty seconds. She had thought the process was exaggerated. Now she knew the truth. To her surprise, she felt her rage quell. Her body stopped shaking. Then came the resolve.

Oddly, she remembered her third-grade geography class. Her mind scampered past sketchy memories. Pictures and lessons from a dog-eared geography book raised an incarnation of sorts. Then a face from the past stepped forward. What was her name? Yes, Mrs. Bowers. Sure. Of course. Emily Bowers.

In a hand-me-down geography book, there had been a photograph of a Native boy and his sister. They were living on a riverbank, in a clay hut with a thatched roof and a small, oblong entrance. She recalled that the Indigenous people there traveled in carved wooden canoes, vessels not that much different from river canoes belonging to the North Coast's First Peoples. Katherine thought she remembered—had she been ten?—smoke from village fires, a dark smudge rising and twisting through masses of trees and brambles in a South American jungle. Everything was painted in verdant green. Twice a day the rains came, showers falling heavily, covering the village like a wet, dense blanket. She remembered reading that, believing in the truth of words. A little girl might drown under rain so thick and unrelenting.

All the memories came flooding back from vaults buried long ago in her mind. From where she now stood—amid the ghost of a jungle that appeared more desolate than any nightmare—Katherine framed the picture. Excitement stirred in her, the cloud of a memory closed for so many years, ever since Mrs. Bowers and her fourth-grade geography class.

From somewhere deep inside came the flutter of a long lost vision, the memory of a dream so real that she felt the breeze in her hair and the sounds of Native people, of drums and dance. She found herself surrounded by thatched clay huts, by water, smoke, and fire. A village deep in a jungle. A previous life, perhaps? Or a genetic memory passed through ancient ancestors. One or the other. Both or neither. A reality blurred by time and space.

She opened her eyes, and the vision faded, replaced by the devastated landscape surrounding her. The burned earth and smoking embers filled her nostrils with the stench of broken dreams.

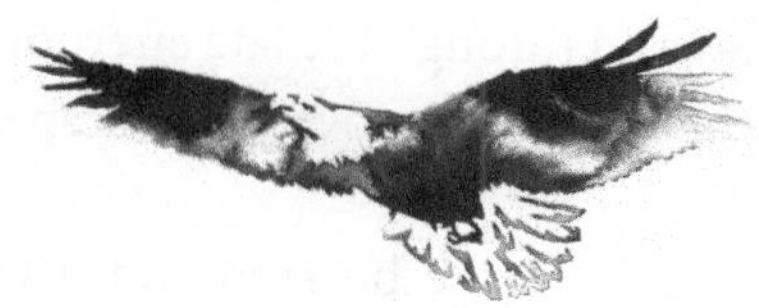

CHAPTER TWENTY-THREE

I gathered my night of knowing, my season of belief.
I plunged through the forest to the canoe in deep grass, untied the knotted bow rope from a spruce, dragged it to the water, set out against the wind. My paddle flashed in spray.

—Kim Stafford,
from *Entering the Grove*

The day closed in fours: four seekers in a wooden vessel, four days of travel, bright, clear, alluring. Four ravens hunkered onto a rocky point shaped like an eagle's wing. Four totems—the last of hundreds that had once graced the valley—rising majestically into the clear evening sky. A sinking sun washed the horizon in crimson and rhododendron hues.

Kolnux: a handful of Native shanties—summer and fishing cabins. Eulachon and salmon swim past there. It had been a gathering place for ages. Along the point was a graveyard for the dead, all Native. The four seekers were surrounded by the sassy chatter of a rookery of ravens and the solemnity of ancient spirits.

Beaver, eagle, whale, and raven: four clans—four clans of the Haisla.

Rebecca spotted chimney smoke long before she distinguished the sharp edges of the rooflines. The evening water laid silky and flat like the fur on a beaver's back. Trappers called the fur "plew." In the spring when the pelts were thick and lustrous, each hide brought three dollars. That was a significant sum of money.

The foursome traveled through the late afternoon and into the evening, a change of plans that revealed a lovely landscape but, unfortunately, left them exposed.

Rebecca looked again to the horizon and discovered a sudden color change. Now the mercurial sunset was a blaze of ruby and the pink color of flushed skin. Above the horizon floated a thin swatch of clouds, cut and suspended like the flayed sides of a smoked salmon. Rebecca remembered the stories of beaches covered with Native drying racks. Tens of thousands of fish drying in the autumn heat. Much had changed so fast. Now the practice was infrequent. *Better days ahead,* she thought. Rebecca's attitude had shifted.

The flooding tide mirrored four faces, all of them colorless. No prejudice from the eternal waters.

Paddles synchronized into a pattern as predictable as the English guard change. British blaze of red, British cadence, British power. British Columbia. This was no longer Native land. This was the queen's land now.

Paddles dipped. Lifted. Held. And dipped again. Spirit Runner chanted a Native canoeing mantra that had been passed up the coast.

"Hey. Mana Naka, say. Ho. Mana Naka, so."

Eagles find me. Eagles protect me.

Lower on the horizon, only a sliver of the falling sun remained. Then it was gone. A nimbus of twilight surrounded the travelers.

The canoe scraped belly first onto round granite stones. The sound had a welcoming feel.

"Pull the canoe high onto the shore. Snow melt tonight." Spirit Runner enforced the message by pointing toward the rugged mountains that lay before them. "Water rising. Hurry now. Night is upon us."

On pea gravel, the canoe settled like a sleek, beached porpoise. A second canoe suggested that someone was nearby. *These are not enemies*, Spirit Runner thought. *These are allies.*

The women went in search of firewood while Spirit Runner nurtured a fire.

Above the beach a campfire warmed the weary travelers. High above them spruce boughs swayed in the updraft where the flames met the cold night air. Man Hides Good disappeared along the shoreline, heading for a spark of lantern light and four simple cabins built of rough cedar boards and square nails. Rebecca speculated to herself that the Haisla knew his destination and probably knew the inhabitants.

Man Hides Good reappeared carrying two spring salmon. He left a second time and appeared with two more, both of them smoked. A third trip revealed an exquisite cedar basket brimming with salmonberries. Nestled into the berries, eulachon grease floated on four large mussel shells, likely gathered from the ocean and ordained as miniature serving bowls. Perhaps the Haisla had forfeited one of his silver dollars. Perhaps the salmon had been a gift between friends.

From the fire the aroma of roasted salmon wafted on the cool night air. A gentle breeze pushed across the fire circle. Inside, the travelers crouched, toasty warm. Spirit Runner picked flaky slabs of succulent flesh from the loin of the fish carcass. Neither woman remembered fish tasting so good.

"Dip the salmon in the grease," Man Hides Good implored, his fingers wrapping around the succulent flesh while pouring eulachon grease from the blue shell onto flakes of tender salmon. He sucked his fingertips with relish.

The conversation faded into silence as the four travelers satisfied their hunger. The stillness of the nearby forest and the richness of the meal called out for a good night's sleep. In the darkness outside the fire circle, the forest spirits crept forward as if they wished to overhear snippets of the conversation. Man Hides Good began to talk. "Berry Woman, she speak of three canoes passing late in winter. Lawmen stopping. Many questions, but men gone soon. Berry Woman watch two other men pass near dawn, just that morning, just ahead of the law. She don't talk to any law. Don't tell her whole story. 'No speak English,' she say. One man with a rifle spit on the ground. She not like his eyes. She not like his manners. *Go away*, she thinks. *Take your bad blood out of my valley*. Three lawmen stand tall in front of her. The fourth, the quiet one, he stand behind, by canoe. She know him. Everyone knows him. Tsimshian. White Bear. Canoeing with wrong clan."

"Coffee?" Rebecca asked, filling the battered tin mug for the initiator of the conversation.

Double-thick black coffee. Four teaspoons of raw brown sugar. The man knew what he liked.

"She didn't see anyone coming back?" Rebecca inquired. She tried to sound calm, fooling no one, least of all herself.

Man Hides Good swallowed two mouthfuls of the thick, steaming brew, then turned his eyes from Rebecca toward the woods as if to gather the correct group of words to answer the wife of Dan Skinner. After a few moments, his eyes settled carefully onto her. "Two Haisla with remains. One Indian canoe."

The ensuing silence was as thick as two-day-old coffee.

"Berry Woman says the remains of three lawmen there, wrapped in canvas. Dan Skinner's younger brother too. Four men altogether, all dead. Haisla stop here. Camp. No sign of the Tsimshian. No sign of your man, Dan Skinner. I think he is still ahead. As alive as you and me. And the Tsimshian? Maybe him too."

All night while the others slept, Rebecca's eyes remained wide open. Waking several times and glancing sympathetically in her direction, Man Hides Good felt her pain. Without moving, he diverted silent prayers her way. He contemplated the force that bound humans together, about human loss and love.

The next morning, Man Hides Good guided Rebecca into a nearby grove. Rebecca had never seen the likes. A Haisla graveyard opened before her. She was startled, her voice subdued. Over numerous graves rested a conundrum of carvings: a cedar whale, a war canoe, two horizontal mortuary totems (one, she thought, resembled a frog), two carvings of life-like men, Natives for sure, with wild faces and huge, round eyes.

"Wild woman of the woods," Man Hides Good said, catching the direction of her gaze.

Deeper in the woods were dozens of individual graves. She looked closely. The graves were decorated with sewing machines, blue-and-white enamel pots, porcelain plates, and bowls—artifacts from both cultures. There: a few bone-white marble gravestones, Christian variety. Wooden crosses. Granite crosses. Common names all: Allen, Hill, George, James,

Wilson, Frank, and Hall. Last names for the first. First for the last. She thought of a Bible lesson: the weak shall inherit the earth. Odd that! Simple names that spoke to the White man's language and customs. Word tattoos imposed upon Native cultures.

Man Hides Good kneeled beside a recent stone, tears beading in his eyes. Rebecca was caught by surprise. Maybe she didn't know that the big Indian cried. "Mother . . . Mother, I have brought a Boston friend. Good woman. I like this woman. I go help find her man. Walk with us, Mother. Walk with us during our journey. I miss you, Mother."

"That's your mother's grave? When did you lose her?" Rebecca couldn't think of anything else to say. Nothing profound.

"Two winters past," he answered. "She called Two Birds."

"I'm so sorry."

"She lucky. Live full life. My father buried there. Die young of the disease." He pointed in the other direction.

Over her shoulder, Rebecca spotted a huge, smooth mound.

Man Hides Good watched her intently. "One hundred twelve of my people buried there. Smallpox. Beyond . . ." He swept his finger again, as if aiming through the lush and sound-constricting forest where another mound, bigger than the last, cast a strained silence over the ancient grove. "More there. Beyond, there are more."

"More?" she gasped, her eyes dilating into soft full moons.

"Yes, three hundred seven!"

She opened her mouth to speak but failed to pry out the words. Her constricted expression hung limply, as if searching for a listener who would never materialize. Man Hides Good turned his head from her but not before she witnessed a face scarred by pain. She understood that his tears had been played out many times before. The memories had to be old. No, she thought. *Raw*!

"When the bad medicine come, we have no time to bury dead. Not honor with proper burial. There were few survivors. So few. We . . ." His voice shuffled off like a man crippled by a blow from a large, gnarled fist. "We not bury properly."

Man Hides Good turned and walked away from her, leaving Rebecca alone, though she understood that she wasn't alone. She lowered herself to the forest floor. Minutes passed before she found the strength to rise. Then she stumbled from the copse.

"Rebecca." Sally's loud voice lacerated the stillness of the holy ground. "Where you been, honey?"

Rebecca turned and walked up the beach, her confidence shattered like broken glass. She walked like a woman proud of who she was, but inside, Rebecca staggered toward her friend, no longer so sure. All she wanted was to be left alone. That or find Man Hides Good. She wanted to comfort him. And she wanted to be comforted. She was still spinning from the story that Man Hides Good had shared with her the night before.

"Man Hides Good took me into the cemetery," she said. "I . . . I never felt the likes of that. I mean, I never felt the presence of so many dead before. Not even after the war. Strange. Man Hides Good was so gentle. Sweet. I think I hurt him. Well . . . memories, and I . . ."

Sally was not so sure about the gist of her friend's conversation. "I went lookin' for you, Rebecca. Couldn't find you anywheres. Back there. Mm hmm."

She pointed to the forest over her shoulder. "Started to go in. Big son of a gun raven jumps down on a limb just above my head. Like a bully, threatenin' me. I swear it. Seemed to be telling me not to enter. Not to go into the forest and look for you. You know? 'White girl, you're not welcome here. Stay out.' That's what he said. Least I think so."

Rebecca remained quiet. She stood erect and began to sweep her right foot from right to left and back again in front of her, girl-like, as if she was designing a pattern in the snow—as she once had as a child—but now into beach gravel. She spoke so quietly that Sally had to push closer to catch her words.

"That's strange, Sally. After Man Hides Good left the cemetery—after I followed him out—I wanted to go back in. Go in alone. For some reason I felt compelled. A few minutes later, I started in by myself. Just like you said. Well, my story is the same as yours. That same raven dropped down, crying out its deep-throated bird voice. Hostile-like. Threatening, maybe? But insistent, for sure. Suggested the same thing to me. Least I suspect so.

Swear to it. I couldn't go back in. Not without Man Hides Good. No, I just couldn't."

"Well, I'll be damned."

Down the beach the Natives signaled the ladies.

"Time to go, honey. Let's go find your man."

Rebecca started to follow her friend but then stopped. She couldn't describe it, but something was calling her back. She turned and stared. On a low branch of a hemlock tree, not twenty yards away, an old crone of a raven, big, black, and sullen, stared at her intently, then released a volley of squawks loud enough to slow a train.

Sally scampered ahead. Rebecca waited, staring at the big, sassy raptor. When she spoke, her voice was leveled straight at the raven. "Okay, mister. Whatever you know, go tell it to my Dan. Tell him I'm on my way. We'll be together soon. Don't wait. You go tell him now."

She turned then and scurried up the beach, just behind her best friend.

Day by day the big river narrowed. The current was stronger now. All four shared the responsibility of piloting the fine cedar vessel. A hard-won monotony settled in. All four travelers were on their own. Each struggled with private thoughts.

Paddles dug into the river. Muscles constricted. The canoe pressed forward. Dig in, push, lift. Dig in.

Hours flew by.

"Hey mana naka, say. Ho mana naka, so."

Muscles swelled and turned sore. The big tendons along the back of the neck were inflamed. No one complained. Rebecca remained lost in thought.

Before Rebecca left home at fifteen, she visited her daddy one last time. The graveyard was wrapped in pickets and covered with headstones of quarried marble and granite. Except around the soldiers, the boys slaughtered in the Civil War. There, white wooden crosses, sentinel-like, graced the yellow-grass meadow, the highest knoll for many miles.

Daddy should rest there, she thought. Rest close to a few of the boys he couldn't save. Boys never forgotten. Her father's gravestone was granite, white and gleaming in the hot midday sun. Most of the flowers had wilted in the prairie heat.

1972

Be Here Now. What sort of book was this? Richard Alpert had converted to a seer with a new name, Ram Dass. How strange. Katherine read the book in just a few hours. Devoured it a second time. She didn't know if the message was a countercultural bible, hoax, or a message from a legitimate spiritual teacher. Was this the same man who had experimented with LSD with Timothy Leary? *My, oh my.* Or was this simple palaver, to borrow for mountain man jargon? And how did East Indian philosophy relate to the Native American culture? Its spirituality? Katherine was stumped. She called her mom.

"Keep an open mind," her mother implored. "Remember your father."

Keep your eyes open and wait, Katherine thought, as she exchanged one book for another, this one ten years old and by Rachel Carson: *Silent Spring*, written in 1962. *Where has this been hiding*? Rebecca shrugged. *Well, right before my eyes. That's where.* There was no magic there. Just cold reality. *To believe or not to believe, that is the question.*

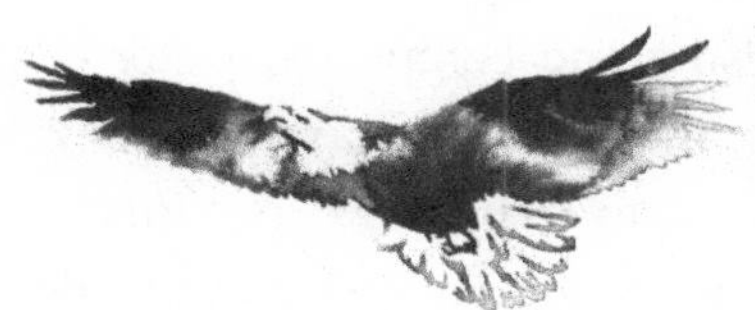

CHAPTER TWENTY-FOUR

Iron wheels. Steel tracks. The new West waited beyond the mountains. God, how Rebecca loved the green glades, those mountain pinnacles, snow-capped like the head of an eagle and just as formidable. She thought the great and immense forests would stand forever. No man could encroach on that much majesty, nor any army of men.

—Katherine Skinner-Patterson

Notes for a novel

The river that had flowed with the four seekers now turned against them. Water came in layers. On top, the freshet—surging down from the mountains—dumped a fine blue-green silt into the river. Below that layer, cold canal water. Sometimes the currents ran side by side, canal water the color of weak coffee, and ice melt, tinted like ancient jade. In the whirl of eddies, the waters married, bluish gray as ocean rain and swirling like one of Dan's favorite desserts, a chocolate-and-vanilla marble cake. *Well,* Rebecca thought, *that will be the first thing I bake for Dan when we get home.* The reflection caused her to smile.

The rock sentinels rose taller and taller each day, and the river swelled higher and higher. The force was palpable. So was the danger.

As the four paddled against strong currents, the canal began to narrow. The rush of the rising and compacted water came soaring. In less than twenty-four hours, the floodwaters raised the river level by several feet, and they were forced to struggle even harder. Soon, the river turned a steely silver green as the glacier melt flooded down the fjord in torrents. Even with the high water, the river bottom was often exposed. The turgid river offered no comfort to the weary travelers.

The Haisla frequently had to push the canoe with two long cedar staffs as they skirted the shallows. Polling was arduous work, and their elation over earlier, hard-won progress dissipated considerably.

After a long day fraught with tension, everyone was grateful when Man Hides Good signaled the end of a day's journey. They traveled by daylight now. Sunken obstacles were impossible to spot in the moonlight or under the blanket of nightfall.

The tide still flowed with them—it would for at least another day or two—but the Haisla perceived the time of change was nearing. *Better get some rest*, they thought. *Move again in six hours.*

No fire that night. No one had the energy to start one, and the weather stayed warm. It was late in the evening when the sun deserted the valley, and the shadows deepened.

It was pre-dawn when they launched into the current. The river was loaded with natural debris. Deadliest were the massive stumps of fallen evergreens, "deadheads" that had been dislodged from the sandbars and low floodplains by the rising water. Many of the stumps had begun to rot. Many were waterlogged. Their massive hulks rested barely above the water's surface, like the head of a beaver. Nearly out of sight but not out of mind.

Sally was told to keep her eyes open for the canoe wreckers. She obliged with enthusiasm. Spirit Runner was positioned at the canoe's stern, pushing with a stout staff. The Haisla had a name for this job. It translated into "one who steers." Man Hides Good took the bow. He, like Rebecca, who was seated behind him, plied the sultry waters with a cedar paddle.

From time to time, Sally would spell Rebecca. Both women continued to spot for their guides.

For a couple more days, they paddled during the two six-hour flood tides and rested the other twelve. Light was visible after six in the morning. Dusk slowly dropped down upon the river at about seven o'clock in the evening. In between the travelers forced their craft upstream.

The river dropped after the fifth day of the freshet. Finally, they were passing tidewater. They were in the mountains now, the granite peaks rising majestically, thousands of feet on either side of their cedar craft. The mountains were higher there, rugged and beautiful, bound in their furs of evergreen bounty.

Rebecca dipped her cupped hands into the river and drank from the sweet, swift water. The ocean's long, flooding arm—the mixture of salt and freshwater—had finally retreated. Hopefully, she thought, they were nearing the end of their journey. Would Dan be waiting ahead?

The currents stiffened. As the water's tempo surged, the passage became even more arduous. The two men favored their staffs. The women sat and surveyed the river for signs of debris and underwater snags, occasionally spelling the men. Frequently, all four dragged the canoe by a pair of long ropes. The going was rough. At times they staggered along the gravel riverbank. The process was further hindered by the long, tendril-like arms of Sitka spruce that reached like groping fingers to the water's edge.

Miles ahead—a half day of steady paddling—the river and the adjacent riverbanks of hard clay and detritus widened. The river slowed. Rebecca glanced at Man Hides Good. The look on his face suggested a certain satisfaction. What Rebecca couldn't perceive was that her guide had identified the entrance to his homeland, the place of his birth and the hereditary homeland of his people.

The Bear Meadows—the sight refreshed the two Haisla. The People of the River, their family and ancestors, had lived there for centuries. Bordering the lush and peaceful meadow, dozens of their cedar houses had once dominated the riverbank. Now cedar and spruce trees with tangled vines and exposed roots intruded to the river's edge.

Rarely did the Natives fall the conifers around their living spaces. The trees protected them during the winter from the freezing northern winds, and then garnered cool shade during the hot days of summer. The Haisla were beholden to their tree cousins.

Rebecca guessed at the popular spots where the encampments had once punctuated the landscape. She did not need a surveyor's badge to spot the signs. Exploring on foot from their campsite, Rebecca and Sally found the weathered blazes that Haisla women had cut into the trunks of the cedar trees. The Native women had scored and peeled strips of cedar bark from the massive evergreens. Separating the soft inner layer from the heavier epidermis, they would pound the pliable fiber. Later, they would braid and weave baskets, blankets, mats, and other items of clothing from the durable, water-repellent fiber. One of the guide's ropes was woven by this process. The rope was prized by Spirit Runner, a gift from his late grandmother.

Proud of the women's quick eyes and acute observations, the guides spent hours unraveling cultural clues. Rectangular chinks whittled into the spruce trees—Rebecca found them everywhere. These trees were bled for pitch, used both for medicinal practices and for starting fires. As the tree slowly released its pitch, the sap was gathered and processed. Both women marveled at the skill and patience of these women.

Sally discovered a petroglyph on the flat, sheltered side of a massive stone slab, hidden away for decades under a tangle of huckleberries and moss.

Natural colored dyes of red, black, and brown outlined the ancient childlike figure of a man. The Haisla guides were deeply touched by the discovery. Sally was ecstatic. Spirit Runner teased her, calling Sally "One Who Seeks." The Haisla were pleased by the genuine enthusiasm the woman showed toward their culture. The petroglyph represented a spiritual contact with their ancestors. The women were startled by the deep emotional effect that it had on their guides.

Lastly, cedar debris. The detritus of rafters and the flat cedar planking that had framed Native lodges. Dust to dust—loam covered the ground around the village's ancient foundations. Many of the planks had been burned for firewood. Many were buried under scrub and salal. Already, nature had taken back the remnants of this proud, ancient civilization. Wooden artifacts were short-lived in the lush, wet forests of the Pacific Northwest.

Another day on the water. Man Hides Good unexpectedly pulled their canoe toward a sheltered riverbank, a shaded, flat embankment lined with spruce trees, huckleberry bushes, and patches of sword fern. In front of a stately copse of spruce, a shallow sandy beach beckoned. The Haisla guide aimed the canoe's bow toward the shoreline as deftly as an archer launches an arrow.

The Haisla were skilled river people. Before stepping from the canoe, Man Hides Good reached his hand into the river, then rubbed the water across his eyelids and over his ears. An explanation followed. "This is a custom of my people. Take the water and wash your eyes, so you may see better. Wash your ears and hear the sounds of my homeland. Hear the songbirds and the stir of our four-legged friends. The river has many, many doors. Many rooms. This…" He raised his hands again, touching the sky. "This is our way. Do this and be grateful for the Creator and his bounty."

He stepped quickly from the canoe and climbed up a steep bank onto a narrow, sheltered outcropping. Behind the landing the cliffs reached toward the sky, dominating the landscape.

Rebecca and Sally saw the decayed remains of some cedar planking, envisioning a small family village.

"My house." Man Hides Good pointed to a pile of decayed timber. "I am home."

The party of travelers napped beside the spot where Man Hides Good's family and ancestors had lived for centuries, a lodge once fondly called "Raven Rests above Its House." Spruce trees and yellow cedar were scattered through the lush forest. Soft, buttery light filtered through the boughs of the evergreen giants.

Man Hides Good turned to the women. "My family and ancestors live here for hundreds of years. Until I was eleven, this was my only world. This was home to my father, my mother, one brother and sister. Here, this very spot.

"Over there," he said, pointing to a flat clearing just twenty yards away, "Grandfather and Grandmother had their small lodge. Uncle, aunt, and three cousins lived just beyond those large alder trees near that spring." He pointed his steady finger into the woods where the two women heard the tumbling sounds of a small waterfall.

Sally broke in, impetuous to the last. "Where did they go? What happened to the houses? Did you have neighbors? Hmmm."

"Whoa, Sally," Rebecca said. "Give the man a chance."

Rebecca had grown fond of her guides, and maybe a little protective. Besides, Sally overwhelmed anybody with her quick-fire questions and bigger-than-life enthusiasm. But the Haisla only laughed. They had become fond of the big-boned woman.

Spirit Runner fell back several steps, then gyrated the palms of his hands as if holding back a swarm of insects. Everybody laughed.

Man Hides Good laughed the loudest, then turned serious. "Disease took most of the old ones here. Caught many of the young and infirm too. My grandparents died of pox. My young cousins. All three. Then my father. The government come five years later and moved all survivors downriver to new settlement. Last week you see deserted cabins. Like Tasska—the queen's people took many villages, ransacking until only scars remain. Tasska is older than memories. So were many other villages belonging to the Haisla and Xenaksiala people. To the Haida and Tsimshian. And Kwakiutl.

"Missionaries burn totems and mortuaries. They are afraid to leave any reminders. They want my people to go to Christian churches. They not like our Creator. I was sent to a residential school. A Christian school. Not good!

"Where the Bostons left a few homes—property they choose not to use—the land fell back to the Great Spirit. Many of my people would never return. Too much pain. Many bad memories."

All four travelers gazed at the deserted village, suddenly at a loss for words. Contemplation tangled their tongues. For several minutes a hush silenced their private thoughts.

Man Hides Good finally spoke. "I come here often. Johnny Johns, Grey Owl. We trap marten and otter many winters. We often alone, other than spirits of the ancient ones. I camp happily here. Even when the lake above froze over, and harsh winters caused much suffering, the beauty of the land sent message straight to my heart. This valley is gift from the Holy Spirit."

There, the four-legged inhabitants and the humans who walked in the great valley were dwarfed by walls of stone that towered above them. The tall, steep cliffs only amplified the echo of the downy woodpecker as its grubbing ricocheted staccato-like through the granite valley.

What message did it send? Man Hides Good listened intently, joy returning to his face. He was back home. Remembering many of the joyful moments that had passed there, he felt gladdened.

Beyond the Bear Meadows, the river narrowed and ran fast. Once again the women were forced to pole the canoe as the men pushed, knee to waist deep in the frigid river. Hard-won progress was further impeded by the frigid high-mountain runoff. It was impossible to acclimate to the near-freezing conditions of the pale green river. And the bullying force of the water.

First came the sting, a bite on the legs that took one's breath away. The initial pain became a dull ache. Numbness followed, as insistent as a beggar. The Haisla accepted the challenge without complaint but could only remain in the water for about fifteen minutes before switching places in the canoe. Every step consumed energy. Everyone was worn to a frazzle.

Every mile represented an obstacle. Frustration pummeled their morale.

Later that morning, the four were startled as they poled around a bend in the river and caught a glimpse of an armed man disappearing back into the woods. With lightning-fast strokes of their paddles, the Haisla turned the canoe back around into the downriver current. In the torrent, the canoe galloped quickly away. Although it was painful to give up the hard-taken ground, any chance of discovery threw the party into a panic.

The women had a sinking feeling that they had been discovered. Both Spirit Runner and Mans Hides Good assured the women that the retreating figure could not have identified their party at such a distance. The time frame was too short. Few men were that quick, and he probably hadn't even been looking. The man likely was a trapper, and he would fade back into the woods. He would be out of touch with civilization for several months at a time. Even if he had seen them, the guides predicted that this man—this interloper—would hold their secret, the discovery of their passage, tight to his chest.

Two miles downstream they cached into a small breach in the riverbank. A large island divided the river, and the lee side sheltered them from the newfound stranger's prying eyes. The four seekers would rest until well past dark. Now they would be forced to travel by night.

Henry Crockett was not the kind of man who spent much time conversing with his neighbors. Indeed, he had few of them. Taciturn didn't even begin to describe the trapper. Crockett stank, talked in grunts, and neither needed nor took pleasure in the company of other humans. Crockett was, in the truest sense, a man of the woods, a member of that profane breed known as "mountain men." He spurned civilization like a mole avoids light.

Like Dan and Tom, he survived in the wilderness for months at a time under impossible conditions and deprivation. He preferred his isolation. His leather clothes were more skin than costume. He bathed only a few times a year. He covered the animal skins with the smoke from his campfire, curing the leather from shrinkage while disguising his scent from animals and enemies. When that smoky scent—as well as months of accumulated dirt and sweat—accompanied him back to the settlements, town folks avoided him like a leper.

In his covert movements, he was nearly invisible. He hadn't enjoyed the company of a woman for decades.

But he shot dead straight, survived in a hostile wilderness with an uncanny intelligence, and separated enemies from friends by a set of tracks. Nutrition was simple: he ate the four-legged animals, sometimes a fish or a basket of crawfish. He carried black coffee and sugar and maybe flour for campfire biscuits. Berries were his only dessert.

Crafty, he was capable of stripping trees and plants of their leaf or bark and boiling it into a brew that more civilized folk wouldn't drink, even under duress. He called flora and fauna "medicine." He had learned the healing herbs from the Natives.

In short, his craft and senses were so keen that when he saw the four in a canoe (he carried a battered copper spyglass) he knew something wasn't right. Crockett faded into the woods with the stealth of a forest animal. He would remain attentive and hidden.

1974

"Okay," Katherine said, speaking to her comrades in their weekly get-together. Her tête-à-tête. "Ideally, we mix a little magic into a reality cocktail. The environment can obviously use some help: a blast of magic, an army of foresters, and a score of human worker-bees. And that's just a start."

She waved her animated hands, her voice rising an octave. "If humans are actually capable of saving it (was the planet a "*her*?"), we need to apply a large dose of practicality to this old, broken equation. In fairness, science is discovering more each day. We simply must apply it. Think of Earth as a sacred body."

Her voice rose yet again, seeking a sympathetic audience. She hoped to generate enthusiasm. "Look at the universe. There is plenty of mystery out there. It's out in the open for all to see. But just dare to define it. Isn't all this about anarchy, the universe spinning out of control? Isn't deep space defined as the unknown?"

She thought of the early seafarers, of Magellan and the Vikings, each sailing into the unknown. Certainly, they had experienced fear. But they had overcome.

Now there were worlds beyond imagination. Well, she had only one in mind, and she was determined to save it.

"Open your eyes, friends, and stand in awe."

CHAPTER TWENTY-FIVE

The universe is an example of love. Like a tree. Like the ocean. Like my body. Like my wheelchair. I see the love.

—Ram Dass

While his three companions slept restlessly, Man Hides Good stood the night watch, pondering the ordeals that might wait ahead. He hadn't told the women how he truly felt about the interruption that afternoon. It worried him plenty. Mountain men were an inquisitive lot.

Man Hides good studied the ebony sky, the half-moon that teased the dark curtain of nightfall, slipping stealthily through thin, ragged clouds.

Whoever this man is, he's a trapper. No other reason to be here. The man would be naturally suspicious.

Man Hides Good held several thoughts close to his chest. He had seen plenty of signs that implicated the Skinner brothers and the deputies. Four times he had spotted their deserted campsites. He suspected where the hunters and the hunted had beached their canoes. Noticed what they ate and wasted. What remained was mostly scattered bones. Even capable woodsmen left some sign. And these men were in a hurry. A big hurry. White men hunting White men—no reason to cover their tracks.

There were many clues. The lawmen weren't considerate campers. Nor did the Skinner boys have time to leave a clean campsite. Grasses and scrubs were flattened and broken. Plenty of tracks were left. None of this came as a surprise to Man Hides Good. Men on the run—or those without principle—often left a dirty trail. And these men were moving far too rapidly not to leave a calling card along the way.

There was a second matter: Man Hides Good had a sneaking suspicion where Dan and the scout had ended up. Already, his sixth sense belayed certain suspicions. In a couple of days, more clues might fall into place. For the moment he just had to be patient and hope the visitor that morning didn't impact the course of things to come.

And what about that eagle? He saw it again that same day, or at least he thought it was the same one. Unless eagles came as twins. No, he was sure. Something about the raptor piqued his interest. Something peculiar. Something beyond its immense size. The eagle was huge, larger than any eagle he had ever seen. *It must be old*, he thought. *Old and wise.* And it appeared to be watching them, or at least it was mighty interested in their comings and goings. As sure as winter rain, the giant bird appeared to be following them upriver. The Haisla had never seen the likes.

Man Hides Good sat quietly, listening to the stir of the wilderness. That night a bushel of activity was pressing around him. Along the river the working sounds of the beaver, otter, and muskrat drifted off the water. The tyee were finally moving, the surest sign of spring. He identified the migration by the slapping sounds their tails made, rippling across the sandbars on their final run upriver.

His favorite song was the call of the wolves and coyotes, each predator wailing across the granite canyons. Lonesome cries pirouetting in the clear mountain air. It was grounding for him, knowing these were the same sounds his people had heard for untold centuries. Maybe this mountain music was embedded in him. Maybe there was an instinctual feeling inside his head that loved the cadence of the night wilderness. Moon music—that's what his grandfather had called it. He couldn't even begin to express his feelings, not to these women. Not to the Whites he had encountered over the years. Such poetry was hard enough to express in his own language, among his own people. A man didn't have to tell Man Hides Good that this was Native land. Had been for thousands of years. He was honored to be there and felt obligated to protect it.

At midnight Man Hides Good roused the others from their sleep. Tonight they would follow the moon. Under the cover of darkness, Man Hides Good hoped to circumvent the unexpected stranger. The moon was nearly full. Low, wispy clouds danced across the bright yellow orb. A gauzy haze moved back and forth over the river. Luck was with them. The cold silver veil offered protection against intruding eyes.

The cold air pressed through their clothing and into the skin. The women shivered inside the buoyant cedar canoe. As the condensation swelled off the water, the women were convinced that they could taste the brackish pungent smells of the adjacent fields, the perfumed grasses and sour, wet clay.

But the going remained difficult, the current swift and unpredictable. They knew that at all costs they must avoid any obstacles the river might throw in their path. Although they felt a sense of urgency, they were grateful for the cover of night.

It took nearly four hours to recover the ground they had forfeited the previous afternoon. As the night lengthened, they pushed hard toward the headwaters. By four o'clock the next morning, they all were exhausted. The decision to cache was adopted by general consent. Rebecca prayed they had escaped the prying eyes of the stranger on the riverbank and that the coming day would be less arduous. She was plagued by anxiety. Exhausted, she fell into a short, restless sleep.

Dreams rallied around her deepest fears. Rebecca believed that she saw Dan bushwhacking through dense forest. In her dream, she raced after him. As she ran hard toward the man, low limbs and thick brambles tore at her bare arms and face. As she neared, the apparition turned. Rebecca was startled to encounter the image of the woodsman they had spotted the day before. She screamed, and as she did, Rebecca awoke abruptly.

From the shoreline, Spirit Runner heard Rebecca stir. He turned and studied her. Like his comrade, Spirit Runner had become protective of the woman. Perhaps he was surprised. He never would have guessed they would form such an enduring friendship.

The water was singing its night song. The sky had cleared. Above, he traced the silhouette of the weaver of baskets, the woman in the moon. The warm yellow light touched him, and Spirit Runner felt content.

The sky lightened. Silhouettes emerged from the night sky. Awakened, Rebecca spotted the alert shape of the Haisla watchman. She waved and then moved toward him. She felt groggy from her short, tormented sleep but realized the nightmare had dislodged any further chance for rest.

Spirit Runner acknowledged her greeting and returned the salutation. Rebecca sauntered slowly toward him, letting the magnificent landscape sweep before her eyes. "Why not get some sleep, friend? I'm wide awake now. Get some rest before the others wake."

She patted him on the shoulder, then winked as he smiled in soft reply. She caught a look of surprise in his eyes, a softening of his sharp gaze. Spirit Runner thanked her, grateful for the opportunity to rest his weary body. He had been surprised by her constant kindness. They had become fast friends, and friends care for each other.

Another day passed. Once again they chose to travel by daylight. The water was surly and unpredictable. A sudden spring rain pelted them from the west. No chance of traveling by nightfall. The unpredictable weather continued to dampen their spirits.

Far too many obstacles lay before them now, particularly the deadheads swirling like sunken serpents as the four struggled upriver. Twice the water turned vicious. Once a strong eddy threatened to overturn their canoe. Later, a nearly submerged log narrowly missed their craft, scraping hard down the starboard side. Two miles ahead the water turned even more threatening. Before testing the unexpected turbulence with the canoe, Spirit Runner and Man Hides Good decided to bring the craft into shore. Both men wished to review the fierce rapids before they pushed ahead. Unmentioned to the women, Spirit Runner had also sighted some debris that needed closer examination.

For an hour or more, the Haisla moved along the stream and through the underbrush. The women waited patiently by the canoe. Both were exhausted and fraught with emotion. Both catnapped.

Finally, the Natives summoned the two women. Rebecca knew immediately what they had found. A look of apprehension was etched on the guides' faces. No man could hide those signs. Rebecca immediately recognized the debris. Before her were mangled pieces of Dan's wooden canoe.

Rebecca let out a low moan and prepared herself for the worst. Turning toward her Haisla guides, she asked the only question paramount on her mind. "Did my Dan die here?"

Man Hides Good shook his head vigorously, but Spirit Runner answered for him. "No man dies here. But soon—probably just ahead—two brothers go on foot."

He raised his arm and pointed a single finger up the imposing granite wall that dominated the human beings below. The summit, thousands of feet over their heads, faded under a scudding of gray clouds and a sudden spring rain. Into a miasma of rain and mist, the cliffs ascended; sheer and terrifying.

"You think they had to climb that?" Sally blurted out.

Both guides nodded. Studying the cliffs before her, Rebecca was sure she was staring death straight in the face.

Sequestered under the shadows of the awesome heights, they set up camp beside a plume of angry water, a confluence of rapids and swift, threatening waterfalls. As suddenly as it began, the rain abated. The two men explored the area while Sally started a small fire. Rebecca sat quietly to one side, visibly shaken.

The men were hardly out of the women's sight when the Haisla heard the rustle of footfall. Both turned simultaneously, only to see Rebecca behind them. The Natives stopped and waited respectfully.

"Sorry," she said when she caught up to them. "I just couldn't sit back there waiting for any more bad news. Do you mind if I follow along?"

Man Hides Good displayed a full wide smile. "Maybe, we expect you." Even his eyes had a way of smiling. "Spirit Runner tell me you come along any minute now."

The Haisla elder's wide, flat face broke into another impish grin.

Rebecca blushed, lifting her head in her proud way. She turned then, smiling apologetically before the quiet men who smiled so brightly but said so little. She expectantly watched as his easy smile began to fade.

"Might not like what we find," he conjectured.

Man Hides Good thought about his statement for a few more seconds, then cast his steady eyes upon Rebecca. His words were reassuring now. "I feel it is alright, Rebecca. I think Dan Skinner can handle himself and all those deputies too. Strong man. I see that many times along the way."

For the third time in minutes, a smile broke across the Haisla's face.

Little sunshine, all day, Rebecca thought. *But this man carries an inner light within him.* For the first time in days, she felt her anxiety fade.

Spirit Runner interjected. "Ma'am, they found those bodies near here, maybe mile or two along. That was the news sent back to Kilnook, from Kolnux. Same news we hear from Berry Woman. You remember?"

How will I ever forget? she thought. She nodded in affirmation.

"It was near here. Right near here, those bodies. Probably not your Dan Skinner. Very hard to tell now."

Rebecca heard compassion mingling with his words. She swiveled her head around as if looking for some sign or apparition to step out of the forest and ease her fears. Something to soothe her strained emotions. Rebeca was unclear about what she might find, but she couldn't resist looking. Inside her head she called Dan's name. Rebecca wanted him more than she had ever wanted anything in her entire life.

The three friends hiked another mile along the shoreline. Beside them the river adopted an angry face. The forest was a foreboding and tangled thicket. Above, the granite cliffs rose dramatically. There was no escaping the reality of danger. And they had come to a dead end. The stream bank narrowed dramatically. The only choice was up.

Rebecca thought about her brother-in-law, thought how she had come to love him, to appreciate his brand of kindness. Likely, he had fallen nearby. Pain stung her acutely. Walking beside her, the two Natives read the signs of anxiety on her face. The Haisla sidled into the bramble, pretending they had some clue to explore. They were allowing Rebecca the chance to grieve. They refused to travel too far ahead, to leave the White woman alone.

An hour later they separated. The Haisla had discovered clues and pressed deeper into the bramble. Alone, Rebecca composed herself. Returning quietly, the Haisla found her staring up the cliff as if she were following the steep ascent of her husband and her brother-in-law, step by step. She turned as they approached, her steady eyes composed with courage and determination.

"We have found the place. Two-Hundred yards ahead. Come now!"

Rebecca didn't have to ask Spirit Runner about "the place." She knew. "Let's go look," she said. "I want to see the signs for myself. Don't worry yet! I'm sure we will find him ahead. We'll find him alive." Those were brave words from a brave woman. The two Haisla threw a furtive glance at each other.

They bushwhacked up an animal trail that cut through the forest, forcing their way through dense thickets and up several steep embankments to the bottom of the sheer cliff. After days in the canoe, their leg muscles protested. The two men fell in behind Rebecca as faithfully as a brace of spaniels.

Under the same wall where André and the Mounties had spent their final hours, the trio found evidence of their fall. Spirit Runner scavenged a broken oak shard from the gun stock and a torn leather strap. Man Hides Good found several tattered pieces of cloth. As Berry Woman had indicated, two Haisla had returned with the scattered possessions of the dead. Little now remained under the cliff.

Beyond they found four stone markers. These were simple memorials to the fallen. *Haisla work*, Man Hides Good thought. On top of the stone memorials were four single eagle feathers. They recognized the offerings of their brothers. Rebecca was too stunned to speak.

She tried to hold back her tears. Already there had been so many. But she failed, and the salty moisture trickled out like river water, not the deluge below her, but silently. Softly.

The Haisla bent, offering prayers in a different language. Red man or White, both cultures knew the commonality of pain. Rebecca's mind raced.

Man Hides Good directed his prayers outward into the soft mountain air. Spirit Runner spoke silently to his Creator. Their words were alive with a power as clear and determined as the currents that shaped the free-flowing river and the wilderness beyond.

Rebecca's thoughts turned back to André, a man who had treated her with a respect equal to that of her husband's. She knew why Dan had taken his brother into the wilderness. This was not abandonment. This was commitment, the strongest of bonds between brothers. If either had asked, she would have dropped everything—left everything—to protect them. She knew why she had come on her dangerous odyssey. Though in different ways, Rebecca loved both men wholly. Now she wondered how a sensitive person could separate love, divide it into degrees, into larger or smaller sizes. She felt no remorse over the complexity of the love issue—Rebecca trusted herself and trusted her intuition. She knew she loved more than just one human being. She thought of the two men beside her now. Two Native people. Rebecca knew they were her guardians and that she trusted them implicitly. *Guardian angels*, she thought. A thin, twisted smile crossed her lips, and her tears departed.

They bushwhacked back to their small camp. There, sitting in front of a blazing campfire, Rebecca became aware that something undefinable was opening before her. Something not easily shared with the others. But further explanation was as elusive as the winds and the currents that shaped the wilderness around her. That definition was as big as love, equal to love. She knew she might never fully define her inclinations. Thoughts scampered beyond her.

Then a second affirmation. Suddenly, she knew the man she loved most—the man she was committed to with every fiber of her soul—had not died on the cliff with his brother. Rebecca couldn't guess where her journey might lead, but she felt sure that she would find her husband again. She would hold him once more in her arms.

She wept unabashedly. The sound swept through the forest like a piece of music that favored neither sorrow nor joy. The two men beside her did not lift their heads until her tears had subsided, until other sounds belonging to the river and the forest began to take shape again. Night descended over the camp. The fire burned brightly, sparks lifting into the clear spring evening, an evening awash in migrating stars, each one a beacon of hope.

Man Hides Good spoke, his words unfolding softly, his eyes fixed on the heavens. "These are the souls of the dead and loved ones who have gone before us."

From across the campfire, Sally concentrated on her best friend's face as shadows danced in the firelight. They danced with a freedom that is hard won. Sally watched the sparks lifting into the night air. She noticed how they telegraphed into brilliant arches like a string of foreign letters.

The sky was kettle black and the sparks fiery red. She was glad to be on the adventure, excited to discover a new appreciation for the wilderness, grateful for the two Haisla guides, and, above all, happy to be sitting next to her dearest friend, watching firebrands fly up from the campfire.

The next morning all four pushed the canoe upstream. Their bodies and minds were weary. They hoped to circumvent the same chute of wild water that had capsized the Skinner brothers' canoe. As they paused to survey the scene, Man Hides Good whispered an ancient blessing to the river, praying for safe passage. As he prayed, he wondered if the two brothers had offered a similar salutation. He imagined the brothers hard-pressed from behind, paddling into the rapids without taking the necessary precautions. They had gambled and lost, and that wager had cost four men their lives.

At noon the eagle reappeared. For an hour or more, the Haisla guides watched as it circled in great wide loops above the river. Twice they glanced at each other, and twice their thoughts intertwined. To the Haisla guides, there was no longer any doubt: the great bird was following them, or just possibly, leading the way.

As they watched, the eagle made an abrupt turn and disappeared upriver into the high mountains. Without sharing their private thoughts with the ladies, they now knew which way the party had to travel. They were closing in on their objective. At least one of the men had a good idea where the trail might end. Their decisions were simpler now. They would follow the direction of the raptor's flight.

No one had to explain to the women that they would no longer be following the trail left by the two brothers. So much for the sheer mountain cliff.

"No way, gentlemen." Sally grimaced after she spit out her edict. For a change, Rebecca wasn't far behind. As far as that went, neither were the guides.

The search for Dan would move upriver and away from the sheer precipice where André and three Mounties had fallen to their deaths.

Rebecca was remembering standing with Dan in their small meadow, a singing river just a stone's throw away from the cabin. Everywhere else, great trees, ferns, and thicket.

Dan and André spent their days feeding the sharp teeth of a two-man cross-saw through six feet of living fiber, through the heartwood. After hours of grappling with the giant, the tree would lean, hanging like a prayer in a pocket of thin sky. Rebecca would bite her lip and wait. So tall was the tree that it took an eternity to drop, twisting and broken like a fluted pillar, felled by a pair of Samsons. A sullen *whoosh* of air and then a powerful sound reverberated through the valley like the angry volley of a cannon, the death knell of an old-growth cedar.

Hundreds of limbs to be bucked—the chore was endless. The fat ends were sectioned into firewood. The rest of the limbs were piled around the stumps for burning. The blaze burned endlessly, the smoke thick and cloying. Another tree. Another day. Around the cabin the sky was gray with the pout of ash.

Dan and Rebecca begged André to join them, to build a second cabin on the property. Plenty of room there, plenty of acres.

"One big family, André, when you settle down. But if you don't, won't make no difference."

Secretly, Rebecca and Dan hoped he would take them up on the offer.

André figured differently but wouldn't say why. Nobody was fooling anybody. Underneath, André wasn't ready to domesticate. Hadn't met a woman he would take as a wife. Hadn't met anyone half the likes of Rebecca. Wasn't that the unspoken truth?

Even though Dan was his brother—his only living relative—André liked the action in town, and it was an awfully long horse ride back to the farm when a pilgrim was loaded on liquor. As far as that went, it was too far a ride to track down a good bottle of whiskey. André had to sow his wild oats first. He would wait until he met a woman like Rebecca. Above all else, he preferred his independence.

"Ain't right," he would repeat. "This is your place, the two of yours alone. You don't need trouble like me." But he was proud to have been asked.

The river snarled and growled, the sky wrinkled by a gauze of pure white nimbus. Over the angry river, it was unnaturally warm. Snow was melting in the mountains, which meant rising water. A day had passed since leaving the gravesites, since leaving André's memorial and those of the lawmen. Downriver, three families were certainly bereaved, but the grief that the four voyageurs felt for the two brothers continued to move upriver, always upriver.

For hundreds of miles, a vast watershed fed the river, swelling in the spring heat as the snow melted like a snake that had shed its skin. Dozens of feeder streams, mountain arteries, square hectares of snowmelt—they all meshed like blood racing through a man's arteries.

The four travelers had reached the upper end of the great Kilnook Valley. Above them was a mountain divide. Through the divide, ancient trails bled into British Columbia's interior and then unraveled north into Alaska. The Natives had different names for their land than the Whites. This was the land of the raven, the eagle, and the great bear. For the Whites it was the chance to pan gold or mine silver, to harvest lumber, furs, and salmon. Greed and opportunity seduced their imaginations. The new culture was defined by industrial and monetary achievements. The Bostons claimed they took their inspiration from the Holy Bible. "The meek shall inherit the earth." They repeated the words like a mantra.

Well, the Whites weren't particularly meek, and their appetite for profits was voracious. There was plenty of opportunity waiting for men with strong backs and grasping hands. For better or worse, Dan was one of those.

Half a day ahead was a long, narrow lake that the Haisla called *Ka'ous*, a word meaning "cathedral" or "sanctuary." Man Hides Good and Spirit Runner knew the lake as the ancestral gathering place of their people. They called it their "summering place." On four sandy beaches, fishermen returned with their catch, five species of salmon. There, the fish were butchered, dried, and smoked in vast quantities—rations for the long winter months when game ran scarce.

Between the four travelers and their goal lay several miles of rapids and then the notorious falls. The travelers would have to maneuver their canoe through a ferocious stretch of water. The next few hours would be the most dangerous miles of their journey.

With the extreme runoff, water roiled around half-submerged rocks. Vexation and toil—that's what a traveler might expect. The angry water crowded high up the riverbanks, washing tons of clay, silt, and the hulks of evergreens and cottonwoods downriver, where all manner of things merged with untold tons of melted ice and snow. There was little to no shoreline now. High, swift currents slowed their progress to nearly a crawl. The women steadied the canoe with paddles while the two Natives forced the vessel upstream, aided only by stout cedar staves, rope, and muscle.

Though the river was savage, the weather turned clear and warm. Cottonwood lining the meadows of the upper Kilnook Valley permeated the air with a sweet, oily fragrance. The forest perfume eased the pain of arduous travel, but the yards crawled along.

Now they were faced with the last obstacle before the lake: a narrow, angry chute of water that dropped thirty or forty feet over a hundred yards. As they approached the falls, all four turned introspective. Before them the narrow stone walls compacted the water, churning out a brand of meanness that only a fool could deny.

With the aid of their prized cedar ropes, Spirit Runner and Man Hides Good dragged the canoe along the slick granite shelf that paralleled the river course. The women polled the cedar vessel, pushing it away from the boulders and riprap that endangered their passage. All the while, wily currents threatened to upset the canoe. Spirit Runner whispered a few words to Man Hides Good in Haisla. Rebecca had never seen them look so anxious. Both men nodded, and the conversation ended.

They continued to challenge the savage water, dragging the canoe up the angry flume with ropes. The women sat at opposite ends of the canoe, using poles to keep it away from the boulders that littered the waterway.

It was the only choice they had. The flow of water was too swift to paddle, and the canoe was too large to portage. The option of giving up and going home was not even considered.

Rope in hand, Spirit Runner took a deep breath, lifted his head, and offered a silent prayer. Above the mist and the blast of pounding water, he saw that the eagle had returned. "Guide us well, sky brother," he whispered.

The time had come. The falls were upon them.

The river quickly metamorphosed into an angry boil. The pounding sensations of tons of river water colliding with stone sent vibrations through Rebecca's body. It approached like a runaway locomotive. She was in it, and the currents roiled around her like the snarl of a hungry animal. River spray formed a thick, moist curtain that hampered her vision. She felt isolated from her companions, surrounded by a surly rush of angry water. Faintly, as if from a great distance, she heard Sally shouting at her from the canoe's stern where she poled the canoe away from submerged boulders.

On either side of the narrow chute, the sun burned down with springtime heat, but in the canoe, the cold shock of river spray embraced the women, soaking their hair and their clothes and clawing at their skin with ice-cold fingers.

The men, testing to the limit of their strength, inched the vessel forward. Their movements were careful, their motions practiced. As they labored, the Haisla watched the women with eyes that betrayed their grim anxiety. There was no choice but to press on.

Thirty minutes passed, and the worst was over. The two Haisla had reached the top of the falls where the river ran smoothly before plunging into a churning chasm. Thirty feet more and they would pull the canoe onto the shore. They fought the temptation to relax. Rest would come soon enough.

From the canoe the women saw the entrance to the lake. Rebecca closed her eyes and bowed her head in relief. The ordeal was over. They had fought the river and won.

As Sally rose to take in the view, Spirit Runner slipped on a slick, moss-covered slab of rock that jutted out from the riverbank. He quickly regained his footing but, as the rope went slack, the canoe was caught by the current and jerked away from the riverbank. The sudden jolt startled Rebecca from her reverie. Both women fell. Rising quickly, her eyes wide open, Rebecca watched in horror as Sally dropped her pole and fell silently into the roiling water.

"Sally! Sally!" Rebecca screamed as she instinctively reached for her fallen friend.

But there was no hand to grasp. Sally had vanished, pulled beneath the water's surface by currents that ran strong and deep. With frantic, pleading eyes, Rebecca turned to the two Native men who stood frozen on the shore.

They, too, had seen Sally fall, but there was nothing to be done that might save her. To release the ropes would have doomed Rebecca and the canoe to the same fate.

"Rebecca!"

The word broke from the water like a trout rising for a fly.

Rebecca turned and saw Sally floundering far beyond all hope as the current swept her downriver toward the abyss.

For a moment, their eyes met. "Sally!" Rebecca screamed, her face pale with fear.

Again, in frantic desperation, she stretched out her arms and grasped at nothing but empty air. Sally raced beyond Rebecca's grasp.

The two Haisla pulled the canoe to shore and eased Rebecca onto the safety of the firm earth. Tears would have to wait.

"Back soon," Man Hides Good whispered, then sprinted down the river behind Spirit Runner.

They were not hopeful.

Sally felt the river envelop her. She felt the pageantry of its voice, the viscosity of its body. Swift was the water and numbing. She heard music. She tried to shout above it. No words came from her mouth. *So cold*, she thought. *So cold*. And she struggled in vain against powerful currents.

Minute by minute, the icy blast discolored her face and skin with the paper-white hue of shock.

For a moment she thought the water might slow ahead. Maybe a freak eddy would pull her close enough to shore that she might latch onto an extended root or limb. But the icy river froze breath and body while pulling her deeper and deeper into its frozen grip.

She felt the current gaining momentum as it bucked her along. Sally conceded to its power and stopped struggling. She was the bride of the river now. Suddenly, she remembered her friend, Rebecca, and wished she might have had time to say goodbye. *Is this how death comes*? she wondered. *So suddenly, so sure*?

The river rolled fast, and she thought she felt its heartbeat. She groped for a meaning, but in the end, she succumbed to something greater, an undefinable force.

Instead of air and water, she began to breathe in a blue-diamond light. The glow christened her. Quickly, the soft-blue hues changed to turquoise and then into a virgin white more intense than the snow fields that glistened like faceted stones on the crowns of the high mountains.

Her body ricocheted hard against a river boulder. She turned over and over in the fierce current. Her body touched down, rose, and descended.

Here was death, staring her in the face. Her friends raced along the riverbank. Rebecca's face reflected anguish. Now, Sally watched from high above the peaceful valley as the river rushed along. The sky color was the deepest, purest blue she ever remembered seeing, and the air was as warm as summer.

Like the great eagle who saw it all and missed nothing, Sally found herself caught up in a spiritual current. She felt a freedom she had never experienced, a freedom she accepted without question. Her last earthly vision was that of Rebecca. Something as annealing as love reached through the soft, opal sky. Sally offered a blessing upon her one true friend. Then light turned to darkness, kettle black, the burnt charcoal of a cold campfire. Then deeper black yet until all color was drawn away.

But ahead was a white light, a long tunnel, and something greater. Sally was touched with wonder.

1987—Brazil

Katherine Skinner-Patterson and a dozen men in business suits gathered in a mahogany-paneled office paid for by the government of Brazil. The men were charming and hospitable. They offered kind words but no solutions to the complexities of ecological devastation that was stripping the Amazon of its ancient jungle.

They had a rationale. Their people needed work. Their citizens deserved opportunity. There just wasn't enough of that in Brazil. Families were hungry. Children were hungry. The fertile fields that lay below the jungle were their only hope—or so they believed. While they talked, the fires smoldered, and unplanted fields awaited cultivation where the world's largest rainforest had once reigned. Crops would grow once the fallen trees were removed and the stumps shorn and burned. After the Natives were displaced.

When Katherine and her companions became impatient, the feeling of graciousness evaporated. In a steady, cool voice, one dignitary offered an insight. "I have been to the Pacific Northwest. I have seen your logging practices. I have seen wilderness stripped of their trees. Replanted yes, but with a single-specie hybrid that is only allowed to grow for thirty years. Why not do something about your own deforestation? Then come tell us where we have gone wrong."

Katherine left the meeting feeling despondent.

She slept fitfully, awoke, and paced about her hotel room. She was feeling the cold burn of humiliation, a banishment of sorts. Katherine counted the long list of defeats associated with her movement, with the "greenies." She thought about her father. She wished she could talk with him now, if only for a few minutes. Or talk with Paul. Seek advice and comfort. She wanted both. Katherine thought of calling her mother. She even checked her watch, then realized it was the middle of the night in Seattle and thought better of it.

As she paced around the room, she reminded herself that she was a strong woman—a fighter. She didn't need a man to fix things. God, she missed them, lover and father. Missed them both so much. She was wearing a path into the carpet. The color was wrong for the room. The texture was hard under her feet.

She turned off the overhead light. A full moon burnished the walls and floor. *Nice,* she thought. She remembered the bureaucrats again, associated their demeanor with the hard knots of carpet underfoot.

For an hour or more, she ruminated over the challenge issued by the bureaucrat. In a state of introspection, Katherine realized that perhaps the Brazilian had been right—partially right, anyway. It was time to go home. Time to focus her energy on the ecological brambles of the Pacific Northwest. The Old West was long gone, along with most of the old-growth forests, but plenty of hope remained. Sometimes the going got tough, but one still had to talk, plan, and initiate change. And at home, one negotiated in one's own language.

Better than 95 percent of the old growth had been felled, mostly replaced with hybrid Douglas fir seedlings and patches of wind-blown hemlock, which crowded in with the alder. In a thirty-year rotation, even those small trees came down.

Plans to manage the salmon runs had been a disaster. The great rivers traversed by Lewis and Clark now produced but a fraction of their former bounty. *Aren't the Columbia and Snake rivers dammed in seventeen places*?

Go home, she thought. *Go home and deal with the problems closest at hand. Why not? Why not, after all*?

As her plane flew over the clear-cut patchwork of forest that quilted the west coast, a plan began to emerge.

CHAPTER TWENTY-SIX

Among these trees till morning comes we sleep, and dream thunders of fern alerting space by the way they wait, eloquent of light's return.

—William Stafford
from the poem, "Camping at Lost Lake"

Dan's dreams were scattered. He would wake suddenly, sidelined by the pain that ran up his leg, an ache that extended even into his sleep. Once awakened, he let his senses stroll around the longhouse, feeling oddly like a thief in the night. The Natives slept peacefully. The lodge was always quiet during the wee hours except for a few communal sounds that added a level of comfort to his ears. But not that night. That night the camp dogs fidgeted and scratched. The children were restless. A few had colds, and their coughing and sniffling was persistent throughout the dark hours. A wind scampered through the forest. A few deadheads fell. He heard the secretive, late-night whispering and then the guarded lovemaking of a young couple. Maybe he felt like a voyeur. Maybe he was embarrassed. Lastly came the yearning, a yearning for his dear companion.

The large central fire crackled and spit as chunks of firewood burned into embers. A grandmother stirred and added another armload of alder. The fresh kindling offered fuel to the cacophony. An infant awakened and nuzzled into a sleepy mother's breast. Everywhere there was constant snoring.

The sounds continued, aggravating like a swarm of no-see-ums on a windless spring evening. An insistent rain continued to fall.

That night Dan's private doubts rumbled on like an iron kettle bubbling and boiling over a campfire. Inside his head, a battle raged.

The truth was, he knew the answer to his conflict.. Deep down, he knew. Common sense dictated that the Natives had little choice in their decisions or their reactions. *Not in this village anyway.* If discovered, their life there would be finished. Dan knew that even if he pledged himself to secrecy, that promise would be greeted with skepticism by his captors. They just couldn't take the chance. Couldn't reasonably trust Dan or any other man, particularly a White man. It was hard enough to trust one of their own. Secrets were always hard to hold close to the chest, even among the best of men. Once out, scathing words would get jostled about. The story would travel. They would be discovered.

He turned, and a jolt of pain raced up his leg. He coughed and grunted from the pain. A hush ran through the lodge. He had been discovered, a voyeur with a shattered leg.

In the forest an owl chortled its late-night mantra. A strong night wind pawed at the tall virgin trees, at their needle-cloaked limbs.

Dan knew that any new attempt to escape would be compounded with fierce retribution. He felt confused. Pain wracked him, and not just physical pain. Part of his mind wrestled with the possibility of spending the rest of his life in the village. Whenever that happened, he thought about Rebecca. After that, any possibility—other than finding her—became intolerable.

Black Wing was old. After his passing, Dan felt he might attempt another escape. Trouble was, by that time—two or three years down the line—Rebecca would likely be gone. After all, why should she stay in Kilnook? Rebecca would be condemned as the wife of a killer. All that was left for her was a hostile community eager to hang her husband by his neck. That was too much to ask of anybody. And to trump it all, most likely, Rebecca figured him dead.

Dan just wasn't going to walk into the general store and ask about the whereabouts of Rebecca Skinner. The more he thought about it, the more he realized she might have already left. The possibility of that scratched and clawed at him during his waking hours and troubled him worse as he tried in vain to sleep.

Sure, Rebecca had a keen attachment to the farm. But with all that hostility leveled toward her, what good was an isolated piece of land? No matter how beautiful the setting, she would feel trapped. Like Dan's immediate predicament, she, too, was held hostage.

All this and more he mulled over in his mind. It would be a minimum of two months before he might use the leg. Possibly three or four. That was if the bones set correctly.

He was fully awake now, pain becoming his constant companion. He cursed his luck but reminded himself that he had lived through worse. And he knew he might have died. Retribution could have been far worse. Other doubts harangued him. What if his leg became infected? The *what ifs* jangled along. *Well, no sense dwelling on doubts.*

Pain wrenched his thinking, and he wondered suddenly what was worse, the leg pain or the agony of her absence?

Then the litany of questions started all over again.

Before first light, the residents of the lodge began to stir. Fires were awakened. The children were sent out to gather firewood and fetch fresh water. Hunters ate a handful of berries and pemmican and washed their bodies in the small stream behind the village. They departed on their individual ways, always deep into the forest, seeking game. Like their fathers before them, they offered a small salutation to the animals they would be hunting. As they cleaned their bodies and prepared for the hunt, they also offered a up prayer.

From his dais, Dan watched and listened as the hunters departed. He wished he was going with them. The men passed in a blur. Many of them nodded to him, their way of offering encouragement. A few mumbled kind words in English. Much of the hostility of the previous days had weaseled away. They liked this man. Mutual respect coursed between them. Like Dan, the Natives were keen hunters and fine woodsmen. They respected their prey, and they also respected this pathfinder who hunted both the big and small mammals.

Animal flesh kept their people alive—that was the simple truth. Few hunters failed to acknowledge the spirits of the four-legged ones, of the swimmers and the flyers. Above all else, they remained grateful.

After the men left on their errands, the women gathered to talk over the happenings of the day, to plot out their chores. Like human beings everywhere, the Native people enjoyed a bit of gossip.

After breakfast, the children were fed and bathed. Later came lessons, games, and duties. The grandparents and elders chipped in. Among the teachers, Black Wing offered his knowledge. Not only did the children listen, but the adults also hovered nearby, just within earshot. "Listen. Learn. Sk'ada, Sk'ada," they would repeat in Haida.

Dan thought it wasn't much different there than at home, except for the children. He and Rebecca had none. The thought festered.

In better times, when he was mobile, Dan spent hours watching the children play their games. Like kids everywhere, they were inventive, curious, and excited about any new opportunity. In the village, a half-dozen bone games elicited laughter and lighthearted frolicking. The Natives professed a fondness for gambling. To some extent their games mimicked the elders' pastimes. This custom extended to the spear and wheel game. The children braided hoops from cedar and green willow limbs, then sectioned them with braided spokes. The spear was intended to pass through the spinning wheel. The youth became deft at the process. Of course, the play skills led to hunting skills, which were practiced predominantly by the young boys. The girls had their private games as well.

Two hours after sunrise, Yellow Bird Singing stopped by for a visit. Despite the pain, Dan's spirit brightened.

"How are you today?" she asked, using her best English.

He answered amicably. "Just fine, I reckon."

She looked at him askance.

"Well," he said, surveying the patch job on his leg. "Kind of incapacitated."

"Incapacitated?" Her face screwed up into an expression that begged for explanation.

"Well, that means I can't go far with this leg being as it is. Being injured and all. *Incapacitated.*" That had been one of Rebecca's chosen words.

He winced as another throb of pain careened along the broken bone.

Yellow Bird Singing wasn't sure "incapacitated" explained anything. Her eyes traveled along his broken leg. She knew the story. Everybody in the village did. She flinched as the pain touched another raw nerve, and Dan reacted with a grimace.

"Yes, I . . . I see. You are badly hurt?" Her voice was soft with the compassion of the young.

Dan raised his head, locating her perceptive gaze. "Yeah. I have some pain for sure. But I've had worse."

The words stuck in his throat. An older woman had given him a bitter tea the night before, a salal tea laced with some strange herb. It had dulled the pain. He wished for more now. He thought of requesting it. The young girl usually passed along his requests. Dan forced his thoughts back to Yellow Bird Singing. Even in his short time there, she had blossomed into a fine young woman. Dan realized suddenly how beautiful she had become.

She lowered her eyes. "I'm sorry," she whispered. "Sorry for your troubles. You don't deserve this, but what can we do?"

It struck Dan how she assumed responsibility for her people. He liked that. Liked her sense of fairness.

"Sometimes nothing is fair."

Having expressed her sentiment, Yellow Bird Singing reached out her hand and rested it on his arm.

A pain larger than the leg injury struck him. Yes, he wanted a daughter. Always had. And at the moment, he wanted Rebecca even worse. Even as encouraging words passed between them, Dan realized he was wishing for unanswered prayers.

Yellow Bird Singing straightened his sleeping mat and then rearranged his bedding and personals. She left but returned minutes later with an herbal tea and some berries. Had she known?

Dan sat motionless, watched the world spin around him. He fell into a meditation that Black Wing had taught him, and his mind quieted. For a time the pain remained distant, but random thoughts continued to pulse through his mind, and ultimately, the pain settled back in.

He thought of Black Wing and realized that he hadn't seen his friend since his return from his aborted escape. Dan's affection for the old man ran deep. His respect for the elder's wisdom ran even deeper, even though he had committed the ultimate betrayal of that wisdom in his attempt to run away from the village. To run away from a people who treated him with courtesy and respect.

Dan felt a sudden urge to see him, to gather in his keen words. The thought rang true, like an arrow on target.

The lodge quieted. The women moved out into the forest and the meadow. Dan wanted to sleep, but his leg throbbed endlessly. He kept hearing Black Wing's warning—his admonitions. For crying out loud, he needed to talk with the elder.

He did not have long to wait. The old man and Charlie were walking up the cedar apse. Dan forced a small, exasperated sound from his lips. Such timing. Was it just one more coincidence?

Charlie guided the elder by the arm. As usual, Black Wing appeared slower than normal as he shuffled along beside his nephew. He appeared older than Dan remembered, a little feebler perhaps. Well, Dan knew better than to trust any such assumption.

"Good morning, my son. Sán uu dáng giidang." Black Wing spoke in English and then Haida. His voice was clear and commanding. Charm and sincerity clung to his person like a Sunday suit.

"Charlie?" the elder said, nodding toward the lodge entrance.

Charlie rose. He smiled at Dan and then quietly left the lodge.

Black Wing settled onto the ground in a cross-legged position. He remained quiet for several minutes. Outside, Dan heard the rustle of a spring shower. Black Wing always sought out the correct words before beginning a conversation.

The smoke was thick in the longhouse. It clung to the ceiling in listless pockets. The color reminded Dan of cold, dirty coffee. A woman wielding a long, thin pole pushed aside a couple of cedar planks, and much of the smoke began to dissipate along the roof line and into the morning air. Although his mind was darting about, Dan waited patiently for Black Wing to speak.

"I hurt for you, Dan Skinner. In the long, dark night, I pray for you. I beg that you not be bitter, that you not hold a hateful place in your heart for my people. I hope your pain will pass quickly. I tell you again, a good man must rise above vengeance."

Dan had changed some—how could he deny such a reflection? Looking at the elder, what might he say? He felt such fondness for him, such empathy.

Dan had lived through plenty of disharmony, and now, he needed a friend more than ever. As he studied Black Wing's lined face, Dan felt his mouth begin to stir, but he held up. He felt he lacked the words to speak truthfully and with sincerity. He touched his fingers to his face. His forehead was sweaty. He felt lightheaded. Was that the pain? He forced out his next thoughts. "You tried to warn me off. Can't much blame you for trying. Don't get me wrong; I'm mad as hell. Well, not at you."

He chewed over the elder's last words. Black Wing had gone quiet, like Tom before he found his new tongue. Lately, the Tsimshian had opened up. He had swung about-face. Dan appreciated the change, a kind of rebirth.

Black Wing wore a shredded cedar-bark cape with a whale design in black and red. He looked older but regal. Elegant in a simple way—Dan liked that.

Dan broke the silence. "Maybe . . . maybe I'm just mad at the world. I didn't plan to spend my life here. You know what I want. Hell, everyone in camp does. You also know that you can trust me not to expose your people. Nobody could beat that out of me!"

Black Wing remained quiet. His blind, piercing eyes, spotted ebony in the dimness of the lodge. They penetrated right into Dan's psyche. A long silence ensued.

After several minutes Black Wing spoke. "I don't believe you will remain alone much longer." His words curled out in a near whisper.

Dan had good ears, but he nearly missed it. He cocked his head closer to the elder. "What? What did you say?"

Black Wing's words surprised him. Dan chewed on them for several seconds. Like a bird dog on scent, Black Wing was onto something. Dan didn't know how to figure out in what direction the elder's quiet words were headed. *Where was Black Wing going this time*? Dan shut his mouth and waited. He was slowly learning that patience was his ally.

After a couple of minutes, Dan realized Back Wing might refrain from further comment. The old man always outlasted Dan. He had the patience of Job. Dan decided to break the log jam. "Do you mind explaining that to me?"

Another long silence ensued before Black Wing answered. "It is time that you begin to trust me. I'm telling you that everything will work out for the best. Trust me in this, for I can do no more. I'm not reading the future. This is common sense. Events speak to me, or maybe I'm just a lucky guesser."

A big smile broke across the elder's face as if he was enjoying his own palaver. Then his smile disappeared, and he became serious. "I put a certain trust in the future. Soon, things get better."

Dan wasn't quite ready for that. His leg hurt, and his pride had been wounded. Gingerly, he shifted his body to accommodate the pain, then chose his next words carefully. "You once told me that you read pieces of the future. Do you see mine now?"

"Pieces. Yes."

"And . . . ?"

"I have felt your gift like a seed that grows into a flower. It is the flower that I see before me. A blossom that comes to my people like the morning star, then grows and blooms. This will sound very strange to you, but I felt the gift of your coming long before our first meeting. And now I see something more. I see life and birth. Still, I'm not sure that either of us will live long enough to see that lovely flower bloom."

Dan was stupefied. His eyes widened as he gazed at the elder. Black Wing's eyes remained calm. Dan's mind began to thrash wildly about, not sure where to go. Black Wing's pronouncement puzzled him.

"Do you mean I'll have children? Me and Rebecca? Why, that's impossible!"

"Visions are never as clear as that," Black Wing answered cautiously. They remind me of the way sunlight filters down through the forest. A man can catch pieces of that fine golden light but only small pieces. I wait, trying to put shape on the mystery that is life. Often I am mystified or lost. Many times I stand alone. Are you not familiar with this?"

Black Wing took a deep breath. As his next words punctured the air, Dan felt his own breath slide away. "Yes, I believe that you and Rebecca will have a child, but it is your grandchild that I have seen."

"What are you talking about?" Dan had never felt so confused.

"I'm talking about your granddaughter. She will bring new hope to my people, to Mother Earth."

"A granddaughter? That's . . . that might take . . . years. And in the meantime, what about Rebecca? A child? What about us, for God's sake? What do you mean? After all, Rebecca is a hundred miles from—"

"Time will tell. That is all I can say for now."

"For crying out loud, that's a big help. Come on, Black Wing. I mean, is there hope for this village? And Rebecca? Here? Why, that's crazy! And while we're on the topic, what's going to happen to all these good people anyway? To you and me?" Dan flayed the air with his hands. Around the longhouse, several women stopped their chores and turned his way. Of course, Dan was talking about the whole tribe, about a way of life that he had come to respect.

Once again, Black Wing smiled broadly, but his smile faded as he spoke. "You know that this village cannot last forever. This . . ." He spread his arms, illuminating his explanation. "A man does not need to read the future to see this much. This village is like a mirage shaped by sunlight."

His voice was low and hushed. Dan leaned closer to hear, his forehead nearly touching the elder's. The rest of Black Wing's sentence followed, full of expectation. "This village can just be for now—for a short time—as was another village here once before. Many have come and gone."

"You're sure about that? Is this another vision?"

"No. It is the way things are—or were! This can't last. I hope I am wrong."

"Why, I'm not so sure—" Dan's declaration stumbled out.

"I have named this village after another place in time. On this very spot long ago, a great village called Wolf Haven stood proudly. This is English translation. I have mentioned this village, in passing. It stood here, right where we sit. It existed for many winters. You have walked over the dust and ashes of this great village every day, not recognizing what is now only legend. But the spirit power still exists. Once before, this village fell. The earth I call 'Mother' took it back, wood to dust. One lodge stood right here where we sit. Another village will stand again—or so I believe—but not for many moons.

"For now you and I are just travelers on a long road. For our people, time is not a mark on a straight line. It moves in a great circle. You are a player in that circle. Like the many creatures that shape our world, you are a gift, an offering from the Creator. You may leave your mark here. Or perhaps at a time and in a place that comes after you. No man can know all."

Like dust settling, Dan thought. A life turned back to dirt. Man came from clay. *Sooner or later, he will return to the ground.* Dan was remembering a lesson from the Bible. His head swam in introspection.

Black Wing's eyes looked so youthful. The elder sat before Dan as a blind man, yet no human being could deny the depth of the elder's vision.

He spoke then, leaning close into Dan, his words like a warm breath on the morning air. "I believe that before there were bodies—before human beings—that spirits roamed freely through the air. Their words were like birdsong. If they chose, they could turn into a human or into another animal form. A bear or wolf. They could take on the body shape of another. These people are known through legends as the Sparrow Hawk People. This story my grandfather shared. Maybe truth. Maybe some fiction.

"Grandfather say that after a time, many of the Bird People trapped themselves in the skin of human beings and no longer returned to the spirit world. Their souls became earthbound. Over many generations, the earthlings forgot about their place in the spirit world. Those spirits were silenced. Instead, men came to covet possessions. Frequently, they spoke angrily. They learned to lie and to steal and to fight savagely. They lost their way."

Dan sat perfectly still. He remained silent, his mouth dry, his mind overflowing with unanswered questions. It felt peculiar to wrestle with such elevated thoughts. *Sparrow Hawk people? Free spirits*? Dan didn't know what to say or how to shape an intelligent response. But then, he knew that Black Wing didn't need a response. The old man was comfortable with himself. If Dan needed more answers, he would have to wait. He also suspected that an explanation might never come, at least not in full, but he had to try.

"Black Wing, are you one of those bird people?"

"No son," he answered firmly, turning his eyes away, deserting Dan to his own thoughts. "Maybe sometimes I see the world through different eyes. I borrow from an eagle or a bear or my friend, the wolf. That is all. Maybe my friends borrow a little from me. This is confusing. No?"

Black Wing stood up and abruptly turned away from Dan. He walked up the dirt aisle unaided, his head held high. The elder found his way out through the opening between the two eagle totems, the foundation of the longhouse, of a proud and ancient culture. Daylight silhouetted the shape of the seer until he was lost from Dan's view. Never had he seen the blind man walk so far alone, but Dan felt little to no surprise.

Three times that afternoon, Dan was served a bowl of herbal tea, stream water boiled with colt's foot, a lovely silver-and-green plant that was found in patches beside well-worn trails. The medicine soothed his discomfort. He was tired. After Black Wing's visit, Dan felt drained. When night came, he slept deeply.

Late in the moonlit night, he dreamt once again of Rebecca.

In the dreamland, he walks up behind her. Her back is turned toward him. She seems to be praying. A moon dances through the trees and backlights her shoulders and neck, her long auburn hair. The moon is early in its cycle. A few nightbirds contribute their song. If music has a voice, Dan is clear that the words echo sadness. He looks around the forest. Through the alder, he deciphers the shapes of two men. Even in his dream, the revelation troubles him. Turning back to his wife, Dan realizes she is crying. In the dreamland, Dan is forced to explore the beauty and pain of life and death.

Above the stately trees, the fierce piercing call of an eagle rings through the night sky.

Pain stirred him from sleep Struggling to find his way out of the dreamworld, he pulled himself into a sitting position and opened his eyes. Pieces of the dream filtered in and out of his consciousness. He remembered seeing Rebecca. Remembered her tears. Is this really an apparition, he wondered? Again, there were few answers. But as hard as he tried, he couldn't remember who or what she was crying over. He shook his head to clear the vision and slipped back into a deep sleep. Across the lodge, smoldering fires burned lower and lower.

Rebecca's sleep was restless. In a knot of deep loss, her dreams focused mostly on Sally. But then there were others, a carousel of actors. Her father stepped before her. And Dan, always Dan. Time flooded by. She woke with a start but remained intent on lingering memories, on the afterworld, and on her father. She always called him "Daddy," even later, even after his death.

Rebecca sat up and looked toward the campfire. Had she talked in her sleep? Had she shouted? The sound of her own voice had startled her awake as the granite wall echoed her lament. "Daddy, Daddy, Sally, Dan. . ." She couldn't remember everything. Maybe she was still dreaming. There had been so many losses.

She looked around the camp and then back at the fire. The embers had nearly played out. By then, her dream had played out too. She lay back on the fern pallet and tried to sleep. That soon became an impossibility. The dreamworld had turned against her. There would be no more sleep that night.

Gazing at the maze of stars, Rebecca lay as still as the forest around her. She remembered how she would sidle up to her father and settle into the comfortable nest that was his lap. He was a big man, and his sheer size enveloped her tiny girl's body, her gangly legs and stick-like arms. On the other hand, she retained a vitality that her father no longer matched. Not since the war. He was a shadow of his former self. The war had stripped him of his vitality and one arm.

When Rebecca turned ten, her daddy was thirty-eight. A year later, he was failing. But hadn't he been failing for years, ever since the war?

Chancellorsville had left him nearly dead, alone on a killing field for two days, ravaged by thirst and desperation. Forever after, he walked with a decisive limp. A third bullet had burned his insides, leaving a permanent pain, but the gravest damage went far beyond those physical limitations.

Rebecca's father suffered from mental wounds that only a foot soldier understands. John Stamp never forgot the ravages of the war, never forgot the slaughter. John was a captain. That commission happened through the process of natural attrition and because of his bravery under fire. A dozen times he had marched against a killing wall of Confederate marksmen. He had survived while others fell.

As dawn arose on the three travelers, Rebecca once again pondered love, luck, and fate.

At age forty, John Stamp took his own life.

1989

Pyramids. From her bed stateside, Katherine dreamed of an Egyptian, a craftsman. She saw him as if she was seeing herself in a mirror. She saw this man—a man, yes. That startled her.

He was a foreman on a crew of builders, stone movers. There were slaves there, but most of the craftsmen were salaried workmen. The man was unhappy. She saw how the desert heat had reshaped his face, etched a mask of acquiescence across the exposed skin of his brown body. He was weary from years of arduous labor. Beleaguered because there was no way out of an intolerable situation, no way to change his life. If her senses were speaking the truth, the man did not have much longer to live. She deciphered all these things instantaneously. Somehow she knew it all. Somehow she knew this person as well as she knew herself.

Who is this? she wondered. *Who is this man*? The answer frightened her. *He is me.*

After the initial dream, she suffered from another recurring nightmare. An assassin was coming for her, coming out of a thick fog. Violence careened through the air.

But he never found her, this apparition. It would come into her house, creep up her stairs, try to open her bedroom door—almost but not quite. And she never saw the face. Every time the dream seared her imagination, she woke up screaming.

She wondered if the apparition of the Egyptian had opened a door that should have remained closed. She wondered why she had experienced such a vision. Why had she seen him at all? *There are mysteries in the world best left alone*, she thought.

For years afterwards the killer would stalk her in her dreams, and she would wake screaming, calling for Paul. Calling for *Daddy*.

Always, she clung to her mission, her work. Katherine moved ahead, a determined woman. She sought answers, but there were never enough.

CHAPTER TWENTY-SEVEN

The elder would implore us to gather around the fire, to close the circle. "This is how we end the day," he would say. "This will bring us together." Then he would pass an eagle feather around the circle. With that feather the speaker owned the camp. No one was allowed to interrupt the monologue. Around the campfire circle, we worked out our problems together. After the campfire the day was finished. We felt healed. One always slept soundly in the summer camp of the Haisla.

—Katherine Skinner-Patterson
From her diary, Memories of a Lost Summer on the Northwest Coast

Another campfire. Another solemn night. Smoke ascended like the memories of her loved ones, straight up into the night sky. Far up the valley, a wolf howled, a siren song, long and cold and chilling. Certainly she had thought that once, but not now. Oddly, she found comfort in the animal's stirrings. Staring into infinite space, Rebecca wrangled with her thoughts, caught as they were between a deep abyss and far-fetched hopes. High above the forested valley, she imagined the wind taking her prayers, lifting them upwards, empowering them like the wolf's cry.

Private loss was as tangible as the smoke, a reality to the three survivors who rested quietly below. For two days they had scoured the riverbanks. Not a single sign of Sally was to be found. Soon, small hope had turned to no hope, but they had searched on, never surrendering to their private doubts.

That evening as they sat around the campfire, Man Hides Good said it was time to move on. He was sure that Sally was dead. He was just as sure that Dan was waiting somewhere ahead. They should push forward, he said. Perhaps the renewed journey would reveal hopeful news.

The following morning, the Haisla scouts stood beside the lakeshore, chanting in a language that Rebecca did not understand. But she perceived the direction of their words.

The men had come to respect Sally. Now they were saying goodbye to their common friend.

The suddenness of Sally's death wounded Rebecca grievously. She felt guilty and wondered why she hadn't talked Sally out of their mission. Earlier in the week, Rebecca had stood before a simple memorial to her brother-in-law. Now Sally was gone too, and there wasn't even a body to mourn. The wound refused to abandon her. Rebecca's single remaining motivation was the belief that she would soon find her husband. Without her belief, Rebecca would have been lost.

The two Natives sensed this and moved about her as quietly as a tiny newborn fawn that stumbled into camp, just at dusk.

"Welcome, little friend."

Man Hides Good spoke in a voice so hushed that Rebecca nearly missed his words. He declined to touch the fawn for fear of leaving a scent that might separate infant from mother. Gently, he shooed the baby back into the forest. For him, the fawn was a sign of rebirth and healing.

"Good sign, Rebecca. Little one, he come to see us. He senses our need. He know we travel with good spirit."

Rebecca thanked him but turned her eyes back toward the fire's embers. The men left her alone. Ambling from the camp, they talked about the coming day and their next course of action. Where would they be heading, and what did they hope to find? Nothing was certain. The Haisla had learned that lesson three days before. If Rebecca agreed, they would head out the next morning and drift deeper into the northern wilderness.

The men reasoned that Dan had climbed the sheer granite wall where they had camped two days earlier. Likely, he had headed north to east. That was the natural flow of the land. They calculated that he was on the run from the last of the posse, and that meant Tom LaCross. They both knew that such odds didn't bode well. Not for Dan. Not for any man.

The Haisla had followed the Tsimshian's reputation for decades. He lived just beyond their village in a small, rough-hewn cottage that bordered the river. Known for his cunning, his skills, and his taciturn personality, Tom was respected by elders and youth alike. Both guides believed that if any man could find Dan in that wilderness, it was the Tsimshian scout. Predicting that confrontation, they speculated on the outcome. They offered a prayer for a peaceful resolution.

Man Hides Good had a secret to share. Walking beside his friend, Spirit Runner, he spoke softly in his Native tongue. "I can only guess, my friend, but I have an idea where we might find the husband of Rebecca Skinner."

They camped in a nest of cottonwood, along a narrow, sandy beach on the long, isolated lake. The water was deep and still. Tall granite mountains reflected off the lake, painting the mirrored surface with mountain color. The sounds of numerous waterfalls tantalized.

The valley was stunning in the early morning light. They called the beach *A-koo-u-wa*. For centuries it had been the summer gathering place of the Eagle clan. Down the lake was the hereditary village of the Blackfish-Salmon clan, a camp called *Kla-eyss*. Farther up there was *Ogu-Walla*, a lovely beach and the ancient village of the Raven clan. Few relics of the camps remained, and that reality distressed the two Natives.

The Haisla had camped on those beaches for generations beyond memory. Man Hides Good summered there as a boy. It was the homeland of his ancestors.

The two guides believed that someday the land would be reclaimed by the First Peoples. The Haisla would return to their homeland. Their culture would once again stand proudly. Prosperity would follow. Hope and prayers guided them. The lake remained holy to the Haisla. None of that was lost on these two friends.

Spirit Runner turned. "Memories," he said. "How many do you have, my friend? How many summers did you spend here?"

Man Hides Good lowered his head, turned, and began to walk up the beach, his friend beside him. "Much pain, much joy," he said. "Along the way, so many tears. Before that, happier times. We lived well. We were strong. I miss that very much."

For centuries the Haisla had processed salmon on these beaches by the tens of thousands. Man Hides Good could still picture the huge cedar smokehouses and drying racks.

Only scattered remnants from that time were still visible. Timbers, decayed lodge poles, and dilapidated cedar planks were strewn along the shoreline and into the nearby forest. Many a harsh winter had grayed and decayed much of the cedar fiber into dust and loam.

The missionaries never ventured into the summering place, but nature had accomplished their fundamentalist mission. Abandonment had overwhelmed the seasonal village with decay and rot.

Gone were the canoes. Gone was the laughter. But a few of the tall carved totems had fared better. Several still stood, tall and proud. The harsh coastal winters had faded the primary colors. Rain and storms had softened the sharp facial outlines. Still, in the clear morning light, the carved images remained haunting and magical. The two Haisla stood in awe. The totems represented another time and place, but the message of Haisla heredity rang loud and clear.

As the two men walked, Man Hides Good talked, mostly speaking his Native tongue. "I have traded with a Haisla named Charlie. Many times over many seasons, I have sold seal and whale flesh to this good man. Whale no longer plentiful. Not the big grays. But seals, yes. Many seals. And salmon and eulachon. He pledged me to hold his secret. Pledged me to my honor. This I have always done until now. It is only because of this woman, Rebecca Skinner, that I now speak to you. And because of the trust I hold sacred between brothers.

"Often I carry meat and fish packed in glacier ice. I travel many days upriver. There, I exchange with Native runners. They vanish beyond this lake into the Ozyetea River, and then beyond, toward the mountain divide. They travel by night. First, I think, these people go far inland. But can't be. These are coastal people. As I say, Charlie is Haisla. And the mountains are harsh during the long winter months. A few men from our village also sell to Charlie. This I see with my own eyes.

"These men hold their tongues. But I notice how they disappear as stealthily as wolves. Often I pass them in the night without the courtesy of the clan's greeting. Their heads bend low as they paddle upriver, invisible like the night creatures. Later, they return with empty canoes. So, I think, yes, up that river is a good-sized camp. I think some of our people live in a secret village, hidden now for many years, hidden from Bostons and their laws. I believe they preserve our old ways."

Man Hides Good slowed and turned facing his friend. The sun rose higher and higher over the placid lake water. "I ask few questions. I think this man, Skinner—I think maybe he end up there." He pointed his finger high into the mountains. "But I do not know if he is welcome or a prisoner. Maybe White Bear there too, or maybe he dead. But Skinner? Only the eagle knows."

Man Hides Good turned his head and looked heavenward, as if anticipating another visitation from the great bird. "I know you watch that great eagle like me. I catch your eyes. This confuses my senses, this keen-eyed bird, this raptor whose face is carved on the totems of my clan. Still, I feel drawn to the direction where that eagle flies. I feel we must go his way. Much is strange here. Very strange. Still, I am convinced . . ."

Spirit Runner listened respectfully to his friend. When the time was right—after he honored Man Hides Good's wise words—only then did he speak. "Yes," he said. "I too feel the eagle is a messenger. Like you, I'm drawn in the direction where the great bird flies. I think we go that way. I also suspect this village you speak of. I, too, notice hunters among us who return empty-handed after weeks in the wilderness. Later, I also notice trade goods. And the stealth of these men—that say plenty to me. I think now that I wish to go with you and find this village."

Nothing else was said. Both men walked back to the camp. There, they found Rebecca sitting before the campfire. Her eyes were steady and dry. Great strength in those eyes, both thought. The men respected this strong woman. Perhaps they felt something beyond that. Few Bostons had impressed the Haisla. This woman was quiet and honest. She treated the men with dignity. Good qualities for a White woman, for any human being. Good medicine.

The next morning the travelers rose before dawn. A warm fire awaited. Man Hides Good had drawn the last watch. He kindled the fire and began to cook a wonderful Tyee salmon that Spirit Runner had trapped in a fast-moving stream that emptied into the lake. The night before, Rebecca listened to the wilderness music until its song lulled her to sleep. But whatever dreams she had, some undefinable force had stolen them away. None-the-less, she woke refreshed and strangely optimistic.

While Man Hides Good roasted the fresh salmon over the coals, Rebecca strolled along the white, sandy beach. Like everywhere else in that country, majestic granite mountains ascended thousands of feet above the bowl of the lake. Just above the granite crowns, the fading crescent moon reflected its yellow eye on the only human visitors in the valley. The mountain vista was mirrored like a collapsed double vision off the water's dark surface.

As her eyes settled on the placid waters, Rebecca couldn't help but notice her image mirrored in the lake's surface. She stood transfixed, studying herself as if meeting this person—this pioneer woman—for the first time. As odd as it seemed, she liked the spirit of the mirrored face. Contemplating her reflection again, she realized that since the beginning of her adventure, she had come to depend on herself more each day. The lake reflected her inner strength. Her single wish was that she might share this revelation with her dear friend, Sally. That Sally was alive and well. *Now*, she thought, *I have memories. Certainly, there is great wealth in that.*

The valley was awash in spring colors, a cascade of golds and yellows, lime-green, and chartreuse. Silver and blue and platinum white; the lake mirrored the forest and the massive granite cliffs. Countless shades of green sparkled off the flora and fauna, pressing reflections upon the still water surface. Overhead and along the waterway, waterfalls toppled like thunder, falling hundreds of feet into the lake basin. Echoes ricocheted across the water with all the backlash of a shotgun blast. A palette of colors, sequined daubs, sun motes, and broad strokes of sunlight revealed a vista to test the greatest talents of nineteenth-century painters. *Masterworks,* she thought, realizing that something would be lost there too. After all, no man would ever capture all of it. No man. Rebecca wished to hold forever in her mind's eye the vision of the great valley and all that fed it.

Never seen the likes, she thought, tantalized by the mountain beauty. The landscape soothed her, releasing many of the tensions from the previous several days, relieving her of an onslaught of pain and anxiety.

They feasted on the succulent salmon and then set out across the lake.

Even as Rebecca basked in the natural beauty that surrounded her, she was reminded of the harshness of the land beyond. Here the back country was sheathed in ice and snow that, even under normal circumstances, could turn deadly with the speed of a cougar.

She took a sweep with the canoe paddle, lifted it, and then dropped the tip carefully back into the dark lake. Behind her, reflections were broken into a million fractured shards. Rebecca studied the dark water. Staring back over her shoulder, she wished that all the unpleasant moments of the last several months might pass away peacefully, that the pristine wilderness might lift her burden.

At the east end of the lake, a great eagle flushed from the high candelabra top of an evergreen, then escalated in widening circles above the becalmed lake. Rebecca marveled at the great bird. She was seeing the eagle in a new light.

They paddled across the great lake known to the Haisla as *Ka'ous.* It was fed by the Ozyetea River and other smaller tributaries. They pushed ahead.

The river water was the color of a Chinese celadon vase. The blue-green glaze appeared translucent, but a smoky-white haze—the result of minerals and snow melt—layered the water with a mysterious veil. To Rebecca it seemed as if the whole land was holding back a secret. What that mystery was, she could only guess, but somehow she felt bound to its mysterious gift.

High above the travelers on the sheer mountain cliffs, the long-haired goats bolted up the craggy granite face, disappearing into pockets of spindly evergreen shrubs that clung tenaciously to the rocky mountainside. Occasionally, Rebecca heard falling rock and scree, as the pieces fell and scattered behind the scampering legs of the fleet-footed goats. She listened as the sound bowled down the valley, through the evergreens and cottonwoods, bouncing like gunshots off the granite walls that lined their passage.

Far overhead the eagle arose again, turned, and caught the updraft. In widening circles, it rose higher and higher. Then it flew up the valley, leaving the humans to their private vexations.

Once into the Ozyetea, the currents challenged them. The river was swift but not nearly as brutal as the white water below Ka'ous Lake. The trio made good progress. Rebecca asked about the half-moon cutouts that scraped out a primitive clay trail along the banks of the shoreline.

"Those are our water cousins, the beaver," Spirit Runner replied. "Tonight we might trap one." He circled and rubbed his tummy.

Even Rebecca had acquired a taste for the tree eaters. Spirit Runner returned early the next morning with two beaver, and another feast ensued.

Rebecca reveled in the call of the flickers, the red-tailed hawks, thrushes, jays, and juncos. Hooded mergansers erupted off the river, scudding for cover, their wings clapping hard off the water's surface. Canada geese hunkered along the waterway. As the canoe approached, a dame crouched over her nest of eggs, her motherly instincts on display to a discerning eye.

Mallard, drake and hen, a river otter and pups, a mother doe and fawn, a black bear with cubs—the water path teemed with waterfowl and wildlife.

Oh, how Rebecca pined for Sally. How she wished to share her experience with her best friend.

Three days above the lake, heavy rain tumbled upon them. Once again the water turned coffee brown. For hours they struggled against the rising currents of the Ozyetea until they were too exhausted to continue. Man Hides Good brought the canoe into the lee side of a sandy beach where they set up camp. Rebecca gathered wood and started a fire while the two men disappeared into the forest with their bows and arrows. The fire was crackling brightly when they returned, laden with wild onions, edible roots, and some tender salmonberry sprouts, all gathered from a nearby meadow. Best of all, the Haisla carried two fat mallards brought down with their arrows over a beaver pond. Rebecca took the bounty, cleaned and quartered the birds, and then added the meat to the thin stew she had made with the last of their dwindling provisions. They feasted on hearty fare, devouring the natural gifts with relish.

As they moved upriver, the day continued warm and balmy. Aching arms and backs powered the canoe upriver. The miles crept by.

The skies remained clear throughout the afternoon. The landscape, refreshed by a recent rain, sparkled and gleamed in the sunlight. The river flowed swiftly again, forcing them to push and pole the cedar canoe through frequent shallows. But the stream was beginning to play out like a weak poker hand.

At noon the following day, the Haisla guided the canoe into a cache that elbowed into a natural cutout in the riverbank. They nestled the canoe under a thick stand of alder trees alongside a smooth gravel beach where tree limbs hovered just above the water.

Nearby, the stream branched into two small tributaries. Spirit Runner explained that they would now be traveling on foot.

"But how will we choose which fork to follow? Where do we go from here?" Rebecca asked, an anxious expression crossing her face.

Instead of offering an answer, Spirit Runner turned his gaze upwards to where the eagle still circled high above them. As he watched, the eagle broke away to the north, drifting effortlessly toward a series of low-lying foothills. Spirit Runner pointed to the northern fork in the river. "There!"

As he gazed into the heights above the valley, the great eagle circled. Here, the most northern fork of the Ozyetea broke away into foothills that appeared less menacing than anything they had encountered over the last week.

"There?"

Rebecca reacted incredulously. "Just what do you mean?" Even Spirit Runner had startled himself over the abruptness of his decision.

Man Hides Good joined the other two. He intuitively sensed the direction of the conversation. Soon, he interjected. "Spirit Runner think we find your man few days from here, maybe up at top of that valley." As he talked, he pointed his finger toward a tall expanding ridge of hills as the eagle ascended farther and farther in the same direction.

"I still don't understand. Why do you think Dan is there? Why would he be?"

Man Hides Good had been standing behind Rebecca, watching and listening. Now he offered more advice. "Spirit Runner think we find your man where the eagle goes."

"I still don't understand. Why do you think Dan is there? And the eagle? What has that to do . . . ?"

Rebecca wondered why Man Hides God had begun to speak in a near whisper. She drew closer to him. He smelled like smoke, body sweat, and earth. Naturally, she thought about Dan, and for a moment, she felt her emotions swell.

"What I have to say may seem strange, but you must listen to me now. Many times, I have sold seal and elk meat to men who disappear into these same mountains. They live, I think, in secret. I believe it's nearby. We will follow our eyes and the skills given us by the Creator."

"Here?" Rebecca asked, not knowing whether to trust the optimism she found in his words.

As she peered into the dark-brown eyes of her two friends, she remembered her initial doubts, the fears and suspicions she had felt when she first met the Haisla at the farm. But times had changed. A mutual trust had formed between them. She waited patiently for his answer.

"We cannot be sure," Spirit Runner replied. "This is our hope. We think long and hard. You see, the river runs out of water. From now on, we must walk."

Man Hides Good spoke next. "All along, we followed clues left behind by the two brothers—your Dan Skinner—and the lawmen. After we passed the cliffs where the men fell, we had to trust our instincts. We continued to follow the river and prayed that the Creator would guide us. Perhaps he sends a messenger now."

He peered upwards, expecting to see the eagle, but, except for a few cumulus clouds hinting at yet another weather change, the sky was empty.

After a moment's pause, he added, "Spirit Runner and I have decided to follow the eagle."

As he spoke, the great bird reappeared, an omen perhaps, and the humans below stared in wonder.

Spirit Runner pointed far down the valley where the eagle was gliding back and forth across the foothills. "This eagle has trailed us for many days. We watch him constantly. We think he watches us back. Eagle leads us to his mountain home. His lair. Both Man Hides Good and I feel need to follow this bird."

"Sweet Jesus," Rebecca began. "I mean . . . how can you be so sure?"

"Trust us, Rebecca. We have not gone wrong yet. We have not led you astray. This no longer about your silver dollars. We, too, wish to find Dan Skinner. We wish to find village of our lost clan."

"What if they don't wish us there?"

"I'm sure they don't. But Man Hides Good has traded with these people, our cousins. They may be as sly as foxes, but I believe they are honorable people."

"And if they're not?"

"Do you wish to go back now, Rebecca Skinner? Go back empty-handed?"

That afternoon the two Haisla headed into the forest. They returned at dusk, satisfied that they were not being watched. They were still unable to agree on what direction would take them toward the village. There were no tracks, no trails, and no signs.

The next morning the three travelers began to follow the northernmost stream as it snaked into the foothills that lay below a high mountain divide, a curvaceous dip that still rose several thousand feet above them. After weeks in the canoe, the solid ground felt alien, but they were delighted to use their legs again.

The trio was high in the mountains now. The forest was lush. Huge clumps of ferns and salal silenced the natural sounds. Stinging devil's club often blocked their way. Evergreen trees twenty feet in circumference rose majestically from the rich forest floor. The limbs were so thick and dense that the brightest rays of sunshine barely penetrated the tangle of foliage. The three travelers' passage was hampered by dense stands of hemlock, Sitka spruce, and western and yellow cedar. As they gained elevation, the composition of the evergreens began to change. There were fewer of the spruce and cedar trees and more of the straight-trunked Douglas fir.

No matter—all the conifers were imposing. Indeed, they stood like great giants, often extending two hundred feet or better into the mountain air.

Beside the streambed, alder and cottonwood crowded the riverbank. Thin golden blazes of light were smothered by soft, rotund shadow. Occasionally, an animal trail meandered beside them. They borrowed the path and plunged ahead. The going was arduous.

The party was forced to follow the natural incline of the land. That meant wading into the frigid mountain water or bushwhacking across deadfalls and slick outcroppings of stones and boulders. By midmorning their legs and backs ached. Though the air was cold, the trio's bodies were covered with sweat. Each began to remove pieces of their dirty clothing.

The terrain continued to rise steadily.

At times, bramble cut off their access, and they were forced to go wide, back into the forest. Eventually, they would rediscover an animal path. As they stumbled closer to the mountain divide, both men became furtive. The Haisla seldom spoke. That was just fine with Rebecca. She didn't have the energy to talk back. Her usual barrage of questions dwindled to nothing. When Rebecca did comment, she was met with grunts or succinct replies, generally in a whisper.

During the day, both men walked with a stealth Rebecca found difficult to imitate, moving in a slide and shuffle and seldom falling on the heels of their feet. They climbed all day without food or rest. By evening all three were exhausted and ravenous.

The men hunted with bow and arrow. They chose not to expose their presence. Anything unnatural might ricochet for miles as the tall stone mountains amplified the sounds. Happily, the hunters returned with two grouse.

A tiny fire flared that evening, one lit after dark to hide any trace of smoke. The men exchanged night watches. For the first night in many, Rebecca slept soundly. She was exhausted.

The second day went much like the first, but for the pleasant fact that the thickets thinned as they climbed higher into the mountains. The sky turned gray, and the weather cooled. To Rebecca's relief the devil's club thinned. Twice during the long day, they stopped to pick ripe orange berries. The salmonberries were in bloom. Thick tangles of salal bushes and huckleberries were heavy with promise. *Shining times in the mountains*, Rebecca thought, remembering one of Dan's favorite expressions.

Late in the afternoon of the second day, the party came upon the spot where Tom LaCross had waited for his midnight ambush on Dan. Up ahead he had stumbled into the trap carefully crafted by his wily student. The snow and trail signs were long gone, but something undefined alerted Man Hides Good. He asked Rebecca and Spirit Runner to wait. Cautiously, he moved up the creek and into the thicket until he was standing before the cairn of rock that surrounded the firepit, the very spot where Dan had lit his fire and waited in ambush for his mentor.

Man Hides Good returned ten minutes later with an enlightened look on his face. First, in Haisla, he spoke briefly to Spirit Runner. After the two Natives exchanged words, Spirit Runner scampered off, leaving Rebecca alone with the older scout. A perplexed look crossed her face. The scout noted her anxiety. Choosing his words carefully, he explained the situation. "Ahead I find where men have struggled. Dan Skinner here. Tom LaCross too. One injured—LaCross, I think. Your man has much cunning to surprise a scout like Tom LaCross. You have never told me how great his skill is."

"Is he alive?" Rebecca felt as if the words were ripped out of her mouth.

"Yes, I am sure now. Maybe you judge yourself. We spend night in the same place where he camped. Too late to go on. I am tired to the bone. No worry; Spirit Runner join us later, maybe early morning. There good shelter here. We make small fire," His smile brightened, as did Rebecca's disposition. The promise of a night's rest with hot food was alluring. Even though her mouth remained bone-dry and her nerves frayed, his optimistic words cheered her.

The day had been cold and the weather unpredictable. There had been pockets of sunshine, followed by thunderclouds. As afternoon settled into evening, the sky, like a rich woven tapestry, became entangled in grays, blues, and silvers. The weather stewed like a swarm of gnats.

Rebecca was damp and uncomfortable and tired to the bone. The thought of a warm campfire appealed mightily to her. A bath would have been even better. She chided herself then. *No sense complaining*, she thought. Her Dan might be just ahead. "Shining times," she whispered to herself, and a smile broke through her exhaustion, as beckoning as the heat of a campfire.

Every nerve was on high alert as Rebecca stepped gingerly into the deserted campsite. The pit remained much as it had months earlier, a gaping hole. Staring at the trap that her husband had crafted, it was hard to imagine anyone surviving such a fall. Rebecca felt a chill curl up her spine. Imagined the deadly stakes tearing through flesh. The snare that had evaded Tom LaCross hung limply, the noose a harbinger of her own anxiety.

Man Hides Good built a fire and saw to it that Rebecca was comfortable. Then he began to disassemble the snare and cover the pit. All the while a story was unfolding before him.

The two men had been there; that was certain, but where had they gone? Certainly, they had disappeared suddenly.

Rebecca confirmed his doubts minutes later. In a voice shaking with emotion, she called Man Hides Good to the campfire. Just a foot behind the fire pit, buried in tall grasses, was the small leather rucksack that Dan always carried with him.

Rebecca was shaken. Man Hides Good took the pack from her quivering hands. Their fingers grazed, then separated. "Saints be damned. I just can't seem to rise above this…this!" Rebecca wiped the back of her hand across her sweat-stained cheeks and steadied herself.

In the sheltered grove beneath the rock buttress, Man Hides Good hugged her like a daughter. Abruptly, he raised his eyes as an eagle soared over the clearing. He knew the eagle by now. The eagle felt like a friend. A look of wonder creased his mouth, followed by a small smile. "It is okay now, Rebecca. Everything will be fine. Your Dan waits just ahead. Eagle, he tell me."

She looked up and began to believe.

The following morning, before daylight bathed the camp, Spirit Runner returned. He found his friend awake, sitting in a cross-legged meditation. He looked relaxed, but Spirit Runner easily ascertained that his friend was fully alert. Beside him, Rebecca remained fast asleep. Man Hides Good had heard the sounds of a man coming up the trail. As a precaution, he'd notched an arrow into his bow. Beside him lay a knife, its blade honed to a razor-sharp edge. A man couldn't be too careful.

"Were you expecting company, my friend?" Spirit Runner asked, laughing.

Man Hides Good grinned his broad smile. "One never knows which way the wind blows."

They both laughed heartily, the happy sounds ricocheting off the stone cistern. Exhausted as she was, Rebecca slept through the revelry.

Spirit Runner kicked the burning firewood together and added a few new dry boughs. He was cold, but like any warrior among his people, he seldom complained about discomfort. Nor would he consider rushing into conversation. Only after the two men had settled comfortably around the rekindled fire did Spirit Runner speak in Haisla. "I find village."

The words hung in the cold mountain air until Man Hides Good had a chance to absorb the news.

"Maybe five or six miles from here. East up a large stream. Then north, up and over two valleys. Thick woods. Then down. A hidden trail plunges into a valley. The land is beautiful. A large plateau there, well hidden. Hundred or so people live there. Looks like the winter camp of our ancestors. Lodges from the past. Haisla or Tsimshian workmanship. Some Haida and Xenaksiala too. Haven't seen the likes in years. I not believe my eyes."

Man Hides Good silently acknowledged each disclosure with a solemn nod. Spirit Runner charged on. "The village hard to approach without being observed. Dusk shielded me. And the teachings of my uncle and father."

Spirit Runner took a deep breath, then settled into a quiet space for another minute before he continued, speaking each word carefully. "I choose not to get too close. I see that the village is well guarded. Seeing it . . . seeing it makes me hurt inside for the old ways. For all we have lost."

Man Hides Good sat quietly, chewing on the news like a deer grazing on thick green grasses. There was much to consider. He turned to look at Rebecca. Whatever was decided, he would not knowingly put her in danger. "Let us rest until after dark."

"Yes. Yes. That is good," Spirit Runner replied.

Time passed slowly. The stars were rising in the heavens. Daylight was seeping in. In the firelight, Man Hides Good's face was steady but serene. Words began to stir deep inside him. Finally, in Haisla, he proposed a plan of action. "Tomorrow, I go with this woman into the village you find. I believe they will not hurt her. Not hurt me. Spirit Runner, I insist you honor me by returning to the canoe. If you not hear from me in three days' time, you must return to your family. To Salmon Village. If warriors come for you, you must flee before them. Listen, my friend. I have no family. You have yours to consider. And I may choose to stay in this village. Do not worry for me.

"I ask you hold the secret of these families who hide in this village. I am pledged to hold their secret. They will be fair with me. You now share their story. You must promise: this stays between us forever.

"You understand, my brother, that neither the White woman nor myself may be allowed to leave this camp."

Spirit Runner understood all this. And he understood the rights of an elder to dictate the laws of his tribe. Even if he disagreed with the decision, Spirit Runner would never consider violating that code. In the end, he nodded. "Yes, I do as you ask. I honor your wishes."

After that, neither man rested. They sat on opposite sides of the fire, turning their eyes from the dying embers toward the approaching dawn. Slowly, the sky lightened. The larger stars remained visible as the first rays of sunshine poked above the tall peaks of the imposing mountains. A meteor streaked suddenly across the heavens.

"Souls of lost ones," Man Hides Good stated, repeating the message he had shared with Rebecca only days before. He was remembering that many of those recent souls, belonged to his family.

Man Hides Good prayed that all would go well the next day. He was not ready to become one of those falling stars. Like most warriors among his people, he did not hold a great fear of dying. He simply wished to pass with dignity. The woman was another matter. He had no intention of leading her into a trap. Like his brother across the campfire, he was honor bound to defend her. He turned his eyes skyward and prayed that the Creator would protect Rebecca.

A sad parting of ways.

"Aix gwa las," Spirit Runner repeated, as he moved quickly away from his brother and from the White woman he had grown so fond of. "May the Creator follow you always, Rebecca Skinner. May the Great Spirit guide you and bring you home safely. May you find your man."

As Spirit Runner turned and headed down the trail, emotions welled. Out of sight, he wiped his eyes with the back of his hand.

Spirit Runner was not alone in his sadness.

1987—Portland, Oregon

Katherine had formed a skeletal organization consisting of four dedicated environmentalists, two economists, one marketing director, and a secretary. Together, they calibrated four northwest regions from satellite maps that illuminated where the largest natural watersheds remained. Of the four, only one had not been logged. This British Columbia wilderness remained the largest undisturbed temperate rainforest in the world. The great timber was under pressure. Logging companies waited impatiently in the wings. If Katherine's new organization was going to make a difference, this was where they had to start. At the same time, they hoped to enlist and engage locals in the remaining three regions.

All four of the watersheds had belonged historically to Native Americans. This had been *their* land. Over the last hundred and fifty years, much of the landscape had been usurped by the United States or the Canadian provincial government. Subsequently, the bulk fell into the hands of private timber conglomerates. In Canada much of the land had been leased to logging companies for nominal fees or sold outright for pennies on the dollar. The bulk of the forests had already been logged, often two or three times. A few logging corporations owned significant chunks of real estate, better than half of the rural landscapes in the Pacific Northwest.

The plan was fraught with complications. Any alliance would be difficult. Their choice was to forge ahead.

Katherine figured her plan of attack had to be coordinated with local volunteers. Local support was mandatory. She knew that in these rural communities, there were key people her organization could work with. Get them excited, Katherine reasoned. Teach by example. Any environmental alliance would have to demonstrate the economic bellwether of sustainable development. She would have to inspire the locals to run their own businesses in a sustainable manner.

She knew that would take plenty of energy. A lot of dollars too. That meant private donors. And they would need some luck as well, more than a little good fortune.

The group started with a tiny office in northwest Portland. The space was so small that a secretary's desk was placed in the hallway outside the director's door. Staff was family. Katherine hired a political refugee from El Salvador. Another local woman to deal with economics. That woman had a degree from Stanford but couldn't find work. Three members of the meager staff headed for a different watershed. Katherine drew the fourth assignment. She would head north. Somehow, she would forge an alliance with the Native people of British Columbia.

They began to round up local players. In principle, they decided that any alliance must represent a cross-section of the entire community.

Katherine believed that locals would not support another environmental group that insisted on logging and fishing bans. After all, that was how many in these communities flushed out decent livings.

She organized the first rendezvous in southwest Washington State and asked two logging executives to serve on the first board. She sought out a fisherman and an oysterman—both taciturn watermen but professionals. She corralled a cranberry grower, then found a couple of local business owners who offered broad economic diversity and common sense. She was surprised by the brainpower and the commonality of purpose. Soon, she had a dozen members. The program began to roll. But as she soon found, the reality of making a difference didn't come easily. Katherine took her lumps. The local papers were suspicious and unfriendly. There was squabbling on the board. A few members left. Others joined. Katherine raced ahead.

In quiet moments she thought about her father—wondered what he might have thought of her aspirations. As the project unfolded, she began to feel his presence. Was he a spirit guardian? In her higher moments, she believed so.

CHAPTER TWENTY-EIGHT

They, the dead, go south and jump through the hole, one by one. One person goes through at a time. They close the door and go out into the sky.

—Yahi legend

Dusk hunkered down, a smoky-gray veil. A Native village lay partially camouflaged in a tangle of huge conifers. Willow and alder stood on the periphery, part of the larger ancient forest. Blue sky holes punctuated the trees. Light dappled through the limbs, and tiny songbirds flitted through lush, leafy growth, so thick that their flight was rendered nearly invisible to the common eye. The old conifers clung to granite and bedrock, their roots spread wide and tenaciously, their stories old. The granite was so ancient that no person in the village guessed its origin. But the humans knew that before the granite, there had been a force that shaped the river and forest and the tall, snow-capped mountains.

The Haida believed that Raven came first. The wily one released the humans from their clamshell imprisonment, creating an alliance between the tribes and the beautiful land the Creator entrusted to their protection and well-being.

Raven's antics were well known to the tribe. Raven was disdainful of the tiny songbirds and often attacked their nests in search of eggs and hatchlings. But the songbirds were more acrobatic than Raven and pestered the predator with swooping air attacks. In the village, Tom watched as a raven used his nimbleness to attack a hawk. For those with eyes to see, nature offered a whirling, wondrous waltz.

Near the spot where Tom watched the raven, Dan sought a pattern to his life, seeking answers to a multitude of questions. He explored the pieces, one by one. The man was immobilized and kept to his woven reed mat. From that lowly vantage, he thought constantly of his wife, and how the pattern of their life together had scattered like stone shards left behind by retreating glaciers. Hopes were crushed. Dreams shattered. A positive man but now his expectations were cast asunder. But still he cogitated, remembering Black Wings recent prediction.

He lay on his back, listening to the songbirds, watching a tail of smoke as it rose dispassionately above the lodge. The evening was windless, and a soft rain began to fall.

He listened to the rain as it etched its slow, insistent pattern into the soft-grained cedar planks that covered the great lodge. The man deciphered their story by the concentric circles, the tight-grained patterns that etched the wood. Strangely, he found consolation in the map of the cedar's life. He identified the lean years, the years of drought and the years of heavy growth. Tree rings held the conifer's story close to the heartwood.

None of these answered the labyrinth of questions that dogged him. Wood rings told of the past. The future remained silent. The man was certain of the former, confused over the latter. Perhaps it was near the end of June.

Dan had mended well over the last month, better than he or anyone might have expected. Tom had broken Dan's leg just below the kneecap, where the two leg bones were strongest. Only the smaller of the two bones had completely fractured. Tom's decision had been intuitive and well chosen. A poultice had been wrapped around the injury to prevent infection. Native women splinted the injury, using cedar spines, leather, and natural healing salves. They possessed uncanny skills. A cast of wet parfleche had been molded around the dressing. Overnight, it dried hard into place. Dan was a strong man, and his captors expected his injury to heal rapidly.

Daily attention from Yellow Bird Singing aided his healing. The young woman became a constant companion. First, Dan and Yellow Bird Singing exchanged words and language, learning from each other through a natural curiosity that each possessed. They taught each other the different customs belonging to their two cultures. In time they became intimate, like a father and daughter. Underlying the affection was mutual respect.

Yellow Bird Singing lost her parents at a young age. Dan had become fatherless at about the same time. He had always wanted a daughter, and Yellow Bird Singing had always desired a father. A flourishing friendship filled the void. That bond was evident to the citizens of the village. The familial union met with their approval.

Black Wing visited frequently. His visits became less and less formal. Frequently accompanied by Charlie, the men smoked and gossiped like old friends. In between visits, the elder disappeared from the village for days at a time. When Dan asked about it, his captors were short on words. "Easier to track the wind," they declared.

At such times Dan missed the companionship of his new mentor and friend.

The People of the Valley respected the trapper. They clearly understood his talent. After all, he had bested the formidable White Bear. Yes, Dan Skinner was a very capable woodsman. The Natives kept a watchful eye on the healing process as well as his whereabouts.

Dan found it remarkable that the villagers didn't appear to harbor any lingering resentment over his aborted escape. As far as they were concerned, the Boston man had paid his penalty, and the incident was settled.

Night found its way into the lodge. Its residents slumbered. The evening sky turned starless and dark, but as summer approached, those hours on the dark side of the moon were quickly retreating into longer, warmer days.

The following morning as the subtle hues of daylight brightened the forest, the four-legged animals that foraged under the cover of nightfall bedded down. Daylight was their sleeping time, and they moved deeper into the grove and away from the hunters' keen eyes.

Birds particularly loved the dawn, and as the sky brightened, they took to the sky. Their songs started just as they had ended the night before, ebullient and inspiring. Theirs was a preamble for the awakening of the human beings. Under the roof of the cedar longhouse, the adults stirred, their children behind them. Black Wing's people began to imprint their brand of order onto the day, and the rich music of the songbirds gladdened them. The sky brightened, turning from gunmetal gray to heron blue.

And into that lovely, sun-washed village walked a Haisla elder and a White woman.

A blind man and his guide were waiting for the visitors at the edge of the village. The White woman and the blind man studied each other respectfully from a discreet distance. She was startled and remained wary. Intuitively, she felt the old man's warmth cross the earthen carpet that separated them.

This was the language strangers frequently offer when they met for the first time. When they sense common understanding. One was blind but could sense the goodness of these strangers. The woman was just beginning to understand the strange spiritual world that eluded her until recently, revealing itself in so many unpredictable ways. She favored fine eyesight, but now, time and place abandoned her. Rebecca had grown immeasurably, had grown physically and spiritually beyond the woman who had greeted the two Haisla just a few months before. And now she was lost in wonder.

She stepped across the space that separated them and reached out her hand, smiling warmly. "Hello," she said. "My name is Rebecca Skinner."

He answered in perfect queen's English, "We welcome you, Rebecca Skinner. You have been expected."

And somehow—some way—she believed that.

She noted the four spears of rock and judged their presence as strange and formidable. With each additional step, she gathered in rich details.

This was a good-sized village. The lodges were handsome in their own way. Hand-hewn totems and intricate carvings graced the construction. Racks of Chinook salmon were drying in the smokehouses and in the high rafters of a half dozen cedar lodges. Rich fish smells spoke to her hunger. At the far end of the village, she saw two artisans carving a fine cedar pole. A gaggle of children stood nearby, watching and learning. And then, they began to gather around the new strangers. This startled Rebecca. She should have guessed. The children were curious.

She turned her gaze away and studied the largest longhouse. The structure called to her. Her eyes grappled with the detail. The craftsmen's skill was obvious. Back in Kilnook many of the structures were disheveled from neglect or had been abandoned. This village was young and prosperous.

The old man studied her quietly before repeating his welcome. "I am called Black Wing. This is Charlie. Charlie care for me always. You come with us now."

She walked through the village, filled with a sense of awe. She was not alone. The Natives were awakening to the fact that two new strangers were in their midst.

Through the walls of the lodge, Dan sensed a new intensity in the drone of voices. The chatter stirred his curiosity.

The gentle blind man guided Rebecca by the forearm, encouraging her forward. Yet, it was hard to figure who was leading whom. Black Wing's directness startled her, but she allowed him to lead her deeper into the village. Her steps were hesitant. She felt anxious. Where did he want her to go? What waited ahead? And above all else, she pondered how it was that a blind man might lead her at all. Perhaps, she thought, it was a question of the blind leading the blind. Perhaps the old man could ferret out his way by the faint sounds of Charlie's moccasins sliding quietly across the earthen floor, just a few steps ahead of her and the elder.

They quickly approached the front of a great lodge. Rebecca stepped through the longhouse portal cautiously, the bright light of the outdoors collapsing behind her, leaving Rebecca temporarily blinded by the dim light. Only the soft flickering of the wood fires offered a sense of direction. She followed their amber glow as she walked deeper into the dimly lit interior. The space startled her in its intimacy. She wasn't sure what to expect.

"Don't worry, Rebecca Skinner. You are safe here."

The old man led on. Ahead of him, Charlie dropped away.

As Rebecca's eyes adjusted to the dim light, she became aware of two massive house posts standing at the far end of the lodge, their features awesome and intimidating. As the miasma of darkness lifted—as her eyes adjusted—the carved cedar eyes on the totems cast their penetrating gaze upon her. Rebecca knew these were the eyes of an eagle. She never could have guessed that her initial reaction mirrored that of her husband's many months earlier. She shuddered involuntarily and then moved forward. Her world was reeling.

Between her and the carvings, a fire blazed. She just made out the dark shape of a man resting against a cedar backboard.

The man in the shadows saw only a silhouette, but the outline was familiar. He recognized the outline of Black Wing quickly enough. The old man was guiding another human, guiding a female by the arm. As the figures came closer, beads of sweat broke across his brow, and his chest muscles tightened. He sat up sharply and felt a cry of rebuttal from his injured leg.

Dan pushed himself awkwardly to his feet. He fumbled with his cedar staff, then suddenly let it drop. He stood on both legs as his eyes raced down the long dirt aisle toward her. The aisle may as well have been a marble apse in a distant cathedral—he never imagined such magic, such a miraculous visage. That miracle moved quickly within his grasp, each advancing step an epiphany. He was sure but unsure. Emotions smote him like hard rain.

Later, Rebecca would describe how she had seen light and prayer transform a dark, vague shape into her beloved husband and how, in that moment of recognition, she had felt the presence of André and Sally and her two guides, all bound together by an affirmation of friendship and love that she would carry in her heart for the rest of her life.

Black Wing saw it differently. From his perspective, he imagined two intersecting lights becoming one. In his blindness he sensed a completion that was new and rich, even to him. After all his lives, a surprise.

As Dan and Rebecca embraced, a surge of power surrounded the couple like a veil. When the veil lifted, the power danced outward, penetrating the house of Black Wing's people, a lance thrown into the heart of a target. Neither of the Bostons were capable of surmounting their emotions, their tears, their surprise, or their newfound joy. Those same emotions scribed the faces of many who watched. A sensitive people who shared communal space, the Natives quietly deserted the lodge until only Dan and Rebecca remained—Dan and Rebecca and the two cedar eagles, awesome and commanding in their stark, regal presence.

When words finally came, their voices were reduced to whispers. The sounds melded like the trickle of a summer brook.

"Danny. Oh, my Danny!"

"Honey, I . . . I can't . . . believe this. I just can't. Jesus! Rebecca. Thank God I didn't leave. Did not . . . Well, I'll explain later. How in the hell did you get here? Explain to me now. How in God's green earth did you find your way here?"

"I'll tell everything, honey. Just give me a little time. Let me catch my breath. Right now I just want to hold you. It's been so long. Just give me a chance to believe this is all happening."

In pieces like verse, the story stumbled out. A radiant quality passed between them, something similar to the inner light of an agate. How, holding the stone before the sun, one perceives a golden translucency.

Dan and Rebecca stepped back from each other and stared as if the person in front of them was an illusion conjured out of thin air. Stared in disbelief. And the murmur that was the wilderness—the racing river and the tall mountains—flooded back into the lodge through the portal under the carved eagles. Poured through the smoke hole in the roof and seeped through the cracks in the walls. Soft light surrounded them like an aura.

Outside, the low shuffling sounds of the Native people—sounds of joy, curiosity, gossip, and the innocence of children's laughter—mingled with the natural sounds of the valley and mountains and the tall evergreen forest.

Minutes passed before she noticed Dan's wound. The sight alarmed her. After all she had been through, Rebecca found it impossible to contain the look of anxiety in her eyes.

"It's nothing," Dan replied. "Just a hunting accident. It'll be fine soon. No need to fret."

While holding her, Dan twisted the past events together in his head. But all the while, he was leaning into the rich taste of newfound joy.

He thought about what Black Wing had intoned about their child, their child to be, his and Rebecca's, and he hugged her once more but kept the secret to himself.

Rebecca spoke again, remembering a greater pain. "I lost Sally, Dan. She drowned in the river. She came with me. She did! I just can't…"

The words stumbled out until she chose to go no further. Rebecca held back the tears. There had been so many already. Maybe she had run dry. And she wanted to be strong for Dan. Strangely, she remembered the eagle. Then she thought about her friends, Spirit Runner and Man Hides Good.

Dan held her tightly, acknowledging her strong body and her tenacity. Her skin was damp, soaked with perspiration. He felt her pain. And he remembered seeing her in a dream, grieving. *Sally Walton.* Now he knew. Now he understood. But they were together. And together they would heal.

But, of course, there was more to be said. "Honey," Rebecca stammered, afraid of how Dan might take the news. "Do you know that . . . André . . . is dead?"

Dan nodded. It was his turn to revisit the pain world.

"It'll be okay, Danny," Rebecca whispered. "It'll be okay. We're together now. And I believe . . . well . . . there will be a reunion with André—with Sally—later."

A long silence ensued, and in the long silence there was partial closure.

"I loved your brother, honey. I loved him deeply. I miss him so. These losses—maybe, somehow, they will make us stronger."

"I hope you're right, Rebecca. I do hope you're right."

And by framing those words, they almost believed.

By now the worst was out. Rebecca could only nod when Dan questioned her on details. Her words were open wounds. She leaned into him, feeling the ripple of his muscles, his hard chest and abdomen. His arms wrapped around her, pulling their bodies into a symbiotic meld of skin and muscle. And love. She had been through so much. Dan too—she was sure. Rebecca wiped her hand across her face. *No tears now. No tears.*

They had traveled the corridors of rivers and mountains. They had been touched by rain and sunshine, death and rebirth.

Finally, she spoke. "I saw the place where he fell. We left a memorial. Spirit Runner and Man Hides Good. You know one, Spirit Runner, a Haisla named Richard Washington."

With the lift of his chin, he acknowledged the association. And Dan realized the reward of kindness, kindness delivered. Kindness taken. "He brought me here. Tell me that you didn't have to climb that cliff. Tell me, Danny."

The thought continued to rattle her.

She saw the answer to that question in his eyes and moved on.

Slowly, the Natives scuffled back, entering the way a tide might turn, at first softly as in the early stages of the flood and then with greater insistence.

The Natives went about their day, naturally and easily, as if nothing noteworthy had transpired. As if the arrival of the Boston woman was a daily event. The village's inhabitants accepted her without question. She was the wife of Dan Skinner, and Black Wing had promised her protection. Knotted together, that was a powerful medicine. No man or woman in the village would consider challenging the elder.

Rebecca and Dan sat as one. Sat as if it was the most natural thing in the world, there, miles and miles from their farm, from the only civilization they had ever known: the White man's world.

Rebecca was spellbound as she watched the Native women prepare the evening meal—prepare it and then ladle the ingredients into handsome, hand-carved bowls. The bowls had been crafted into the shapes of the many creatures from the animal kingdom: otter, whale, and seal, to mention a few. The vessels were filled with rich broth and wild meats. Roots and greens supplied further nutrition and a rich, aromatic taste. She was surprised at how good the soup tasted. Ripe berries were then offered. Rebecca was overwhelmed.

As was the Native way, guests were served first. This was old tradition passed down from the elders, passed down generation after generation. In many Native cultures, a host would often postpone eating until the visitor had completed the meal. Rebecca felt humbled.

Outside the lodge the Native men gathered around Man Hides Good. They had a decision to make that would decide his fate. Unlike Dan just weeks before, there was none of the hostility. The village had a choice to make. It was essentially the same decision that both Dan and Tom had faced. Man Hides Good would have to stay, or he would be punished. The village's safety depended on that simple law.

But Charlie thought differently. His opinion startled the village. His words were firm and sure. His peers respected this quiet, intelligent man. Charlie had developed into a leader among his people. Now his eyes settled sternly on his brothers. As he spoke, his words gathered momentum. "Man Hides Good has been our brother. He has shared our secret for many winters. He has held that secret tight against his chest. During the moon of deep snow, he has brought us provisions to fill our bellies, those of our grandparents and our children. He has traded seal and elk and venison. In our time of hunger, he aided us. Now he brings this woman, the wife of our brother, Dan Skinner. Using great skill he has found our village. I am sure he suspected it all along but kept our secret to himself. The travelers have suffered much to get here. They have faced danger and death, but this warrior has never wavered.

"I ask my brothers to allow Man Hides Good to become a member of our tribe. I ask that he be allowed the same privileges as our people, the same freedom to come and go as he pleases.

"Man Hides Good may wish to stay. This answer I do not know. I do know this man can be trusted. He is a brave and honorable man, and I hold kindly to his friendship."

Spoken in the Haisla language, his next words startled more than a few. "My brothers, I wish to extend this privilege to others. It is time to allow that same freedom to our White brother and his wife. It is time to release our hold on these good people. I would ask that these three guests be allowed to make their choices without retribution. That they may come and go of their own free will, back to their homes if they choose, or stay here with us as allies within the tribe."

For a long moment, Charlie's words hung in the clear mountain air. Patiently, he let his message penetrate. "I ask you to remember that to be a true brother among our people, a man must be free. Remember, here in the village of Black Wing, we are freemen. To remain a whole person, a man cannot be bound to a place or to a people like a slave. If these brothers and sisters choose to remain with us, I will feel greatly honored. If they go, I will hold a special place for them deep in my heart. Either way, they remain my friends. Either way, I trust that our secret will remain safe."

Charlie stopped, taking a deep breath. Black Wing had come up behind the assembly. He stood in rapt attention, gathering in every word.

Out of the corner of his eye, Charlie recognized the elder, but he didn't relinquish his podium. Every man in the crowd saw how Charlie had grown. He didn't need his mentor's support. His words held the countenance of a chief, a leader among his people.

Charlie's words converged with the cadence of rustling leaves. His audience listened raptly. "Here in our circle stands a fourth man who is new among us but who has quickly become an ally. He is a powerful brother, a warrior of distinction. White Bear has told Black Wing of his wish to become a member of our tribe and his intention to remain among us. My brothers and sisters, I wish to honor this warrior with a ceremony given by our tribe during the salmon moon, just as the fish return and the berries begin to ripen.

"I ask that you sleep and meditate on my thoughts for seven days. On the evening of the last day, Black Wing will hold a council. You must share your decisions then."

With those words the villagers were bound to care for the guests until the counsel. The visitors were trusted to remain in camp. Man Hides Good realized that meant that Spirit Runner would return to Kilnook without him. The decision tore at his heart. If Man Hides Good stayed, he would lose a friend. But if he remained in the village, he would gain a family. Either way, Spirit Runner was off. At best, it might be many moons before Man Hides Good saw his brother again.

1987

Katherine was interviewed by the editor of one of the local conservative newspapers. Unbeknownst to her, the editor secretly set up a tape recorder and asked damaging questions. With her guard down, Katherine was steered into a compromising position. He hand-picked her responses, editing her answers to betray her true feelings. The result shocked her. Many county residents were already suspicious of the "environmentalists." Now they joined in a small-scale protest. Katherine was disgusted at herself. She had been caught with her guard down.

Working with a large conservancy, Rebecca helped to procure two valuable river estuaries. The rivers were pristine watersheds. Elk wandered on the periphery. Otters swam up and down the waterways. Ducks and geese nested. Would anybody feel threatened by such a purchase? As it turned out, there were many.

Katherine ducked her head and went back to work. A decade later, public sentiment would change. In time, Katherine and her conservancy would be applauded.

The rivers were ultimately considered to be two of the most natural treasures in Pacific County. Unfortunately, that didn't help the present situation.

Katherine trudged ahead.

CHAPTER TWENTY-NINE

I wish the world was twice as big—and half of it was still unexplored.

—David Attenborough

Henry Crockett never intended to abandon the deep, wild woods, at least not until the trapping season wound down in the early summer, when the furs played out, thin and dull.

Something was bothering the trapper—something like an itch that got under a pilgrim's buckskin, a burr that scratched. Besides, that spring, the beavers were poor. Maybe he had trapped that part of the river dry. Maybe somebody had beaten him to the plew. *Time to move on*, he thought. But his mind kept returning to the canoe with the two White women aboard.

"Damn it to hell!" he swore. "Them were women thar, and two Indians fer sure. And if that weren't strange now."

He'd keep his eyes peeled, him and his brass eyepiece. No pilgrim was going to sneak around Henry Crockett. "No man," he muttered. "No man, by God."

He walked east toward the lake. Two fat streams there. He'd find some shiny plew. Any pilgrim would wager on that. And maybe he would stumble across those strangers. *Be careful*, he reminded himself. *Those Native people could be plenty cagey. Be careful, old man.*

He headed out with the stealth of a cougar, each step the first in a pattern of deception, each catlike. He followed the tree line along the river. At all times he would stay hidden. This was no longer hostile country, but Crockett had stayed alive for near-on sixty years by utilizing his keen mountain skills. He wasn't about to change any of that, *no how*.

He moved up the river, his eyes alert all day for sign. But Crockett hadn't traveled far when he caught the color of trouble. Thirty yards from the riverbank, entangled in a beached snag half in the water and half out, lay a heap of color that didn't belong in his world. The color appeared like a hunk of cotton print. The cloth was wrapped around something. *Dang it. Damn it to hell.*

Crockett brought the brass telescope up to his eye, focusing its sliding lens on the misplaced object. He caught his breath. Then he lowered the eyepiece, waiting and thinking. He brought it up a second time, as if he was uncertain what he was seeing. He readjusted the lens. Sure enough, through the glass eye, Crockett brought Sally Walton's body into focus. The sight wasn't pretty. The woman was dead for sure. Dead for days, he reckoned. It appeared that her drifting body had snagged onto a waterlogged trunk of a fallen tree and then both had slipped many miles downriver.

He buried the body along the same sandy beach that Sally had poled past several days before. The trapper said a prayer as best he knew how. Sure, he was a heathen to the proper folk back in the settlements, an eccentric and a hermit to boot. Few would even share a drink with him. None of that mattered much to Crockett. But say what they might, the trapper had a streak of decency in him, even if it was a short one, even if Crockett wasn't articulate enough to define the attribute.

He started walking in the direction he figured the trouble had come from. Walking upstream on a fine spring day, he was a trapper with a mission.

Crockett was figuring murder—what else could have happened to the woman? He decided he would get to the bottom of it. He'd track down them two red varmints and set things straight. He hoped to find the other woman alive.

Something else was chewing on his mind. The woman he buried—the shape of her face, her large body—kept coming back to him. Then memory struck. Suddenly, he placed her. He remembered her business, the café, and the afternoon when he had wandered inside.

Crockett had just sold two bundles of pelts. He wanted a hot meal and some real coffee, not campfire coffee. A man always got tired of his own cooking, and Crockett wasn't exactly the best chef on the river. Besides, no pioneer baked a proper buttermilk biscuit over an open campfire, and Crockett had run plumb out of blackberry jam.

The café was nearly full. As he elbowed through the door, silence as big as a bull elk fell upon him. At first he was confused. Then he realized it was him that the stillness crowded around. He thought of just walking out, but pride got in the way. Crockett figured he was as good as any man in that flea-bitten town. *Christ*, he thought, *there isn't a man here who can hold his own with Henry Crockett.*

"Not in this wilderness, anyway," he mumbled to no one in particular. *No. There ain't no man I can't take with fists, knife or by shooting dead true.*

Crockett had mingled with the toughest trappers. *You ask any of them thar if 'in a body among them is still alive.*

He sat at a small table by himself, mumbling under his breath.

One man started in on him right away. "Whew, that is a powerful odor, old fella." He turned to the others. "Is this here varmint or human?"

The place rattled with that tinny laughter that always sounded cowardly to Henry Crockett. Crockett sat straight in his chair but acted as if he hadn't heard a thing. Crockett didn't want to start a fight, but he was feeling pushed toward the edge. Truth was, it didn't take much to get Crockett riled up. The bully just didn't know it. Crockett's blood was already boiling.

Crockett sneaked his left arm down his pant leg, settling his fingers on the hilt of a concealed knife, a Green River, a blade of distinction that held preference among the free trappers. The knife could be thrown like a projectile or used to stab and maim, generally fatally, at close range.

Then she came up, the big-boned woman with a large voice and an ample chest to fit it all into. She smiled. "Bet you could use a cup of hot coffee, trapper. Maybe some of my buttermilk biscuits with homemade jam."

She smiled again. Hers was a handsome, engaging smile. Her mouth was big and wide and appealing. He stared at her chest. Though fully clothed, the swell of the gingham dress left little for a man to imagine. She favored a handsome pair. Crockett was hungry in more ways than one.

As his attention swiveled in her direction, he lost track of the man behind him, and he released his grip on his knife. Over her smile he caught her eyes sending out a warning to the loudmouth pilgrim behind him.

Then she spoke, her words vibrant with authority. "Shut your fat mouth, Walter Hedge. I don't tolerate no trouble in my place, and you'll only get hurt anyways."

Crockett knew this kind of man, a soft-faced city pilgrim. A coward who stood tall only in a crowd. Hedges should have known that the old trapper was capable of cutting him down in the blink of an eye. Crockett threw a blade with unerring accuracy—threw the honed knife nearly sixty feet. He had killed a man at that distance. Killed twice. He might do that again. Head out the door and soon be lost back in a wilderness that sprawled for endless miles into the deep country.

Most of the customers cleared out shortly, making subtle, behind-the-back gestures as they closed the door and sidled off. Crockett slowly finished his breakfast, eating it noisily and with great gusto. He chewed the food with his mouth wide open. His teeth weren't any too pretty, but who could criticize a trapper for his natural appetite? Eating without constraint was normal to Crockett. He didn't know any better. And food rarely tasted so good.

Then she brought out a bowl of venison stew. Said it was on the house. Said a trapper might miss some of the finer comforts in the wilderness. She even sat and visited for a minute or two. Crockett liked her a lot. Felt pampered for the first time in years, leastways by a White woman.

Just then—standing next to her grave—he wished he had done her better. All he hoped for now was to get even.

After three days, Spirit Runner was ready to push off. He had waited patiently for his friend. From the very beginning, he had doubted that Man Hides Good would return. The Haisla was twenty years his senior and remembered many of the old forgotten ways. Up there in the mountains beyond the river fork, something was calling to his friend.

In the first hour of morning light, Spirit Runner bathed his body in the cold mountain water. So cold was the snow melt that he had to suppress an urge to run for shore.

On the beach as the light pressed over the mountains, he prayed for his friend, calling up a friendship song. Turning slowly, he faced west where his family waited. He sent a silent blessing to his loved ones. Spirit Runner was plenty anxious to see his family. He had been away for quite a spell.

He pushed the canoe off the white, sandy beach and let the currents bridle the sleek cedar hull. He had only to guide the canoe now. The current was with him, behind him. Heading downriver would be relatively easy. The wild currents would push him home. He knew he would cover those same miles that had spelled out so much hardship in but a fraction of the time.

The shoreline passed rapidly. A soft, warm wind massaged his back. On a warm spring day, the weather added a sense of comfort.

In the low, rocky shallows, Spirit Runner spotted hundreds of tyee salmon as they nosed upriver against the persistent currents. The salmon were moving once again, as they had done for millions of years. They were returning home. Spirit Runner knew the salmon would not be following him back to the ocean. This was their final journey. A year from now, their offspring would have grown into fingerlings, and then the smolts would journey to the ocean and scatter far out to sea. In three or four years, the fish would be back. He hoped his adventure would go as well.

By the second day, Spirit Runner had passed into the Ka'ous. He chose another campsite near the southeast side of the lovely lake. For centuries the Eagle clan had summered there, gathering in the great runs of salmon, eating and preserving the fish. Thus ended another chapter in the long-running sequel of his people and the most prevalent sustainers of all, the five runs of Pacific salmon.

An ancient ceremony preceded the fishing season.

The first tyee was harvested from the lake and ceremonially baked, its succulent flesh shared and then its bones lowered carefully back into the water. The chief pointed the salmon's head toward the ocean. Currents took the remains to the home of all salmon. The Natives believed that the relatives of the skeletal fish would return the following spring, the way they always had, the way it would always be—if the bones were complete. If the blessings were honorable. If . . .

Haisla tribal law dictated that the first runs of salmon be allowed safe passage upriver to their historical redds. The philosophy was simple enough. Left alone, early runs secured the productivity of the future runs. These salmon would breed. Their offspring would return in four more years. Sacrifice guaranteed full bellies.

Under a sky awash with stars, Spirit Runner passed the night peacefully. The easterly wind lulled at dusk. The lake's mirrored surface quivered gently under the bone-white light of a full moon. Deep in the Kilnook wilderness, the sounds of night animals rang out, far and wide.

Spirit Runner's fire burned low. Sometime late in the night, he stirred from his sleep, reacting to a disturbing dream. He poked the embers back to life, added an armload of driftwood to the campfire, and settled back into a comfortable position and awaited the dawn. He remained cautious. Ahead waited the falls.

The lake was double reflected in the early morning light. Sunrise lifted over the violet mountain peaks. A sudden flutter of wind pressed down off the mountains, stirring the glassy surface. Everything natural wallowed in a bastion of intense colors: azalea, rhododendron, and the brilliant yellow of the flowering skunk cabbage.

The wind was at his back. As he glided across the lake, Spirit Runner offered thanks. Such was the Haisla way.

By midafternoon he approached the west end of the lake. Already the currents were pulling the canoe toward the falls. Spirit Runner began to brace himself for the big chute of water that he knew awaited, river currents that would test his canoe and his water skills. He paddled his vessel into the shore, then walked ahead to survey the falls.

Much had changed over the last two weeks. The angry water had subsided and the water level had dropped. He was thankful enough for the small changes. He calculated the deepest channel, weaving a mental map for his descent through the cascading water. As Spirit Runner returned to the canoe, he gathered a handful of salmonberries. He also gathered in a recent memory. He would never forget Sally Walton. He said a prayer for his special friend. Spirit Runner would honor the brash woman as his canoe swept down the river.

The fruit was bright and sweet. In his hands he cupped the clear glacial water. Spirit Runner drank deeply and felt replenished.

Then he aimed the canoe's bow into the wily falls and felt the tug of the swift currents as it cradled man and canoe like a baby in the arms of a mother.

1988—Pacific County, Washington

Katherine wandered off trail and entered one of the few ancient glades of old-growth cedar left in the southwest corner of Washington State. The grove was nestled into the middle of a protected island in Willapa Bay. The county was called Pacific, and the bay drained twice a day into the Pacific Ocean.

Standing motionless inside the copse, she heard the distant gurgle of a small stream. Its song called to her. She moved carefully through two hundred yards of dense underbrush until she found the water. The rustle of the soft currents cleared her head. The stream had found her, called her name—of this she was sure. The creek bed was as natural, as beautiful, as any place she had ever seen.

She moved up and down the stream for two hours. The world there was lush and green, untouched by human hands, a hidden place where ferns and lichens had been left free to evolve over eons. The ancient soul of the forest lingered there.

She moved like a dancer through the underbrush and into the water. She was a careful and respectful observer.

Katherine felt a kinship with nature that would be difficult to describe to the corporations that so prized the valuable timber around her. She thought momentarily of John Muir and wished she might express herself with such eloquent language.

She placed her shoes into her day pack and waded knee deep into the stream. Through the clear, chilly water, Katherine saw a bed of luminous, multi-colored stones. She bent and picked a small handful, stuffing a few of the radiant pebbles into her pocket. She studied the tiny fairy ferns cloistered along the dead hulk of a massive fallen cedar, a dying tree that formed a wooden barricade where the stream slowed and pooled. A protected home for salmon smolts. Miniature mushrooms and lichen appeared suddenly before her, abundant, unnamed, and precious. Tiny minnows darted for cover.

Katherine had co-founded an environmentally based organization in Portland, an extension of her dreams, hard labor, and a decade of commitment. Wading up the stream, she realized how much work lay ahead.

That afternoon she wrestled with the reality of social change. How might she leverage such a small conservancy into a stronger environmental organization? She knew: above all else, changes had to begin at the roots. That meant the education of its citizens, particularly the young students in elementary and high school. Not Katherine—not even the president of the United States—could elicit ecological change unless the nation was ready to endorse its basic principles. She needed help. Plenty of help.

She plunged deeper into the grove, following the streambed. The afternoon sun began to fall into the ocean. She could just decipher the fading colors through the mass of trees that masked the horizon. The light was as radiant as the intense bright hues of the summer berries.

Go softly, she thought, suddenly recalling a verse from Dylan Thomas, putting a spin on his words. "Go softly into the night."

She realized she had never wandered through an old-growth forest by herself. She imagined she was alone on that island, and perhaps, she was right. Alone, yes, but in a space that felt like home to her, a place where she belonged. She realized that few people had ever seen a grove like this. They hadn't been so fortunate. And perhaps that was part of the problem, part of the denial. *To see is to believe.*

As she turned and began to retreat toward the canoe, she pondered the significance of an uninhabited island in a pristine bay and how uncommon that was. She remembered Gary Snyder's poetry book, *Turtle Island,* the title a Native interpretation for North America. She considered for the first time that all continents were simply large islands. She stepped onto the beach where she had grounded her canoe, looked across the vast expanse of water, and heard her heart whisper, *We are all islands.* The thought inspired her.

She sat on the beach for another hour, watching the sun settle over the horizon. She began to write in her notebook. Those words outlined a plan of attack for her new organization, essentially a path to lead *them* forward. Katherine knew she had miles to go. She fostered aspirations of changing her world into a planet where people were committed to healing its human-induced wounds. That might take eons. But she had to try, didn't she? *Baby steps and then…* She had to start somewhere, alright. Hadn't this been her dream from her teens? Hadn't *this* been her lifetime passion?

She thought some more about the grove, the stream, and the rare jewel of an island. *One step at a time,* she warned herself.

A story flowed out of her, flowed from a place deep inside, as if she had been given a key to unlock her thoughts and free her mind. She wrote in a frenzy. She wrote until she felt drained.

The sun was setting as she pushed the canoe toward the mainland. Not since her relationship with Paul had she felt happier and more confident.

Beyond the golden horizon, the sun fell like thunder.

CHAPTER THIRTY

Dreams have luminous edges, like a flash of some object in a copse of trees.

—Gary Miranda
"Reconnaissance"
from *Listeners at the Breathing Place*

In the darkest hour of the night, Rebecca woke fitfully on Dan's mattress of boughs and skins. Had she been dreaming? Was she alone again? *No.* She sat up straight. The inside of the longhouse felt balmy. A half dozen fires burned low, but the thin layers of smoke smarted her eyes. The night sounds were unfamiliar but not unpleasant. She lowered herself and squeezed close to her husband until she believed again that he was real; that they were really there, together at last. His skin was warm and sweaty, his muscles as hard as parfleche. She ran her fingers along the small of his back. His even breathing was interrupted as she nuzzled into his backside. Awakened, he felt her breasts and the taut muscles of her legs. His breathing quickened as he opened his eyes, turned, and reached for her.

He rolled over slowly, trying not to aggravate his leg injury. The pain was still uncomfortable when he moved carelessly. This time he was cautious. They kissed quietly for several minutes. As their lips touched, she felt the pain of the past several months slipping away. She felt her passion rising like smoke above the lodge fires.

Rebecca kissed her way down his neck until she came to his chest. She kissed him again, aware that his skin was salty. Dan needed a bath. Well, she would take care of that afterwards. Right now she had other things on her mind. Rebecca ran her fingers over his nipples. He reacted with a start, pulling her in as close as his strength would allow without aggravating his leg.

Dan returned her offerings, caressing her gently but firmly. His strokes were a bit clumsy, his fingers awkward but expressive. His hands were large and callused, but his fingers had a memory of their own. His passion was a force that had been caged up for many months. His yearning was a hunger.

Her touch was sure and smooth and light on his flesh. His fingers sidled onto her breasts. Dan's lips and tongue tickled her throat. Rebecca arched her back and squeezed even closer. His hands slid deeper then, splitting her legs. He cupped her buttocks. She responded with a sound that came from deep within. She pressed into him until their bodies became inseparable, her hands and lips marauding.

Their lovemaking was soundless but consummated with a muffled explosion that shook both bodies. Afterwards, they held each other tightly. Light began to seep into the lodge. Each whispered words they had both longed to hear for many months.

That morning Yellow Bird Singing came to visit the Skinners, to welcome Dan's wife to the village. Like the rest of her clan, the young woman was inquisitive. She displayed Native manners. She was clearly surprised by the turn of events.

Yellow Bird Singing was shy at first, standing with her eyes lowered in front of the Boston couple. She struggled with something to say. But that was normal for the young woman. Dan reached out and led her by the elbow to Rebecca, who was sitting regally in Dan's favorite position, legs folded under her.

"Honey," he said, "This is Yellow Bird Singing, the young woman I have told you about. She has been my tutor and a wonderful friend. She watches over me like family."

Rebecca was instantly taken with the girl. She sat up, making room beside her on the raised platform. Rebecca patted the cattail mat with the palm of her hand to indicate that Yellow Bird Singing should sit next to her. Apprehensively, Yellow Bird Singing joined her. Settling beside Rebecca, she said, "Why, thank you, madam," in the queen's proper English.

The Native girl had suddenly blossomed into a young woman. Even through her bashfulness, she exhibited a certain poise that manifested beyond her early teen years. Rebecca asked her age, and Yellow Bird Singing replied. Rebecca responded with a second question. "Is your family here in the lodge?"

"Yes, ma'am. Well, not my birth family. My mother died ten winters ago of influenza. My aunt brought me up. I think of her as 'Mom.' My father died only a few weeks before I was born. Would you like to meet my aunt?"

Rebecca found Dan's gaze and raised her eyebrows in acknowledgment of the young woman's elocution as well as her natural charm. Then Rebecca smiled, her eyes rich and wondrous, and Dan smiled back. Rebecca was smitten.

She turned to Yellow Bird singing. "Yes, I would be honored to visit your aunt. Yes.

"And how do I thank you for taking such good care of Dan? "

The young Haisla smiled happily. "My pleasure, Ma'am. He has become a true friend."

That morning, her first in the lodge, Rebecca paid particular attention to the bustle surrounding her. Not thirty feet away, a family was preparing breakfast. A young boy brought in a load of firewood and stoked the embers. Nearby, a young mother coddled her newborn baby. Rebecca refused to lift her gaze from the child. Yellow Bird Singing noticed Rebecca's distraction and excused herself briefly. She returned moments later with an infant girl in her arms. When Yellow Bird Singing handed her the baby, a smile broke across Rebecca's face that brightened up the entire lodge.

"You like this little one? Yes?"

Rebecca's wide smile was answer enough. The mother appeared then, accompanied by two more daughters, and in her Native tongue, asked a question of Rebecca.

Again, Yellow Bird Singing translated. "Blue Bird Woman asks if you have children of your own."

And bravely, Rebecca answered. "No, unfortunately, that hasn't happened yet." Though Rebecca's face held steady, all saw a shadow of sadness cross her eyes. They avoided further questions, refusing to embarrass their guest.

"The children are so quiet here," Rebecca noted.

Yellow Bird Singing responded again, explaining how this conditioning was a necessity for the tribe's welfare.

"Babies are raised this way from birth. Always before, in the old days, this was for the protection of our people. The tribe's rights came before any individual, even the chiefs. In times of crisis, a crying baby might expose us to an enemy."

Rebecca returned the baby to her mother. She allowed her eyes to wander about the longhouse, examining the people and the environment with covert glances. She noted that the Native women were handsome with beautiful dark eyes and exquisite raven-black hair. Many of the mothers were stocky, but their straight-backed stature and their natural dignity made them appear tall. Their smiles were broad and inviting. Most of the men who remained in the camp were older, grandfathers now. The younger men were out hunting, a daily occupation. The children listened to the elders' stories with rapt attention that suggested familial respect.

Rebecca turned to Yellow Bird Singing. "This afternoon while Dan rests, would you show me about the village? I would love to meet my new neighbors."

Yellow Bird Singing indicated with a shy smile and a nod that she would be delighted. Around the circle all the women smiled. The mood between Rebecca and Yellow Bird Singing remained infectious. Dan watched all this with quiet pride. Again, he thought about Black Wing's prediction, about the child to be. He dared to hope.

While Dan napped, Yellow Bird Singing escorted Rebecca around the village. There were several split-cedar lodges, and Yellow Bird Singing explained that each clan shared its individual space with extended family. She took Rebecca past the large ceremonial lodge, hinting that Rebecca might see the inside sometime in the near future. Intuitively, Rebecca realized that she needed a formal invitation to enter the sacred hall. *Well,* she thought, *all that can wait.* She was with Dan, and times were shining.

Rebecca was surprised. The Native people radiated self-confidence. This was not a culture she had closely witnessed, not until she had come to know and trust her two guides. Rebecca realized the strain that had been placed between the two nations. She realized that in this valley, she was meeting Native people who chose to sustain their old ways. Native ways, not Caucasian—not Boston. Not the queen's. Misconceptions and prejudice had guided Rebecca's reactions ever since she had moved to the Pacific Northwest.

This was a Native culture that had been reborn, a resurrection of the best of what had once been. Had the old man influenced these people? She was enchanted and more than a little startled. Rebecca remained curious.

She thought then of her two friends, her guides. She had grown so fond of the pair. They were good people, no matter the color of their skin—no matter what others thought back in the settlements.

When Rebecca and Yellow Bird Singing returned to the lodge, Black Wing was sitting quietly beside Dan. Yellow Bird Singing offered a respectful salutation and then left to return to her family. The men sat cross-legged around a small fire just a few yards from Dan's sleeping platform. Dan was fondling a cedar cane with an intricate eagle gracing the top, handsomely carved from yellow cedar. At first Rebecca avoided the men and busied herself around her new surroundings. Dan quickly called her over. "Look," he said, then proudly held out the beautiful walking stick before her. "A gift from Black Wing. He says in a few days I should be able to walk with it. He says the healing goes well. Well . . . I might have told him that, if he would just listen."

He grinned mischievously at the elder. Dan's spirit had elevated noticeably since Rebecca's arrival the previous day.

Rebecca sat quietly between the two men. After ribbing the elder, Dan went quiet. Neither man spoke for several minutes. Rebecca had become familiar with the pattern. She had seen plenty of similar wordplay—or lack of—bantered stealthily between Man Hides Good and Spirit Runner. She wondered about her two friends. When the time seemed right, she decided to share her concerns with Black Wing. "Please sir . . ."

The White woman's formality and earnestness made Black Wing smile.

"Can you tell me about my friends, Man Hides Good and Spirit Runner?"

"Of Spirit Runner I cannot speak with certainty," Black Wing replied, "but I suspect he is heading home to his family. Man Hides Good believes his friend is on his way to the village of Old Kilnook. Man Hides Good has gone hunting with some of the younger men. His reputation as a hunter is highly regarded, even here, far from his home."

As the old man spoke, Rebecca let her eyes wander into the deep, etched lines on his weathered face. When their eyes met, she stopped. Black Wing's face captivated her just as his words impressed. Rebecca would have been hard put to explain all this, but even after such a short encounter, she realized the elder was unusually patient and wise.

"Rebecca," Dan said, catching her attention. "Black Wing speaks of a council that will be held next week. This is big medicine. The tribe will decide whether we will be allowed to leave this village. This is entirely in their hands. It's something we may have to live with for a while. Well, maybe for a long while. But . . ."

Rebecca nodded. At that point she didn't much care. After all, she was with Dan, and that meant everything to her. They couldn't return to Kilnook anyway. If they chose to return to the coast, Rebecca understood the reality. If discovered they would be arrested. Beyond that she chose not to speculate. Even if they avoided Kilnook, she realized they might be forever on the run. The village felt good. Good for now.

On the other hand, she didn't like the proposition of being tied to one place forever. Particularly when that one place was a Native village secreted hundreds of miles from nowhere. She figured that mirrored Dan's feelings. But things change. She had seen plenty of that over the last year. For now she would have to trust her fate, hers and Dan's, to these people. Sensing that Black Wing was studying her, she turned toward the elder.

Rebecca saw his blind eyes were fixated on her face. Then she watched as his eyes turned and settled back onto Dan's. Rebecca continued to find this disconcerting and several times avoided his gaze. *This is silly,* she thought. *He can't see me anyway.* When he spoke again, however, she felt turned inside out.

"This woman of yours is strong, Dan Skinner. She has passed through many obstacles to find you. She is a fine wife."

I'll bet you can't guess the half of it, Rebecca thought.

Black Wing switched his gaze back to her. "I am sorry for the loss of your woman friend, this sister of yours."

As he spoke, Rebecca paled, then turned toward Dan.

Dan must have mentioned that to him, she thought.

But Dan was reading her reaction as well and just shook his head.

Black Wing continued. "Your journey was long and hard from this farm of yours into these mountains, to our village. Our Haisla brothers guided you well. The loss of your friend was a terrible accident. It surprises me that you hold no blame toward your guides. Your heart is strong and wise."

Rebecca let his words sink in. Dan had warned her that this man had strange powers, powers that leveled a person with his blind eyes or with his sagacious words. She saw that clearly now.

She also saw something else that startled her. Walking toward them was Tom LaCross.

The scout sat in an empty space that swelled the circle of attendees to four. Tom liked that number. It was the sacred number. The two Whites and two Natives sat evenly, almost like compass points that played out into the four sacred directions.

Tom swung his eyes around the circle. Every time they touched on a person, they stopped and lingered. His eyes were steady and deep and as dark as obsidian points against the reflection of the cooking fires. After examining one person, he nodded formally, then settled onto the next.

When he got to Rebecca, he studied the woman's strong, beautiful face. Her eyes held him firmly and would not give an inch.

Well, he thought, *I don't want no showdown.*

The hostility he saw etched in her face did not surprise him, but the clear presence of such strong character and curiosity were unexpected.

Her facial lines told him she was no longer a young woman.

Hard journey for a young man, he thought. *Plenty hard. Nearly killed me, but I've lost my youth. This woman has courage aplenty.*

Tom saw strength and liked what he saw. He asked himself why he should be surprised. After all, she was Dan Skinner's wife. After what they had been through, she was nothing if not strong.

And she was there now, in the village. That took plenty of courage. And a little help from friends.

He dropped his head and pondered the circumstances of her arrival.

Strange that he had never met the woman before, but Tom had been the kind of man who kept to himself. Whenever he stumbled into town, he skulked along, avoiding contact with nearly everyone, especially the Bostons. When he worked for them—for the lawmen—he kept to himself, sleeping and eating apart. With the Whites his speech was curt and to the point. It was in the wilderness—alone by himself—that he felt most comfortable.

Rebecca had seen Tom from a distance. Dan had pointed him out to her a few times when they were shopping in town. She had seen his stern face, his furtive gestures. She knew he was a man of talents. According to Dan, in the wilderness, there was none better. She believed Dan. Both men kept to their own side of the street, and she had wondered why. Hadn't they been close? Hadn't Tom taught Dan his trade? Had something happened that Dan kept to himself?

All that secretiveness took its toll on a proud man, but it kept Tom out of trouble. Besides, he hadn't found too much to like about these foreigners, these Bostons. He hadn't found much to trust either. But the boy? A man now. Well, that was different. One betrayal, yes, but. . .

There in the mountains—in the village he had come to love—Tom was in his element. He would never consider lowering his gaze around these people, *his* people. Instead, he walked tall, his posture tentpole straight. His words were steady, kind, and sagacious. Among his Native brothers, he was respected. He was White Bear, not a "breed." He was a craftsman of the wilderness, an artist of the deep woods. He was both scout and hunter, par-excellence. *Incroyable.* To borrow a word from his long-dead father.

Tom settled his dark eyes on Rebecca. She watched his mouth open and listened as his words carefully tumbled out. "I honor you," he said. "I am surprised, yes—you come so far. Your trail was difficult. That I know from experience. It nearly killed me."

He reflected on his last few words for several moments. The silence was awkward.

"Well, you take good guides with you. That was very smart. Man Hides Good speaks only good about you. Says you are a strong woman. I see this!

"Do not look upon me as an enemy of your husband. Yes, I led lawmen to your husband's brother. They make the shot, not me. I am sorry for this. Sorry for André Skinner. Sorry for you.

"I carry no weapon. I leave my rifle in my small cabin. I ask now, what would you have done? I am hired scout. Lawmen pay me to do this job. This happens many times before. Maybe I should say, 'no.' Should have but didn't. Your man, Dan Skinner, he is my friend. I respect him since he was a cub. I track him skillfully. He tracks me. My surprise. He is very good—the best I ever see. Maybe better than me. Let others judge." An extended silence passed around the circle.

"Now all that is finished. I am your husband's friend again. I ask you, will you have me as yours?"

As Dan listened to Tom, he was aware of the changes that had transpired in the last several months. The tough-skinned scout had softened. Changed.

Tom sat patiently, remembering a similar question asked of a White father. Years before. Asking for her hand. Asking for a chance at love.

Dan watched and imagined Rebecca's head nodding carefully—warily—as if her movements had a life of their own. One steeped in cause and effect. Steeped in integrity. She knew her words—her response—must become her bond. She had come to Tom LaCross loaded for bear. She was a strong woman. She knew herself. But studying both her husband and the scout, Rebecca was wrangling for an answer to a puzzle.

She turned and looked at Dan and then back at the man who had tried to kill her husband. The two men were close again, and all that despite what had happened to André. She wasn't sure she could completely forgive Tom, or should she call him White Bear?

She looked again at Dan. Felt the love that bound them together. Felt her heart soften, and then she made her decision. If she couldn't do it for herself, she would do it for Dan.

She turned to Tom and nodded, but everyone saw the hesitation.

Tom watched with an expression that seemed to Rebecca to be a mixture of bemusement and apprehension. She waited patiently, sorting through a conundrum of thoughts. Rebecca was realizing just how much she had learned from her guides. Patience had become her new gift, an ally. She nodded a second time. "Yes," she said, plain and simple.

It was Tom who fidgeted first, surprising everyone, including himself. He shifted and dropped his head. Face down, he remained motionless. Then his eyes came up slowly, settling on her. "I will now live in this village with my people. I track no more for the White man."

His hand chopped horizontally through the air. Tension suddenly filled the space around the campfire.

"Although you nod my way, I sense your confusion. You need not answer me. Not now. Your wound is fresh. Later, as you come to trust me, then you decide. I wait. We talk later."

And with that, Tom stood up and left the lodge. Rebecca stared at the place where he had been, her whole world careening once more. Then she remembered: she was with Dan.

1989

The organization grew. An air of cooperation spread between several other conservancies. Local government shared more than a passing interest. Ideas were shared. Land purchases coordinated.

Katherine became a popular figure among the growing environmental constituencies. More properties were saved from the wrath of unparalleled growth, from the voracious appetites of timber companies whose final appraisals generally fell on the side of profits. She worked long, hard hours and seldom complained, and then only to her mother.

She was proud and effective.

What might go wrong? She was on a path forward.

CHAPTER THIRTY-ONE

Never take the last. Take only what you need.
Take only that which is given. Never take more than half.
Leave some for others.

—Robin Wall Kimmerer, author of *Braiding Sweetgrass*

Dancing water. Rapids with sharp stone teeth. Spirit Runner's canoe plunged into the falls like an arrow point, severing the white-capped waves.

While wily currents lunged and parried, he was rifled downstream. He steadied the fragile wooden hull with a skillful sweep of his cedar paddle, with an exact twist, a perfect thrust. He was commandeering a vessel built for four. Harder to control—one false move and the rapids would tear the vessel to pieces, pulling Spirit Runner with it. Drowning him beneath the turbulent water.

However dangerous, the river's song was lovely. The day was unusually serene. The falling and decaying leaves smelled of rich, clean earth, of fertile decay. The sun rose gracefully above the violet mountains, casting its spell.

The narrow granite sluice squeezed the rapids into a roly-poly circus of three and four-foot waves. When the cedar vessel reached the zenith of the wave crest, Spirit Runner backpaddled the canoe, pausing on top of the surging water, and then let the current rush under and past him.

Then he would thrust the canoe forward through the deep-water trough that lay between the two wave crests. And again, with a strong stroke of the paddle, he rose to the top of the next wave, backpaddled, and waited as the roiling waters rushed by, flushed under him. He knew that breaching the vessel would mean sudden death. In his strong arms, he controlled the canoe with precision. Here was the turning point, a life-and-death struggle between buoyant cedar and torrents of angry water. There was no turning back.

In a salutation borne of reverence, he called to the Creator, asking for guidance. The angry currents drew him along. He respected the water as an adversary, a current with a life of its own. With his father's own paddle, he steadied the canoe and fought bravely through a churning maelstrom. This was not the time for indecision. He held the course, his mind alert for imminent danger, for debris, for sunken logs, the canoe wreckers. And finally, he guided the vessel into calm water. His challenge was over. In several days he would be home.

Just a few miles below the falls, another man was bushwhacking along the forest edge. The trail clung to the river's rocky perimeter like moss to the north side of a sheltered tree. The trail belonged to the animals. As always the man's rifle was primed with a lead ball ready to fly, a survival habit from harder times. Old habits died slowly with Henry Crockett.

He caught the motion of the canoe out of the corner of his keen eye as the vessel burst into view on its race downriver. He didn't need his brass telescope to know this was the same canoe he had seen just the week before. He was sure this was the one belonging to the Indians who had killed the woman he had just buried a few miles back. He remembered her kindly, but now his mind whispered deep suspicions. Where was the second woman? Had the Red man killed her too? He'd bet the farm on that. And where was the second brave?

He swung his head from left to right, studying the lay of the land as if half expecting the other warrior to materialize suddenly behind him. Then he turned his eyes back on the canoe.

His rifle came up in one fluid motion. Swinging through a clearing in the trees, the bead moved from left to right, past the Native's head, and swept ahead of the canoe, like leading a duck. His finger began to squeeze the trigger as softly as a man's footfall falls upon the duff and moss of the forest floor. It was an easy shot for a master marksman. The canoe was fifty yards away. He couldn't miss.

Suddenly, Crockett heard a bellow and then the sounds of something large and in full motion, coming up quickly behind him. His finger froze on the trigger. The sound struck him like the shock of a projectile: a bullet or an arrow. As was his habit, Crockett sensed the disturbance before it overwhelmed him. Something was charging madly through the trees. And that something wasn't human, of that he was sure. This something was as big as a horse and racing out of control.

Crockett swung his musket into the oncoming path of a giant grizzly, stopped, sighted, and held. This one was as white as snow. *Kermode*, he thought. *The Spirit Bear.* Wagh! This was something, alright. But he knew one shot might not bring this beast down. Likely wouldn't. Damn, the bear was huge! A single shot might only slow it and further provoke the powerful mammal. And Old Ephraim was charging at a speed that would have startled common folks. Hard to draw a steady bead on the galloping monster.

Crockett knew that after his first shot, all he had was his knife. For the first time in years, he wished he had a repeating rifle. He cussed his pride. Wished he had a cannon. Wished he was sitting in the warm café back in Kilnook drinking coffee with Sally Walton.

The bear pulled up, rose onto two gigantic hind legs (its torso seemed nearly as large as an ancient tree stump) and bellowed out a savage and intimidating war cry. Crockett had seen many a bear but never the famous Spirit Bear. What did that matter now? Crockett was as good as dead. Most likely, there would be no bragging rights. And nothing approached the size of this giant. Nothing near the anger either. The bear's small and deep-seated eyes seared into Crockett. Held steadily. Deadly. Well, the trapper had faced death before, and he wasn't backing down now. No way, by God! A man had his pride.

The bear's ivory teeth flashed. Crockett smelled bear sweat, the lather of anger, dirt, and saliva. The smell alone nearly backed him down. All Crockett's senses screamed at him to flee, but such action would only confirm his fate. The bear would take him down in seconds. Crockett felt a strong sense of doom. His finger flirted cautiously on the trigger.

Just ahead of the flint shard, dry powder waited patiently in the rifle's steel pan. The bear's arrival silenced Crockett's heavy breathing. He unconsciously sucked in a deep breath. Death waited as anxiously as a gravedigger who was low on cash. One of them would fall, man or bear, probably the former. Crockett thought of the grave he had just dug for Sally. Who would dig his?

The trapper began to pull the trigger. *Nothing lives forever,* he told himself. Then suddenly, mysteriously—Wagh! Never seen the likes—the bear lowered itself to the ground onto four massive legs, turned in one rapid dusty half circle, and retreated back into the forest.

Crockett was struck by the pungent smell alone—that was all the evidence left behind. The bear was gone in seconds. Had it all been a mirage? A dream? His eyes scampered through the fine earth dust as it shuffled into the rich mountain air. Sunshine cut through the haze, as thick and as yellow as freshly churned butter.

In the forest, natural sounds began to filter back in. Crockett was alone. Spirit Runner was far down river. Two hundred yards into the forest, Crockett heard the Grizz, retreating—well, not retreating. No animal that big ever retreated. Thick fauna shook and quivered, stunned by the force of the massive animal.

"Wagh!" He shook his head. His heart was racing. *Shinin' times*, he thought. *Not seen such shinin' times. Never*. Crockett was grateful to be alive. Grateful for another tall tale that no other trapper could trump. "Wagh!" he shouted again, louder now. Loud enough for the whole forest to hear. Loud enough for the retreating bear to hear and remember the mountain man's salutation. This was Crockett's way of thanking the giant for its change of menu. This was as close as he ever got to an actual God-fearing prayer.

Crockett sucked air into his lungs. He was high with exhilaration. He let one final bellow fly. This one for the Kermode and for any pilgrim close enough to hear.

"WAGHHH!"

Once again the forest fell into silence. Once again the natural sounds tumbled back.

Crockett walked back to the river and swung his head in the direction where the Indian had fled, by then far downriver. There was no Indian, no canoe. Just a huge eagle sitting on a snag. *Strange that*, he thought. *Strange to be sitting here amidst all the commotion. Strange, indeed.*

Crockett calmly continued upriver, never looking back.

By then Spirit Runner was far downstream. He never heard Crockett's great bellow. Never felt the deadly volley of a round lead ball. Spirit Runner smiled. He was on his way back to his family.

A gathering place. A ceremonial lodge built at the west end of the Native village, a secret enclave hidden deep in the mountains. Wolf Haven. A human sized, oval-cut entrance faced west, toward an ocean, miles and miles away.

The façade stood as tall and erect as the great beams that supported it. The wooden surface was windowless, the wide planks adzed with small, beaver-like bites of chiseled perfection. A huge thunderbird design had been painted across the wide cedar face. Inside the lodge, four carved totems soared skyward. Two faced east and two west. At the top of each totem was a carved animal crest. Four sets of eyes like the four wind directions beamed down on the First Peoples.

At the east end of the lodge was a raised cedar dais. Behind that, a wall with more painted designs: faces of wolves and eagles and whales, and, of course, the indomitable grizzly bear, its ivory teeth fierce, formidable, and ferocious.

In the middle of the cedar wall, another man-sized oval opening. And evenly centered in the room was a large, welcoming fire, a fire that promised protection from the night, from mischievous spirits that wandered through the forest. A haven for the people of the valley.

Black Wing sat motionless, centered on the dais like a stone statue. He was dressed handsomely with the aura of a chief or shaman. Around his shoulders and down his back hung an elegant button blanket, decorated with disks cut from abalone shells. Under the blanket, an apron of cloth and more shells. Rather than wear a White man's shirt, he reigned bare-chested. Most elegant of all was a cedar headdress ornamented with a crown of baleen.

Rebecca was moved. The carved cedar mask mimicked the head of an eagle, and its eyes, abalone rounds, blazed an admonishment to any who doubted. None dared. Small abalone squares formed a brilliant rectangle around the mask's perimeter. Ermine fur graced either side, as bright as a snowdrift. The headdress was tied on the chief's forehead with a band of swan's skin. The mask had been passed down for decades, from father to son.

Rebecca marveled at the precision and imagination of those who had carved the mask. In the pulsating firelight of the lodge, everything seemed magical, everything larger than life.

If Rebecca was impressed with the headdress, Tom was stunned. As he entered the lodge, and his eyes fell upon Black Wing, the scout was plunged backwards to the night, months before, when he'd fought for survival on a sheer mountain wall.

During that long night, Tom had cat napped. Torn between moments of terror and self-reproach, he had envisioned the exact headdress that Black Wing was now wearing. Tom shifted his keen eyesight onto the elder's face. Strange as it seemed, he knew that Black Wing was connected to his dreamworld.

The entire village participated in the potlatch. It was a night to welcome new members into the tribe. No White man had ever been tested. And now there were two: one man and one woman. It was a night of ritual and initiation. A night of dance, music, and feasting. Firelight dodged between devouring flames and the dark interior shadows. Dan and Rebecca chose one of the carved cedar benches to watch the proceedings. They were happy to be together, happy but a bit apprehensive.

Whether painted on broad cedar planks or poles, or applied to the bright intricate costumes, the native designs struck them as powerful. It was fine craftsmanship and much more. It was art.

Because of the tenderness in his leg, Dan didn't plan on dancing. He chose the bench strategically, insisting on a good view. He knew Rebecca had never seen anything like this ceremony and wished every advantage for her.

At the back of the cedar stage, four drummers beat out a haunting melody. The music dodged to and fro, wrapping about each of the players. Bass sounds soared, and then scampered outside and into the surrounding forest. In the treetops, a raven listened, curious always, a raptor of intelligence and more than a bit mischievous.

When the drumming subsided, Black Wing asked the representatives of the four clans to step forward and inform the village of their decisions regarding Man Hides Good, White Bear, and the Skinners. Four warriors in elaborate ceremonial costumes stepped onto the raised cedar dais. Each elder in turn spoke words much akin to those that Charlie had spoken seven days before. "Make no secret about it," echoed a leader named Silver Wolf in his native language. "Sharing the secret of this family, this village, will warrant an indictment of death to the guilty man or woman. Discretion and honor are woven together. Each man and woman must impart an oath of secrecy. Wherever a brother or sister goes," he turned to the Skinners and Man Hides Good, "our secret must remain sacred. You are forever honor bound."

Dan caught passages of the speech and translated the gist of it for Rebecca. It didn't take a college professor to understand the meaning. This was big medicine. Every person in the village was dependent on their pledge to protect the tribe's welfare. That included the two White people. Still, amid the seriousness of these commitments, the mood in the longhouse remained festive.

In turn, Rebecca, Dan, and Man Hides Good were escorted to the center of the stage. The Skinners addressed the gathering, pledging their words of honor. After the Skinners returned to the cedar bench, the Haisla went on speaking in the ancient language of his ancestors.

"Brothers and cousins, grandmothers and sisters, recent times have crippled the old ways, our ancient customs. I stand before you in this last known place—this village—given to the ancient ways of our ancestors. I ask you, why should I return to the White settlements? They refuse to speak our story. They scorn the words of our elders and our traditions, those carefully preserved, decade after decade. I ask you to hear my words and honor my commitment. As long as you shelter me, I wish to remain among you, to hold your secret here, next to my heart."

At that, he crossed his chest with his big hand. "I thank you for the trust you offer me. The thought of such a brotherhood brings me joy. From this day forward, I will remain one with you."

When he finished, Man Hides Good moved through the crowd and sat next to Rebecca and Dan. He thought about Sally and wished she was with them, sharing the sacred moment. He continued to feel the loss deeply.

Sensing his well of emotions, Rebecca touched the back of Man Hide Good's hand. Watched his unbridled pride as emotions crisscrossed his thoughtful face. The origin of his joy was mingled with pain, and the two twined together like knots in a Chilkat weaving. *Joy seldom comes easily*, she thought.

The music began again, lifting higher and moving faster and faster. Mixed with the drumming were the sounds of the high-pitched cedar whistles and the yelps and chants of the congregation. Gathering momentum, the sounds blended into a marriage of music and celebration. Dancers in fantastical carved masks stepped up to the beat, succumbing to the enchantment of the music.

Between dances and speeches, another hour passed. It was Tom's turn to talk, but before he began, he was required to dance to the satisfaction of the gathering. That was the first prerequisite, an initiation. Later, he would offer words. After that—if the village welcomed his offerings—he would become a member of their society. No one had to imagine what might happen if he were not accepted. And no one doubted that he would be. The Tsimshian loved to dance. And dance he did.

White Bear was a dervish of motion. His hardened arms began to replicate the great beating wings of an eagle, soaring higher and higher.

Then he stalked like a bear. Ran like a coyote. The music swelled from the drums and whistles as naturally as the water dance of the thick-furred otters. White Bear was lost in dance. He was at one with his brothers and sisters, and they with him.

Music, dance, and wily shadows cast by the firelight filled the great hall. The Skinners were transfixed. And then came the feast.

As night passed into morning, the dancing and feasting subsided. Then White Bear told the story in the language of his family and his people, the Tsimshian. He related how he had become a warrior among his people. He recited the story of when and where he had learned bravery, facing it for the first time on the banks of the Skeena River. Throughout the long hall, no one listened more intently than Black Wing.

White Bear's face was serious, his words falling into a low, moving oratory. He chose his first language. "I was a young boy, eight winters. Eight winters when my uncle taught me the way of a warrior.

"Together we walk far up the great Skeena River. We hope to fish the summer run of the huge Tyee. This is the season of the ripe berries. The river returns her gift to us, each year, as faithful as true love.

"This time of year, the killer whales come in great numbers. They roam just inland in search of salmon and seals. In a small turbulent stream that fell suddenly out of the sheer mountains, a killer whale cornered a magnificent salmon in the shallow gravel of the streambed. The salmon lay just beyond the reach of the whale's huge, mashing teeth.

"My uncle said, 'Little Cub'—I go by different name then—'drop down into the mouth of this stream and bring me that salmon.' At first I not answer him. I do not have the courage to refuse. I do not have the courage to go forward. I am stuck. Then Uncle repeats his request a second time. I indicated that I had a hungry fear of the black-and-white swimmer. But Uncle said, 'Go now, and bring me that salmon. Hurry, for I am very hungry.' He smiled then, though I missed the flicker of amusement that crossed his face. 'We must all learn to grow past these fears that guide us unknowingly,' he said. 'Your fear is now greater than that of the stranded salmon.'

"I went forward until I stood before the thrashing salmon. Stood before the killer whale, before its wide mouth, his row of glittering white teeth. I stood there in my towering fear, praying to the Creator for guidance. I prayed hard. Yes, I studied the two water animals just as hard. The whale, sensing a thief, lifted his huge hulk above the river stones. Threw his huge body forward and down. The cold water surged, trying to wash us away, the salmon and me. The whale growled much as dogs will do in any Tsimshian village when faced with an enemy.

"Uncle shouted, 'Remember that your courage is greater than your fear! Find it quickly! I qu.aa yax x'wán. Go forward. Go forward with courage! Be proud.'

"I confronted the Tyee. It was a great fish, a grandfather of nearly fifty pounds. After wrestling with it for several minutes, I pushed my small arm through its cheek and gills and then dragged it up the bank where my uncle waited. The salmon shook its head and tail at me, and many times I fell, slipping and sliding until I stood beside Uncle. And that whale, he be angry. The spray from his topknot smoldered like smoke. Once on the bank, I stared into its dark, ferocious eyes. There before me, was the whale that our people honored. Many tribes. I knew then that Uncle tested me. I had overcome my fear and passed the challenge. I was grateful not to have dishonored my family.

"My uncle smiled broadly. He had known about the test all along. Knew that one waited for me. He was patient. He was proud. That day he taught me that bravery is the powerful cousin to fear, like two limbs on the same tree but both pointed in different directions."

The audience had turned silent. Around the gathering, the flames from the fires tossed light and shadow across the ceiling. The coals crackled and hissed. Tom shifted his weight from one leg to the other. One leg still felt the impact of his injury, particularly after his animated dance, but he refused to acknowledge any discomfort. His expression steadied as the firelight's glow was reflected in his dark eyes.

Rebecca saw that Tom was engaging the young people who were scattered around the lodge. She saw how the lesson impacted the youthful audience. The adults saw it happening too. No one doubted that White Bear would become a valuable elder in the tribe.

An hour later, Black Wing gave the Tsimshian his new name. He had carried three names during his lifetime. This would be his last. He was no longer White Bear. From that day on, he would be known as Dancing Eagle.

As the village began a welcoming song, the sun crept above the granite mountains. The sky shifted into a shimmering blue. Still hanging in the morning sky, a crescent moon quickly faded away.

1990—The Pacific Northwest

Lives are often shaped by doubt. Often when Katherine felt the weight of emotions quell her spirit, she rallied and attacked whatever problems that festered. She had felt despair before. She'd lived it for months after Paul died.

When her mother passed away on that December morning in 1990, her world, once again, came crashing down. Grief swallowed her, lock, stock, and barrel. She refused to climb out of her malaise. She was absent from work for a week and then two. She remained alone in her apartment. When she returned to the office, support awaited her. Katherine had trouble fielding it.

At her mother's funeral, Katherine prayed for a reaffirming vision. She found only tears. She believed her father would come and surround her with all the same comfort her mother had always offered, a steady and kind hand until the end. This time there was no magic. If her father came into her dreamworld, those communications fled long before the night faded. A woman who refrained from all drugs, she found herself taking sleeping pills to get through the night. She felt deserted and hollow. She refused to call friends. When they called, Katherine terminated the conversation abruptly. Most of her friends remained patient. A few gave up.

At the office, the answering machine was backlogged. There was a call from the small Native village of Old Kilnook. There were two villages now: one Caucasian and the other Native, one prosperous and the other struggling. It was time to rendezvous there, in British Columbia. Katherine had planned the trip before her mother's passing. The voice on her answering machine belonged to a respected elder from the village, a spokesman. Members of Katherine's staff had talked with him and spoke highly of his manner. They spoke almost reverently of his person and his strong emotional message.

On the phone, his gentle voice touched and soothed her across the long miles that separated them. He invited her to visit. He had a dream, he said. He saw hands reaching out to help his people. One set of hands was white. Those hands belonged to the Boston people. He would welcome them as brothers and sisters. He would share with them his land. Share the bounty given to his people by the Creator. His words gripped her. His elocution was gentle but empowering. Katherine called and made reservations, then went home to pack.

The phone call energized her. She felt better than she had in weeks.

As she walked up the wooden steps that led to the front door of her apartment, an object caught her attention. She stooped and picked it up—a large black feather with a long, strong quill. She recognized it immediately as a feather fallen from a large eagle, a bird rarely seen in her neighborhood. She turned it in her fingers and pondered her good luck.

CHAPTER THIRTY-TWO

Wherever you go, I go, always, padding out an echo across time. Remember me, your friend.

—Katherine Skinner-Patterson

Letter to a friend

In the big meadow behind the village, older children were taunting and shouting to their younger brothers and sisters, hurling epitaphs at their friends. All in fun. The game was performed with a cedar disk, drilled twice and spun between two braided leather thongs. Dancing Eagle had shown the children how to construct the toy. He remembered the game from when he was a child among the Tsimshian. The children played with enthusiasm—played as children everywhere play. The rules were different but the same: invent and compete. Laugh a lot. Grin ear to ear.

Dan and Rebecca had wandered away from the village. Nearly two months had passed since Rebecca had walked into camp with Man Hides Good. Dan had healed rapidly. He moved with little visible impairment. If it still stung from time to time, well, he could live with that. Always a taciturn man, he kept the discomfort to himself. Each day he felt stronger. Each day offered a new promise. Still, he was anxious. He knew they must soon make a choice. He and Rebecca must decide whether to stay or leave the Native enclave known to but a few as Wolf Haven.

As the days grew shorter, autumn announced its calling card. On clear, starry nights, Dan and Rebecca felt the sting of mountain frost, a premonition of the long winter to come. The days were still warm and clear, but everyone in the mountains felt the coming of winter.

Autumn was the traditional time for foraging and gathering. The days were filled with preparations. The village bustled with activity from dawn to dusk. The women and children cleaned, scaled, and beheaded the fish, then cleaved the fillets into two slabs, red-orange fillets attached by a central partition of skin and sinew. The fillets were hung in neat rows between green-wood posts in the same smokehouse where Dan had been imprisoned many months before. One skilled woman spent hours at a time turning and rearranging the dried fish, a prerequisite for ensuring the longevity of the life-sustaining flesh. When winter came, the tribe's prosperity would depend on the woman's dedication and skill.

It was also berry-gathering time: the moon of storing and drying. Women and children slipped deep into the woods in search of huckleberries, wild currants, and blackberries. Elderberries—poisonous if not cooked—were parboiled and preserved. Most of the other berries were sun dried on reed mats. The tribe's survival depended on such preservation. Winters were long and cold so high in the mountains.

An aura of harvesting defined the warm autumn days. Salal berries were crushed and mashed and then mixed with crumbled pieces of smoked salmon. The small cakes were dried in the hot September sun. The cured cakes were coveted by the coastal tribes. If there was an abundance of smoked salmon, eulachon grease, or other delicacies, the bounty was traded. Friendly tribes who lived farther eastward into British Columbia's interior were the most preferred trading partners. Venturing farther afield, the Haida had historically traded as far south as the Columbia River with the notorious coastal traders, the Tsinuk. They were notorious canoe men and fishermen and coveted the rich grease, which was rendered from the candlefish.

For weeks, the preparations continued until the storage baskets were full. Entire ceilings above the lodges were covered with the hanging carcasses of dried fish. As had been the Native practice for thousands of years, a large number of returning salmon were allowed to escape beyond the lake and into the Ozyetea River. There, the salmon laid their spawning nests, their redds, in the numerous waterways that laced the enormous wilderness. The people's preservation depended on a strong run of the fish each year. The Natives were stewards of the five runs of salmon that inhabited each of the rivers that snaked through the majestic Kilnook valley.

Rebecca had chosen a warm September day to be alone with Dan. Together, they hiked deep into the old-growth forest. As had become their habit, they made love in a protected copse of trees. It was pleasant for Rebecca to undress in the warm still air of autumn, to stand naked before Dan and God. She particularly enjoyed the privacy of the forest. Afterwards, they would bathe together in the same small stream where Dan had wandered upon Black Wing praying, many months before.

Black Wing had been ill for nearly ten days. No one in the village remembered such an occurrence. Dan and Rebecca missed the frequent visits from the elder, his keen observations and stories. Twice they had wandered to his lodge for a visit, and both times Charlie met them and insisted that they not worry—Black Wing would be fine. The elder was old now, near ninety winters. His cold had turned deeper. Again, Charlie repeated, the elder was fine.

Two weeks earlier, at Black Wing's invitation, Dan and Rebecca had visited. For some reason, Black Wing had asked several questions regarding Rebecca's health, a line of inquiry that surprised her. On that mild, clear day in October, she spoke of a change in her body.

"Dan," Rebecca said in a tone of voice that alerted him to the fact that she had something important to share.

"Dan, I . . . I don't quite know what to do with this.

He was alert for sure now.

"I haven't bled for three months. Honey, you don't think I might . . ." She bit her lip, and Dan watched her eyes turn soft and vulnerable. Suppressed joy scribed her smooth, lovely face and crinkled the tiny lines around her expressive mouth and eyes.

Dan felt a slow chill running down his spine. He had never told Rebecca about Black Wing's premonition—hadn't dared raise her expectations. There was too much pain waiting there. Too much disappointment if the elder happened to be wrong. Now he turned toward her, studying his wife's hopeful expression. *Could it be*? He let his thoughts run wild. He felt a flurry of emotions, something—he figured—like what was exciting her, something in her telling expression.

Again his eyes dove into hers. She had a susceptibility that warmed his heart. Dan sat her down on the exposed root of a giant spruce tree and told her calmly about the prophecy that Black Wing had shared with him, the premonition of their forthcoming baby.

Rebecca cried, this time joyfully.

Dan held her in his arms, rocking her gently back and forth, then reached down and touched her belly. He placed his strong hands onto her smooth, taut skin as if he already felt life budding inside.

Later, silently, they made love a second time. A deep peace settled over the valley.

The next day, Black Wing was about, accompanied as usual by Charlie. For the first time since meeting Black Wing, Dan sensed the frailty of old age cloying at the elder.

Hell, he thought. *Black Wing is no kid.*

He realized that even Black Wing had to suffer the indignities of aging. Dan had to admit that he had never considered the possibility of losing him and felt blinded by the thought.

Good God, he thought, *what will his loss do to the tribe?*

It comforted him when he realized that it would likely be years. But that thought was quickly followed by another: *Not even the stones live forever*. Hadn't Black Wing offered that up sometime early in one of their conversations?

He told himself it wasn't the day to be unhappy. Indeed, Dan could hardly contain his joy. He nearly shouted at the old man. "Black Wing, listen: I think Rebecca is pregnant."

And, of course, the elder teased him. "How, my son, can I help but listen? Your words are like a strong wind driven down the valley from the mountains. A Chinook wind, as strong as a big bull elk."

The elder grinned broadly. Clapped his hands. Then in a steady gaze, he met Dan's eyes. "Yes," he said, "I too feel new life stirring in your wife's body. This woman has joy in her voice that tells me an infant rests inside her womb. The Creator has blessed you both. I share this great happiness with you."

To Dan's amazement, he was sure that he caught the reflection of moisture as it surfaced from the corners of Black Wing's blind eyes.

The valley wind changed direction and blew hard from the northwest. The promise of winter floated on the autumn air. The Natives felt it and sensed the change in the many natural signals that spoke to them and their four-legged friends.

Dan and Rebecca had spent some of the happiest months of their marriage in the village. The pace of life, the respect and kindness from the Natives—many things contributed to a love they felt for these people. Still, neither Dan nor Rebecca had decided how long they might stay.

They reached one conclusion: they would remain through the winter and have the baby in the village. After that only God, and possibly Black Wing, knew.

Questions piqued them. Where might they go? And how would they get there? If they went north, how far might they run before somebody recognized them? South? Well, more of the same uncertainties confronted them. There were no clear answers. At times they would ask themselves, why go anywhere? Maybe they had found their place in paradise. Sure, this wasn't the life they had envisioned when they were first married, but it was a good life, and they might never find better.

And so, their days passed happily, but their future was clouded with unanswered questions. One answer remained clear: they decided to explore life one day at a time.

Winter 1992

Katherine saw her parents in a dream, kicking up their heels on the dance floor in Ballard. They were alive. They were vital. They were in love. In a strange, contorted way, Katherine envied them. From where she stood, a surge of loneliness smote her. And then another emotion—Katherine was suddenly drawn into a fracas of dance and music and something more, something larger. Was that renewed hope?

As she watched, a half-smile crossed her father's lips. Her mother displayed a full smile, her teeth as bright as an ivory bracelet. Her mother was lively, vivacious, excited. And youthful. Had Katherine ever seen her quite like this? Of course, Katherine hadn't been born yet. She was still a far-off dream in her mother's mind. In her heart.

Then her father turned, and his keen eyes settled onto Katherine's, as if messaging. Whatever his thoughts were, she failed to completely divine them, but she knew that love waited: soft, comforting, and tall.

Katherine watched all: the dancing lights, the dancers' flashing legs. The music swelled. The saxophone blared. The trumpet shouted and soared. Her own eyes glittered with glee. She was caught in a gyre.

An alarm wracked her from sleep. She sat up, still pondering her dream. *Was that a revelation? A visitation? An epiphany?*

She headed to the shower, the hiss of silver water washing away her doubts. She smiled under a plunder of warm water, feeling a new surge of hope. She was back.

CHAPTER THIRTY-THREE

Those whom we love never leave us.
Death cannot destroy our devotion.

—Katherine Skinner Patterson

Notes

Four men stalked through the forest. All four were armed. Below them, down at the three forks of the Ozyetea River, Henry Crockett waited. He had brought them this far but stayed behind as they continued on. The armed men trusted the trapper's instincts, his story, and his sense of direction. Sure, he was a crazy old coot, but he knew this country better than anyone they had ever met before. Anyone except Tom LaCross, a man they thought dead. And the old trapper had a story to tell—smelly old codger—odd as that seemed. The lawmen had followed him to get some answers.

The weather had turned cold. The mountain air stung their faces. The posse shivered in the brisk, pre-dawn frost. They had risen before light and followed the old trapper's directions to a trail that spelled out a meeting they had never expected. Anxiety gnawed at their bellies.

The trail came to an end. Before them stood four pillars of stone, just as the old trapper had said. Behind the pillars was a large village of Indians.

They were startled, alright, the officers with the guns. They had no idea where the hell these people had come from.

There wasn't any time to answer their questions.

The children spotted the lawmen first. By then, it was midafternoon. The posse had bushwhacked long and far. For nearly two weeks, they had followed the trapper upriver.

Weeks earlier, Crockett had followed his instincts and stumbled upon the hidden village. Lying on his belly in tangled bramble, he watched their movements. He had drawn a mental picture in his mind and then headed back to the settlement, where he shared his suspicions with the lawmen.

The Mounties were tired, but adrenaline rushed through their veins. They were alert for trouble. Each man released the safety on his rifle, holding his weapon at the ready. As they stepped into the clearing, the village stirred like a hive of angry bees.

The women rounded up the children and headed for cover. Mothers implored the always curious youth to hurry, to run from the Whites, from their brass-encased bullets. Rushing from the village like a murder of crows, the men raced toward the Mounties. As odd as it seemed to the four lawmen, the Natives were armed with only bows and arrows. Those were scary enough. Only one man among them had ever seen warriors in such dress, ever seen a bow and arrow in actual combat. *Hell,* he thought, fear racing through his mind. *These are the Indians of old, the ones Grandpa talked about before the Whites whooped 'em.* Something strange was going on, and none of the four lawmen were sure what it was, but they didn't have time to contemplate.

A man rushed before them. He held out his hands in a peaceful salutation. His actions were urgent. A deputy named Willis recognized the man and caught his breath.

By God, that's Tom LaCross, and he has gone wild. Tom, the tracker. The famous scout. He's thought dead, for Christ's sake. Dead. Died with . . .

Willis didn't have time to ponder the thought. The new lawman from Kilnook stepped forward and hit the Tsimshian in the face with his rifle butt, then aimed the barrel toward the man's chest. Panic drummed on the trigger.

"Dumb fool," Willis croaked. But it was too late.

The Tsimshian sank to the ground, bleeding hard from the face. Stunned. He came up just as fast as he had gone down. Before anyone reacted, Tom brandished a knife hidden behind the back of his leather-fringed pants and buried it in the lawman's ribs. Willis leveled his .30-30 repeating rifle at Tom and pulled the trigger. Tom spun to a halt. He was a dead man, the bullet exploding into his heart, in the gentle heart that Tom LaCross had recently resurrected. A man finally set free.

The deputy swung the rifle at the next blur. Pumped a second shell into the chamber. Before he squeezed the trigger, three arrows tore into his chest, and he fell, his breath torn away.

Rebecca and Dan watched hell unfold. They had been approaching the village from the other direction when the shouting started. Painful leg or not, Dan broke into a full run toward the Mounties, shouting for Rebecca to take cover. She tried to hold him back. She knew it was impossible. Fear was screaming at her. He covered the fifty yards in seconds, just in time to see Tom fall. Dan headed straight for the gunman, but before he got there, arrows brought the lawman down.

Rebecca stood and watched in slow motion as another lawman swung his rifle toward Dan. She began a long, silent scream. Deep inside her, the baby cried out in pain. Her motion was suddenly limited to a deep internal howl.

Dan saw the rifle and tumbled into a front roll, coming to his feet just in front of the deputy. He had no weapon but kicked savagely with his left foot. The man went down, and his rifle spun into the dirt. Dan leaped for it.

As the deputy rose, Rebecca saw him slide a hand into the holster at his waist. He had a pistol there.

"Dan!"

Dan swung at the deputy, but he wasn't fast enough. Rebecca watched in horror as smoke cleared the pistol's barrel. She saw Dan fall backwards. Blown backwards. She was screaming out loud now. Screaming his name. His chest was bloody. She saw that clearly enough. A dead-gray exit wound in the center of his back filled quickly with a bubbly pink froth, then turned deep wine red. Dan staggered and fell.

Arrows fell in dense volleys on the Whites, on the two who remained. They had no chance to turn and run. No chance to flee. The thunder of rifle fire bled down the valley, playing out like the mating bellow of a bull elk. In their final seconds, the remaining lawmen turned abruptly toward each other, face to face. It was a look mixed with fear and surprise. There was also a strange understanding to the look, a finality. As they fell, all the colors of the forest and sky melded together.

The sighing sound of arrows singed the air, followed by an abrupt, unnatural silence. Rebecca ran to her husband, then fell to her knees.

"Rebecca." Dan's last word floated out weakly and then seemed to evaporate.

She clutched her hands around her abdomen where the baby waited. Mother and child were singing Dan's name.

Dancing Eagle can see his relatives plainly now. They are calling him home. His mother is there, standing toward the back of a huge cedar canoe. He has forgotten how beautiful her blue eyes are, the roundness of her smooth face and mahogany skin. Her arms and hands are extended. He feels the most powerful love he has felt since his infancy.

His uncle is there too. Dancing Eagle's heart jumps. Behind him, his family waits in a pair of handsome canoes at the edge of the sea. Dancing Eagle is going home at last. The canoe will take him across the deep, wide sea. What waits after that, he doesn't rightly know, but he reasons that it can't be nearly as painful as the life he has just left. He trusts it will be fine and whispers an old Native prayer. "Hey Mana, naka say. Ho Mana naka so." A Salish prayer. "Eagles find me," he prays. "Eagles protect me."

Over the dying bodies, the eagle dropped, its high, piercing call gathering force as it descended, lower and lower, until Rebecca couldn't help but tear her eyes away from her beloved husband and fasten them onto the magnificent bird. She knelt beside Dan and held his head on her lap, praying for a miracle. There had been so many recently. She wept silently. In the forest, a jay broke into a rattling objection. "Kak-kak-kak-kak."

Grief plunged into her soul.

Far below the chaos, the old trapper heard a volley of shots and then dead silence. He predicted the outcome and scurried away. Following the same pattern as Spirit Runner, he pushed the canoe into the current and headed for Kilnook. He had heard enough.

The raptor settled into the middle of the killing field, its head and yellow beak swiveling madly back and forth, back and forth. Instead of the eagle's wild call, Rebecca swore she heard deep remorse, a cry of pain. And then the eagle bounded into the air, an agonizing, bleating sound trailing after him.

Higher and higher it rose until the raptor was only a tiny spot in a large sky. The bird swooned into circles, wider and wider. Then higher yet. And then gone.

Gone except for a visible iridescence, a violet hole where the eagle was last seen, a willowy illumination already filling Rebecca's memory. She knew the bird. "Why, oh why?" she murmured, as if speaking to the eagle. "Why, now?"

A gentle rain settled across the valley. Below lay her beloved husband. Around her the bodies of the lawmen and Tom LaCross. The baby stirred in her belly. She wondered how she and the child might survive such pain. She remembered Dan's pioneer spirit. His constant courage. Pain swept through her. Rebecca sucked in a deep breath and pulled deeper inside. *We will survive together. We must. Me and Dan's baby.*

She touched her abdomen. Tears fell unbridled. Her Dan was gone, but the baby waited.

Over the village came a hollow, unnatural sound. The villagers began to scatter. Once again the village would be deserted.

Months later, Rebeca stood in a tall grassy meadow behind her old farm—hers and Dan's. The swallows were back, breaking and somersaulting through the pleasant summer air. Rebecca was holding a boy child. And she was saying hello and goodbye to the valley she so loved.

Spring 1992—Old Kilnook

Katherine stood next to her rental car, surrounded by a Native enclave, twentieth-century style. The collection of homes was called Old Kilnook.

A newer city of the same name had moved inland where all the trees were felled. Where the Whites congregated and started new businesses and schools and churches and bars. And a new supermarket.

There were four Americans in her party, all Caucasian. Two were men and two women. They had arrived before her and began to case out the village and visit with some of the Native people. They met at the house of the Haisla spokesman.

The house before her was spartan, and that assessment was generous. The clapboard structure had little lawn, and plenty of weeds. Bits of debris littered the yard. A broken washing machine sat on the front porch—looked like it had been there quite a spell. A metal boat rested on an aluminum trailer next to a Ford pickup, looking forlorn, like an abandoned street waif. Other than a flat tire and a cracked window, the vessel and trailer appeared in reasonable repair. Katherine realized that the boat was an essential mode of travel. She noticed immediately that there were few flowers in the village, few plants. By her standards, the space appeared unkempt.

Later, an elder explained that his people, a First Nations people, had occupied thousands of square miles of one of the most natural undeveloped rainforests in the world. It had been stolen from them. This forced residence felt "like a concentration camp." The Natives had been given a leftover scrap. These First Nations people were tangled up in bitterness and rage.

At the mouth of the bay was an aluminum plant. Waters diverted from the mountains propelled the huge turbines, ultimately churning out the coveted metal that the nation fed upon voraciously, no matter what the environmental consequences.

An elder, in his faded flannel shirt and dark trousers, stepped through a flaking painted door and introduced himself to the group. This was the man whom Katherine had talked with on the phone. He had beautiful bright teeth. His smile was infectious. He was the honorable spokesman of the Killer Whale clan. He stood just above six feet, and his posture was arrow straight.

The spokesman's eyes sweep slowly from face to face, as if seeking an understanding of who these people were. Who they really were.

When his eyes reached Katherine, they settled slowly, retreating into brown pools of understanding. She felt a strange, out-of-body detachment. It was if his gaze rendered her vulnerable. She felt like her thoughts were being dissected. But his disposition appeared as one of gentleness and compassion. Rebecca was confused.

Startling her—startling her comrades—he declared, "I have seen you coming in my dreams. I told my mother about you, at Kolnux, where she rests in the forest, a cemetery filled with my ancestors, over four hundred felled by smallpox, felled in one week. I told Mother that your coming is to be welcomed, that it fulfills a promise to my people."

He took a cigarette from his pocket and sidled into the ritual of lighting it. He blew the smoke back through his mouth and watched as it rose, higher and higher into the brisk air.

Katherine watched as the smoke curled into the sky. The pause was pregnant with expectation. All the while, silence built up like a storm.

He talked for ten minutes, each word measured for impact. His story was like a book unfurling. He told his guests about his people, the Haisla and the Xenaksiala, their history, their suffering, and their strengths. He had expectations. The Bostons had come to help them save their land, hundreds of thousands of acres that spread up the great valley. Timber companies were lobbying to cut the virgin trees, to plunder the largest temperate rainforest in the world. Their land was sacred, he said. It was given to his people by the Creator, by God. Given to their care. It was their duty to preserve it for the grandchildren and their grandchildren. Careful attention was needed, attention and good allies. And yes, the help of the Great Spirit.

Katherine felt separated again, mind from body, and realized she had been crying. So were the others. She saw that her companions had been touched, just as she had been, by this humble but strong man. She drew a deep breath and settled herself.

She swept her gaze to her three companions, then back to the elder. Something unsung banded them together.

Katherine had a revelation. Somehow she and her compatriots had just been handed a gift, and, as yet, they didn't fully understand the true value.

We are here, she thought. *We will overcome.* She remembered a quote attributed to Jesus: "*Unless you see signs and wonders, you will not believe.*"

Well, she thought. *Maybe. Just maybe?*

Her eyes remained on the elder. His eyes were reservoirs of dark reflection. His face was creased like an old leather hat. *He has suffered,* she thought, *but he has grown from that suffering. He has grown strong and gentle simultaneously.* She felt drawn to this man, drawn to this place, as if this vast homeland had always held a piece of her. As if she had always known him.

A door opened and closed. Katherine recognized the creak of tongue-and-groove floorboards as footsteps crossed the wooden space. Standing on the porch was a fine-looking man. Spry. Katherine's age. His face said half-White, half-Native. His bronze skin favored his First Nations heritage. From under the sleeves of his T-shirt, smooth muscles rippled along his bare arms, into his tight chest and thick neck. The young man was handsome and appeared intelligent. His eyes bright and penetrating.

Silky, raven-black hair covered his ears. As with the elder, his smile was infectious. Katherine felt a stir inside her belly like the kick of a mule.

The elder retreated to the bottom of the stairs, looked up, and then introduced his nephew. Katherine's emotions were swimming. That familiar, hollow space was filling like a summer rain seeping into a stone cistern. She wanted to drink from the vessel.

The nephew sidled down from the porch and extended his hand. She identified a dancer by his light, athletic steps and remembered her father's proclivity. *So graceful*, she thought. As he walked toward her, she noticed how he slid up onto his toes like a ballet dancer. An abstract truth struck her suddenly.

The elder spoke again, and Katherine reluctantly turned away from the young man. "My nephew's grandfather," the elder said. "Long ago, a famous scout. Grandmother, a White woman, Ruth Anne McCaul. . ."

"Tom LaCross!" she shouted, spilling out the words in a fury, startling the entourage. "The Tsimshian!"

The elder eyed her peculiarly, his gaze penetrating. But Katherine's gaze had moved back to the young man, her memory back to her daddy.

The elder's words stopped her reverie. "Yes, White Bear. Dancing Eagle. How do you know this? How do you know this man?" Suddenly, there was urgency in his words. "I have a story to tell you. We will share."

"Do you know about my grandfather and grandmother?"

"Yes," he said. "I know story."

She turned and stared at the deep northwest sky. In the distance, great white-capped mountains graced the landscape. A sea of ancient cedars greeted her, their tops twisted and shaped into green-tipped candelabras. This was why they had come, but now there was more. Tears pooled behind her eyes. Unseen.

Something caught her gaze and swept past her effortlessly. She turned, startled. A great bird. Yes. A mature bald eagle. The largest she had ever seen, gliding overhead in a wide circle as effortlessly as breathing, examining each man and woman through gold-rimmed eyes. Then rising, catching an updraft, and gyrating into a periwinkle-blue sky. It spun east into the Kilnook Valley, its huge wings steady and powerful.

Silence settled over Katherine's world. She turned back to the elder. "My father," she blurted out. "He told me a story of a Tsimshian warrior, a man named Tom LaCross."

"Yes, White Bear. Dancing Eagle,"

The elder turned his full attention onto Rebecca. Around the circle, the others stared, unclear as to the significance of this new revelation.

"Tom LaCross was a close friend of my grandfather's."

"Yes, Dan Skinner. His wife, Rebecca. And a child."

"That child was my daddy, Martin Skinner."

The young Haisla followed the eagle with his eyes. Katherine followed his. He waved a hand in a salutation toward the eagle. Breaking another silence, he declared, "The eagle is my friend."

Then he turned to her, and their eyes locked.

She felt a bite of something as undefinable as love. Something that wouldn't let her be. Her whole body was reacting. She felt him intimately. One door closed, another opened.

The elder's gaze jumped from his nephew to the young woman. His face broke into a wide, generous smile.

In the distance the eagle's high, piercing call floated on the wind like glass shattering and falling.

And rising again.

ABOUT THE AUTHOR

PHOTO BY DOUG MACKENZIE

DAVID CAMPICHE is a published poet, a professional potter, an avid outdoorsman, retired innkeeper of forty-two years, and a passionate student of Indigenous cultures, art history, painting, and nature. He is a member of the National Audubon Society and Sea Resources and serves on the board of the Willapa National Wildlife Refuge. On trips into northern British Columbia, both privately and with the organization, EcoTrust, he conferred with leaders in the environmental efforts to protect areas of BC's wilderness.

David has published a book of poetry (Sidekicks) with the author, Jim Tweedie, two novellas, and has written many columns and stories centering around the Pacific Northwest for *The Chinook Observer* and *The Daily Astorian.* He and his wife, Laurie Anderson, live on the Long Beach Peninsula in Southwest Washington State. Photo of the author by Doug Mackenzie.

Printed in the USA
CPSIA information can be obtained
at www.ICGtesting.com
LVHW041650230823
756019LV00048B/268

9 781039 141452